They tried to improve the human genome, but nature took things into its own hands!

Echoes: For every ten embryos they genetically enhance, nature would return nine to their unaltered state. They remained echoes of humanity's limitations.

Deltas: Only one in ten would be born with and keep all of its altered traits. They were an improvement to humanity, but only within limits that were considered a reasonable step beyond normal evolutionary growth.

Charlies and Betas: But for 1% of those Deltas, nature wasn't done; it threw a genetic curveball brought on by puberty. They were faster, stronger, and smarter than was thought to be humanly possible.

If that had been the end of it, science would have been satisfied: its goal had been achieved. But they just couldn't leave it alone. And what they did next would start the final war—the war to end all wars.

THE REGNANT WAR

BOOK TWO
THE REGNANT WAR

CITY OF ANGELS

R. J. Hunter

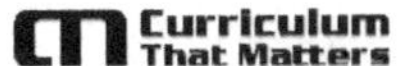

City of Angeles

Cover art by Kaitlynn Hunter
Cover art © 2025 by Kaitlynn Hunter

Interior illustrations by Rayanna Hunter
Interior illustrations © 2025 by Rayanna Hunter

ISBN: 978-1-7353113-5-7

First Edition: January 2025

For all my students who kept telling me to hurry up and get the next book done, because they couldn't wait to find out what happened next. (You know who you are!) And for those who begged me to give Thatcher a bigger role in the story.

This book is dedicated to you.

Also by R.J. Hunter

THE REGNANT WAR

"It has been argued that no other city in the world has a name whose origin story is so obscured as to be practically untraceable than does the city of Los Angeles. Some claim the city's name came from a quaint little chapel on that same land that housed a painting of the Virgin Mary surrounded by angels in the 18th century. Others claim that the naming of the city was nothing more than the continuation of a mistake made on a map by one of the original explorers of the area. But few can disagree that the city's name was prophetic in its choosing when that city of thirteen million people died in the blink of an eye, their bodies sent instantly Heavenward in the brilliant flash of that fateful nuclear explosion. They became, in that instant, an actual City of Angels.

"Today we have come together to discuss the naming of the new city that has been proposed to be built upon the ruins of that once-great city. The good counsel from France has proposed that we call it UFC City, a purposely non-culturally specific name so that it might belong to all countries, as it is intended to represent all countries. But I must respectfully suggest that doing so would demean the sacrifice of those who died there, and who, in dying, laid the foundation for the formation of this great federation of countries that we enjoy today.

"And so, I would place before you for your consideration a name that, although not multicultural in its birth, is universal in its meaning. It is one that would indefinitely honor those angels who lost their lives so that we might have a better future. I propose that it be known forever more as the New Los Angeles: The City of Angels."

-The argument made by John Eddington, a special representative from America to the UFC Directorate Council on 5 June, 218 in favor of retaining Los Angeles' original name with the added honorific nod to those who died there at the start of the Pernicious Bellum War, also known as The Regnant War.

THE REGNANT WAR

CITY OF ANGELS

The

United Federation

7

1

2

3

4

5

6

Directorate Zones

Zone 1: NW. North America
Zone 2: NE. North America
Zone 3: SW. North America
Zone 4: SE. North America
Zone 5: Central America/
N. South America
Zone 6: S. South America
Zone 7: W. Europe

UNITED FEDERATION OF COUNTRIES

# of Countries

Directorate Zone Map

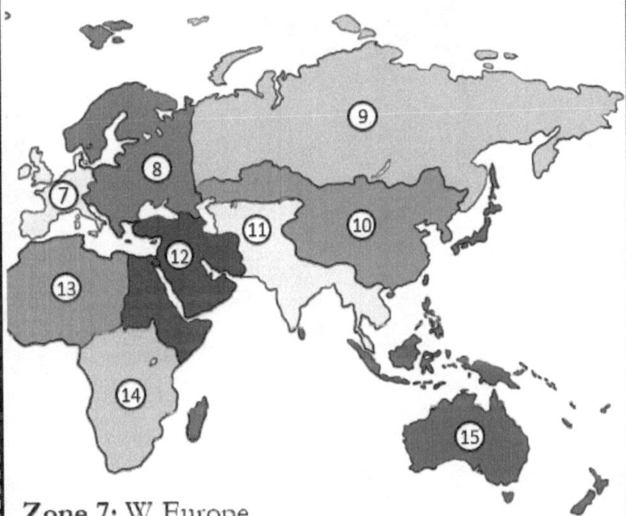

Zone 7: W. Europe
Zone 8: E. Europe
Zone 9: N. Asia
Zone 10: Central Asia
Zone 11: S. Asia
Zone 12: NW. Africa/W. Asia
Zone 13: N. Africa
Zone 14: S. Africa
Zone 15: Australia/Oceana

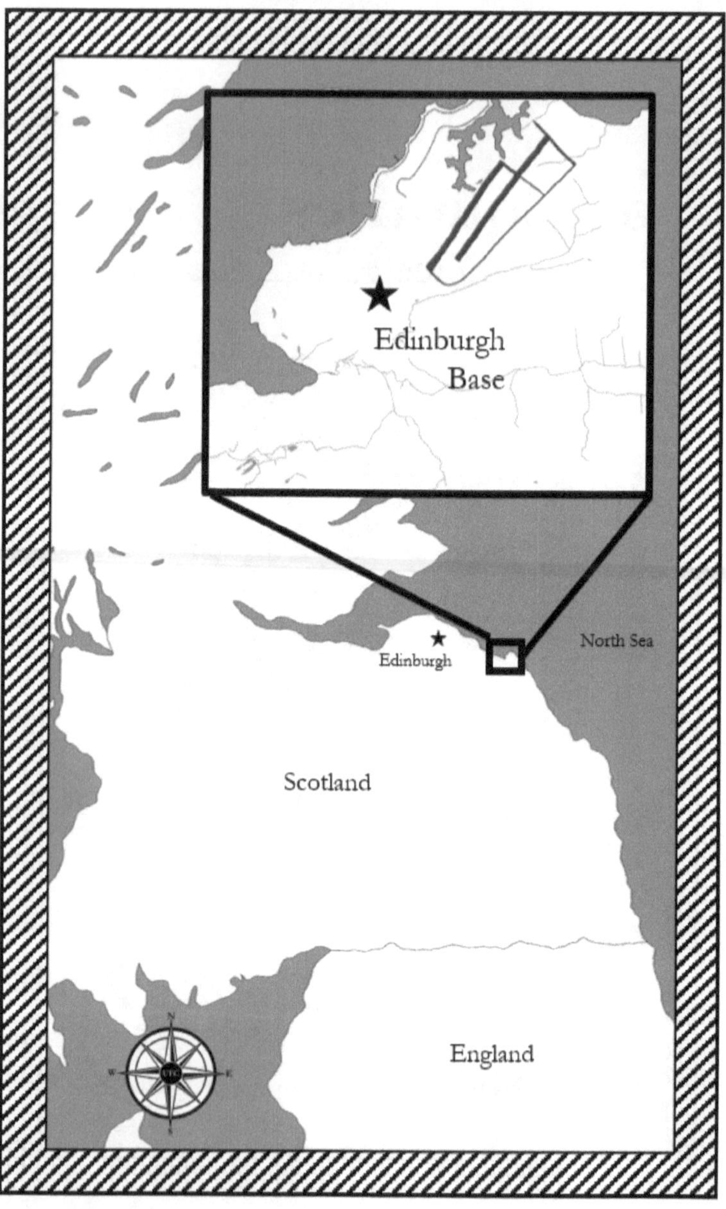

Edinburgh
Base
Edinburgh
North Sea
Scotland
England

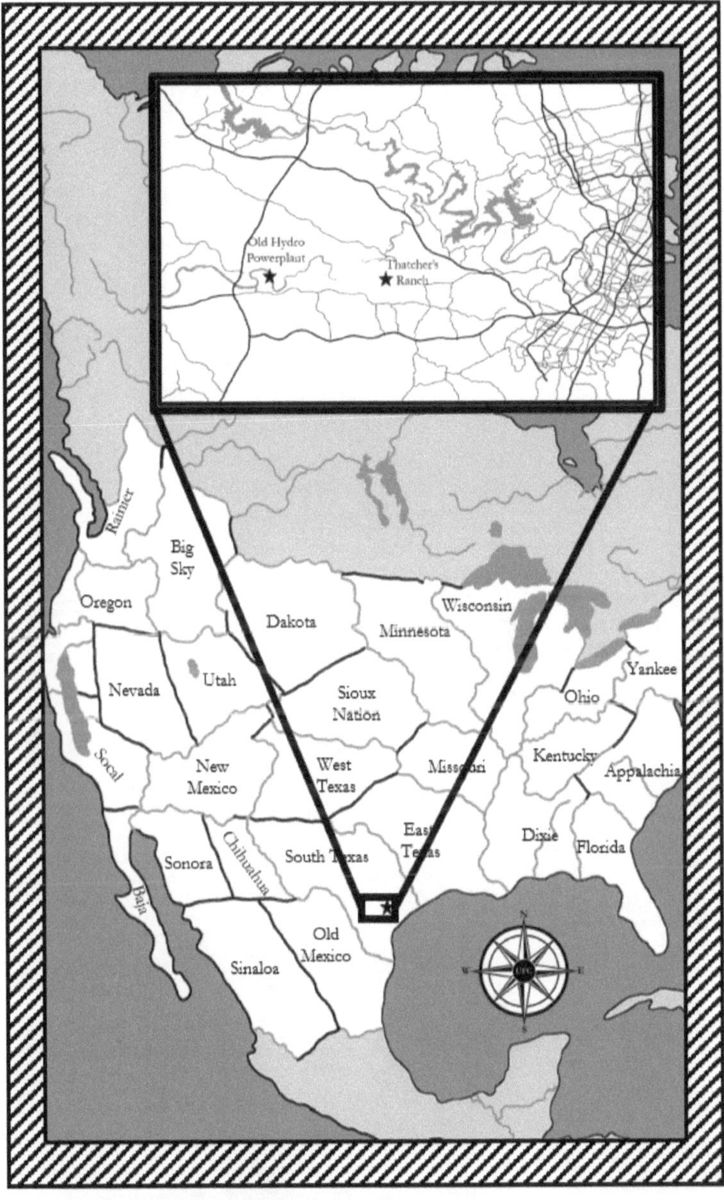

Old Hydro
Powerplant
Thatcher's
Ranch
Rainier
Big
Sky
Oregon
Dakota
Wisconsin
Minnesota
Nevada
Utah
Yankee
Sioux
Nation
Ohio
Socal
New
Mexico
West
Texas
Missouri
Kentucky
Appalachia
East
Texas
Dixie
Florida
Chihuahua
South Texas
Sonora
Baja
Old
Mexico
Sinaloa
N
W
E
S

Prologue: Aiden Haskell 

BETWEEN THE REGNANT War and the M-Gen War, the world was in desperate shape coming into the close of the first century Post Bellum. Five percent of the world's population had been killed in the first war; fifty percent were killed in the second. For those that remained behind, food shortages and a lack of basic essentials would see even more dead before any type of recovery could begin.

But recovery did eventually come in the form of the first international government. While not every country chose to join or even recognize the leadership of this new form of governance, enough of the major countries did that its domination in making worldwide decisions was undeniable. Thankfully this new governance, called the United Federation of Countries, or UFC for short, was founded on the belief that the world would only progress as a planet when every country, race, and people were lifted together. So, for many years, its decisions did just that with the goal of helping everyone, not just the countries that had chosen to join it.

The fifteen directorates at its head, each elected from and representing a specific region of people, were responsible to ensure that their region's needs were being appropriately met.

Together they led the world into an age of prosperity that was, for the first time in the known history of the world, truly universal. The phrase "No One Left Behind" became the government's motto and guided its actions in establishing programs and centers for learning that helped everyone, or at least it did for many years.

But a wise man once said that power corrupts, and absolute power corrupts absolutely. While the UFC continued to claim that it was keeping its constitutional beliefs intact, there began to be hints that it was not as benevolent as it had once been. Hints of internal corruption, suggestions that military force was being used to coerce non-member countries, and even leaders who somehow managed to stay in office long after their terms had expired began to be the norm. Those who spoke openly of their concerns quietly disappeared and UFC business went on as usual.

One man saw the corruption and silently began gathering allies who agreed to do something about it. That man was Ewan Buccleuch, Duke of Scotland. He led the resistance against the UFC with the goal of bringing down the corrupt leaders and replacing them with newly elected ones who would return the UFC to its constitutional foundations and the values of equity and justice that it had been established on.

Unfortunately, on the day the resistance became an open rebellion, and the Scottish forces became actively engaged with UFC troops in order to remove the corrupt leaders, Scotland was abandoned by those who had promised to be their allies. No one stepped in to help them and their troops were insufficient to match the strength of the UFC forces alone. Their rebellion failed and Scotland was labeled a country of traitors. Ewan was executed for his part in the rebellion. The Scottish people paid for their actions with their firstborn sons through the Scottish Accords, unanimously signed by all fifteen directorates. It required a mandatory draft into the UFC military for all of Scotland's firstborn sons upon the day of their fifteenth birthday. I am one of those sons. My name is Alistair Buccleuch, the grandson of Ewan Buccleuch.

 Chapter 1: Aiden Haskell

NO ONE SAID anything as we drove through the darkness. It had been nearly an hour since we had left my family's property. And, while the first few minutes of adrenaline-heightened awareness had kept us talking and discussing the night's events, the discussions had eventually given way to quiet reflection. With the retreat of the adrenaline had come the reminder that we were each nursing injuries that would need further treatment once we reached a base. Thatcher had taken a phaser blast to the arm, McLagan had a gash in his leg, Wren had a deep cut above his eye, and I…well, I hurt everywhere. My muscles were still aching from the torture, my knee was screaming at me, my wrists were on fire, my rib ached enough that it hurt just to breathe, and my head was pounding. But none of that mattered to me right now.

Alex was still unconscious in my arms; she was my primary concern. Our escape had been due to her efforts. The number of gravity fields she had been simultaneously controlling there at the end, and the level of control she had maintained over them, was greater than anything I had seen her manage before; it had been truly incredible. She had almost singlehandedly turned the tables on Remington's forces. But it had come at a cost: the effort had left her physically drained. On top of that, the emotional trauma she had suffered while watching Remington torture me had become debilitating in the end. She had retaliated at Remington by seeing the shock collar placed around his neck after it had been removed from mine. Or at least that's what I thought had happened. Now I wasn't so sure.

Hearing Remington's screams of pain had sent her back into shock, reminding me just how fragile she was. For all her training and abilities, she did not belong in battle. Estradé had seen that much quicker than I had and had done something about it.

Alex was an Alpha, and an extremely strong one at that. She was one of those Alphas that Icarus had genetically modified to become weapons. Genetic manipulation was a regular practice in our day and age, but most only produced Betas and Charlies. I myself am a Charlie. I can run far faster than anyone else, but that is the extent of my Alpha abilities. If I had gained any other advanced abilities then they would have classified me as a Beta.

Alphas are different. Not only are they genetically modified, but a surgery was performed when they were in their mother's womb that caused a sixth lobe to develop in their brains; a lobe that allows them to see and control waves no one else can. Because the surgery is so dangerous, there are very few Alphas in the world. The Alphas Icarus created in his lab are by far the strongest. That is why the UFC wants Alex so bad. They want her to be their weapon.

Fortunately, Estradé had contacted those who could help Alex and arranged to set her free of the UFC's control. She had even arranged for me to see what the UFC had done to

Alex, and helped me to finally understand what she really meant to me.

But, in spite of Estradé's careful preparations, I had managed to mess everything up by dragging Alex smack dab into the middle of my own problems. I shook my head in self-recrimination; I should have never let her stay.

Thatcher must have seen the movement. "You doing okay there?" he asked softly.

"Aye," I answered. "Just frustrated with meself for lettin' this all happen."

He looked at me for a long moment before turning his attention back to the road. I could only imagine what he was thinking. He had tried to insist that she be taken to safety the moment he had learned about my situation. It was my fault she had even been given the option to stay, thereby compromising the integrity of our mission. I didn't imagine he was going to be overly forgiving about that. As the silence stretched on, that certainty was confirmed in my mind. I was surprised when he suddenly broke the silence.

"When I was sixteen, my father asked me to check the fence around our prize bull's pasture. It was a job I was more than capable of doing on my own, but about halfway around it I saw the cute neighbor girl and thought I'd try to impress her by pretending to be a matador with the bull. She cheered me on and was rather impressed with my tomfoolery, right up until I misjudged the bull's speed and got caught by its horn right across my thigh. I went flying, landing hard enough to knock me unconscious. My pa, who had been coming to check on my progress, saw what was happening and charged in with his horse to save me from my own stupidity. He ended up having to shoot the enraged bull to keep it from killing me.

"Later, when I woke up, safe in my own bed with only a jagged scar on my leg and a big lump on my head to show for my near-death foolishness, he told me how disappointed he was in my choice and how much the bull's loss was going to cost the family. He also told me that the young lady I had been trying so hard to impress had cared so little for me that she had gone running for home the moment she had realized that I was in real danger. She'd gone there, not to get help, but rather to hide from the trouble that she was afraid she would get into when someone discovered that she had been encouraging me on in my childish antics. I was left to understand exactly how much I had given up that day for so little in return. I felt about as small and worthless as a worn-out horseshoe.

"A few days after that my mother taught me another lesson that I won't soon forget. What my pa hadn't shared with me was that he was harboring his own wound from the incident. The bull had not gone down with the first blast and my father had been forced to ram his horse into the bull in order to push it off the path that would have taken it over my prone body. In the process, his leg was crushed between the bull and his horse. He still walks with a limp today because of it. The lesson she made perfectly clear was the difference between the love my pa had for me and the infatuation I had with that girl. One was worth dying for, the other was not.

"Pa didn't say anything more on the subject after that, but I knew it was my fault and the guilt ate at me until it made me sick. Trying to make up for my guilt, I pushed myself hard to cover the chores he wasn't able to do. I was barely sleeping trying to get it all done, not even taking time to stop for meals. I began to lose weight and constantly had dark bags under my eyes. Finally, one night several weeks later, long after I should have gone to bed, my father found me outside frustratedly trying to repair the gate on one of the cattle chutes we were going to need the next day. It should have been a simple fix, but I was too tired to do it correctly.

"He limped over and took the tool out of my hand, forcing me to stop working and face him. Then, without a word, he reached around me to fix the gate with a simple maneuver of the wrench, then handed the tool back to me and told me to go put it away. When I came back, he was standing there with his arms folded across his chest, six-foot-four of angry cowboy glaring down at me.

"'Son,' he said to me, 'we don't have the luxury of wallowing in our self-recriminations. You did something you shouldn't have, but you've already paid the price of it and learned from your mistake. Now it's time to move on.'

"I tried to argue with him and tell him how it was also my fault that he had been injured and how I needed to make amends for it, but that was when he really got angry with me. He told me that it had been his choice to go into that bull's pasture and that I had no right to try to take the responsibility for that choice away from him."

For several moments Thatcher went silent. Then he finally said, "You are not responsible for what happened to her out there tonight."

I shook my head, disagreeing. He was wrong, I was responsible. "Look, Thatcher, I appreciate what yae're tryin' tae say, but I'm the reason yae all stayed. I should have forced Alex tae leave with yae this mornin'. Then…"

Thatcher's deep growl cut me off. "Haskell, you could have no more forced Alex to leave than I was able to. It was my job to get her to safety; I failed to do that. You do not get to relieve me of my responsibility for my choices or my failures. Alex chose to take the battle to Remington and free her team. You do not get to take the responsibility for her choices away from her either. Remington already made you pay for the choices you were responsible for. Now it's time for you to move on."

"Amen," McLagan added unexpectedly from the backseat. "No bloody noble gets tae claim responsibility for me choices; yae least of all, Buccleuch."

I found myself chuckling in resignation. "Okay. I get th' point." Then, after a few seconds, I added, "Thank yae, for not abandoning us."

"No one left behind, not even yae," McLagan muttered under his breath, making me chuckle again.

The command pad beeped softly, its mapping function telling us it was time to change direction. Thatcher slowed the jeep and began looking for the side trail the pad said was off to the left. It turned out to be harder to find than we expected. We had to backtrack several meters because we missed it the first time.

"Well, at least it will be hard for someone else to see as well," Wren suggested. "Pull in a few meters and let me out. I'll make sure there are no tire tracks to be seen from the road."

The trail turned out to be little more than a pair of overgrown ruts in the ground that led us into a large copse of trees. In the middle of the trees, Thatcher brought the jeep to a stop as the headlights came to rest on the crumbling remains of an old castle surrounded by a large moat of water. The trail leading up to the castle's old wooden door was a walking bridge too narrow for the jeep to drive onto.

Wren climbed out again, taking his gun with him, and walked up to the door; it was unlocked. He pushed it open and walked inside. A few minutes later he came back and gave the all-clear. Caerlaverock Castle was much older than the one I had grown up in; it was also much smaller. This one had been built in the thirteenth century AD with an unusual triangular shape inside of a man-made moat almost as wide as the castle itself. It housed early Scottish Earls until sometime in the seventeenth century AD when the drafty, cold place was eventually abandoned.

Repair work in the twentieth century AD kept it sufficiently viable as a tourist site so that non-M-Gens were able to take refuge in it during the M-Gen war. Unfortunately, as a result, it took a beating from the M-Gens trying to get at those sheltered inside. The result was that many of the walls had large openings where bombs and other shrapnel had struck, and the interiors of nearly all the rooms were open to the sky above. But it would do as a place of refuge for the night until Captain Marcellus' scheduled transport arrived to pick us up in the morning.

We set up camp between two walls just wide enough to allow for the four-man tent that had been packed. I've always found it interesting that a tent labeled as a four-man tent only truly has room for four sleeping bags with nothing left for the gear. That might have been a problem considering that there were five of us, but it was a given that one of us would be remaining on watch outside the tent while the others slept. Wren offered to take the first watch, stating that he was the least injured of the group. None of the rest of us were up to arguing with him.

Thatcher helped me take the boots off of Alex's feet and then get her settled into the bag at the center of the tent. She only stirred once during the process, her head shifting slightly when I took my arms out from under her. McLagan was asleep in the bag across the entrance to the tent before we even finished zipping up her bag. That left the bags on either side of her. Thatcher took the one on the left; I took the one on the right.

I laid there for some time, staring into the darkness, listening to the rhythm of Alex's breathing, and trying to ignore the aching of my body. I was exhausted, but sleep was slow in coming. Instead, my mind insisted on replaying the events that had brought me so close to losing everyone I loved. At some point, though, I must have drifted off because I woke with a start to the realization that something wasn't right.

"Thatcher," I said in alarm, "where's Alex?"

I heard him reach out to touch the empty sleeping bag between us and then curse loudly. We were both out of our bags and moving in the space of a heartbeat. It was still dark inside the tent, but that wouldn't have stopped us if we hadn't both stepped on McLagan in the process. McLagan yelled in pain and bucked upwards sending us sprawling into a tangled mess of arms and legs.

McLagan began swearing up a storm and yelling at us to watch where we stepped, only to be pulled up short as Thatcher shoved him roughly back to the ground and out of the way. Outside the tent, the first hints of the pre-dawn morning could be seen in the dark gray cast of the sky above us. There was just enough light from the crescent moon for us to avoid tripping over anything else as we raced through the corridors shouting for Alex and Wren.

"Up here," Wren's voice called faintly from some distance above. "She's with me." I felt a wave of relief wash through me with those words but didn't slow my pace as I searched for a way to get up to where they were. I found the stairwell in the corner tower and took the steps three at a time, heedless of the rubble that was strewn across them. I only slowed long enough at the top to duck through the fallen, rotting beams of the tower's collapsed ceiling.

As soon as I was beyond the landing and out onto the wall, I was able to see Alex silhouetted against the pale light of the early dawn. She was facing away from me, her attention appearing to be focused on a point far off in the distance. Wren stepped out of the shadows next to me.

"I followed her up here about thirty minutes ago," his voice was soft. "She's just been standing there the whole time."

"Why did she come up here?"

"Don't know," he shrugged. "I tried talking to her a few times, but she only looks at me for a moment before turning away again."

Thatcher finally made it, breathing hard as he came through the doorway; he joined us out on the battlement. I could see his jaw twitch as he studied Alex, his mind processing what he was seeing.

"Haskell, go talk to her," he finally said. "Find out what's going on." I nodded; it was the same thing I had been thinking.

I could feel the strong chill of the air out on the open battlement as I approached her. It would warm up once the sun had risen, but Scotland was in the grips of the late fall season with early winter fast approaching. On top of the battlement, the cold winds that blew across the moors this time of year were strong enough to lift her hair off her shoulders and stream it out behind her in a continuous dance. She turned to look at me as I approached. Then, without a word, she turned back away to continue watching whatever had her attention out beyond the walls.

Several thoughts passed through my mind in that instant. First, there had been a complete lack of expression on her face. No expression, and no recognition in her eyes. Second, she was shivering but was making no effort to warm herself. It was as though she was not even aware of how cold she was. Finally, standing this close to her, I could feel the faint shifting of the gravity underneath me. Looking down, I realized that neither of our feet were actually touching the ground, nor were any of the tiny pieces of rubble that were immediately around us. It couldn't have been more than an inch or two, but it also didn't appear that she was consciously making it happen.

What was going on? Hesitantly, I reached out to touch her shoulder. She didn't flinch, nor did she turn to look at me again. "Alex, what are yae doin'?" I asked somewhat nervously. She didn't respond. "Alex, can yae hear me?" Again, she didn't respond. She just kept staring out toward the moor beyond the trees. *What was she looking at?* I followed her line of vision and felt my jaw drop. Barely visible in the shadowy pre-dawn, several vehicle-sized boulders were floating in the air, slowly shifting positions with each other as though they were performing some type of intricate dance. Any one of them alone had to be heavier than the four hundred pounds she had told me she was currently capable of lifting. All of them together should have been impossible for her. But, impossible or not, she was doing it.

"Thatcher?" I called softly, "Yae're goin' tae want tae see this."

Thatcher and Wren followed my hand as I pointed out toward the moor. Wren let out a low whistle. Up until this point, it had probably been too dark for him to see what she was doing. Thatcher looked back at Alex, studying her again for a long moment.

"Inadvertent control," he finally said.

"What?"

"The graph Durnham showed us. Her inadvertent control is much stronger than her purposeful control."

Thatcher walked over and waved his hand in front of her eyes; she didn't so much as blink. He grunted. "She's asleep."

Asleep?! I turned to look at him in confusion. "Her eyes are open; how can she be asleep?"

"She's sleepwalking. My cousin Jim used to do it. He'd get up in the middle of the night, walk to the kitchen, eat a big piece of the chocolate cake Aunt Mallory had made for Sunday dinner the next day, and then go back to bed. In the morning he'd wake up with cake crumbs all over his bed and chocolate frosting on his face without any clue how it had gotten there."

I thought about the graph General Durnham had shown us. There had been two lines on it: one for the gravity she purposely controlled and the other for the gravity she inadvertently controlled. The second line had suggested that she could unconsciously control much more than she consciously could. I looked back out at the floating boulders. It would certainly explain how she was doing that.

"If she's asleep, then how dae we wake her up?" I asked.

Thatcher shrugged. "In my cousin's case, they didn't. They would just turn him around by the shoulders and walk him back to bed."

"Why not wake him up?"

"They tried to the first few times, but they discovered that he would become agitated when they did so, and it was much harder to get him back to bed. So, they quit trying."

Wren, who had joined us and was listening to our discussion, nodded his head in understanding. "Then we walk her back to bed."

He reached out and took Alex by the hand. She looked down at his hand as he did so but didn't say anything. Speaking calmly and firmly he said to her, "It is time to go down. Come with me."

Still holding her hand, he began to walk toward the tower and the staircase. To my surprise, she followed him. Out on the moor, the boulders settled gently back down. As she walked away from me, the gravity underneath me shifted as well and I felt my feet touching the ground once more. Suddenly standing with bare feet on the cold stone walkway, it occurred to me that this was probably why she had been holding herself off the ground. In my rush to get to her, I hadn't even noticed the freezing cold of the stones, but I sure felt it now.

Wren led her all the way back to the tent with Thatcher and I following close behind. McLagan was waiting there for us. He held the tent flap open with a quizzical expression as

Wren led her back to her sleeping bag, but he held his questions until we got her settled. Once she was laying back down, Wren began singing a low, soft song. The words were not in a language I understood, but the purpose was unmistakable: it was a lullaby. Within moments, Alex's eyes grew heavy and then finally closed. Wren let his song fade.

We left the tent as quietly as we could. Outside we kept our voices low as we discussed what had happened.

"Light help us," McLagan muttered under his breath as we finished. I had to agree.

"Now what?" he asked.

"Now," Thatcher answered him, "you're taking watch."

McLagan grumbled under his breath but didn't argue. In truth, Wren should have woken him up to take over the watch some time ago.

"As for you two," he indicated Wren and me, "get back in the tent and get some more rest. We have a few more hours before the transport is scheduled to arrive."

"What about yae?" I asked when he failed to follow us toward the tent.

"I'm going to stand watch out here and make sure she doesn't decide to go for another walk. Now get in there; you still look exhausted."

He was right. The adrenaline was gone and my heart rate had finally slowed from the pounding staccato Alex's disappearance had set it to, meaning that there was nothing left now but my exhaustion. As I lay back down beside Alex, I considered what I had seen up there on the battlement; she was far stronger than she knew. But more than that, in spite of the fact that she had clearly been the reason those boulders were in the air, I had not seen any indication that she had experienced any physical or mental difficulty as a result of it. Hadn't she told me that supporting that much weight was both physically and mentally exhausting for her? Wasn't that the reason she had passed out in the clearing and then collapsed again last night? But on the battlement she hadn't been straining. She hadn't even broken a sweat. I wasn't sure I understood what that meant, but there was a faint tickling in the back of my mind that suggested there was something important in that line of thought; it just wasn't going to make itself clear right now.

I rolled over in my bag, shifting off the sore rib that had started screaming at me. The only problem with the new position was that it made my knee ache more. I shifted my knee trying to find a more comfortable position, but after several moments I had to sigh in resignation; there wasn't one. I gave up and just held still, allowing my body to scream at me while I tried to sleep.

Chapter 2: Alexandria Jaquette

AS ALWAYS SEEMED to be the case, I was aware of the sounds around me before I was fully awake. What I heard was two sets of steady breathing, the type that came with sleep. I opened my eyes to see Aiden next to me. There was a peacefulness in his sleeping features that brought a smile to my lips. But there was also a purpling bruise creeping out from the shadow of his hairline and a trail of dried blood from the small split in the skin that brought back the memories of what had happened.

I squeezed my eyes shut as images flashed through my mind of the engagement party and the interruption of the invading soldiers, followed by Thatcher trying to lead me away from danger and the DuCains finding us, then seeing Aiden being tortured and the fury I had felt. Finally, I remembered the decision to stop running and to rescue my team, changing into the dead soldier's uniform, and all that had come after that, even Remington's screaming.

I shuddered. There was an ache deep in my chest that accompanied that last memory. In a moment of fury, I had sent the shock collar to Roisin. I had given in to an emotion that I should have never allowed to take over. It wasn't the first time it had happened, but every time it did, I did something I regretted. I needed better control.

With a deep sigh, I sat up and looked around. *A tent?* We must not be at Aiden's home anymore. I had no memory of leaving. For that matter, I didn't remember anything after Remington's screams. But, obviously, quite a bit of time had passed because the light outside the tent indicated that the night was over.

Moving carefully so as not to wake Aiden or the person buried inside the bag on my other side, I stepped out of the tent. I paused only long enough to grab the smaller pair of boots that had been set just inside the tent's flap; it was cold and I had no desire to freeze in bare feet.

"Good morning," Thatcher greeted me. "You awake?"

I rolled my eyes. "I'm standing up and walking, aren't I?"

He grunted but didn't smile, making me wonder if he'd woken up on the wrong side of his bag. Come to think of it, there were dark circles under his eyes. *Had he gotten any sleep?*

"Where are we?"

"We're at the rendezvous point. We have about an hour until our ride arrives. How are you feeling?"

I shrugged. "Sore from sleeping on the ground, but otherwise fine. You? You don't look like you got much sleep."

He grunted again. "It was an interesting night. Sleep wasn't my highest priority."

"Interesting?! Is that what we're calling it?" He smiled that crooked smile of his that always made me wonder if he knew something I didn't, but he didn't say anything more.

My stomach chose that moment to grumble. Thatcher nodded knowingly and pushed himself off the wall he had been leaning against. He grabbed one of the bags that was stacked near the tent and tossed me the ration bar he pulled out of it. "It's not fancy, but it will tide you over till we can get some real food."

"Thanks," I said sarcastically as I caught it. Though in truth, anything edible sounded good right about now. Even a dry ration bar.

I looked around while I ate. The tent had been set up in the narrow space between two stone walls that showed indications of not having been cared for in quite some time. There were chunks of rubble scattered all around that had fallen from the walls at some point. I was actually a little surprised that they had found a rubble-free space big enough for the tent. There was no ceiling, though there were indications that there had been one at some time in the past. At least the walls offered some shelter from the wind that I could hear blowing beyond them. Even so, it was cold. I rubbed my hands against my arms to warm them. Thatcher saw it and reached for another bag; he handed me the jacket he pulled from it. This time there was no sarcasm when I thanked him.

Someone stirred inside the tent. "Thatcher," Aiden's voice called out. "She out there with yae?"

"Yep," Thatcher answered back.

"Good." I was surprised to hear a hint of relief in his voice. *Did he think I would take off without my team?* I shook my head and laughed to myself; how little he knew me. When he joined us a few minutes later, I couldn't help but notice that there was a distinct limp with each step he took, and he grimaced slightly as he pulled on one of the jackets.

"You okay?" I asked him in concern.

"Yeah," he replied automatically, not bothering to look at me while he zipped the jacket. "I'm a little sore, but that's not really surprisin' considerin' that th' girl in th' bag next tae me kept kickin' me all night."

"What?! I did not…" My voice trailed off as Aiden looked up, his straight face cracking into one of his old roguish smiles accompanied by a warm chuckle. I glowered at him but couldn't help the small skip of a beat that my heart did at seeing that smile.

Still grinning, he turned to Thatcher, "Why don't yae go get a little more sleep before our ride shows up? I'll keep her out of trouble for a while." I shook my head in exasperation and turned to walk away from them. I didn't really have anywhere specific in mind, but there was only one direction that led easily away from the tent, so I took it. I hadn't even reached the archway in the wall when he caught up with me.

"Goin' anywhere in particular?" he asked.

"Depends;" I teased him. "Which way are you going so I can go the opposite?"

He chuckled again then suggested, "There's a stairwell in that tower over there. If yae've nothin' else in mind, it will take us up tae th' castle's battlement where yae'll have a decent view of th' land around us. Yae should at least get tae see some of Scotland before we leave."

"Sounds good," I smiled back. "Lead the way."

The battlement turned out to be a long narrow walkway between the castle's two remaining towers. There had been four towers once upon a time: two at the narrow front framing the castle's entrance and two more at each point of the unusually shaped castle, but the two on the east side had collapsed long ago. On the inside wall of the battlement, there was a straight drop down to what had likely once been a large room in the castle; now it wasn't much more than an overgrown courtyard between two walls. The other side was a sheer drop down into the wide moat below. Beyond the moat was a small forest of trees, and beyond that was miles upon miles of beautiful grassland. Aiden was right: the view from up here was incredible.

I glanced back to tell him so, only to find him watching me, an expression of nervousness on his face.

"What is it?" I asked.

He hesitated, as though there was something he wanted to say but didn't know how to approach it. Finally, he cleared his throat. "Um, Alex, th' reason for th' engagement, I don't think it exists anymore."

His words caught me off guard. He was right; it just hadn't occurred to me yet. The purpose of our engagement had been to convince Remington that Aiden was not free to enter into an engagement with his daughter. But, with Remington's accusation that Aiden and his family were traitors, the danger that he would force Aiden into the undesirable marriage was gone.

I looked down at the delicately braided ring he had placed on my finger less than twenty-four hours ago. There was no excuse to keep it on if we weren't going to go through with the engagement. With a surprising pang of regret, I slowly slid the ring off my finger and held it out for him. It was a family heirloom after all, and he should have it for whomever he did eventually marry.

Aiden stared at the ring in my hand but made no move to take it back. Instead, he looked up at me and cleared his throat again, "Actually, I was kind of hopin' yae would keep it on; that yae would still let me have that chance tae earn th' rest of yer heart."

My heart skipped a beat. He still wanted that? Even when he didn't need it to avoid an unwanted marriage? Then my heart fell as I wondered: would he still want it when he realized how much I really was like my siblings? And did I really want to wait around long enough to watch him figure it out?

He must have sensed my hesitation, because he hurried on to say, "Look. I know yae only agreed tae th' engagement because of th' situation I was in and yae can still walk away at any time. All I'm askin' for is a chance. If I'm not successful…well, then yae can take it off and dae whatever yae'd like with it. It's yers now." He looked toward the grassland as he finished speaking, but I was almost certain I heard him softly whisper, "I won't be needin' it back if yae're not th' one wearin' it."

I lowered my hand, though I didn't make a move to put the ring back on. I realized that, just like before, I still had a choice in what I did. Only now, Aiden did as well, and he was choosing to move forward with what he had begun. But was this still what I wanted? Should I give him the ring back, or should I give him the chance he was asking for?

In the past twenty-four hours, I had come to realize that the barriers I had built around my heart to protect myself had been breached. Aiden had somehow slipped through my defenses and stolen a piece of my heart. It was a smaller piece, but the sense of betrayal I had felt when he had turned his back on me had hurt enough to warn me that I never wanted to feel that way again. Even so, if I walked away now, I would heal. It would be painful, but what I had gone through already had proved to me that I would survive it. If I let him stay, though, I risked allowing him to eventually have enough of my heart that I wouldn't be able to recover if he ever abandoned me again. That thought terrified me, almost as much as it had crippled me to see him tortured and to realize that I could do nothing to stop it.

At the same time, I had been surprised to find that allowing the DuCains in had made me stronger. *Could it be the same way with Aiden?* I looked down at the ring in my hand. Four braided metals that each represented a side of love: purity, strength, and passion intertwined. But it was the fourth side, hope, that held my focus now. Hope that the love would grow. Hope that it would be returned in equal measure. Hope that it would prove to be worth it in the end. Hope that hope would continue to exist for me and never be taken away.

Nervously, I slid the ring back onto my finger. It was hope that made the decision for me. I needed that hope to keep me going, to keep me believing that I could be different from my other siblings and that I could prove I was stronger than Icarus' claim on me. I needed to be able to hope that Aiden would succeed in his wish to earn the rest of my heart. Because, without that hope, I had already lost the battle.

Chapter 3: Alexandria Jaquette

THE TRANSPORT ARRIVED right on schedule, bringing with it a whole squad of UFC soldiers. My phase rifle had been fired triggering the alarm relay; the response squad had arrived at Aiden's home forty minutes later only to find that we had already left. Eithine had assured them that our group was in a safe location but had refused to give them the coordinates until our pre-arranged time this morning. Instead, she had put them to work cleaning up from Remington's invasion. Specifically, she had them transporting the UFC soldiers who had been following Remington's commands back to their base of origin. And, being who Eithine was, they had only succeeded at offering minor arguments against what she had demanded before finally doing exactly what she had told them to do. Of course, the commander of the recovery squad didn't admit to it in those exact words, but I was able to piece together enough of what had occurred from the conversations among the other soldiers to put two and two together into a complete picture.

They delivered us into the care of the Edinburgh base's commanding officer who was waiting for us at the landing pad. The woman had a prominent beaked nose that was framed by steel-gray eyes hard enough to crack a mountain. She looked the team up and down for several seconds, taking in the bandages and limps before turning to the aide at her side. "I want them taken to MEDDAC first. Make sure they get priority attention." Then she indicated that we were to follow her to a vehicle waiting just off the tarmac. As we walked, she talked.

"Welcome to Edinburgh Base. My name is Corporal Worthington. I don't know what your team has been up to, and I don't want to know…" she eyed the silver case in Wren's hands suspiciously as she said it, "…but it's rare that we see the type of security clearances that came through to get your team evacuated. Someone high up wants you well taken care of. I've been instructed to make sure you have everything you need before sending you out on the first flight to America. That plane will be leaving at zero five hundred hours tomorrow morning, so plan to be on it. Which one of you is Haskell?"

"I am," Aiden replied.

"Captain Marcellus said to tell you that your next set of instructions should already be on your command pad and will become available once you reach the appropriate altitude. I'm assuming you know what that means?"

"Aye, sir," Aiden nodded.

"Good. Then I'll leave you in the hands of Lieutenant Klark. She'll escort you to the MEDDAC and then show you where you'll be staying for the night. Whatever you need, just let her know and she'll take care of you."

"Thank yae, sir." Aiden saluted her before climbing into the transport vehicle; she snapped a quick salute back then left us for a second vehicle that was waiting to take her elsewhere.

MEDDAC, as it turned out, was the base's medical facility; the acronym stood for Medical Department Activity. It was basically a five-story military hospital that serviced the large base. At the facility, the Lieutenant escorted us to a medical room where several doctors were waiting. I was quickly cleared, but the rest of the team took more time. Thatcher's arm was the most serious. The attending physician took one look at the wound and then got on the phone to schedule a surgery room.

"Whoever bandaged you up did a good job with the supplies they had on hand, but this is going to require hands more skilled than mine to fix. Lawry is a good surgeon. He'll have you fixed up in a jiffy and back with your team in time for your flight tomorrow morning."

As the doctor finished entering the orders into his digi-pad, Thatcher turned to Aiden with a frustrated scowl, "Haskell, you've got the team till I get back. Make sure there are no more midnight outings."

Midnight outings? What was that about? But Aiden simply nodded and said, "I'll take care of it."

As the doctor led him from the room, it occurred to me that he was probably frustrated that his arm was not going to be a simple fix. He seemed like the type who would rather just shrug off an injury and keep going than spend time in a doctor's office getting it fixed. But I also couldn't imagine that the military was about to take any chances with his arm or that aim of his, and they would take steps to ensure that it would heal properly. He was too valuable a marksman for them to do otherwise.

Aiden's knee, which he had originally injured fighting Sobrien in the caves, had been further injured last night by a kick to the back of it. It didn't need surgery, but it did need physical therapy, which the doctor said he would have to get at his next location as we weren't staying on base. He entered orders into his digi-pad pre-authorizing it for when Aiden arrived at his next post. It also turned out that Aiden had a cracked rib, explaining his grimace when he put on his jacket this morning and the occasional wince I had seen him trying to hide when he took too deep of a breath. He was given pain medication, a brace for his knee, a bandage wrap around his torso, and a bag of ice for his ribs, but there wasn't much else to be done while he healed. He was still on active duty and would be required to remain so. They just recommended that he take it easy whenever his duties gave him the chance. I started to protest, only to have him hold up his hands to stop me.

"I'm Scottish, Alex. This is normal procedure for us."

That didn't set well with me. But he followed it up with a grin. "Besides, yae'll not be rid of me that easily. Relievin' me of duty, even temporarily for an injury, would mean I wouldn't be goin' with th' team when yae continue on, and I'm not about tae let yae leave here without me."

I shook my head in exasperation. I was less and less impressed with this side of the UFC that I had learned about in the last twenty-four hours, but I didn't want him to be forced to stay behind either, so I kept my mouth shut, at least for now.

The gash in McLagan's leg was stitched up after which he was basically told the same thing they had told Aiden; rest it where he could and get back to work. The cut on Wren's forehead was stitched up, as was the small cut at Aiden's hairline, and then we were told we were good to go.

Next, the Lieutenant showed us to the dormitories. While we walked, she explained that we had each been assigned rooms for the night in the base's coed dormitory. She handed Aiden an envelope with our key cards in it then explained that we were also welcome to take advantage of the base's entertainment facilities which included several parks, a theater, a bowling alley, a rec hall, a gym, and a commissary.

The last one, she joked, was particularly exciting on nights the mess hall served one of its infamous *goolop* meals, a conglomerate casserole made up from the week's leftovers. It turned out that no one ever seemed to want to risk the mystery meal, and everyone rushed to the commissary to find something a little more promising for dinner. On the other hand, they'd had one only a few nights ago, so it was unlikely that we would get to see it tonight. She left us in the hall next to our rooms with a final farewell and a credit card that she said would pay for our meals in the mess hall and anything we needed from the commissary.

After she left, Aiden told us to stow our gear in our rooms while we went to the depot to get replacement supplies. Because of Eithine's foresight, we had basic camping gear with military rations and jackets, but the travel bags Marcellus had supplied us with were still in the rooms where we had left them and the dress clothes that most of the team was still wearing had not survived the night's events unscathed. We needed a change of clothes, basic toiletries, and replacement weapons for the ones we had been forced to leave behind. Technically, we did have three rifles between us, but Aiden wanted the whole team fully stocked before we left in the morning. It wasn't that he expected trouble; he had just learned from personal experience that it was always better to be prepared for the worst so that you could relax and enjoy the best.

We also had that worthless silver case. Aiden had been tortured over it, yet both he and Thatcher had insisted that we still needed to bring it with us in order to maintain our cover. I had adamantly made clear my displeasure with their decision. Unfortunately, I was overruled. So, I did my best to ignore the fact that it was there. Fortunately, when we left the dorms to get new supplies, they left it behind in the rooms.

The depot officer was expecting us when we arrived; the commander's secretary had called ahead to let him know we were coming and instructed him to cooperate with us fully. We left with five new packs filled with several changes of fatigues each, toiletries, and replacement weapons ranging from phase rifles and pistols to knives and scabbards. Well, actually, he'd readily supplied the packs, fatigues, and toiletries, but he'd sent us down the hall to the armory for the weapons. That part didn't go quite as smoothly.

The armorer had also been called ahead, but he balked when Aiden refused to give him our names and unit in exchange for the weapons.

"Name and unit are required for every weapon issued. No name, no weapons."

Aiden sighed heavily. "For th' last time, yae don't have a high enough security clearance for that information. If yae have a problem with it, yae'll need tae call Corporal Worthington's office."

He did, and he did. Corporal Worthington was less than amused. I could hear her voice over the line even at the ten feet away we were standing.

"Were you or were you not given instructions from my secretary to take care of this team's needs?"

"Yes, sir. But…"

"And were you or were you not told that you were to do so without asking questions?"

"Yes, sir. But…"

"Then do it! Give them what they ask for! Put my name in your log book and send me the forms to sign. Do I make myself clear?"

"Yes, sir."

He was much more subdued as he closed the line. We left with everything we asked for and no further problems.

Showers and lunch had been the next order of business. It felt good to wash away the grime of yesterday's events. Not that I was actually all that dirty, but I felt dirty from everything that had happened so that the hot water had the same effect, scrubbing away much of the emotional grime that had taken a toll on me. There was still a dark place in the back of my mind that recalled what I had done to Remington, but it remained silent for now, content to hide in the shadowy recesses of my mind.

The new fatigues fit me snuggly. With the pistol in its holster and a knife strapped to my leg, I was ready to meet up again with my team. Aiden had instructed us that we were to have our pistols and knives on us at all times from here on out. It seemed unnecessary to me, but he had more experience with these things than I did, so I strapped them on before leaving my room.

The others were waiting in the hall; at least, Aiden and Wren were. They said McLagan had decided to catch a nap. He'd had the final watch last night, so it wasn't all that surprising. That left Wren, Aiden, and me free to find something to do with the rest of our afternoon. With Aiden's injuries, the gym and the bowling alley were out and I wasn't really interested in watching a movie, so I suggested the Rec Hall.

The hall, as it turned out, was surprisingly similar to the one on Ghana Base. It had the classics: billiards, ping-pong, foosball, skeerdeball, and a few video games. It also had a multimedia area set up with groupings of tables and chairs, and a few couches arranged around the entertainment system. Against the wall next to the display screen was a cabinet full of games, a shelf with a few books, and a sign that read "Clean up after yourself! Your mom's not here to do it for you!"

"How about a game of cards?" I suggested.

"I'm game," Aiden grinned. Wren and I groaned at his pun.

We played a few different games including one Wren taught us that was based on speed and strategy. Wren's game required several piles of cards in the center of the table that were to be played on, more piles around the table to be drawn from, a pile of cards in front of each player that they needed to get rid of in order to win, and a set of cards in each player's hand that we could use to mess up our opponents' plans. The strategy aspect required the players to track what everyone else was doing; the fast pace of the game made it almost impossible to do so. The more players there were, the more difficult it got. Three players, Wren explained, was a good size group to start learning with, but six or seven made the game far more interesting. I couldn't imagine playing with that many. It was difficult enough to keep track of everything that was happening with only the three of us.

Wren won most of the rounds soundly, but Aiden got in a few good ones as well and racked up a respectable score by the end. My score was just plain miserable. I had never been great at card games, but this one was especially difficult for me compared to Wren and Aiden who seemed to take to the game instinctively. When Wren won for the umpteenth time, I threw up my hands and called it quits.

"Enough! I surrender." I was half laughing, half groaning.

Aiden chuckled as he set his cards down on the table as well. "I think that's it for me tae. Good game, Wren. We'll have tae play it again sometime. What did yae say it was called?"

"Cuckoo's Nest," Wren offered as he began gathering up the cards and separating them back out into their individual decks; he had combined several to make the one deck needed for the game.

I stood up and stretched; we had been playing for quite a while and I was starting to feel stiff from sitting still. As I did so, an appreciative whistle sounded from across the hall, startling me. I looked back to see a dark-haired and dark-skinned soldier staring at me from across the billiard table where he had been about to take a shot. He stood up slowly, never taking his eyes off me. The man was tall, with broad shoulders that nicely filled in the lines of the black T-shirt he was wearing. He continued to stare at me as though entranced by what he saw. I turned around to fully face him.

"Oy, Jackal, quit stalling and finish your shot," his opponent hollered at him. The man shook his head as though to clear it, finally breaking the gaze. Then a slow grin grew on his face as he confidently turned to his opponent and said, "Two-ball in the side pocket."

I expected him to stop talking and take his shot. Instead, he glanced back toward me once again as he continued, "Followed by the five-ball in the left corner and the eight-ball in the right corner."

His opponent scoffed, "Jackal, you're making this too easy on me. You might as well pay me that twenty credits and give up if that's your intent."

The man's grin grew smugger. "Tell you what, if you're that confident I won't be able to make the shot, why don't we just double the bet?"

His opponent laughed. "Sure, why not. I have no problem taking money away from fools." The man set his cue stick back into its slot on the rack. Clearly, he didn't expect to need it again. Then he leaned back against the wall and folded his arms across his chest with a confident air. "Let's see it then."

The man spared a quick glance back in my direction before bending back over the table. His grin grew when he noted that I was still watching. He drew back his cue stick and snapped it forward. The cue ball shot into the center of the small grouping of balls. The solid blue ball went spinning into the side pocket. The orange five-ball shot straight for the left corner pocket followed by the black eight-ball ricocheting off the sidebar to drop straight into the opposite corner pocket. His opponent swore in frustration as he pushed off the wall. "You and your Light-cursed luck," he complained while throwing several credits down onto the table before stalking away.

The man casually picked up the credits and slid them into his pocket before setting his cue stick down and strolling across the room to our table. To my amusement, Aiden stood as he approached. I wasn't naïve; I could see what was happening. But it had occurred to me that I was curious to know how Aiden would handle competition, so I didn't say anything to reassure him.

"That was a nice shot," Aiden said a little coldly.

The man glanced toward him, seeming to notice him for the first time. "Thanks," he said. But then he turned back to me as though he found Aiden and Lakota to be unimportant. He held out his hand to me. "Nate Evans."

I smiled, slightly amused, and accepted it. I remembered at the last second to give him my new name. "Claire DuCain."

Not releasing my hand, he went on, "I've just come into a few credits. Perhaps I could convince you to join me at the bar for a drink."

I shook my head, still smiling. "Thanks, but no. I don't drink."

Nate wasn't dissuaded. "That's not a problem. They serve non-alcoholic drinks there as well. The barista makes a nice little non-alcoholic strawberry daiquiri. I'd love the opportunity to talk. Maybe, get to know you a little better?"

I raised my eyebrow at the suggestion in his words. I most definitely wasn't interested in that, but it didn't stop me from countering, "I must admit you've made an interesting offer. Perhaps another time I'd even consider taking you up on it…" I heard Aiden almost choke behind me. I had to hold in my grin as I continued with a hint of regret, "…but I think my teammates had something else planned for this afternoon." I took my hand back and started to turn away, only to stop as Nate started talking again. I turned back to realize that he was finally giving Aiden an appraising look. He took in Aiden's stance and the scowl on his face.

Nate's smile faltered for half a second. "I see."

Then his grin returned, and he looked at me again. "I'll tell you what. How about we play a game of billiards? You win, I'll admit my defeat and sadly leave you to your team's afternoon plans. But, if I win, you join me for that drink."

He turned to look Aiden straight in the eyes as he added with a wink, "I promise I'll have her back in time for curfew."

Aiden's face grew darker. I almost felt bad for what I was doing, but if he wanted me to continue with the engagement, then I wanted to know just how he meant to handle it.

Smiling innocently, I seemed to consider Nate's offer for a long moment before finally saying petulantly, "I'm afraid I'm not very good at that game. But perhaps," I turned to look at Aiden as though suddenly seeing another way, "you would care to play for me?"

Aiden hesitated, a slight hint of shock in his expression. Then he forced it into a smile and said, "Gladly." I wondered if he suspected what I was up to.

Nate frowned at the change to his plans, but went along with them. "All right. So long as you agree that his loss will mean my gain."

I laughed, nodding my head in agreement.

Nate set up the table and offered Aiden the breaking shot. It was a clean break, though nothing special as a single solid colored ball rolled into a side pocket and all the others came to rest in scattered locations. Unfortunately, however, Aiden missed his second shot turning the table over to Nate. Nate proceeded to sink three of his own balls before one of his striped balls bounced away from the pocket it had seemed almost certain to drop into, having instead caught the edge of the pocket's corner.

Aiden stepped back up to examine the table's setting. He was looking for the best angle to shoot from when Nate slapped him on the back, making Aiden draw in a sharp breath. Not knowing the pain he had just inflicted, Nate said with a grin, "Thought it would only be fair to give you another chance before I cleared the board and your afternoon plans."

I frowned as I watched Aiden tuck his arm against his ribs. Suddenly, I didn't find this very amusing. I was about to say something when Aiden met my eyes. He shook his head ever so slightly; he didn't want me to interfere.

Aiden took a slow breath and then picked up his cue stick again. He made the next few shots easily, smoothly dropping four more of his balls into their respective pockets before he finally missed one. His jaw clenched for the briefest of seconds, then he forced the smile back into place. "Guess it's yer turn again," he shrugged deceptively lightheartedly.

Nate grinned at me as he stepped forward to take over. He confidently took his next few shots, appearing poised to clean up the board. The only thing left for him was to drop the eight-ball. "You played a good game, but I'm afraid it's over. Eight-ball, corner pocket," he said confidently as he took the shot.

There was a distinct look of disappointment in Aiden's eyes as the eight-ball rolled in a straight line for the pocket Nate had called, but he valiantly forced a smile back onto his face as he looked at me with an apologetic shrug. I returned his look with a steady gaze, not making any effort to hide the twinkle in my eyes when Nate suddenly swore. Aiden's eyes shot away from mine and back to the table where the eight-ball had suddenly come to an inexplicable stop, half an inch from the pocket.

A slow smile crept onto Aiden's face as he said, with the faintest hint of satisfaction, "Wow. That's really tough."

Nate grumbled, but sportingly stepped back to allow Aiden to have the table. Aiden didn't miss his final two shots as he sunk his last colored ball and then the eight-ball. Nate shook his head ruefully in defeat as the final ball fell into the pocket. In spite of the loss, he kept a smile on his face as he walked up to me. "Guess I'll have to get that drink alone. Maybe you'll give me another shot sometime?" His expression was so hopeful, I hated to completely shut him down. So, I simply smiled back and said, "Perhaps another time."

I think he realized what was not being said as he sighed in resignation before turning back to shake Aiden's hand. "Congratulations. I'll, uh, leave you to your winnings." Then he regretfully left the hall, only glancing back once with a slight shake of his head.

As the door closed, Aiden turned to face me. "Why dae I get th' feelin' yae've been takin' lessons from Roisin?"

I shrugged with an innocent smile causing him to start laughing. "I think I should have never let th' two of yae meet."

Somehow, I kept the smile on my face, but his teasing accusation struck a nerve and left me feeling sick. I didn't like the suggestion that what I had done was anything like the games Roisin played; it wasn't something I had planned out the way she seemed to. I had simply reacted to the situation Nate had presented. It had been an opportunity to see if Aiden was the jealous type or if he was confident enough to withstand a challenger, and he had responded brilliantly. His displeasure at Nate's attention had been charming and his disappointment when he thought he had lost the game had been endearing. But mostly, he had not interrupted when I was talking to Nate or attempted to assert dominance in any way, nor had he interfered until I had invited him to do so. I couldn't have been more pleased with his reaction to the situation. I just wasn't pleased with how I had gone about getting it. I shouldn't have done that.

My disappointment in myself dominated my thoughts as we left the rec hall. All my life I've known that I was a child of Icarus and that everyone was watching, waiting for me to start acting like one. For the second day in a row, I had done something that seemed to be taking me down that path. It worried me. That was not what I wanted to become.

Chapter 4: Alexandria Jaquette

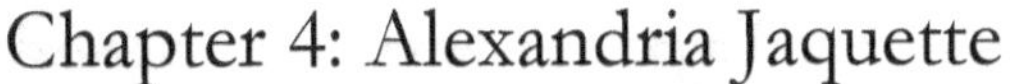

WHEN WE ARRIVED back at the dorms, we found McLagan waiting for us. We still had an hour or so until dinner time, but there wasn't anything we wanted to go do, so we just sat around in the dorm's common area instead. It was little more than a big room with scattered couches, tables, and chairs that had been haphazardly arranged and likely rearranged on multiple occasions to suit the needs of whoever was currently using it.

We chose a small grouping of armchairs away from the others in the room and started talking. It wasn't long before what had happened in the rec hall came up. Wren, with his normal straight-faced humor, shared the story with McLagan. In short order, I was blushing and McLagan was laughing, "Girlie, I dae believe I'd like tae buy yae a drink sometime, for keepin' this boy on his toes so effectively."

Aiden only shrugged with a helpless smile as McLagan teased him, but I noticed there was also a faint hint of pride as he looked at me. Somehow, it made me feel worse. I had failed him by setting him up like that. It was obvious that he found the situation amusing this time, but that didn't make me any less disappointed in myself. *Why had I done that?*

I was startled out of my thoughts by Aiden leaning over to ask me, "What's botherin' yae?" He had spoken quietly, not interrupting the conversation on knife sharpening techniques that McLagan and Wren were engaged in.

"What makes you think something's bothering me?" I nervously asked. I wasn't sure I wanted him to know my thoughts just yet, at least not until I had worked through them myself.

He smiled wryly as he looked pointedly down at my hands and then back up at me. I knew immediately what had clued him in: I was twisting the ring again. I let it go and purposely folded my hands.

"It's nothing," I lied.

His smile faltered as he considered my answer. "Why don't we go for a walk," he finally said.

When I hesitated, he added with a mischievous grin, "I did win th' game after all. The least yae can dae is go for a walk with me." Then, not waiting for my answer, he called over his shoulder to McLagan and Wren, "We're goin' tae go outside. We'll be back in a bit."

Caught up in their conversation, they waved goodbye without even looking our way. With a rueful shake of my head, I gave in and accepted his proffered hand.

Aiden continued to hold my hand as we walked; he hadn't let go of it after helping me up. To be honest, I liked how it felt. But right now, I was too worried about what I had done to recognize how comfortable it was.

To his credit, Aiden didn't try to force a conversation. Instead, he seemed content to walk with me in silence, giving me time to try and put my thoughts together. But the longer we walked, the harder it seemed to be for me to start talking.

There was a growing fear in the back of my mind that Aiden should be mad at me and that his silence was an indicator that he was. Perhaps it was an irrational fear, but there it was.

We walked for long enough that I no longer had any idea where we were. The sidewalk we had started out on had given way to first one road and then another so many times that I almost wondered if Aiden was taking us in circles; it wouldn't have surprised me. But, in truth, the base was large enough that we could have walked in a straight line for several hours and still not reached the other end.

Edinburgh Base was located on over twenty-thousand acres just a few miles to the east of the city it was named for. It had been established in 71 PB at the outset of the M-Gen War but had since become Scotland's main operating base because of its central location and its position on the coastline. Today it housed some fifteen-thousand active-duty soldiers. I assumed that many of the forces here were the ground troops that Scotland was obliged to enlist and train, but there were also a lot of non-Scottish troops here. There was even a small naval installation and an airfield that operated with their corresponding soldiers.

To the best that I had been able to determine from our short time on the base, it was laid out similarly to Ghana Base. The roads ran in a grid pattern with specific grids set apart for specific functions. The vast majority of the base consisted of training grounds. At Ghana it had been primarily jungle; here it was forest and fields. But there were also sections set apart for operations facilities, storage, maintenance, housing, and recreation.

It was the recreational facilities section that we seemed to be in now. The sidewalk we were on was adjacent to a football pitch where a game was in full swing. While it looked to be an unofficial match between friends, they had attracted quite a gathering of spectators to cheer them on. Beyond that was a second field where several people were tossing a flybee back and forth.

We followed the sidewalk around the fields and had just reached the far side when Aiden finally decided it was time to break the silence. "Alex, whatever is botherin' yae, yae can talk tae me about it. Maybe I can help yae with it."

He hadn't looked at me as he said it. He just kept walking, continuing to hold my hand. Somehow, by not looking at me, he gave the impression that whatever was worrying me wasn't so big of a deal that he couldn't handle it. Even so, it still took a few minutes more before I finally gathered enough courage to force something out.

"It's what happened in the rec hall," I finally said. "I shouldn't have done that to you. I'm sorry for putting you through that."

Aiden stopped, mid-stride and turned to look at me. His expression was somewhere between shock and amusement.

"That's what has yae upset? Th' game yae played in there?"

That was not the reaction I had been expecting. *He's amused?! I'm concerned that he should be angry with me, and he's amused?* I was suddenly mad at him, as though it were his fault for not feeling the way I thought he should.

I yanked my hand free and turned to face him. "Yes," I answered heatedly. "That is what has me upset. Games like that are just plain mean."

His smile slid away. "Alex, I didn't mean…"

I cut him off. "No one should play games like that with someone else's heart. You should be furious with me right now. Instead, you seem to think it's all some type of joke. It's not okay, Aiden. I knew it wasn't okay, and yet I still did it. Just like with Remington. Just like…" I suddenly stiffened as what was really bothering me clicked into place. *"Just like a child of Icarus,"* I finished in a horrified whisper.

My anger was gone in an instant, frozen into a solid chunk of ice by that thought. "Aiden, what I did last night, what I did today, it scares me. What if I really am just like them?"

He was shaking his head before I even finished. There was no longer any hint of amusement on his face or in his voice, "No, Alex. Yae can stop that line of thinkin' right there. What yae did in th' Rec Hall was no different than what Roisin would have done in th' same situation. Aye, yae played me against him, but when it became clear that I was goin' tae lose tae him, yae stopped that ball. Yae made sure I would still win. A Child of Icarus would not have done that. They would not have cared if I lost or how it made me feel. In fact, they would have let me lose so that they could revel in me pain."

"But what I did to Remington…"

He was shaking his head again as he reached up to place a hand on my shoulder. "Alex, yae didn't dae that; Roisin did. She put th' collar on him and started it; yae didn't. Yae were angry and upset, just like th' rest of us; it would have been unnatural if yae hadn't been. But yae weren't causin' pain for th' mere pleasure of it and yae most certainly weren't enjoyin' hearin' his screams. If anyone behaved like a Child of Icarus last night, it was Remington and Roisin. And as for what happened in th' Rec Hall," his expression softened back into one of his wry smiles, "I'll admit I didn't expect that from yae, but it was nice tae know that yae would choose me over a tall, dark, and handsome stranger."

45

I stared at him in surprise for a full three seconds. *I'd chosen him over Nate? Well, yes, I guess I had.* I felt my smile return just a little and I teasingly shrugged. "I guess he just wasn't my type. I'll have to keep my eyes open though; in case a better offer comes along."

Aiden adopted an injured tone. "Hey now; that's not…" The rest of what he was going to say was cut off by the sound of an explosion. We both spun in the direction of the sound. We couldn't see what had caused it, but there was a plume of thick black smoke just starting to rise from somewhere off to the west. The football players had also stopped to stare in that direction.

One of the players called out, "What's going on?"

A woman on the sidelines, with her hands shading her eyes against the late afternoon sun, answered, "Looks like it's coming from the airfield."

Even as she was still speaking, a pair of jets approached from the east. They streaked over the airfield and dropped two small shapes. We watched in stunned silence as the cylindrical objects plummeted in the direction of the airfield and then were lost from view behind a pair of buildings. Half a second later more explosions rocked the silence, followed in quick succession by the winding up cry of an air raid siren.

Aiden didn't stick around to find out what would happen next. He grabbed my arm and pulled me into a sprint straight across the fields, back in the direction we had come from. The brace on his leg didn't slow him down even a little. He wasn't the only one to jump into action. The football game came to an abrupt end as men and women scattered, presumably to their respective stations.

As we ran, I saw more jets become visible, streaking into view and releasing more of those shapes in different locations. Explosions were happening all over the base. In tandem with those blasts, we began to hear shouts and phaser fire coming from more than one direction around us. It crossed my mind that this was a large-scale invasion. There were too many sounds of battle, coming from too many places, to be anything less. What I couldn't understand was how this was possible on such a large military base.

Even as multiple explosions began to rock the base, a deep reverberating *thrum* sounded nearby, accompanied by the pounding cadence of something heavy. I couldn't place the sound; it was unlike anything I had ever heard before, but Aiden recognized it immediately. Still running, he looked sharply to our right. A startled look crossed his face then he rapidly swung back to wrap his arms around me as he threw us both to the ground. We rolled to a stop with him protectively holding onto me.

Brilliant white light seared the air just above where we had been. More phaser fire streaked across the field to strike several of the buildings on the other side. I had no idea what those buildings held, but they erupted into fireballs of flames, compounded moments later by more percussive explosions as whatever was inside of them erupted from the fire.

My ears were ringing from the explosions as I shook my head and tried to get my bearings. The phaser blasts had come from a military-style vehicle unlike anything I had ever seen before. It had a large black body balanced easily on its two thick legs which stomped down the road at a slow, steady gate. All the while, its thick-barreled gun kept up a steady stream of phaser fire aimed at anything that moved, whether it be people or vehicles.

The moment its gun turned away from us, Aiden yanked me to my feet and pushed me forward. *"Run!"* he ordered.

We'd only made it perhaps twenty yards before he lunged forward to knock me back to the ground, just in time to fall below another brilliant blast of light. We lay there, breathing hard, waiting for it to turn its attention elsewhere again. Then, as soon as it did, he pulled me back up and we repeated the process. It took several minutes, and several desperate dives to the ground, to cover the remaining hundred yards of the open field before we were able to make the final surge across the road and behind one of the parked vehicles.

"What is that thing?" I shouted to be heard above the sounds of battle.

"Talos," Aiden shouted back without taking his eyes off the machine. He had taken up a position at the end of the car and was cautiously peaking around the bumper.

"What's a Talos?" The name meant nothing to me.

"Not what, who. Talos is one of Icarus' children."

I looked at him in utter confusion. "It's a machine. How can it be one of his children?"

Aiden barked a bitter laugh but didn't answer right away. Instead, he grabbed me by the arm and lunged to his feet once more; the machine had just turned away. We ran for the side of the building closest to us, not quite making it around the corner before the machine turned back. It must have seen us because it fired several more shots in our direction. Aiden yanked me around the corner and shoved me to the ground, covering me with his own body as the blast sent bricks and mortar flying from the building. I heard him grunt as some of those bricks landed on his back.

The moment the phaser fire stopped he rolled off with a slight groan but immediately pushed himself back to his feet. "Keep moving," he grunted. I could tell he was hurting, but he didn't let it slow him down. He grabbed my hand and we took off again.

As I watched him running through his pain, I was reminded once more that he wasn't just another specialist training to potentially use his gifts in battle; he was already a battle-hardened soldier who had spent the last five years serving in the UFC's special forces, fighting daily on the front lines in the war against Icarus. He had trained his whole life for that role and now that training was likely all that was keeping us alive.

Even so, we were hard-pressed to get more than a block or two at a time before we ran into some new obstacle. There were soldiers in black uniforms everywhere. No, not quite black. They were the same Multicam uniforms the soldiers in the jungle had been wearing two weeks ago.

How could Icarus' forces have possibly gotten onto this base? Why hadn't there been any warning? Shouldn't someone have seen this large of a force coming? Great Britain was an island for Light's sake! I thought about the soldiers who had been in the jungle. They had been specifically looking for Icarus' missing Alpha. Were these ones doing the same thing? Or was this a random attack and we just happened to be in the wrong place at the wrong time?

These questions and many more raced through my mind, but they were relegated to the back as more pressing concerns took precedence. Most important was the need to find the rest of my team and to avoid alerting others to our presence as we carefully threaded our way between and around the many enemy soldiers that seemed to be everywhere.

Aiden led the way, seeming to instinctively know what needed to be done to avoid detection in each situation. If the soldiers were simply patrolling past us, he would have us hold perfectly still, blending into the evening's shadows while they passed. If they were stationed at a specific location and showed no indication of moving on, we usually backtracked and found a different way around.

But twice now, when we had not been able to find an alternative route, we had returned to the blockade where he hid me in the shadows and then removed his knife from its scabbard to dispatch the soldiers there. The efficiency and ease with which he did so was a little unnerving. At the same time, it was also comforting; comforting to know that he had the skills needed to get us through this.

Before long, we'd been forced to backtrack and find new ways so many times that I was no longer certain I knew which direction we were traveling. Aiden seemed to though; he kept us moving with surprising confidence. By the time we made it back to the dorms, the sun had already set. There was only the faintest hint of daylight left in the sky, but it was enough to reveal multiple blast marks on the building. The four large gouges in the brick walls had taken something bigger than a phase rifle to create. It seemed that the invading forces had already come through here. Three dead bodies, left where they had fallen, reinforced the belief.

Aiden pulled his phase gun free of its holster while we searched for any indication that there were still enemies nearby. The street was relatively quiet now. The sounds of battle were more than a few blocks away. Then again, I wasn't sure whether or not that was a good sign. If the battle had ended here, it was most likely because there was no longer anyone left here to resist the invaders. *What did that mean for Wren and McLagan?*

Cautiously, Aiden glided away from our cover, checking in all directions as he went. He had told me to stay behind while he made certain the way was clear. Like his, my gun was drawn. Unlike his, mine was still held at my side, ensuring that no light could glint off of its barrel to give away my location. When he reached the other side without anyone coming out to block his way, he signaled for me to follow. The door that had been the entrance to the dorms was gone, having been blown away. We slipped into the building through the gaping hole that was all that remained.

We searched the first-floor hall using the search pattern that Aiden had taught the recruits back in Ghana. He led; I followed. At each intersection, I would ease up to the corner as he went around it first. The halls appeared to be empty; no sign of Wren or McLagan. But then, there were also several indications that the battle had moved inside the building at some point and had extended even to here. My stomach tightened with worry. Were they still alive?

There were signs of struggle everywhere. Phase blasts on the walls, broken furniture, and even a few more dead bodies. But none of those bodies belonged to our friends. Every door we passed showed signs of having been forced open and the room beyond searched. Yet, aside from the few dead bodies, there was no sign of the hundred some odd men and women who resided in this building. Likely, many of them had been elsewhere on the base at the time of the attack, but there had still been quite a few in the building when we had left to start our walk.

"Where is everyone?" I asked in a careful whisper.

"I'm not sure. They don't usually take prisoners."

He didn't say anything more as we worked our way up the two flights of stairs to the floor our rooms were on, but what he hadn't needed to say was that there weren't nearly enough bodies for the attacking forces to have done their usual practice of just killing everyone. Something else was going on. Even so, the hallways on the third floor showed the same signs of resistance the ones downstairs had shown: they had not been taken without a fight. When we reached our rooms, we found that the doors had been forced open, just like the rest. But unlike my own room, Wren's room showed signs of a battle having taken place inside.

Aiden looked at the room for a long moment before finally saying, "Get yer rifle and yer field pack; leave th' rest."

Aiden had insisted that we each obtain and prepare a field bag when we had been restocking our supplies. At the time, I had thought it a little silly to assume we could possibly need it between now and our arrival at the school; I didn't think so anymore. I slung it over my shoulders and cinched down its straps, grateful for Aiden's foresight. The small packs carried emergency rations and other field gear that would keep us alive for several days if we had to leave here on foot.

Back in the hall, Aiden was already waiting for me, his own bag strapped to his back. I wasn't sure if it was my imagination or not, but his bag seemed slightly fuller than it should have been. Of course, it wasn't an important observation given our situation, so I dismissed it almost as quickly as it occurred.

The next hour was a blur as we crept back through the night, slowly working our way toward the medical center where we had left Thatcher. Our hope was that we would at least find him there, but what we found instead made me sick.

The sun had set long ago, but the parking lot's lights were on and portable floodlights had been brought in so that the area was well lit. We could easily make out over two-thousand UFC soldiers with their hands bound behind them, kneeling in large groups throughout the parking lot and on the grassy area in front of the MEDDAC. Guarding them were some two-hundred armed soldiers with perhaps another five or six snipers on top of the hospital.

From where we were hidden down the street, I could make out the faces of the closer prisoners. Many of them showed varying signs of injuries ranging from bruises on their faces to phaser burns on different limbs. One by one, prisoners were being forced to their feet and taken away. They had their fingers pricked and their blood tested. But it quickly became obvious that whatever Icarus' soldiers were looking for, it wasn't in those prisoners' blood.

The soldiers holding the medical units would read the results, shake their heads in the negative, and then call out "next." The prisoner whose blood had not passed the test was then forced at gunpoint to join another group down the road from the hospital where I noted with a start that the Talos machine was towering over them with its gun trained on them. Its own lights were illuminating the scene there. Almost a hundred individuals were kneeling on the ground in front of it, their backs to the machine.

My anxiety spiking, I forced my eyes away from the machine and started searching for the faces of my team members among the prisoners. With so many, it almost felt like I was searching for a needle in a haystack, but I eventually picked out Wren's angular features near the center of one of the groups about twenty yards from us. I was fairly positive that the man next to him was McLagan. Wren was kneeling straight-backed with his chin held high. I got the impression that he would be ready to fight back the instant an opportunity presented itself. McLagan, in contrast, looked stunned, as though he was unable to comprehend what was happening to them. Aiden nodded when I pointed them out.

Thatcher took me longer to find, but only because I had been looking for him in the wrong place and he was quite a bit further away. I finally found him kneeling in the midst of forty or so other hospital patients and doctors closer to the hospital entrance. Like so many of the other prisoners, his head was up and his shoulders were squared. His posture was one of defiance, refusing to be cowed by the phase rifles that were pointed at him. He was dressed only in the blue hospital pants that he had probably been given for the surgery. He also had a sling hanging around his neck that would have been used to hold his arm stable following the procedure, but his newly bandaged arm was not in it. Like everyone else, his hands had been bound behind his back.

For half a heartbeat, I was relieved to find him. But that relief was short-lived as I realized that his group was one of those being drawn from for testing and that its smaller size meant that he had, at best, only a few minutes until it was his turn to be pricked and then sent to join the group by Talos. My hands clenched into fists. I was not going to allow that. Without fully thinking through what I was doing, I began searching out the waves of gravity under the soldiers guarding

Thatcher's group. I had just grabbed hold of several of those waves, with the vague idea that I was going to send those soldiers flying, when I felt a hand on my shoulder and heard Aiden's voice urgently whispering into my ear, "Alex, don't!"

I turned to look at him with a start only to have my attention immediately pulled back to the scene in front of us by an arrogantly sneering voice calling out, "So, you are here!"

Everyone's heads turned almost as one to stare at the figure who stepped forward from the car he had been lazily leaning against. The boy's exact age was not easy to determine from as far away as he was, but the tenor of his voice suggested he was at least in his late teens. What I could make out was the blond hair tipped with red that had been artfully spiked into a crown shape around his head. He was wearing tight-fitting denim pants and a leather bomber-style jacket, heavy black boots studded with metal spikes, and a silver chain that connected a ring in his nose to the one in his ear.

The soldiers closest to him tensed up in sudden, nervous alertness as he moved toward them. He ignored their tenseness and stepped past them into the mass of kneeling prisoners. Randomly, he started grabbing faces that he forced to look up at him before he roughly pushed them away and grabbed the next one. As he did so, he continued talking.

"Did you know that radio waves are affected by large levels of gravity? It's a faint reaction, but I could see them begin wavering the moment the gravity shifted. What were you planning to do with it, I wonder? I'd wager you're not strong enough to do more than lift ten people at a time; that's not going to be enough to help you escape this."

He paused, looking carefully into the face of a dark-haired soldier whose chin he had just grabbed. Almost pityingly he crooned, "Look at them, Alexander. Their lives are in your hands. Reveal yourself and I will spare them. Continue trying to hide and you will only condemn more of them."

The soldier jerked his head away, hatred in his eyes, but the Alpha just laughed. "What's it going to be? You or these pitifully worthless cattle headed for the slaughter?"

Aiden squeezed my shoulder, pulling my attention back to him. His expression was hard as he whispered, "Come on. We're leaving."

Surprised, I whispered back, "But our team? We can't just leave them."

"Alex, we don't have a choice; he knows yer here," he said that last part as though it explained everything. But when I still hesitated, he added with a hint of desperation, "Alex, please, we have tae get yae away from here."

Before I could respond, the Alpha's cold voice cut through the air with a tone of excited anticipation, "As you wish."

My head shot back around as the Talos machine came to life in a staccato blaze of pure white energy that sliced through the group of men who had been forced to kneel in front of it. I watched in horror as they were cut down before they even had the chance to cry out. In that moment, Aiden's hand on my shoulder was all that allowed me to keep it together as my own hands flew to my mouth to hold back the sob that fought to escape.

The rapture on the boy's face belied the casual tone in his voice as the gun went silent at last. "Come now. Surely you don't intend to let all these men die for you. I can assure you that they will if you don't show yourself."

Not waiting for a response, he nodded his head to those who had been testing the prisoners. Reacting instantly to his unspoken command, they jumped forward to grab the next set of prisoners to be tested; one of them grabbed Thatcher by his injured arm and yanked him to his feet. He grimaced in pain but said nothing as he was forced over to the soldiers operating the machines.

In the space of a heartbeat, my horror transformed into a fury so hot that it burned away everything in my mind except for the need to act. *No! I will not hide in the shadows while they kill my friends.* But if that boy thought he would see me coming, he was very wrong. He said that he knew I was there because of the fluctuations I had caused in the radio waves? Then it must be radio waves that he was able to see and manipulate. That gave me two advantages. First, the Earth's larger gravity waves, the only ones strong enough to interfere with radio waves, were not the only gravity waves available to me.

Gravity is not a one-way force; I'd learned that in grade school. Anything with mass has gravity. The Earth's mass, being the largest, obviously pulls the hardest. But even the smallest ant has minuscule waves of gravity emanating from it that pull on everything else around it. Alone they are too weak to do anything. But pulled on at the same time? Well, that was a different story. What was more, by shifting those waves instead of the Earth's bigger waves, he would not be able to see what I was doing until it was already done.

Even more, radio waves have no destructive capabilities in and of themselves. He could use them to control his machine, but only if his waves could reach it first. If simply taking hold of the gravity waves had caused his radio waves to fluctuate, imagine what would happen to them when I turned the full force of the gravity waves on them.

This time, Aiden made no effort to stop me as I took hold of the smaller waves emanating from all of the invading soldier's weapons and yanked. Well, almost all of the weapons. In truth, I wasn't strong enough or skilled enough to get all of them at once. I could only get the ones I could see and then only about twenty of them at a time. But the moment I had the first twenty in motion, I was already moving on to the next twenty. And once I had hold of a gun's waves, I didn't need to let them go in order to grab at more. In a matter of seconds, more than a hundred of Talos' soldiers were weaponless, their rifles having been yanked from their hands to drop to the ground like stones in a pond.

Just as I expected, he hadn't seen it coming. The Alpha's eyes narrowed, but not before I had the satisfaction of seeing an expression of shock cross his face as I continued to drop more and more of the weapons. My satisfaction was short-lived, though, as he sneered, "Fine, if that is how you want to play this."

The Talos machine's gun was suddenly in motion again, swiveling toward the prisoners in the parking lot. Aiden's hand tightened on my shoulder as he saw it, but I was already reacting. *I am not going to allow that machine to kill any more people!*

It stopped moving mid-motion as I slammed down the gravity waves between the Alpha and his machine. I wasn't just tweaking the Earth's gravity waves, I was increasing them a hundredfold. I felt the flush of perspiration bead up on my forehead in response to the strain.

Out of the corner of my eye, I could see the Alpha straining to maintain control of his machine, trying to push the radio waves back into the position he wanted, even as I forced them to do something different. It occurred to me that he had probably never met resistance like this before. The realization brought a faint, feral smile to my lips. I guess I thought it was about time that one of Icarus' children met some resistance. They had been hurting innocent people for too long without anyone able to do anything to stop them.

I stretched my reach out further, inching the increased gravity toward his machine. With a loud crack, the gun's barrel snapped in half and fell to the ground like metal drawn straight to a magnet. The Alpha's eyes widened in surprise as he finally understood that he wasn't the stronger Alpha in this situation.

As for me, if I had stopped to consider how much gravity I was controlling, I would have been shocked. But at that moment, I was only focused on what it would take to ensure that he could not harm anyone else. I focused on the body of his machine next, pulling on the waves there until the legs began to buckle. I imagine his machine was a little heavier than the ten men he assumed was the limit of my strength. My feral grin grew as first one of the legs broke and then the other. *Any bets he hadn't seen that one coming?*

The collapse of the Talos machine into a pile of crushed metal was like a rallying cry. The prisoners had no idea what had caused it, but they saw in it the chance they had hoped for and surged to their feet to fight back against their newly unarmed captors. Those who could, broke their bonds; those who could not, used their legs and shoulders.

Suddenly desperate, several of the invaders tried to dive for their fallen weapons. That proved to be a futile effort as I had not yet released my grasp on their waves; they were impossible to move. It was only as prisoners began falling to phaser fire from above that I realized I had forgotten about the snipers on top of the hospital.

I growled in frustration at my failure to deal with them sooner, but reacted quickly to do so now. In rapid succession, I sent four of them flying over the roof's edge, not pausing to consider that there was little chance they would survive the five-story drop. As I lifted the fourth one into the air, the thought flashed through my mind that there should have been at least one more sniper up there for me to throw. I started to scan the roof line once more only to have my attention pulled away again by Aiden squeezing my shoulder.

I turned to look at him. His expression was filled with a mixture of satisfaction, pride, and concern. He had to raise his voice to be heard over the shouts of the fighting soldiers. "You can let it go now, Alex. They have it under control."

It was as though his words were permission for me to feel again. I realized that my muscles were shaking with exhaustion and my head had that insistent throb that came just before I started to lose my vision and consciousness. It had only been a few minutes, but that had been a lot of weight to control. Adrenaline had given me more strength than I normally had, but I had still been physically manipulating those waves. There were limits to how much physical strain my muscles were capable of enduring, and struggling against Talos had pushed me to that edge.

I nodded wearily, sighing in unanticipated relief as I let go of all of the waves at last. I was a little surprised to realize just

how many I had been simultaneously supporting as hundreds
of the weaker waves snapped away from my control and back
into their positions under the weapons. Not to mention the
Earth's larger waves that now shifted back into their normal
place. I don't think I had ever consciously tried to control so
many at once. I sagged back against the wall behind me as the
last one left my grasp. I was drained, but I was also
exhilarated by the realization of what I had accomplished.

"I think," Aiden said with a big grin, "that his mistake was
in tellin' yae what tae dae. If he'd avoided that, he might have
fared better."

I laughed, shaking my head at his sense of humor.

"Come on," I said with a weary smile. "Let's go get our
team."

The smile faded from Aiden's face in an instant. "No," he
said firmly. "Yae're stayin' right here."

My own smile faltered, "Now who's trying to tell me what
to do? I'm not going to hide while…"

To my surprise, he cut me off with a dry chuckle. "Aye,
yae are. Yer exhausted. But more than that, they have no idea
that yae even exist. They think th' Alpha they are lookin' for
is me and we're goin' tae leave it that way."

That caught me off guard. "They think what?"

His smile broadened into something I couldn't quite read,
though there was a definite hint of satisfaction mixed into it.

"Didn't yae notice that all those prisoners are men and
that almost all the bodies we came across were women? Or
that Talos called for Alexander tae show himself, not
Alexandria? They're lookin' for a male Alpha, Alex. They
don't know about yae and I want tae keep it that way. Yae are
stayin' right here, out of sight. I will go get our team."

Understanding dawned on me. In the jungle, it had been Aiden that had appeared to be controlling the gravity fields. He had been the one standing in the clearing while I had been hidden up in the tree. Anyone watching that video feed would have had no reason to think he was not the Alpha. Last night we had done it again. It had been at Thatcher's insistence, but once more, it had been made to appear that Aiden was the Alpha controlling the gravity waves. No one had even known I was there.

I considered arguing anyway; I didn't like the idea of hiding. But the look in his eyes was determined. Besides that, he was right; I really was exhausted. Closing my eyes in frustration, I let my head lean back against the wall. "Fine," I said with a sigh. "Be quick about it."

He squeezed my shoulder as he left. He probably intended it more as a means of comfort than as any type of apology because, even in the darkness of our hiding place, I couldn't miss the smug smile on his face as he slid out from behind the bushes and headed into the melee. I couldn't decide if I was more annoyed or amused by his satisfaction over having convinced me to stay. Maybe it was a little of both.

Chapter 5: Aiden Haskell 

I DIDN'T LIKE leaving Alex alone back there, but I liked even less the idea of her being out here and exposed; this battle was far from over. Edinburgh Base was neither small nor unprotected. For a strike of this size to take place without any warning, and for this much time to have passed without backup arriving, there were several things that had to have taken place, and betrayal was a certainty.

First, the base's defensive systems and communications systems would have both had to have been knocked out before the attack could begin. Both were highly secured and set up on a continuous systems check relay with alarms that should have gone off the moment there was any interruption in that relay. There were not many people with the authority or the ability to shut those relays off, but someone clearly had.

Second, even if the base's relays had been disabled, Scotland's defensive system should have identified the transport vehicles before their arrival. There was no way an invading force of this size could have approached Scotland, let alone the base, without someone seeing them coming. At the bare minimum, there were watch towers all along

Scotland's coastline; towers that had been established for exactly this purpose. At least one of them should have seen and reported the approach of such a large force.

Finally, assuming the force had been sighted prior to the attack, which it must have been, someone high up had to be smothering the alarms and warnings so that they weren't being delivered to those who could have done something about it. Was this because of what had happened last night? Was Scotland being punished for what would surely be perceived as a rebellion? But if that was the case, there were a lot of non-Scottish personnel who were being caught up in this punishment. Yes, Edinburgh Base was on Scottish soil, but it was under UFC control. The Scottish draftees were purposely split among many different bases around the world so that we could not establish any central training grounds. There wouldn't be more than a few hundred Scottish draftees assigned to this base.

On top of that, it was obvious that Icarus' forces had somehow known she was here. I hadn't said anything to Alex, because I didn't want to worry her. But this rounding up of prisoners and the testing of their blood was how they were trying to find her. With that being the case, and considering how many people were on this base, this could not possibly be the only staging site for the gathering of prisoners. And, if Talos had been sent here to oversee this specific site, then it was quite probable that there were Alphas at the other locations as well.

Alex had evened the odds for this group of soldiers, but what I had seen on our way here had indicated that this was a massive attack with coordinated strikes throughout the base. This was not the only battle zone, and it was quite likely that Icarus' forces already had reinforcements on their way to quell this rebellion.

What Alex had done had been incredible; way beyond what she had managed in the jungle clearing or even against Remington's forces. It seemed like every time she used her abilities, she was stronger than the time before. Perhaps her increased strength was driven by an increased need each time, but her body clearly had its limits and she seemed to be pushing herself dangerously close to those limits each time. I wasn't sure how much strength she had left to deal with the reinforcements when they arrived, and I had no intention of finding out. I wanted to find our team members and get us all out of here before they showed up.

I found Thatcher first. He wasn't far from where the testing stations had been established. He was trying to cut his bonds on a shard of glass from a broken car window but was struggling to get his bonds positioned right with the odd angle of the glass and the recently repaired muscles that weren't fully ready for use. I used my knife to get the job done for him.

"Thanks," he said, wincing as he straightened his injured arm. "Where's Alex? I assume this was her work."

"She's safe. Exhausted, but secure for now."

Thatcher nodded his approval. "Good. Any chance Wren and McLagan are with you?"

"No. They were caught up in the initial attack, but I saw Wren over that way. Hopefully, McLagan is with him." When Alex had pointed them out, I had been able to see Wren for certain, but the man she thought was McLagan I wasn't so sure about.

"Then let's find them and get out of here."

I couldn't have agreed more.

We worked our way through the groups of soldiers who were being organized into teams by one of the senior officers. Someone had discovered that the weapons could now be picked up and the officer was busy putting those with weapons into a defensive perimeter around the MEDDAC.

The former captors had been gathered into a group under one of the parking lot lights with a couple of armed guards to insure they stayed there. As we passed them, a chill ran down my spine. I looked over sharply to find Talos watching me. There was a predatory grin on his face that made me uneasy. Seeing that I was looking at him, he nodded slowly, his grin transforming into a smirk. At my side, Thatcher's low voice said softly, "You two ever met before?"

"No," I answered just as softly.

"Then I'd say he just identified you as the Alpha."

"Good," I replied. There was a sense of satisfaction in that; one more proof that our deception had been successful. I decided to reinforce his belief with a hard stare back at him, then pointedly turned away, purposely ignoring him. Thatcher nodded his approval at my side.

"Any thoughts on how we can get out of here?" he asked when we were well beyond the prisoners.

"Figured we'd make our way tae th' western fence. If we can get through that, we can hike tae Edinburgh and catch a ride out from there."

Thatcher nodded, "Sounds good to me."

We found the others, not long after, patiently waiting under one of the lights. Or at least, Wren was patiently waiting, his arms folded across his chest. McLagan was pacing back and forth muttering under his breath. Alex had been right; it had been him.

"It's about bloody time," he growled as we walked up. But then his eyes narrowed and, for half a heartbeat, I thought I saw panic in them. "Where's Alex?"

"She's safe," Thatcher assured him. "Safe and waiting for us to join her. Let's get going."

Wren nodded as though he had expected to hear nothing less. But I was a little surprised by how much relief showed on McLagan's face. At the same time, I was glad. The more concern her team had for her safety, the better the job they would do protecting her.

"This way," I said, intending to lead them back to Alex and then off the base. But I had only taken a few steps when a faint buzzing sound that my subconsciousness had already picked up on suddenly registered in my mind. My body reacted instinctively, automatically transitioning back into battle mode as my mind finally connected the sound to its source.

"Drones!" I yelled raising my rifle and looking to the sky. Even as I yelled the word, the drones flew into view and opened fire. There had to be at least twenty of them, swarming in the darkness as they shot person after person. Like me, several soldiers with rifles began shooting back, trying to knock them down. But these buggers were small and almost impossible to see in the darkness, not to mention they were quick and changed directions almost as fast as they could fire. Very few, if any, of our shots actually hit their targets. The one exception was Thatcher. His aim was accurate, though his phase pistol's shots only bounced off the drones' armor, too weak to pierce their plating.

"Think yae can handle th' rifle?" I shouted to him over my shoulder.

He shook his head in frustration. "I won't be able to take a clear shot with it. My arm isn't recovered enough to hold the rifle steady."

"Then we've got to move," Wren shouted. "We're too exposed."

He was right; this was a death trap. I quickly searched for our best route. "This way," I shouted and took off toward the closest building. We could find shelter there and then work our way back to Alex.

I'd only made it fifteen feet when one of the drones broke off from its attack to block my path. I flung myself to the side, rolled back to my feet, and took off in a new direction. The others followed my lead, responding almost as quickly as I had. There was a car parked just up ahead. It wasn't much, but it was better than being out in the open. I started to make for it, only to have a second drone break off to block that path.

Before I could change direction, a third drone came at us from the left, followed by a fourth on our right. In seconds, nearly all the drones were surrounding us as we backed up against each other in a tight circle.

From across the parking lot, I heard the sharp slap of hands clapping mockingly. I looked over to see Talos stalking toward us, an expression of satisfied glee on his face.

"And there you are at last, Alexander," he sneered. "I must admit that you are quite a bit stronger than I expected, though I sincerely doubt you could down all of my drones before I can shoot your companions. So, it looks like I win."

"What dae yae want?" I growled.

Talos shook his head laughing, "Why you of course. I would have thought that was obvious by now. Father has been waiting a very long time to meet you."

"I have no desire tae meet him," I scoffed.

Talos only laughed more. "I really don't think it matters what you want. But I'll tell you what. I'll give you a choice: You surrender yourself willingly and I'll only kill two of your friends. I'll even let you choose which one will live."

A cold sense of dread settled in my chest. How were we going to get out of this one?

"I have a better idea," Alex's cold voice came unexpectedly from the shadows behind Talos. "I destroy your drones and you can tell father to go to…" The last part of what she said was drowned out by the sudden metallic squealing of the drone's mechanics fighting a failing battle to stay aloft against the invisible force that was suddenly shoving them down. Almost as one, they slammed into the ground, shattering into thousands of pieces.

Talos' eyes widened as he spun around. "How?" he asked in disbelief. "The video showed him?"

"Surprise!" Alex said sarcastically. Then she threw a punch that sent Talos spinning to the ground. I couldn't help the surge of pride or the grin that tugged at the corner of my lips. What I would have given to be able to record the moment that one of Icarus' children finally got what they deserved. But as her swing finished, so did her strength. She stumbled to one knee, exhaustion replacing the fury on her face. My grin evaporated and I surged toward her, only to have to pull back sharply as a phaser blast shattered the cement right in front of my feet.

"Don't move!" a man's voice commanded from across the parking lot. Coming out of the shadows between the buildings were about twenty soldiers dressed in Icarus' black uniforms. My heart sank; the reinforcements had arrived.

Talos stood up slowly, murder in his eyes as he wiped the blood away from his split lip. "You little vixen," he said coldly. Then his eyes narrowed as he took in Alex, down on her knee, and he seemed to see her with the sudden light of new understanding. His voice carried a hint of astonishment. "You're still holding back! You did all that while fighting against yourself!" His shock morphed into glee. "Just wait till father hears about this! We thought you were strong before, but we had no idea you were still…" His words stopped abruptly. He spun in a complete circle, his eyes growing wide with panic, "It's not possible! Nothing is strong enough to do this."

Alex looked up slowly, her violet eyes burning with a new intensity. There was a satisfied grin on her lips. There were also beads of perspiration glistening on her forehead and her muscles had begun shaking again, but her gaze and her voice were steady. "You taught me a new trick today. You're not going to be able to use your radio waves to tell anyone anything!"

"Let them go!" Talos growled in fury and frustration, his eyes almost wild. "Release the waves or I'll have you shot."

"Try it!" Alex's expression took on a predatory twist of challenge. "I think you'll find that your soldiers are in no position to do anything for you."

I was surprised to see that they were indeed struggling, trying to lift their feet off the ground while all of their weapons were now floating in the air well out of their reach.

What was more, approaching them from behind was a group of about ten UFC soldiers, battered, but in one piece, aiming their own set of weapons at the suddenly helpless group. I was further surprised to realize that I recognized one of the closer soldiers: it was Evans, the soldier from the Rec Hall who had been flirting with Alex. He nodded when he saw me. Any other time I might have been annoyed to see him, but right now all I felt was relief to have help.

There was mirth in Alex's voice as she continued to address Talos. "You didn't think I was so foolish as to come here alone, did you?" But I knew her well enough that I could also hear the tightness at the edge of her voice; she was struggling.

I didn't hesitate any longer as I brushed past Talos, not caring that I knocked him in the shoulder. I ducked my head under her arm and helped her to stand. "How are yae doing?" I asked softly.

She answered back just as quietly, the strain in her voice increasing with each sentence, "I can't hold this for much longer. We should probably get going before he figures that out." Then she added, almost as an afterthought, "Nate has a way for us to get off base."

"Nate?" Now that was a surprise.

She smiled weakly. "Turns out he was supposed to be our pilot tomorrow morning. He and his copilot were with the base commander receiving instructions about our flight when the fighting broke out. Her final act was to give them orders to find us and get us off base, then she led a charge giving the two of them the time to sneak out a back window."

I nodded slowly, thinking it through. The authorization for our earlier evacuation had likely come directly from

Beckwith's office. The commander had probably connected the dots between those orders, us, and this attack, and concluded that anything important enough to draw Icarus' forces was important enough to deny him at all costs.

"Thatcher," I raised my voice, "we're leavin' now."

"You're not going to get away," Talos retorted. "I know the truth now and we'll keep coming for her."

I stiffened. If Talos reported back that Alex was the Alpha and not me, then everything we had done so far to protect her identity would be compromised. Coming to a decision, I said softly, "Alex, turn away and keep yer back turned. There's somethin' I need tae take care of."

She looked up sharply, her mouth opened to protest. But, before she could say anything, the sound of a phase pistol firing split the silence followed by a thud.

Our heads shot up to find Talos' body on the ground, a phaser burn through his head. Further back, Thatcher was lowering his pistol. His face was a mask of hardness. I suspected that he didn't like killing any more than I did, but that, like me, he wouldn't hesitate to do what was necessary to protect others. Talos had been a threat to Alex's safety that could not be permitted to report back to Icarus. The grim resolve on Wren's and McLagan's faces suggested they felt the same way.

As Alex buried her head in my shoulder, a shuddering draw of breath shaking her frame, I nodded my thanks to Thatcher, then wrapped my arms around her and held her while she silently cried. DuCain had been right: as strong as she was, she was too tenderhearted for the horrors of war.

Out of the corner of my eye, I saw Nate and one other man breaking off from the UFC soldiers to jog our way.

Nate's face was determined as he approached us. "Corporal Worthington gave us orders to get your team off base. If you're ready to go, there's a MET vehicle on top of the hospital. We can use it to get us out of here before any more trouble arrives."

"MET vehicle?" I wasn't familiar with that acronym.

"Medical Emergency Transport," he answered dismissively. "It won't take us across the ocean, but it has the maneuverability and speed to get us into the air and off this base. There's a secondary airfield not far from here where we can commandeer a bigger transport that will get us the rest of the way to America."

I nodded; that would be good enough. "Alex?" I asked gently. I would have preferred to not rush her, but there were still the sounds of battle coming from other parts of the base; it wasn't safe to delay any longer than was absolutely necessary.

She nodded her head against my chest, having heard our discussion, then pushed back so that she was standing on her own once more. Wiping the moistness from her eyes, she said wearily, "Let's go."

Nate led the way into the hospital. The second man, who he introduced as his co-pilot, Hockett, followed right behind him. Wren took up the rear position while Thatcher, McLagan, and I formed a loose circle around Alex. I was worried about her as she occasionally stumbled from exhaustion, but she always recovered quickly and kept moving. If I hadn't been worried that more of Icarus' forces would show up, I might have swept her up and carried her. As it was, it was more important that my hands were free to work the rifle I was carrying, in case we came under attack again. She'd have to manage the distance from here to there with what remained of her own strength.

We took the elevator to the rooftop where the landing pad was. Evans had been required to enter special credentials before the elevator would begin the journey to that location; the rooftop was not accessible to just anyone. I was only slightly surprised to see that it was the base commander's ID that he used to gain us access.

"I take it that hospital transports are not yer usual mode of transportation."

He laughed heartily in response, but it was his co-pilot who answered, "Jackal here can fly just about anything, but the Hawk Wing 7 is his normal vehicle of choice."

I wasn't overly excited to admit it, but if Evans was the pilot of a Hawk Wing 7, then he really was quite impressive. The Hawk Wing 7 was the UFC's latest and greatest flight vehicle. It was said to be the fastest and most maneuverable plane ever made. It took a direct implant link for the pilot to be able to control it and even then, the pilot had to be especially skilled to do anything with it. I glanced at Nate's arms. Sure enough, there was an implant jack, barely visible under the sleeve of his upper right arm.

"Jackal?" Alex asked curiously from where she was leaning back against the elevator wall.

Nate shrugged with a big grin. "It's a call sign. I got it during survival training after I woke up one night to find a jackal sleeping on the foot of my bag. Any time I tried to get up, it growled at me. I stayed in my bag for over two hours before it decided it was done resting and finally took off. The squad started calling me Jackal after that and the name stuck."

She laughed lightly. "Guess it's appropriate then." His grin grew; I frowned.

The doors slid open a few seconds later to an almost dark roof top. Only the blinking green and orange landing lights cast faintly flashing shadows. Nate had explained that there were normally floodlights to fully light the landing pad, but it would be best if they remained off so that our departure was not so obvious.

As we stepped out onto the roof, Nate started issuing orders. "I'll get it started; you guys remove the tie-down cables. Hockett, do a quick preflight."

The cables were attached to the sides of the vehicle and had to be cranked to release them. They were there to keep the vehicle from being rocked by the winds that regularly blew across Scotland. Thatcher and Wren took the ones on the far side while McLagan and I took the closer ones. I had just pulled my cable free of its hook when I heard McLagan's sharp intake of breath. My head shot up and I felt my heart drop. Only a few feet behind us, in the flashing shadows of the landing lights, there was a soldier holding a gun to Alex's head.

"Everyone out where I can see you," the man said firmly. To Nate he added, "Shut the craft down and come out with your hands up."

I raised my hands slowly, the muscles in my jaw twitching. *How could I have let this happen?* I had known they had placed snipers on the roof; I'd even watched Alex throw several of them off. How could I have failed to remember that? Worse, securing the roof should have been our first order of business when the elevator doors opened. I knew that; we all did! It was a lapse in judgment that was going to cost us dearly.

I heard the engines begin to power back down. From the corner of my eye, I saw Evans climb down from the pilot seat and come to stand next to me; his fists were clenched in anger.

I harbored a faint hope that somehow Thatcher or Wren would notice what was happening and do something about it, but just at that moment they and Evans' co-pilot came around the nose of the vehicle. Their hands were above their heads as a second sniper herded them forward at gunpoint.

"Next, you're going to put your weapons on the ground," the man ordered.

When we hesitated, he added, "Icarus, wants you alive. But this one," he pushed his gun into Alex's head, forcefully moving it with the pressure, "well...our orders said we can kill the women. So, if you want her to live, you'll do as you're told. Lay them down slowly and kick them away."

My fists clenched in an effort to control my frustration. We had them outnumbered, but most of us had slung our rifles behind our backs while unhooking the cables. There was no chance we could swing them around and bring them up faster than he could shoot Alex; not even Thatcher could manage that. Not seeing any way around it, I unslung my rifle and set it on the ground. The others did as well.

I still had my pistol tucked into its holster in the small of my back. Maybe I could...the hope faded as the second sniper began patting each person down in turn, searching for hidden weapons. He confiscated my pistol and threw it over the roof along with the other weapons before finally sauntering back to take up a position closer to his partner.

The whole time, Alex watched with silent fury. I suspected that her anger was the only thing keeping her standing right now. It made my own frustration burn all the worse. She needed rest. She needed her team to protect her. Instead, we had failed her miserably.

"Now," the man ordered, "put your hands behind your heads and get down on your knees."

I could feel the muscles in my jaw clenching as I folded my hands behind my head and slowly knelt. It was so infuriating. We had been so close to getting her off the base.

"I said, kneel down!" the man holding the gun against Alex repeated angrily.

I looked in surprise to find Thatcher still standing just behind my shoulder. There was a calm, calculating gleam in his eyes as he studied the snipers. "Release her, and I'll let you walk away with your lives," his slow Texan drawl gave his declaration an ominous tone.

The man only scoffed, pressing his gun harder against Alex. "Do as you're told or she dies!"

"So be it," Thatcher sighed. "Alex, don't move."

A hint of suspicion flashed across the sniper's face, but that suspicion didn't help him to react fast enough when the lights flashed back off and things happened suddenly. In the split-second of darkness between one flash of landing lights and the next, the sound of phaser fire split the air as three streaks of bright lights seared an afterimage into my vision. One streak struck someone next to me; their body toppled to the ground. The other two streaks stuck the snipers with deadly accuracy.

When the lights flashed back on, Thatcher was lowering a handgun that had not been there seconds before. I had no idea how he had gotten it, but with his perfect aim, he had shot the soldier holding Alex cleanly in the center of the forehead and then spun and fired at the other man. His aim had been true, just not quite fast enough. The second sniper had gotten off a shot in the split second before Thatcher's had taken him in the heart. He had probably been aiming at Thatcher, but his aim must have dropped, striking the person kneeling in front of Thatcher instead.

I looked down expecting to find Evans on the ground; he had been the one kneeling in front of Thatcher. But the body on the ground was Hockett's, a circle of red spreading outward from a wound in his chest.

"No!" Evans cried out, seeing his fallen co-pilot. He lurched forward, pressing his hands to the wound to try and stop the bleeding. In the split second before the guns had fired, Hockett must have surged in front of Evans and taken the shot that would have otherwise been his.

"Why?" Evans muttered as he pulled off his shirt to use as a compress against the wound.

Hockett coughed, flecks of blood appearing on his lips. Weakly, he laughed, "Now you owe me one."

Evans muttered something choice under his breath as Thatcher turned to McLagan. "Get the med kit out of the vehicle." McLagan nodded and hurried to search for it.

Beside me, I felt a hand slip into mine. I looked over to see Alex. She leaned her head against my arm, a single tear sliding down her cheek, faintly gleaming in the flashing lights. On the ground, Hockett struggled to take a breath; there was a faint gurgling sound to it.

Panic in his unsteady voice, Evans commanded, "Stay with me Hockett. Don't you dare die."

Hockett coughed and faintly laughed, "No can do…sorry, bud." He coughed again. Then, with a final wheezing sound, his chest stopped moving.

McLagan came running back, carrying a red case. But as he dropped to his knees and started to open it, Evans shook his head and reached forward to close Hockett's eyes; Hockett had died. Thatcher placed his hand on Evan's shoulder, offering comfort. "I'm sorry," he said softly. Evan nodded, his eyes still on Hocket. Then, shaking his head as though to clear it, he slowly stood up. "Come on," he finally muttered. "Let's get out of here."

He didn't say much more after that as we took our seats and he guided the MET vehicle into the air. Thatcher took Hockett's seat in the front. He didn't have any flight experience, none of us did, but Evans said he would tell him what to do.

As we flew over the base, I was able to see the damage it had taken. In the darkness, it was easy to see the buildings that were burning and the two other staging sites where Icarus' forces were still gathering and testing UFC soldiers. I could also make out the reinforcements that were quickly approaching the hospital; we were leaving just in time.

But, while I knew we needed to get Alex away from here, there was a big part of my mind that felt guilty for abandoning the other soldiers. *No One Left Behind, right?* Only this time, we were abandoning thousands.

Chapter 6: Alexandria Jaquette

IT FELT LIKE I had just barely closed my eyes when Nate's voice woke me.

"Dumfries Tower, Air Evac two-three-niner, mayday, mayday, mayday. I have six souls on board coming at you from five miles north-by-northeast."

There was a short pause, then a voice came over the line. "Air Evac two-three-niner, this is Dumfries Tower. Where are you coming from and what's your emergency?"

"We're coming from main base. I repeat, requesting an emergency landing," he answered, though he didn't say what the emergency was.

After a pause, probably waiting for him to say something more, the base finally responded, "Copy that. Please hold." Then a moment later, "Air Evac two-three-niner, landing pad two has been cleared for you and the lights are being turned on. You should see them any second. See you on the ground."

I sat up from where I had been sleeping with my head on Aiden's shoulder.

"How are yae feelin'?" he asked softly.

"Tired," I answered as I stifled a yawn. "How long has it been?"

"About fifteen minutes. We'll change planes here and then yae can get some real sleep."

I nodded, stifling another yawn as I glanced out the window; there wasn't much to see. The countryside was dark with little in the way of a moon to highlight it, but I was pretty sure that I could just make out the outline of a runway because of what looked like a long, straight-lined break in the shadowed trees. Then again, it could have just been my tired eyes playing tricks on me. What wasn't a trick was the flood lights that flared to life in front of a single, small building and the flashing green and orange landing lights that came on to frame a square landing pad next to that building.

Nate gently landed the MET transport onto the pad. As he began shutting down the engines, I noticed that several people were approaching from the darkness outside of the landing pad's lit area. It didn't escape me that they were pointing their rifles in our direction. Even as tired as I was, I instinctively began searching out the waves around them, just in case.

Nate must have seen the soldiers as well, but he didn't hesitate to open the pilot's door and climb out. He also didn't fully close the door behind him, making it possible for us to hear what was said. He walked straight up to the barrel-chested man with a handlebar mustache who stood expectantly at the edge of the landing pad, flanked by two more soldiers carrying rifles.

"Major," Nate saluted him sharply.

The man saluted back, though not nearly so crisply, then raised his chin to indicate the vehicle we had flown in on.

"Not your normal mode of transportation, Jackal. What's going on here? Where's Hockett, and where's your shirt? You told my tower operator that you needed an emergency landing?"

"Yes, sir," Nate answered him with just the faintest hint of a growl. "But before I say anything more, I'd appreciate it if you would do something for me."

"What's that?" the man asked warily.

Nate's tone became suddenly ominous, the growl no longer faint. "Explain why in the blazing Light you didn't send any support to main base?"

"Send support? What nonsense are you talking about?" The major scoffed, though he did look somewhat taken aback by the fury in Nate's voice. At the edge of the light, several of the armed soldiers looked at each other with similar expressions of confusion.

"I'm talking about the support we needed and didn't get!" Nate wasn't quite yelling at the Major, but it was about as close as it was possible to get without crossing that line. "The base was invaded by Icarus's forces. Corporal Worthington and hundreds of good men and women are dead! Hockett is dead! He died in my arms while you and this traitorous lot of yours hid in the darkness!"

I was only slightly surprised when the major took an uneasy step back. The fury that was radiating from Nate was almost tangible. The major was not the only one to unobtrusively take a step back.

"Now hold on a moment," the major said defensively as he seemed to realize that he had retreated and felt the need to recover the ground he had just given up. "You don't get to come in here with guns blazing and make accusations like that. We were doing exactly what we were supposed to be doing. We received orders to put this base on a lockdown drill while main base ran their air raid drill, and we did just that."

"It was no drill," Nate barked back. "You sheeple don't have a thick enough brain between you or you would have realized that."

Next to me, Aiden suddenly swore under his breath. Turning to the rest of us he curtly said, "Stay here." Then, without further explanation, he opened the side door and climbed down from the plane, closing it securely behind him. As he strode toward Nate and the major, his voice carried easily. "Major, yae said yae had orders tae perform a drill, who issued those orders?"

The man's frustration became a scowl as he turned to size up Aiden. "Just who in the nuclear forsaken Light are you?"

"Sir Alistair Buccleuch," Aiden answered commandingly without breaking stride. There was a surprising tone of authority to his voice that I had never heard there before; I was not the only one surprised by it.

The major's jaw dropped. If he had been defensive at Nate's accusation, he was stunned by Aiden's declaration. Several of the surrounding soldiers lowered their weapons nervously in response as well, suddenly seeming hesitant to point them at Aiden. Even Nate's head turned sharply to watch his approach, as though he were suddenly seeing Aiden for the first time.

Aiden ignored Nate, but held the major's eyes with a steely gaze as he came to a stop in front of him and asked more firmly, "Who issued th' orders?"

The major stuttered with surprising nervousness, "I…it came through on a coded line. It had the…uh, the proper authorization codes." He clearly knew who Alistair Buccleuch was and was unsettled by his unexpected presence and demand for answers.

Aiden's eyebrow raised, "You're certain it had th' proper codes?"

"Yes, sir," the man nodded vigorously.

"Show me!" Aiden's tone left no question that he was giving a command, not making a request.

"Of course." The man was still nodding his head. "If you'll follow me into the office." Not hesitating, Nate followed them in.

It was more than twenty minutes before they came back out. Even from a distance, I could see that Aiden's face looked like a raging storm. The expressions on Nate's and the Major's faces didn't look any calmer. The major started shouting orders the moment he stepped outside. His words sent soldiers scrambling. In an instant, the base came alive. The lights to the runway were the first thing to turn on. Flood lights throughout the base quickly followed.

The base was much bigger than I had first thought. There were several barracks nestled among the trees from which men and women came pouring out, racing for another, much larger building just off of the runway. As the big doors were opened, I was able to see that it was a hanger for the planes.

Aiden and Nate came straight to our transport and climbed in. Nate was the first to speak. "They're getting a plane ready for us. We'll be wheels up in fifteen minutes." He had found a shirt while they were inside the building and held a second one out for Thatcher as he spoke.

Thatcher accepted the shirt with a nod, but turned to address Aiden. "What did you find out?"

Aiden gave a frustrated shake of his head. "Th' codes were legit, but th' man who sent them has disappeared. Th' traitorous scum also sent out orders tae every base, station, and tower in Britain tae ignore any calls for help comin' out of Edinburuh, statin' that the UFC was runnin' a massive drill in Scotland and that emergency practice calls were tae be part of that drill. It took quite a bit of work tae get a call through tae th' Directorates' Office. Even then, they almost didn't listen."

Nate gave Aiden another appraising look as he added, "Your boy here was quite persuasive when it came to getting through the bureaucracy and forcing them to listen. To be honest, I'm not sure the secretary at the Directorate's Office knew what to do when the heir to the Scottish title gave his name, rank, and authorization code; no one seems to think that Scotland has authority anymore."

Aiden stiffened but met Nate's gaze without backing down. Nate held that gaze for just a moment before continuing with a tone that could have been either awe or disgust; I wasn't sure which. "Your boy left no doubt in anyone's mind today that Scotland still has power. This airfield is sending immediate air support out to the base and more forces are on their way up from Glasgow Base. We also have authorization to commandeer any plane from here that we need. Speaking of which," he nodded his head toward a medium-sized craft that had just been rolled out of the hanger, "that one will be ours. I'm going to go run pre-flight checks. If you want to gather your things and join me, we'll get you out of here."

He turned to leave, only to pause with his hand on the handle. As he slowly turned back toward us, there was an unreadable expression on his face. He looked from Aiden, to me, to Wren, to McLagan, to Thatcher, and then finally back to Aiden before he hesitantly said, "I think I'd like to know more about this team that includes the heir to the Scottish title, a sharpshooter so skilled that he could hit drones no one else could, and an Alpha that is so powerful that Icarus views her as a threat. I've never seen anyone able to stand up to one of Icarus' children that way, let alone beat them the way your team did. And you!" He looked at Aiden with that appraising look again. "You could have demanded a plane and simply gotten your team out of here. Instead, you used your authority to demand help for the people still on the base and you didn't back down until they got the support they needed. That is the type of leader I can respect and follow."

If Aiden was surprised to hear Nate say that, his face didn't give it away. What it did show was a stony expression that I couldn't read. Thatcher, on the other hand, looked thoughtful, as though he was carefully considering what Nate was saying.

Not oblivious to their expressions, Nate continued more hesitantly, "I don't know what your team was put together to do, but I think…I think when this is over, it's something I'd like to be part of, if you'll let me."

We looked at each other in startled surprise; none of us seemed to have expected that last request. But Nate didn't wait for any of us to respond before he turned sharply and climbed out of the plane. It was as though he were afraid that we would refuse him outright, and he wanted to avoid that disappointment a little longer.

As we watched him go, McLagan was the first to finally say something. "Well, if that isn't a bugger of a surprise. Can we trust him?"

Aiden, who was still watching Nate through the window with that stony expression, responded with a reluctant nod of his head, "Much as it vexes me tae admit it, I trust him."

I was amused to hear just a hint of jealousy in his tone. I might have even teased him about it if I hadn't been so tired. As it was, it was taking just about all I had to stay awake; my exhaustion was rapidly approaching its limit. It took its final toll moments later when we climbed out of the plane to join Nate in the other aircraft. I was stepping off the landing pad when the muscles in my legs suddenly spasmed and buckled. I would have fallen if Aiden hadn't surged forward to steady me. I mumbled a thanks as I righted myself and tried to start walking again.

I had only made it a few more unsteady steps before I was startled by strong arms that swept me up and pulled me in like a baby. I started to protest only to have the words die on my lips as I looked up to find Aiden sternly staring back at me in challenge. The hard look in his eyes silenced my protests; it was clear that he intended to carry me and was not going to take no for an answer.

"Fine," I muttered under my breath, giving in. I was annoyed to see the corner of his lips twitch up into a small smile; it was the second time today he had gotten his way. But I was also too tired to stay annoyed for very long. I found myself shaking my head briefly in wry amusement before finally letting it fall wearily against his chest. My eyes fluttered closed; I was asleep before we even reached the plane.

Chapter 7: Icarus Argyros 

MY GRIP ON the digi-pad tightened, causing it to creak and groan as the screen spiderwebbed into hundreds of hairline fractures. My child had fallen to an "En Passant"—a little-known move in the game of chess—but one that I had not thought my opponents to be capable of. Talos, my child, had been the cost of that mistake. My frustration over his pointless loss burned deep into my soul.

I would have willingly exchanged him had it resulted in the capture of Alexander. But, instead, I was left with nothing in return. No; that wasn't exactly true. I looked back down thoughtfully at the fractured screen in my hands. The image beneath the cracks was still visible, if only barely. It showed Alexander standing back-to-back with three other men, the friends he had risked himself to save. Talos' last message had included this image, telling me that he had Alexander trapped and would be bringing him to me soon.

I set down the digi-pad and turned to my computer console to send a copy of the image to my pawn at Ghana Base. Within moments, they sent back a list of names: *Lakota Wren, Cody Thatcher,* and *Logan McLagan.* Very well. It wasn't a complete loss. I now knew which people Alexander was most likely to risk his freedom for.

As I pondered the best way to utilize that information, another message came through: *Alexander is listed as Aiden Haskell in the system.*

Intrigued, I opened the file on this fictitious character. A slow smile spread over my lips as I realized that I was facing an opponent with a respectable capacity to think and plan ahead. The decision to hide my child as a firstborn son of Scotland was a stroke of genius.

I was more and more certain that Beckwith was that opponent. The orders to send support and provide Alexander's team with supplies had come from his office, albeit through a coded line. One of my pawns had relayed a copy of the decoded communique to me. But, aside from revealing who was issuing the orders, it had not really contained anything I had not already known.

I would be interested in seeing what Beckwith's next move would be. But in truth, I was already several steps ahead of him. Not only had I known Alexander would be going to that base, but I knew where he and his team were going next, and my pieces were already in place there.

Satisfied that the game was playing out according to my plans, I sat back to wait.

Chapter 7 – Aiden Haskell 

THE JET WE had commandeered turned out to be a private plane that the UFC used as needed to transport important military personnel to meetings oversees. It had room to seat ten passengers comfortably, each passenger having their own leather recliner. Thatcher had entered the plane ahead of me and moved now to get one of them ready for Alex. I was careful to not wake her as I set her down, though in truth, I wasn't sure she would have woken up even if I had dropped her; she was exhausted.

As I settled into the seat across from her, I felt the plane start to move. Nate was taxiing us out onto the runway. He'd need to know where we were heading soon, so I opened the field bag I had been careful to keep with me; it was carrying more than just the survival gear I had told everyone else to pack. What I needed right now was near the top. I pulled the command pad out, intending to give it to Thatcher. I couldn't do anything with it now that it was coded to him. But as I turned to give it to him, I found him already standing next to me, and his hand already had something in it: my phase pistol.

"I believe this is yours," he said softly, holding it out for me.

I was stunned. When the sniper had thrown it over the roof, I had assumed it was gone for good.

"How did yae get it back?"

"Alex," he grunted softly.

Alex? Seeing my confusion, he explained, "She didn't let it drop when the guard threw it over. Instead, she floated it back to me. Not sure exactly how she kept everyone else from seeing it, but I didn't know it was coming till it bumped into my hand."

I glanced at Alex, impressed that she had maintained the presence of mind to pull that off. Not many people could have done so with a gun being held to their head, especially considering how exhausted she had been.

Thatcher looked over at her as well. "That's the fourth time she's had to step in to save us from a hopeless situation. Can't say as I'm complaining, but let's try not to let it become a habit. We're supposed to be protecting her, not the other way around."

I could only nod my head in agreement. Then Thatcher turned back to me, holding out the gun once more.

"Here," he said simply.

I took it with my free hand while holding out the command pad for him with the other. "Trade yae," I offered with a wry shake of my head. Thatcher grunted again, but didn't say anything more as he took it from my hand and then turned to go to the cockpit.

I was left to my own thoughts as the plane's engines revved up and Evans took us into the air. I hadn't meant to drift off, but I woke sometime later to Thatcher tapping me on the shoulder.

"We've got our next set of instructions," he said with a distinct frown.

I sat up straighter; his expression had my immediate attention. "Where?"

"Texas," he said simply.

A sinking feeling settled in my stomach. "Home?" I asked.

"Yup," he nodded. "Not sure what's going on, but there was a note from my pa."

"What did it say?"

Instead of telling me, he handed the command pad to me. There was a picture of a handwritten note with four words on it:

Need you home son.

D. Thatcher

"What are they playin' at?" I was suddenly angry. First, they had purposely sent her into the middle of the trouble at my home, now they were sending her into what had the stench of trouble at Thatcher's. What did they think they were doing? To be fair, what had occurred at my home was more my fault than theirs. Even so, it still didn't set well with me. I didn't think for a moment that Beckwith had been oblivious to Remington's plans. He had sent Alex there knowing the situation was a powder keg ready to explode.

Thatcher shook his head. I suspected he was thinking along the same lines. "I'm not sure. But whatever it is, I'm not pleased with it. If my pa is asking for help, it's not a small problem. When we get there, I want you to keep her as far out of the way as you can. You take care of her; let me handle whatever is going on there."

I nodded my head in agreement; I would do exactly that. Whatever Beckwith's game was, she did not need to be part of it. At the same time though, if there was going to be more trouble, we could use more hands. A part of me wished I could dismiss Evans' request and send him packing even though I knew that wouldn't be the wisest course of action, all things considered. But until we got her to the school, I would take help no matter what form it came in.

"Evans?" I finally asked.

"Yup." Thatcher nodded. "You want to tell him, or shall I?"

"I'll dae it," I sighed. "I want tae have a talk with him anyway."

Thatcher's lips twisted up into the faintest hint of a smile. "Thought you might." Without another word, he moved to the seat behind me and stretched out. I had the briefest image flash through my mind of a cowboy sitting back against a bale of hay, stretching out his long legs and lowering his hat over his eyes. Shaking my head, I got up and headed for the cockpit.

Evans only glanced up briefly when I opened the door. Seeing who it was, he released an almost inaudible sigh and returned to watching the instrument panels. Not waiting for an invitation, I took the seat next to him.

His eyes still on the panels, he said, "She stopped that ball from going into the pocket, didn't she?"

I didn't like admitting to him that his loss had not really been because I'd played better than him, but my conscious told me I owed him the truth. So, I nodded my head in affirmation.

"I thought as much," he laughed half-heartedly. "I saw the way she watched you. The ring on her finger? That yours too?"

"It's complicated," I said evasively. It wasn't really a subject I wanted to get into with him.

"Complicated in what way?"

"It's a long story we don't have time for."

I had intended to say something more that would help me to bypass his question, but he cut in with a shoulder shrug and upraised hands, making a big display of looking around the cabin. "It's not like I have anything better to do; this plane is pretty much flying itself right now. Why don't you tell me what's going on. Maybe it's something I can help you with."

I laughed bitterly before I could catch myself. *He was going to help me?* "Look. I don't doubt that yae mean well, but I can handle me own problems. Yae, on th' other hand, are a different type of problem."

He raised an eyebrow as he sat back stiffly. Now he looked nervous. "How so?"

"Our team's missions are top secret. We're supposed tae be untraceable. We were only on that base because we ran intae some trouble and one of our emergency signals was triggered. If we hadn't surfaced and reported in, search parties would have been sent out and that would have put our future missions intae jeopardy." It wasn't completely true, but it was close enough. I wasn't about to tell him that our mission was keeping Alex hidden and safe.

"Unfortunately, it looks like there's a leak somewhere. No one except our direct supervisor should've known we were on that base. I don't think it was a coincidence that Icarus' forces attacked when they did. We've caused him a bit of trouble in th' past so he would really like tae take our team down. And, as yae saw, he went through a lot of effort tae isolate th' base in order tae dae just that."

Evans seemed to consider what I had said, but then he shook his head. "Not buying it. That boy said that Icarus was your father. Only he got it wrong, didn't he? Claire is the one they should have been looking for. She's one of his Alpha's, isn't she? And when that other kid figured it out, your boy shot him to keep him silent."

My expression hardened and I didn't even try to control the dangerous tone in my voice as I demanded, "How many of th' people in yer group overheard enough tae figure that out?"

Evans' chin lifted in defiance. "Hockett and I were close enough to overhear it; the rest of our group was too far behind. As for Icarus' soldiers, they likely overheard as well, but I left orders for them to be shot after we were in the building. So, you don't have to worry about them. That means there's just me."

Just him?! My expression didn't soften as I considered his words. My gut feeling told me I could trust him; I'd already told the team as much, and my instincts about people were almost always correct. So, if he really was the only one left who had overheard, then her secret was probably still relatively safe. I just didn't like the fact that he knew who she really was. I growled softly to myself really wishing that I could tell him to get lost, then took a deep breath and forced myself to relax as I nodded to show my acceptance of his answer. "No one knows that outside of this team, our chain of command, and a few select others. It needs tae stay that way for her safety."

Much to my annoyance, a slow smile spread across Evans' face. "Then there's an easy solution: bring me into your team."

I grunted, not sure if I was more impressed by his confidence or annoyed by it. "That does seem tae be our best option for th' time bein'. However, I can't promise that those in charge of our team will approve yer official placement when they find out. But for now, well…th' truth is that we could use yer help."

"I'm in!" He grinned back in satisfaction.

I nodded again, this time in resignation, and affirmed his words, though perhaps with a twinge of frustration that I should have tried harder to keep out of my voice, "Yer in."

He must have suspected the reason behind my frustration because his face grew serious. "Look, I know a lost cause when I see one; she's all yours. She didn't think twice about my offer. I was only a tool she used to get your attention. And I'm definitely not the one she challenged an Alpha over."

I scoffed audibly. "She challenged Talos tae protect her team and all those other men he had been threatenin'; she would have done it whether or not I had been there. She's like that."

His eyebrow came up and a smirk began to shape his lips as though he was amused by my denial. "Whatever you say. But I see the way she looks at you. She's not looking at the rest of her team the way she looks at you, and she most certainly isn't looking at me that way."

As much as I wished that were true, there were facts he didn't know. Like the damage I had done when I walked away from her in the hospital and the trauma I had put her through because I had not been strong enough to hold in my cries of pain. I had a long way to go to make up for those things. I just hoped that the damage I had done wasn't irreversible and that I wouldn't find some new way to hurt her in the meantime.

"Anyway," I finally said, feeling the need to change the subject, "unless there's somethin' more yae need, I'm goin' tae head back and get some sleep."

"Nope. I've got everything under control here. Like I said, she pretty much flies herself."

"Must be borin' compared tae Hawk Wings," I muttered under my breath as I stood to go.

My hand was on the door when his next comment pulled me up short. The amusement in his voice had been replaced by earnestness. "I meant what I said back there. What you did for the people on that base…well, you're the type of leader we need more of. Thank you for giving me a chance."

I didn't know how to respond to that, so I just nodded my head then opened the door and left. Walking back to my seat, I thought about what he had said. *A leader?* All I seemed capable of leading was my team from one disaster to another. Besides, I wasn't even the true leader of the team anymore; Thatcher was. No. The reality was that I wasn't a leader. I would give everything I had to protect my people, my family, and my friends; I just didn't have what it took to lead them.

Somewhat stiffly, I sat back down in my seat. The painkiller the doctor had given me this morning was finally starting to wear off and my body was beginning to ache again. Wryly, I thought about how much my body was going to make me pay tomorrow for everything I had put it through today. To be honest, if the doctor had not given me that painkiller, I probably would not have been physically capable of keeping Alex out of Talos' line of fire or getting her safely across the base the way I had done. I felt a surge of gratitude toward the man as I glanced over at Alex's peacefully sleeping form. She was safe for now. I just prayed that I had the strength to continue ensuring that she remained so.

Chapter 8: Cody Thatcher

I WATCHED AIDEN returning from the cockpit through half-closed eyes. The expression on his face caused a slight smile of amusement to tug at the corner of my lips. Wren had filled me in on the contest that had taken place between our pilot and Aiden earlier today, so I understood where the tension between the two of them was coming from. They were like two bulls in their prime, locking horns over a heifer.

At the moment, Aiden didn't look overly pleased with the outcome of their most recent confrontation. However, there was no doubt in my mind how this contest would end. Aiden and Alex might be like a pair of squirrels whose courting ritual included chasing each other away at times, but in the end it was obvious to anyone with eyes that they would wind up together. They were the only ones who weren't certain of the outcome yet.

As Aiden settled into his seat, I allowed my mind to return to the problem that had been my real focus for the last twenty minutes. That hand written note on the command pad troubled me; Pa would not have said he needed me home unless it was serious. Like most Texans, there was little he couldn't handle on his own. And what little he couldn't, could usually be resolved with the help of one or two good neighbors. Whatever was going on, I knew he wouldn't have called on me for help unless he had tried everything else first.

Of course, it was always possible that either he or Ma were ill enough to warrant bringing me home, but that seemed highly unlikely. A phone call would have been far more likely in that situation then a handwritten letter. No; something else was going on.

I thought about Pa. His face was weathered and lined from years of working out in the sun, but those years had not slowed him down one bit. He was up at the crack of dawn every morning to start his chores and he didn't stop working until long after the sun had set. His broad shoulders and strong hands had carried our ranch through multiple hard patches over the years and would likely continue to do so for many more years to come. At the same time, those rough hands of his were gentle enough to knead life into a stillborn calf and to patiently coax it back to strength.

He was a God-fearing man; Ma wouldn't have married him if he weren't. But he was the type of man who was more likely to talk to God from the back of his horse than from any church pew. I'd once heard part of a prayer he was muttering to himself while we were getting our gear ready to go search for a part of the herd that had disappeared up in the mountains. I'd assumed he was just muttering under his breath until I'd gone to grab my saddle and tack and just happened to overhear part of his words.

"God," he'd said, "my boy and I are about to go find our missing cattle. Yer welcome to come along for the ride and I'd appreciate having you with us. But if yer too busy, I understand." Later, when we were on the trail, I'd asked him about what I'd heard. He'd just nodded his head and explained that I should always invite God to be with me, but that I needed to understand that most of the time God was busy helping those who needed his help more, so I'd just have to do the best I could to take care of things until he was able to join me.

Pa's one weakness was his pride. He'd invite God to come along for the ride, but he'd face down the hosts of hell single-handedly before he'd ask anyone else for help. Ma was always giving him a bad time about it, reminding him that he didn't have to be a lone wolf. Pa would just grunt one of his soft grunts and continue to tackle the problem alone.

If he has asked for my help, then Pa had already done everything he could to try and solve the problem alone. It just turned out that the problem, whatever it was, was too big; he needed two Thatcher men for this job. That, or Ma had backed him into a corner with her rolling pin and threatened to bludgeon him over the head with it if he didn't contact me.

Ma, like Pa, was God-fearing. Only she attended church regularly and spent time each day reading from her well-worn book of scriptures. She and God had a special relationship: she did what he told her to and he did what she asked. Together they made an impressive team.

That's why I was in the military. She said God had told her in a dream that I was needed here for a time and that He had promised her in return that He would make sure I came safely home when he was done with me. No one said no to Ma when she said something needed to be done, so Pa had dropped me off at the recruiting office the next morning and I'd found myself on my way to boot camp that very afternoon.

Three weeks into the training, the week they referred to as blood week, they had placed a phase rifle into my hands and I had shown them what I'd been doing in my spare time on the ranch. A few days later they brought some people out to watch me shoot. Then they brought some more. By the end of the week, I'd been called out to the range on five different occasions to give a demonstration of my skills.

After that, things appeared to calm down and there were no more demonstrations. But on the day of graduation, they pulled me from the normal recruit path and sent me to a special training ground in an undisclosed location where my K-51 was fitted to me and I was taught how to use it. For the next two years I was shipped from place to place on special missions where they needed an expert marksman who could make the split-second judgment calls that a computerized drone could not be trusted to make. Then, four months ago, I had suddenly received orders to transfer to Ghana Base. The transfer had come without warning and without explanation.

Up until a week ago, I had been uncertain why I was there. I still wasn't entirely sure, but now I at least had some suspicions. The number one suspicion being that girl asleep across the way. She needed help; there was no question about it. The UFC had clearly labeled her as their property and intended to make a weapon out of her. Equally clear was that she had neither the desire to be, nor the disposition toward being what they wanted her to be. Her instincts seemed inclined toward gentleness and helping others rather than toward causing harm. Then again, I had seen hints in the last few days that there was something more lurking in the background of her instincts. Talos had suggested that she was still fighting against herself. That seemed as good a way as any to describe what I had noticed each time I watched her use her abilities against someone.

In each case, she had been acting to protect others; that was consistent with the type of person I had found her to be. But I had also noted a change in her behavior during those times, as though her anger against those she was responding to had momentarily overruled her gentler side, leading her to acts of aggression she might not have otherwise committed. I had seen it most clearly at Aiden's home when I had pulled her back from the window. She had physically lashed out at me when I interrupted her and the look in her eyes in that moment had been one of cold, hard fury to a degree I would not have thought her capable of had I not seen it for myself. Then, realizing what she was doing, the look had suddenly evaporated from her face, replaced by a look of horror.

I had come to the conclusion that there must be two sides to her: a gentle, innocent side and a violent, feral side. The two appeared to battle inside of her for dominance each time she was pushed to use her abilities to an extreme. I also got the distinct impression that the more she became self-aware of that dual battle, the more it frightened her.

So, there were in fact, two things she needed help with. The first was preventing the UFC from forcing her into something that conflicted with her gentle nature. The second was preventing her violent side from turning her into something contrary to what she wanted to be.

If the plan to get her to the school in New Los Angeles worked, then the first problem would likely be under control and it was more likely that the second problem would never evolve into more than a potential threat. But if not, then I would find a way to help her with that as well.

Either way, when we got to the ranch, I wanted her as far away from whatever was happening there as I could get her. I had the sinking suspicion that Beckwith was purposely placing her into situations that would goad her into action. But was he doing it to show her that she could help others with her abilities or was he doing it to force her into being a weapon in spite of what he had claimed? Also, did he know about the undercurrent of cold hardness that she was battling or the true level of her abilities? Right now, I didn't have any answers to those questions; just suspicions.

There was another concern as well. How had Remington known we were transporting something of power and how had Icarus' forces known she was on that base? Back in Ghana, the Brig had said that there appeared to be a leak. It looked like that leak might have followed us. Was it possible she'd had more than one tracker implanted? If she did, it was not one the UFC knew about and the Brig had said they'd had her in their possession since she was a baby. So that didn't seem very likely.

No. More likely was that there was another source. There could be a tracker in the silver case we were transporting. If that was the situation, then the problem was solved because we had left it behind this time.

The one possibility I didn't like to consider was that someone on our team could be a traitor reporting her position. I automatically ruled Aiden out; there was no chance in the Light that he would betray her. That left Wren and McLagan. I didn't know either of them very well. What little I did know of them seemed honest and trustworthy, and they had also already been vetted by Beckwith's staff or they would not have been invited to join our team. What was more, they had both been chained up alongside Aiden yesterday and they had both been captured during the invasion today. So, it seemed unlikely that either one of them was a spy. But also, I couldn't entirely dismiss either of them; they'd both had opportunities away from the rest of the team when they could have betrayed us. I'd just have to keep an eye on them.

The remainder of the flight went reasonably quickly. I drifted off and on throughout it, always keeping my mind half alert, never allowing myself to totally give in to sleep. It's not that I was expecting trouble; I just didn't think it was a good idea for all of us to be asleep at the same time. We'd had enough surprises in the last twenty-four hours that I wasn't particularly interested in being caught unprepared by another one.

To that end, Nate and I had decided early in the flight that he would land us at the UFC base in Appalachia. He'd checked the plane's previous flight logs and found that it had gone there before. Our hope was that the plane's appearance would be less suspicious that way. It also helped that we were landing at about two in the morning. The time differences between where we had been and where we were now meant that we would have spent twelve hours in the air, but only six hours would have passed on the clock by the time we landed. It also meant that there would be fewer people out and about to notice us. The fewer there were who saw us, the fewer there were who could pass along information about us if someone came asking.

As luck would have it, there was only one person to check us in at the base tower when we finally did arrive, and he did a lazy job of it after Nate showed him the commander's ID badge and explained that all she wanted was a vehicle so that she and her staff could get to their hotel as quickly as possible.

Once off base, we headed directly for the closest open public transportation depot we could find and ditched the car. Where the transport was going wasn't important; we just wanted a way to disappear and to ensure that no one was following us.

Unfortunately, the only thing running at that time of night was a last chance bus that was finishing up its final route before heading back to the bus yard. We took it anyway, staying on it for several stops before choosing a random one to get off at.

As the bus drove away, leaving the six of us on an empty street corner, I considered where to go next. Ideally, we'd make our way to the Streamline station and catch an early bird train to Austin. The Streamline was a series of interconnected maglev rails that America had built during its post-war reconstruction period. It connected every major city across the country, traveling at speeds upwards of five hundred miles per hour.

But, before we could do that, we'd need money for the tickets and I would need some pants and shoes. The only problem was that if any of us used our IDs to take out credits, we ran the risk of creating a digital trail someone could follow. Nate solved that problem when he pointed out that there was no record connecting him to our team, so we could safely use his ID to pay for things. At least, we could do so once we found a store that was open.

In the end, it was a long night and a lot of walking before we finally made it to the Streamline station and were able to find open seats in the back of one of the cars.

Aiden must had suspected that I hadn't really slept on the flight because he offered to stay awake this time so that I could get some rest. Truth be told, I was grateful for his offer and it didn't take more than a few minutes before I was out. Sleep helped the ride to Austin go quickly.

The Austin Streamline station was located on the north side of the city where the smaller businesses started giving way to the larger skyscrapers. The immediate proximity around it was a series of other hubs planned out so that passengers could easily transfer to any one of Austin's many public transportation services in order to get where they needed to go. I figured we could take the city tram from there to the south side of the city and then catch the county shuttle to Blanco's city center. But even doing that, we'd still have a long walk from there to reach Pa's ranch; there weren't any forms of public transportation that went as far out as the ranches.

We had just crossed the street in front of the Streamline station and were heading for the tram hub when a loud whistle drew my attention. It had come from a man sitting inside a beat-up old truck.

"Well, look who's home!" called out the silver-haired man with a matching sidebar mustache and sun-weathered skin who had his arms folded lazily atop the truck's open window frame. His face was split into a large grin as he continued, "If it ain't Dale Thatcher's boy."

My lips twisted up into a half smile of their own and I walked over to shake his hand, "Mr. Hillock. It's good to see you, sir."

"What brings you into town, son? Heard your pa dropped you off at some recruiting station a few years back. And, since your ma has been sittin' alone at church each Sunday since then, well, I reckoned it was true."

"Yes, sir," I nodded. "Ma said God wanted me to do a tour for the UFC, and you know Ma."

"Sure do," Mr. Hillock chuckled. "Made the mistake a few years back of telling her no to something. Only made that mistake once."

As he spoke, he glanced from me to my companions. Unlike myself, they were still in the military fatigues they had gotten back on the base. Mr. Hillock's keen eyes seemed to take that in and he slowly turned back to me with a thoughtful expression. "Yer pa ask you to come home?"

I'd known Mr. Hillock since I was a little kid. His ranch wasn't too far from ours and he and Pa had been about as close to being friends as I'd ever seen Pa get. Normally I would have answered his question without a second thought, but something in his expression gave me pause. He knew something, and, looking at my friends, he suspected something more: something I thought I ought to find out before I led my team into a bad situation.

My smile slid away as I asked pointedly, "Something goin' on that I should know about before I step in it, Mr. Hillock?"

He was quiet for a long moment, seeming to carefully consider his next words before finally letting out a deep breath and nodding his head faintly. "There is, but I think I better let your pa be the one to tell you what's been going on around these parts. If he hasn't told you yet, then it's not my place to say. Though I reckon it just might be a good thing to have you and your friends in town for a bit. And it looks like your ma must have asked God to arrange for your transportation home because the likelihood of me being here just as you arrived would have been pretty much slim-to-none otherwise. Why don't you and your friends hop in and I'll give you a ride. It's probably best if the wrong people didn't know just yet that the lot of you are in town."

My eyebrows went up at that last part. It wasn't a real answer to my question, but it hinted at enough. I nodded my head and waved for my team to join us.

Haskell, Wren, Evans, and McLagan climbed into the bed of the truck, leaving the front for Alex and myself. We didn't talk much as we drove; Mr. Hillock seemed to have a lot on his mind. But, as he pulled up to the start of my parents' drive he said, "Would you tell your pa that I said hello, and let him know that I dropped Garrett off at the bus depot this morning; he won't be coming back."

I simply nodded my agreement. I would have liked to have asked why he had dropped him off and why he wouldn't be coming back, only I got the feeling that Mr. Hillock would have said more if he had wanted me to know more. Though it did seem likely it had something to do with whatever it was Mr. Hillock felt it wasn't his place to tell me about. I'd just have to wait for Pa to fill me in.

Ma was in the garden picking weeds as we came up the road. Our two dogs had been sitting not far from her; they climbed to their feet when they noticed us. Alerted by the dogs, Ma stood and wiped her hands on her apron, watching us as well.

There was a wariness in the way she watched that immediately caught my attention. While Ma was always aware of what was happening around her, this was somehow different. It was almost as though she were expecting trouble and was waiting for it to start. She had one hand shading her eyes and the other on her hip. It was only then that I realized that the early morning sun was behind us and would make it difficult for her to see who was coming up the road.

Not wanting her to worry, I whistled for the dogs to let them know who was here. Mazey and Turk were Blue Lacys, a breed of dog that had originated right here in Texas for the purpose of helping out ranchers. Turk, the taller of the two, was a rich charcoal color with a white chest, while Mazey was a gentle cream all over. Hearing my whistle, they both started to bound down the road with their tails wagging. I knelt down and waited for them to come. Behind them, I was satisfied to see Ma's stance relax; she knew I was home.

"This is Ma," I introduced my team a few minutes later. "She'll answer to that for you as well as she does for me, but you can call her Beth if you prefer."

Ma laughed warmly. "Ma will do just fine. Only strangers call me Beth. You're friends of my Cody, so that makes you family round here. Now, have you kids eaten? Breakfast was an hour ago, but I can put something together right quick if y'all haven't eaten yet. And Lilith will be wanting to know you've arrived. We weren't expecting y'all to show up till tomorrow morning."

"Lilith?" I asked somewhat confused. I wasn't aware of anyone in these parts with that name, and we'd only ever hired men as ranch hands before, so she wasn't likely to be one of those. I suppose Ma could have brought someone in to help in the house; she was getting older. But Ma had always declared that the house was her domain and that she wasn't about to let anyone else tamper with it, so that didn't seem likely.

For a moment, I thought Ma was going to ignore my question; she was staring at the sling holding my arm and had one of those expressions on her face that warned me she was about to start a lecture. But then she seemed to change her mind with a shake of her head and instead turned to lead us back to the house. As she walked, she talked.

"A real sweet young lady, that one. Tall, thin, dark haired. Doesn't wear much makeup but looks just fine without it. Has a real knack for getting things organized and running smoothly, and a no-nonsense attitude. She arrived a few days ago with a letter from Director Beckwith asking me to house her for the week in exchange for having you and some friends come home tomorrow."

"You mean Miss Alcott? The nurse?" I asked, somewhat surprised. Lilith Alcott was the UFC nurse Director Beckwith had brought in to care for Alex during the team's time at the lodge. I'd had the pleasure of her company for a short time following lunch that first day, but our conversation had been cut short when she'd been called away to assist Alex back to her room. I had not expected to see her again any time soon.

Ma cocked her head as she suddenly stopped to look over at me. "Why, I do believe that is her last name." There was a distinct gleam of calculation in her eyes as she continued to study me for a long moment, but then a slow smile replaced that calculating look and she turned away from me to start walking again.

"Tell you what. I'll get your friends settled in the kitchen. Why don't you go out to the bunk house and let her know you've arrived. She was working out there today to get those beds ready for you boys."

"Yes, ma'am," I responded automatically; you don't say no to Ma.

As she led everyone else into the house, I headed out back. The bunk house was a medium-sized structure near the back of the developed property that was used for housing the ranch hands who came to work for us. It had a single central room with bunk beds lining the walls and storage cabinets for each person, plus an arrangement of couches, chairs, and tables for the hands to relax at when the day's work was done. There was also a good-sized washroom through a door in the back and a wood stove in the corner for cold winter nights. As I got close to it, I noticed that someone had opened the windows and the door to air it out.

Walking up to the door, I could see Lilith straightening a blanket she had just spread out onto one of the beds. She tucked its ends in crisply and tightly. The last time I had seen her, she had been wearing smartly ironed scrubs with her hair pulled back in a no-nonsense ponytail. She had been every inch the professional nurse that she had been hired to be. Today, the tight-fitting denim jeans she was wearing, combined with stitched boots, a fitted white shirt, and loosely braided hair, gave off more of the girl-next-door vibes. It looked surprisingly good on her.

I could have just walked in, only somehow it seemed more proper to knock.

"Miss Alcott?" I rapped my knuckles on the door frame. "Mind if I come in?"

She looked back over her shoulder and her face lit up in a bright smile.

"Well, now. You're a bit earlier than we were expecting." Her soft Southern accent gave her words an added measure of warmth. I found myself smiling back.

"We had to adjust our plans somewhat. Just arrived a few minutes ago and everyone else is in the kitchen while Ma gets them some breakfast. She sent me out here to get you. I have to say, I'm surprised to find you here."

She laughed warmly. "Well, you shouldn't be. Your weapons were fired. They wanted someone to check on you, find out what happened, and make sure everyone is in good shape. From the sling on your arm, I'd say it's probably a good thing they did send me. Why don't you come in and tell me what happened?"

As I entered the bunk house, I considered for just a moment how much to tell her. There were things she would need to pass on to Captain Marcellus, the military leader in charge of our team, and there were other things that might be best left untold, especially given that Alex wouldn't take it well if Aiden were reassigned as a result of what had occurred at his home. I wouldn't lie about it, but that didn't mean I had to volunteer everything that had occurred.

However, my hesitation must have tipped her off. Before I could even open my mouth, she had raised an eyebrow in challenge. Seeing it, I couldn't help chuckling to myself; she and Ma had that look in common. It was like they knew when a half-truth was about to be told and decided to cut it off before it could even escape the lips. Well, so much for downplaying the trouble. I started to shrug in resignation, only to stop mid-shrug as my breath caught and I winced from the shrug pulling on the muscles the surgeon had knitted back together.

Seeing it, Lilith frowned and pointed firmly to one of the nearby seats. "Let's take a look at that."

She helped me take off the sling and pull my arm free of the shirt's sleeve then deftly began to unwrap the bandage, being especially cautious of the places that dried blood was causing it to stick to either my skin or the stitches. Icarus' soldiers hadn't been very gentle in their treatment of the prisoners. The result of their roughness had been some stressed stitches and additional bleeding at the wound site. But her fingers were surprisingly gentle, especially given how firmly she probed the skin above the repaired muscles.

"No inflammation of the skin in spite of those stressed stitches," she said softly. "It doesn't look like I need to re-tie any of them, but you shouldn't have been doing whatever it was you did to cause so much strain so soon after the surgery."

Not pausing to give me a chance to explain, she continued her exam. "Brachialis and Bicep Brachialis both repaired...slight divot right here...the surgeon utilized the Hansen Stitch coupled with the Nelson Procedure to pull the muscles back together and to patch the gap created in the injury..."

"You can tell all that just from feeling it?" I asked impressed.

She met my eyes with a mischievous twinkle. "Not really. I pulled up the surgeon's report this morning; it told me what was done. Mostly I was just feeling for any heat in the skin or tenderness that might indicate an infection."

Stepping back, she patted my shoulder. "For now, you can pull your sleeve back on and the sling as well. We'll replace the bandaging when we get to the house. I also have some painkiller I can give you that will ease some of the aching. But you will need to limit the use of that arm from here on out; it needs time to heal. I suspect there will be plenty of temptations around here to use it—but don't!" She said the last part as though issuing an order; her stern expression reinforced that idea.

I grunted softly in reply. I wasn't going to lie to her, but I also wasn't about to make a promise I didn't yet know if I would be able to keep. Fortunately, if she noticed, she didn't challenge it. Instead, she sat down in the chair across from me and said, "Now, why don't you tell me what happened out there."

Ten minutes later, all hints of her smile were gone. "Two attacks in two days? How did Icarus' forces know where to find her?"

"Don't know yet. But it seems obvious to me that we have a leak somewhere; someone had to be reporting her position for us to be found so quickly. That, or she had more than one tracking device implanted. Though, come to think of it, those soldiers didn't know exactly where she was. No. I think we need to consider that someone on our team might be a spy."

She nodded. "Any thoughts on who it might be?"

I shook my head in disgust. "It has to be either Wren or McLagan. There is no chance under the Light that Aiden would betray her. It took an explosive situation to finally get those two to talk to each other. But even before that, there was no question that the attraction between them runs deeper than the oil under Texas."

"Glad to hear that at least that particular issue has been resolved," she said it with a wry twist of her lips.

I had to nod in agreement. "The problem is, I haven't seen any indication that Wren or McLagan are the spy either. They were both chained up next to Haskell at his home, and they both were captured on the base. Nor do either of them strike me as the type who would willingly betray a teammate. It's also possible that the decoy case we were carrying was somehow bugged. If that's true, then the problem is solved because it was left on the base."

She nodded again. "Very well. Let's assume for the moment that it's either Wren or McLagan. I'll have Harry do some research and see what he can learn about the two of them. Maybe something will show up there to give us a clue."

Harry was the team's computer expert, responsible for securing Alex's identity and location digitally as well as all communications between the teams while we were in transit to the school. If there were clues in the data, he would find them.

"In the meantime, I suggest that they be left out of any discussions about the team's plans, and we make sure that neither of them is ever left alone with Alex…forgive me. Claire. This new name thing is going to take some getting used to," she laughed lightly. I had to agree. Between finding out that Aiden's name was an alias and that Alex was being given a new name, it was a wonder I was managing to keep up with the changes.

"We will probably also want to make sure Wren and McLagan don't get any more time to themselves. If either of them is the spy, we don't want to give them time to contact whoever they are working with."

I nodded again.

"Aside from that, how is everyone holding up? I know that the doctor on base wrote a prescription for Aiden to receive physical therapy on his leg and it sounds like I will need to schedule Claire for counseling, but is there anything else I don't know about that I should?"

"We have a new team member." It occurred to me that she probably didn't know about Evans.

Her eyebrows shot up. "Someone not under contract?"

"Nate Evans," I explained. "He was instrumental in getting us off the base and flying us here. He's already proven himself to my satisfaction, so we asked him to join us, pending final approval from command, that is. I thought it best to bring in another trained set of hands."

"All right," she said thoughtfully. "I'll have Harry look into him as well. I'll also let them know that Aiden transferred team command to you. Anything else?" she asked the last part almost hesitantly, as though dreading that I might have more surprises to share.

"Nope. Aside from that, the team's a little beat up, but we're all in one piece."

She laughed somewhat sarcastically at my description. "That's like saying a mirror has arrived in one piece when in reality the glass is spiderwebbed into a thousand pieces that just happen to still be held together by the frame. Very well then, Cowboy," she said with a sigh. "Let's go find out just how many pieces there actually are that I need to start bandaging back together."

"Cowboy?" I asked in mild amusement. She only smiled mysteriously in reply, then stood to leave the bunk house.

Chapter 9: Cody Thatcher

WHEN WE GOT back to the house, we found the rest of our team exactly where I had said they would be: around the kitchen table, eating Ma's flapjacks. Ma's food was a far cry better than any I'd had in the military, so I wasn't ashamed to admit that I had missed it. Everyone else seemed to be enjoying it as well. I introduced Evans to Lilith, then sat down and grabbed a stack of my own.

After breakfast, and after she had rebandaged my arm, Lilith decided that she was going to call each member of the team to her room one at a time so that she could perform a full evaluation, starting with Alex.

I was not surprised to find that Ma had set up the guest room in the house for Lilith and Alex; she would have never allowed them to sleep in the bunk house with the men. What did surprise me was how easily Lilith and Ma seemed to be working together, and how easily they communicated.

"Beth," Lilith said before leaving the room with Alex, "I'll have the boys clear the table before they head outside, but is there anything else you needed done inside before I start doing their evals?"

Ma smiled warmly. "That will be good enough. Though, if you could get one of them to carry in some firewood, I'd be much obliged."

Lilith nodded. "Haskell, Wren, Thatcher, you three can clear the table and then head out back to the bunk house until I send for you. Evans, McLagan, if the two of you will follow me, I'll show you where the wood pile is and where she needs it stacked. Claire, you can follow me as well and we'll get your eval done while the boys are doing their work."

After clearing the table, I showed Haskell and Wren to the bunkhouse. Then, knowing that the team was going to be busy for a while, I decided to take the opportunity to talk to Ma. I found her standing in front of the kitchen sink, washing the breakfast dishes. So, I grabbed a towel out of the drawer and began drying the ones she had already rinsed.

"Ma?" I finally asked while picking up another plate, "What's going on? Why am I needed at home?"

We'd never been a family that wasted words. Perhaps Ma was a little more verbal than Pa was, but we were used to getting straight to the point and giving direct answers in return. So, I wasn't surprised that she didn't answer me right away; I was surprised by the cup that slipped from her hands and back into the soapy water. I couldn't think of a time I'd ever seen her drop a dish before.

I stopped drying the plate I had just picked up and turned to look at her. "That bad?"

After another moment of hesitation, she nodded then sighed. "Your pa should be home at sunset. He'll tell you all about it when he gets here. In the meantime, if you and your friends need something to do, your pa could use some help with the chores around the barn. Our last ranch hand resigned last week and Pa has been doing all the chores alone since then."

"The last one? What about Blake and Paul?" Most of our ranch hands were hired on during the spring season and then let go after the fall cattle drive was done, but Paul and Blake were our permanent help. Paul was our foreman. He had been with us for almost twenty years now and considered the ranch to be his home. Blake was a year younger than me, but had already been with us for several years. We had been friends in school, so Pa had offered to take him on when his parents died in a vehicle crash. He was a good friend and an even better worker. Both of them were like family around here.

When I left, they had promised to take care of Ma and Pa for me. I had a hard time believing that either of them would choose to leave, especially not with the end of the season so close. Pa would be depending on them to help him get things buckled down for the winter.

I was further shocked to see a tiny tear pooling in the corner of Ma's eye. I could only remember two times that I had ever seen tears in her eyes. The first time had been the day her mother had died. The other had been the day of her father's funeral.

"Ma?" I asked in concern.

She quickly brushed at her eyes and hurried to grab the next plate, but the slight quaver in her voice betrayed the emotions she tried to hide. "There was a stampede during the last cattle drive. Not sure what started it, but Blake's horse stumbled. He lost his hold and was thrown into the mass of panicking cattle. Paul tried to save him, but he…well, he couldn't get him to the hospital fast enough. It crushed Paul to lose that kid."

Blake was dead?! The thought was almost mind numbing; it didn't hardly seem possible. But as shocking as it was to me, his death would have hit Paul the hardest. Paul had taken Blake under his wing, treated him like his own son. And to have been there when it happened and not been able to prevent it? Somberly I asked, "Where's Paul now?"

Ma slowly set the cup into the clean water, her face a mask of tightness.

"Pa will need to be the one to talk about Paul; it's why he sent for you."

I cocked my head, waiting patiently for her to say more; she didn't. Nor did she turn to look at me. Instead, she sighed as she reached back into the water to pick up the next dish. We washed the rest of the dishes in silence. I would have liked to have asked her more, but I was familiar with that set to her shoulders; she was done talking.

After we finished, I headed out to the barn to see what needed to be done. As I expected, everything was in order. Pa would not have allowed it to be otherwise, no matter how little sleep he would get because of it. However, on the way out to the barn I had noticed that the flatbed trailer was still loaded down with hay that had yet to be unloaded. Pa rarely allowed a trailer to stay loaded for more than a few hours. That meant he'd been too busy to get to it. Well, that was something I could help him with.

I grabbed a pair of gloves from off the shelf and headed back outside. For just a moment, I debated the wisdom of going to the bunkhouse to ask the rest of the team to help, then I quickly dismissed that option. It's not that I was being stubborn or prideful, it was just that I recognized that they all had their own injuries and needed time to heal. Besides that, the work that needed to be done around here was not their responsibility; it was mine. No. I'd let them rest while they could.

As I walked, I considered how to accomplish the task I had set for myself. The normal load for this trailer was eighty-six bales of hay. Each of those sixty-pound bales had been tucked tight and wrapped with two parallel rows of baling twine to prevent them from falling apart. Normally, I could easily buck those bales by grabbing the twine with each hand and lifting up so that it balanced against my thigh. Unfortunately, with my left arm in a sling, that wasn't going to be an option.

While I was certain I could still lift sixty pounds even one-handed, doing so would require me to carry an unbalanced load that I knew from past experience would tweak my back before too long. Instead, what I needed was a way to utilize the strength of my left shoulder and balance out the load while still avoiding the use of the arm itself. Several possibilities crossed my mind in rapid succession. The one that seemed most likely to work was the one that involved tying a rope into a shoulder harness. I grabbed one of the ropes off of the shed wall and started working it into the shape I had in mind.

Next, I had to get a few of the hay bales off the trailer so that I could try the harness out. When it came to getting the bales down, the easiest and most efficient method was to simply push them off. The first bale to hit the ground was always the most damaged because of its impact with the hard ground. But once it was down, it could be used as a cushion for the rest of the bales. It would soften their falls and even, if done correctly, springboard the rest of them closer to the barn. Unfortunately, while I was well practiced at this with two hands, it turned out to be much harder to aim when I only used one. The second bale I pushed off missed its mark completely. *So much for only damaging one bale with the initial drop*, I thought wryly.

Thankfully, with two bales now on the ground, the rest had an easier time bouncing off of at least one of them. After dropping down about ten bales, I climbed back down to finally try out the harness. It worked reasonably well, though not perfectly. The rope, pulled down by the weight of the hay, cut into my unpadded shoulder so that the skin there quickly became raw and tender. I solved that problem by placing the glove I wasn't using into the space between the rope and my shoulder.

An hour later I had succeeded at bucking fourteen of the hay bales up into the hay loft before I had to take a break. In spite of my best efforts, my arm was starting to feel sore. The harness allowed me to keep it in the sling, but it didn't stop the bales from occasionally banging against it while I moved them.

As I sat down on one of the springboard bales, looking up at the work I still had to do, I pulled my arm out of the sling and absently started rubbing its bandaged muscles. At this rate it would take me at least three more hours to get them all unloaded; longer if the pain continued to grow and I had to take more breaks. Normally, I would have worked straight through until the job was done. But then, normally, I would have been almost finished with the job by now. *Well, no use complaining,* I sighed to myself. *Time to get back to work.*

But, just as I started to stand, it felt like someone plopped a hundred-pound sack of chicken scratch down onto my lap. I landed back down onto the bale with a thud and even started to sink into it.

"What in the blazes…" I started in confusion, only to be cut off by Lilith's angry voice behind me.

"You can just stay right there, Cowboy!"

I turned my head sharply to look back as best I could, though the weight had not been lifted from my lap so that I was unable to turn around completely. At that angle, I could barely make out several figures standing behind me. Lilith, the easiest to see, had her hands on her hips and was glaring at me with the same expression Ma occasionally used on Pa when he had done something she thought to be particularly stupid. Inwardly, I groaned; I had a pretty good idea what was coming next.

"What were you thinking, trying to move those bales with your arm in the condition it's in? Are you trying to do more damage to it? Didn't I tell you that you were not to use that arm to do work around here? Did you think at all?"

"I didn't…" I started to explain that I wasn't a total fool and had made the harness to protect my arm, but she cut me off.

"That's exactly right! You didn't think! Out of your whole team, it's your injury that is the least stable. One foolish action on your part and you could permanently damage that arm of yours. Then where would that leave you? Yet here you are, bound and determined to do as much damage to it as possible."

As she continued to berate me, my annoyance began to fade away. I found that I couldn't stop a slow smile as it began to tug at the corners of my lips. She really did sound just like Ma. It made me think that there was a good chance that, if I didn't choose my next words carefully, I'd likely spend the rest of my day ducking away from the rolling pin she'd be carrying around for the purpose of teaching me a lesson. I didn't want that. So, taking a page from Pa's book, I bowed my head contritely and made a sincere apology the first opportunity she gave me.

"Sorry, ma'am," I offered with the necessary contriteness. "It's hard to sit back when Pa needs help, but I should have been more cautious of my arm."

Her eyes narrowed and she lifted her chin slightly, as though trying to gauge the level of my sincerity. But she also appeared to be considering what I had said. Without warning, she turned to one of those figures next to her. "Claire, would you mind moving him out of the way? You can set him over there against the fence. No need to be too gentle." She said the last part with a cold stare back at me.

I had to admit to myself that she had mastered that particular stare. Knowing it was aimed at me, there was a small part of my mind that was telling me to run and hide. But, before I could do much more than think about up and running, I felt myself being lifted into the air, bale and all. In spite of Lilith's words about not needing to be gentle, there was only a slight thump when Alex settled me back to the ground some twenty feet away from the trailer. Well, now I at least knew why I hadn't been able to stand up.

Lilith, whose cold gaze was still on me, said curtly, "Stay there!"

Then she turned back to the others that were with her and started issuing orders. I could now see that the figures I had not been able to make out before were in fact the rest of my team.

"McLagan, Haskell, Evans, go get gloves. You'll find them on the shelf just inside the barn. Wren, take Thatcher's gloves away from him then climb up there and start pushing bales off. If you drop them onto that one on the ground, they'll…"

Wren interrupted her softly, "I know how to unload bales." Then he walked over and held out his hands for my gloves. His angular features were in an even harder line than normal. It was obvious that he disapproved of my choices as well. Shaking my head in defeat, I handed the gloves to him.

It quickly became clear that Wren did indeed know what he was doing as he took the time to push the springboard bale into better positioning then climbed up to begin expertly tossing more bales down. Every one of those bales bounced perfectly off the springboard bale and over toward the barn. There was no doubt in my mind that Wren had done this before. Come to think of it, if I remembered right, I had overheard him mentioning that his family raised horses, so it made sense that he would know how to do this.

Lilith nodded her head in satisfaction as she watched him work, then turned back to me. "Where are these bales going?" She said it with a clipped tone that left no doubt she was still angry.

"Up into the hay loft above the barn." I carefully kept my voice neutral; I didn't want to give her any more reasons to bite my head off.

Haskell, Evans, and McLagan returned with gloves on their own hands and began to pick up the bales that Wren had bounced down. Lilith showed them where to take them, then asked Alex if she wouldn't mind lifting them up into the loft to make the job easier on them. Thirty minutes later, the trailer had been unloaded and the bales were neatly stacked. I was permitted to get off of my bale only after they had finished everything else and were ready to put that final one away as well. Lilith then required them to clean up, instructing them to sweep off the trailer and to rake up the fallen pieces of hay so that the area was pristine once more.

As the rest of the team carried the tools back to the barn, Lilith finally approached me. "What's next, Cowboy? What other foolish notions did you have in your head to get done? Get it out now because as soon as we're done here, I'm marching you over to that bunk house and you'll be starting an enforced bedrest until dinner time."

Suddenly I wasn't very amused. Ma had said that Pa needed help out here. I was willing to acknowledge that trying to move the hay bales alone may not have been my best choice, but I was not interested in wasting the rest of the day in bed when there was work to be done. At the same time, I wasn't sure I wanted to give Lilith the satisfaction of being able to make me sit around and watch everyone else do the work for me.

My voice was somewhat tight as I answered, "The fences."

Those would need to be looked over to ensure that there were no broken posts or snapped wires. If Pa had not had time to unload the trailer, then I could be fairly certain he'd not had time to check the fence lines either.

"You want to put in fences?" She asked it with an arched eyebrow, her expression clearly suggesting what she thought of that idea.

"No, ma'am." I was trying to keep my voice level; I was not fool enough to purposely make my situation worse by allowing my annoyance to show through in my voice. "I want to make sure the fence lines around the pastures are unbroken and secure, ready to receive the cattle when Pa brings them in from the hills."

She studied me for a long moment before finally saying, "Very well. Wren, would you go saddle up three horses? This cowboy wants to check the fence lines next."

I gritted my teeth but didn't otherwise respond. *Where had this name come from? And why was she insisting on using it to refer to me?*

"The rest of you go report to Ma. She'll let you know what she could use help with. Also let her know what we're doing and that we'll be back in time for lunch."

As they acknowledged her instructions and left for the house, Lilith turned back to me. "Come along, Cowboy. Show me where the tools are for this job."

"There's no need for you to get the tools, ma'am," I countered automatically. "I can do that."

I had meant it as a respectful suggestion that it was my job to do the heavy lifting, not hers. But I knew instantly that I had made a mistake.

"Cowboy," she said dangerously, "let's get something straight right now. I am no fragile spring chick who needs to be coddled or protected. I grew up with five older brothers and was expected to work the farm right alongside them. There's not a chore on this ranch that I didn't grow up doing, including checking the fence lines. You, on the other hand, appear to be hellbent on damaging that arm of yours. So let me make myself perfectly clear. If you so much as think about picking up another tool, I will hog tie you, throw you over your saddle, and deliver you to your ma with the explanation that anything less than absolute bed rest for the next week has the potential to damage your arm such that you would not be able to complete the tour God told her you were needed for. Have I made myself sufficiently clear?"

I studied her for a long moment, carefully considering my next words. I was of half a mind to tell her exactly what she could do with her threat. But at the same time, I suspected that if I did, she would not hesitate to follow through with it. *Five brothers, huh? And she'd grown up on a farm working alongside them? So be it.* I'd let her do the work. My ma had taught me manners, but she had also taught me to respect a woman's strength. Lilith had not only instructed the team on how to unload the bales, but she had also climbed up into the loft to show them how to buck them properly so that they would be tight and secure. I had to grudgingly admit to myself that she was stronger than I had first given her credit for. Even more, I had to grudgingly admit that she was probably right about my arm.

"Yes, ma'am," I finally grunted.

"Yes, ma'am what?" she said in a clipped tone.

I sighed. "Yes, ma'am. I will not attempt to pick up or use any more tools. And I will not make the mistake again of assuming you are not capable of the job at hand."

She nodded her head with satisfaction. "Good. Then let's go check out those fence lines and make sure they're ready."

Pa's ranch had five separate pastures, each one encompassing between twenty to fifty acres. Each of those pastures were framed in by posts and stretched barbed wire. The first three pastures were all in good order and ready for the cattle. But the fourth one, the biggest one, held a few unpleasant surprises that I had not anticipated.

"These wires have been cut," Wren said with a disapproving tone.

Not broken. Not damaged by weather or animals. *Cut!* Who would cut pasture fences? Certainly no one from around these parts. Fences were considered sacred boundaries between neighbors around here. They were built, not to keep others out, but to keep relationships good between people by preventing boundary disputes and damages caused by escaped animals. But whoever had cut them had done so in such a way that whole sections of wire had been cut up into small pieces and multiple posts were either broken or bent beyond use. This would take me more hours to repair than the day had hours left in it, even if I had been fully healed.

Appearing to be thinking along the same lines, Lilith sighed. "Looks like we better go back and get the team. It's time for lunch anyway and we're going to need their help if we're going to get this patched up before nightfall. Your pa keep wire in the shed?"

"Yes, ma'am." Pa always kept extra supplies on hand, but never had we needed so much at one time unless it was for a planned fence replacement. I hoped the spool was full.

It turned out that both Lilith and Wren had previous experience stretching wire and tying it off, so they took on that job while the others took care of pounding new posts into the ground to replace the ones that had been bent beyond use.

As I had expected, I was not permitted to do much more then watch everyone else do the work. At least Lilith finally stopped treating me like an errant child. I couldn't say for sure, but it seemed that seeing the purposely damaged fences had made her decide that my desire to check the fence line had not been so ridiculous after all.

Lilith wasn't the only one affected by seeing the damage. As we worked, there was a distinct undercurrent of disgust in everyone's postures and expressions; no one was impressed by what had been done. The result was tight lips and near silence as they worked. After about forty-five minutes of this, Lilith had had enough.

"All right," she said loudly, placing her hands on her hips. "We can all agree that someone is a total nuclear fool for having done this. But there's no need to add to their damage by giving each other the silent treatment as well. So, let's get some conversations going, starting with the newcomer. Evans, tell us about yourself. Where are you from, what got you into the military, and something about yourself that the rest of us ought to know."

We were all caught a little off guard by Lilith's sudden announcement, but Evans only glanced around once before shrugging and deciding to play along.

"Okay, then. Hi. My name is Nate Evans and I come from Exeter, England." He said it like he was introducing himself to a group of strangers, which in reality wasn't too far from the truth. "I joined the UFC Aircorp following in the footsteps of my dad and my older brothers who are all pilots as well. And something you ought to know about me…" he paused for a moment to think, then chuckled to himself as a mischievous smile spread across his face. "I have a reputation for finding the hottest girls in the room and stealing them away from their boyfriends. Up until yesterday, I had never failed to get the girl."

Aiden's head shot up and he stared coldly at Evans for several seconds before finally taking a possessive step closer to Alex. Evans' grin didn't falter for even a moment as he watched Aiden; if anything, it grew bigger. I got the distinct impression that he had chosen his words specifically to get that reaction.

Alex, for her part, was swiftly developing a deeper than normal flush in her cheeks. But then she surprised us all when she muttered under her breath, "Hi. My name is Claire DuCain. I'm from Sussex, England, and I'm already with the hottest guy in the room, so you didn't stand a chance."

There was a full three seconds of stunned silence while her words sunk in, and then everyone burst out laughing. It was like someone had shaken up a bottle of soda and then popped the lid; the laughter just kept bubbling out.

I don't think any of us had been expecting it; Alex least of all. I was guessing that she hadn't thought through what she was going to say before she said it because there was a look of shock on her face that couldn't be explained any other way. That was perhaps what made it even funnier. But, when she saw the grin on Haskell's face and heard his chuckle, her embarrassed expression slowly gave way to a shy smile.

Even Wren, who was normally straight faced through everything, cracked the hint of a smile as he turned to Evans. "Want some ice to go with that burn?"

"Well, I'm glad to see that no one has lost their sense of humor," Lilith said when the laughter finally began to calm down. "Wren, you're next."

The work went much faster after that as we shared our back stories interspersed with some lighthearted joking and teasing.

The sun had already crested the horizon by the time we finally finished up and headed back to the house. Ma was putting the finishing touches on dinner when we walked through the door. She'd pulled out all the stops: roasted potatoes, roast beef, snap peas, and cornbread. It was one of her best meals and I suspected she had cooked it as a way to thank everyone for the hard work they had put in.

While we ate, we talked. Or rather, others talked; I listened. You can learn a lot just by listening. Well, listening and watching to be more precise. People have a way of saying as much in the things they do as they do in the things they say. When the conversation turned to the cut fence wires, I watched Ma closely.

She'd already been told about the cut wires earlier, so hearing about it now wasn't going to be a surprise to her. But the way she sighed and slowly shook her head as she listened was another piece of information for me to tuck away and consider. It was something she did when someone did something she had expected them to do, but for which she was none the less disappointed. Like the time Joey Harper had lit the fireworks under the pews during the church meeting. She had not been surprised he had done it; just disappointed. Whatever was going on around these parts, destruction of property was no longer a surprise to her; it was something she had come to expect.

I was thinking about that when the sound of a vehicle rapidly approaching the house caught my attention. I looked up, meeting Ma's eyes.

"It's about time for Pa to be home," she said it cautiously as though not quite certain that the approaching vehicle was his. But with the sound of the tires skidding to an abrupt stop, her brows creased together in concern. Pa was not one to race down the drive or skid to a halt.

I pushed back my chair and slowly stood. Everyone else had stopped talking and was either looking toward the kitchen door or was following my example and likewise starting to stand.

Outside, the vehicle door opened and then slammed closed, followed by the sound of a second door opening. I was already moving, followed closely behind by Aiden and Wren. Just before I grabbed the handle, the kitchen door slammed open, hitting the wall behind it with a loud *bang*.

"Beth?" a stern voice called sharply from the hulking figure that stumbled through the doorway.

No. Not one hulking figure, two separate figures with the second being supported by the first; Pa was carrying another man over his shoulders. The unconscious man's face was bloodied and his labored breathing had a ragged edge to it.

Pa took in the group without missing a step, a slight twitch at his jawline the only indication that he had seen me.

"Beth, get the first aid kit," his deep voice reverberated with a tightness that revealed both concern and frustration. "The rest of you get that table cleared. Now!"

I hurried forward to help him with the man he was carrying. My lips drew into a tight frown as I recognized the face: it was Mr. Hillock. We laid him down as gently as we could, but it was Lilith who took over, firmly shooing us out of her way.

"What happened?" she asked in her no-nonsense way, not pausing as she pulled up his shirt to reveal a multitude of purpling bruises that riddled his ribs and abdomen. Still not waiting for an answer, she placed her ear to his chest and listened for several seconds before finally turning back to squarely meet Pa's eyes.

His voice was clipped and angry. "I stopped by Garth's house to check on him like I do every evening. I found his door busted in and he was lying on the floor in the kitchen, unconscious. Don't know much more than that."

Lilith's dark eyes narrowed, but she didn't challenge Pa's lack of knowledge. Instead, she turned back to her patient and began to gently probe his abdomen.

Ma came hurrying back though the kitchen door carrying the first aid kit. She set it on the table at Mr. Hillock's feet along with the nurse's bag that Lilith kept her medical supplies in. I had seen Lilith packing that same bag back at the lodge when I had gone to tell Alex it was time for our team to leave.

In her no-nonsense tone, Lilith said, "It feels like he has a few broken ribs. From this bruising, I'd say there is some internal bleeding as well. He didn't get these injuries from falling off a chair in his kitchen; someone did this to him." She looked back up at Pa. "Can we transport him to the hospital?"

Pa shook his head sharply, "Don't think that would be a good idea. I'm not sure who can be trusted anymore."

Lilith shook her head in disgust. "Fine. I'll treat him here."

Her lack of argument suggested she knew at least something of what he was referring to. *He didn't know who could be trusted? But why would the hospital not be a place he could trust? And why did Lilith appear to simply accept that as a fact?*

"Claire," Lilith didn't look up as she continued to check Mr. Hillock's vitals, "there's a box of supplies in our bedroom closet. Open it up and get me one of the bags labeled IV kit.

Haskell, go get the coat rack from the entry hall. The rest of you get out of this room and let me work. Beth, you can stay."

She said that last part not quite as an afterthought, but more like she had taken it for granted that Ma would be staying, only it had occurred to her at the last second that she might need to actually clarify it so there was no confusion.

Shooed from the kitchen by Ma, we gathered anxiously in the living room. Someone had worked Mr. Hillock over and then left him there to die. From the sounds of it, if Pa had not checked on him, that is exactly what would have happened.

In the background of my mind, pieces were starting to shift together into a picture I didn't like the looks of. Ma's nervousness when we had first arrived and she had not yet been able to see who was approaching the house, the lack of ranch hands during a season when there was normally an abundance of individuals looking for work, purposely destroyed fence lines, and an attack on a man who had said that it was probably best if the wrong people didn't know my team was in town. No—I didn't like the picture that was forming one bit.

Pa had moved to the front of the fireplace mantle, his back to the group. I watched him for a moment as his fists slowly clenched and unclenched. Pa was not a man who was quick to anger. It took a lot to goad him into any type of argument, let alone a fight. But the clenching of his fists suggested to me that someone may have just crossed his line. If a fight was coming, then I needed to know what it was about and how to protect my team from it. I nodded my head to myself. It was time to find out what was going on around here.

"Pa," I said softly as I stepped up next to him, "Ma said you'd fill me in when you got home. I think now might be a good time for that."

For a moment, I wasn't sure he intended to respond as he didn't even turn to look at me. But then his hands unclenched and he nodded slightly to himself. "I suppose it is." Turning to look at me at last, he asked, "How much has your ma already told you?"

"Only that Blake died in a stampede and that all of the ranch hands are gone, including Paul. But she wouldn't say why."

Pa nodded again, as though to suggest he had already known that was all Ma would say.

"Well, I can't say as I have all the answers for you, but I'll tell you what I can. You recognize this?"

Pa pulled something small and silver out of his shirt pocket, holding it up for me to examine. My heart sank; I knew exactly what it was. The military had developed them a little over a year ago, a few months after I had started training with my K-51. It was a Chem-Mat cylinder; the final stage of a three-stage delivery system designed to inject chemicals into the bloodstream of animals and an occasional human. We used it to cause what appeared to be "accidental" deaths when the UFC needed a target to be removed from the scene without any suspicion of foul play. With our K-51s, we could deliver the chemical from several miles away, never even needing to get close to our intended target.

But, as far as I knew, there were few outside of the scientists who had designed it, the group of snipers that were trained to use it, and our direct supervisors who told us when to use it, that were even aware of the technology's existence.

There were even fewer reasons that one of those cylinders would show up here in Texas. My own hands clenched as I asked my next question, one I wasn't sure I wanted to know the answer to.

"Where did you find this, Pa?"

"In the flank of Blake's horse," Pa said it with a short tone that left no doubt in my mind he had his own suspicions as to what its purpose was.

I closed my eyes and took a slow breath to calm the sudden fury that had flared with that answer.

"Why was Blake targeted?"

"Blake knew something someone didn't want him to share," Pa said it matter-of-factly, even as he slowly slid the tiny cylinder back into his pocket.

"Right before we left on the cattle drive, he tried to pull me aside. Said he had something he needed to tell me in private. He was insistent, but I was too dadgum busy getting the horses loaded and making sure the gear was ready. I told him it would have to wait."

He turned away from me to stare blindly at the bricks in front of him. I could see from the clenching of his jaw that he was mad at himself for not having given Blake the time he'd asked for.

"Any idea what he needed to talk to you about?"

Pa shook his head, still not turning to look at me. "Nothing I can be certain about; just suspicions."

Pa didn't usually share his suspicions, any more than he shared rumors he overheard. He was of the opinion that rumors and suspicions were dangerous; they had the potential to ruin people's lives when carelessly repeated. But I had also learned while growing up that Pa's suspicions were well-founded in facts and were rarely wrong. I also knew that I could neither coax nor force him into sharing them unless he decided to do so of his own accord. So, I waited patiently for him. I didn't have to wait long.

He finally took a slow, deep breath. "Someone is trying to chase the ranchers around here off their land. I think Blake figured out who it is and why they are doing it."

"What do you mean trying to chase you off? Why would anyone want to do that?"

"Someone wants our land, and they seem to be willing to go to any lengths to get it. It started with an investor who came around a few months back, offering to buy everyone's property. But no one in these parts was interested in selling."

That was unsurprising. The ranches in this area had been owned by the families who worked them for more generations than most of us could remember. Our own ranch had been in the Thatcher family for more than three-hundred years. No one in these parts was going to sell to an investor; they'd be more likely to sell it to each other first.

"After that, things started happening that couldn't be explained. Barns caught fire. Fences were cut. Cattle disappeared. Equipment was sabotaged. Some of the damage got pretty costly for folks. The Edwards Ranch was the first to fall.

"Cole couldn't afford to keep his ranch going, and his kids weren't old enough yet to buy him out. So, he approached some of us about buying his property. Merrick decided to take the opportunity to increase the size of a few of his pastures since their property abuts. But when he went to the banks about a loan, he was told he didn't qualify.

"Funny thing is, he had the collateral to back the loan. As far as we could see, there wasn't any reason for him to be turned down. But the banks wouldn't give him the loan, so he couldn't help."

My eyes narrowed. That didn't sound right. The banks were usually only too happy to give loans to the ranchers around here. They knew the folks in these parts were good for it and always repaid their loans. But Pa kept talking, so I filed the thought in the back of my mind for later consideration.

"Edwards had to sell to an outsider. To everyone's surprise, the buyer tore down the house and the barns as soon as the contracts were signed. The property is still sitting vacant as far as anyone can tell, and no one has seen hide nor hair of the new owners."

So, someone was purposely damaging property, as I had suspected, and they were likely doing it in an attempt to run off the local ranchers. They were even doing it to Pa, if the fence lines we had repaired today were any indication. But what was their end goal? Surely it wasn't just to leave the property vacant.

"Someone cut the wires on the south pasture. We fixed it up for you, but it took most of the spool in the shed."

Pa shook his head in frustration, though he didn't look surprised. "Kind of figured that was coming. That's why I had a full spool in there. I'll have to pick up another one tomorrow."

So, Pa wasn't any more surprised to hear about the cut fences then Ma had been; they were both expecting trouble. Then another thought occurred to me: How much was it costing them to repair the damage that was being done and to keep the ranch operating in spite of it?

Come to think of it, I hadn't paid much attention before this moment, but now that I looked around, there were some key items missing from this room that should have been there. I hadn't heard Grandpa's clock chime once since I had arrived home and the antique hutch that Ma had always taken such pride in was gone. Both were valuable pieces that could be easily sold in a bind.

Is that why Paul had left? Pa didn't have the money to pay him anymore? Is that why Mr. Hillock had taken Garrett to the bus station this morning? He couldn't afford to keep him on?

"Pa, is money the reason all the ranch hands are gone? No one can afford to pay them anymore?"

Pa shook his head. "No. That's something else, though the two reasons are related."

I cocked my head, waiting for him to explain.

"A few months ago, some of our hands started getting into fights when they went into town. They would come back from them in pretty bad shape. No one was certain who was starting the fights, but in each case, the boys were claiming that they had been jumped from behind.

"Then, a few weeks ago, a group of them went to the dance hall and got in to some pretty big trouble. Blake was with that group. Said he was dancing with Suzie Bartlett when some city slick cut in. He figured the girl had the right to dance with whoever she wanted to, but that slick wouldn't keep his hands off her, even after she told him to stop. So, Blake did what any man should have done and stepped back in, ensuring that the slick took his hands elsewhere.

"Problem was, when Blake and the boys were heading out to the truck to come home, that slicker was back; this time with a group of his friends. There was an all-out brawl in the parking lot that ended with the police arresting several of our boys. Interestingly enough, not one of the city-slickers wound up in the jail that night.

"After that, the boys started getting threatening messages; phone calls and notes delivered anonymously, but each containing private information about their families and threatening harm if they didn't leave. Most of the boys refused to be intimidated and stuck it out. A few of them even started looking into where the messages were coming from and who was sending them. I suspect it was something they learned that got Blake killed."

Pa sighed and looked up at the ceiling for a long moment before continuing.

"Happened while we were moving the herd to the fall pasture. Some of the cattle got spooked and started to run; that got the rest of the herd stampeding and Blake was caught in the middle of it.

"He should have been just fine; he's a good rider and has a steady head on his shoulders. But, just when it looked like he was on his way out, his roan stumbled and went down. Blake was hurt pretty bad.

"We called for an air evac, only none were able to get to us fast enough. Turned out they had all been sent in other directions to what ended up being false alarms. By the time one of them made it to us, it was too late."

Pa's voice faltered and he stopped talking just long enough to get a grip on his emotions. He would never admit it out loud, but I suspected he'd cared about Blake as much as he cared about me. When he did finally start talking again, there was an angry edge to his voice.

"Anyway, after his funeral, some of the hands got to talking. It was odd for Blake's horse to go down the way it did; that roan of his was about as sure footed as they come. And the fact that all those air evacs had received false calls? Well, those things didn't sit well with the boys. So, they took a closer look at Blake's roan and found that capsule I showed you, buried deep in its flank and covered over by a fresh scab."

I nodded my head to myself as something seemed to click in my mind. It wasn't a thought that made me happy, but it was a fairly certain one. Whoever was behind this, they had the backing of the UFC.

"The boys took their suspicions to the police. The investigating officer brushed them off saying that it was an open and shut case. Blake's horse had stumbled at the wrong moment; case closed. Only now we were pretty sure that wasn't the truth. Paul was angry about the officer's refusal to listen. They even had to hold him back because he took a swing at the officer."

Paul had swung at the officer?! That went against everything I had ever known about Paul. Growing up, he had always told me that a man's fists were only to be used as a last resort. He was a lot like Pa in that way: slow to anger and quick to find other solutions.

"Where's Paul now?"

Pa shook his head in frustration. "He got it in his head that the officer was being bribed to sweep Blake's death under the rug and wouldn't let the notion go. Even took it on himself to follow the officer around in hopes of finding out who had bribed him. The officer filed a restraining order against Paul as soon as he found out what he was doing. We were basically told that if he left the ranch, he would be arrested on sight.

"Then, about a week ago, one of Hillock's boys came over to talk to Paul. The two of them left in a hurry a short time later; they didn't say where they were going or when they'd be back. Only they never did come back and no one has heard from either of them since. I checked down at the station. He was never booked on any charges and no one seems to know anything about his whereabouts."

Well, now I understood why Paul wasn't here. But what about everyone else?

"And the rest of the ranch hands? Mr. Hillock said to let you know that he dropped Garrett off at the station this morning and that he wouldn't be coming back."

"I guess that explains why he was home alone. I wondered about that." Pa swore softly under his breath. "Stubborn old goat. No one is supposed to be alone right now and he knew it."

Still shaking his head, he continued, "All the ranchers got together and we decided it was time to send the rest of the boys home. The threats were getting worse and we couldn't see our way straight to allowing them to stay. So, we let them all go and told them to go take care of their families."

Then he sighed heavily and added in a low voice, "Son, I'm glad to see you, but I really wish you hadn't come. I've lost too much already."

His words stunned me. I would have never thought he'd say something like that.

"Pa, why did you send for me if you didn't want me here?"

He looked up at the ceiling again, as though looking to heaven for answers. Truth be told, he probably was.

"Your ma told me it was time to send for you. Said that she had been praying for help, and that was the answer she had received. I tried to explain to her that you belonged to the military now and that it wasn't as simple as just sending for you. She shook her head at me the way she does and said God would take care of the details; I just needed to send the message."

I nodded my head, mostly to myself. No one says no to Ma, even when it wasn't something they wanted to do. But before I could say anything more, a soft voice behind us made us both turn.

"Mr. Thatcher, your son isn't here alone. He's part of our team and we're not going to allow anything to happen to him." Alex was standing just behind us, a determined set to her stance. "And we are not going to allow anyone to run you off your land either."

Pa studied her for a moment, his expression taking on a mix of amusement and indulgence. "I appreciate your willingness to stand up for my son, miss, but I'm not sure there is much you can do to help. We still don't even know who the real troublemaker is."

She laughed lightly at his dismissal. "We can do a lot more than you might think."

"That's enough, Claire," I interrupted her firmly with a slight shake of my head. I didn't want her saying anything more that might give away who she really was. My father was a keen man and more than capable of reading between the lines. I trusted him, even with the knowledge of who Alex really was, but she needed to get into the practice of keeping certain things secret. I didn't want her saying the wrong thing to the wrong person at a later time.

"Pa, this is Claire DuCain. One of my team's most stubborn and willful members."

Pa chuckled then tipped his hat to her. "Pleasure to meet you, Miss DuCain."

"Claire specializes in languages, but is fairly new to the military. She doesn't know yet how dangerous some things can be."

Ignoring the roll of her eyes, I quickly moved on to introduce the rest of my team.

"This is Aiden Haskell, an expert in hand-to-hand and a career soldier; Logan McLagan, another career soldier; Lakota Wren, a skilled tracker and horse handler; and Nate Evans, our pilot."

Pa shook each of their hands in turn.

"Welcome to my home boys, just wish it was under better circumstances."

A few of them chuckled to themselves, probably thinking about the situations we had just left at Aiden's home and on the military base.

Haskell simply said, "We've seen worse, sir."

Pa, who had just opened his mouth to say something more, was interrupted by the kitchen door opening. Lilith came through it.

"Your friend is stable for now, Mr. Thatcher, but I'll need to keep a close eye on him for the next twenty-four hours. Boys, I'm going to need your help transferring him to a bed."

As we carried Mr. Hillock to the only other available bed in the house, my own bed, I found Pa's words repeating themselves over and over in my mind. Someone wanted this land and they were utilizing UFC resources to accomplish it. I couldn't help wondering if Director Beckwith knew something about what was going on here, and if he had purposely placed Alex in the middle of it in hopes that she would be forced into doing something about it.

Chapter 10: Alexandria Jaquette

LONG AFTER NEARLY everyone else had gone to bed, I found myself lying in the dark, staring up at the ceiling, unable to shut my mind off. I couldn't stop thinking about what I had overheard. And the look on Mr. Thatcher's face when he'd said that he wished his son hadn't come?! That he'd already lost too much?! Seeing and hearing that, I hadn't been able to hold myself back.

I had acted on impulse telling him that his son was not alone, that he was part of our team and that we would protect him, but I had meant it. I would not stand by and allow Thatcher or his family to suffer any more losses.

Only Thatcher had stopped me from saying anything more; I was still annoyed with him for that. At the same time, I had to admit that he had probably been right to do so. The whole reason my team had come here was to keep me hidden while they got me to the school and transitioned me into my new identity. Telling people who I was and what I was capable of doing wasn't exactly the smartest way to help my team do their job.

No. I thought somewhat bitterly. I might not like being told what to do that way, but that didn't make him wrong.

Thatcher had cut me off to protect me. The reality of the situation was that Thatcher had put my safety ahead of his father's sense of security and I had not exactly been gracious about it.

I thought about how I had rolled my eyes at him. It had been a childish display of willfulness and disrespect that he hadn't deserved. I really did need to stop doing that. I needed to grow up and stop acting like an ungrateful brat.

The door to the room opened quietly, allowing in just a hint of the light from the bedroom across the way. In that faint light I was able to make out Lilith's shape as she slipped through the door and softly closed it behind her. She was checking on Mr. Hillock every twenty minutes. So far there had been no change in his condition, but she had explained that he was in bad shape and that she would probably keep this schedule up for most of the night just to make sure he made it through till morning.

Something must have clued her in that I was still awake because her voice suddenly floated across the room, "Go to sleep Alex…," she corrected herself, "…Claire. You need your sleep."

"Yes, mom," I responded jokingly.

She scoffed lightly, but otherwise let it go.

The truth was that I would have liked to have gone to sleep, but there were just too many thoughts jumbled together in my head. It wasn't only what was happening here, it was what I had seen at Aiden's home as well. In both places, someone was purposely hurting others.

Okay, I know that sounds naïve. Yes, I know that there are bullies in this world; I'd seen my share of them growing up. I also knew from my history classes that there have always been those who would take advantage of others' circumstances. But this wasn't some story from a history book. These were real people that I was in a position to help.

That last thought was the one that was truly keeping me awake. Could I really keep my mouth shut and walk away when I knew that I had the ability to help them? And was there really any difference between using my abilities to hurt others and refusing to use my abilities to stop someone else from hurting others? Did one choice make me a better person because I wasn't the one causing the harm, or did it simply make me a coward because I was hiding behind an excuse?

What I had done at Aiden's home terrified me, but Aiden and his family were alive because of it. And what I had done at the base had saved not just my team, but hundreds of soldiers as well. Weren't their lives worth more than my conscious?

Those were the questions that were really keeping me awake. Was I only a child of Icarus, or was it possible that maybe, just maybe, I could choose to be something more? Something that could change the world for the better instead of just destroying it?

Chapter 11: Aiden Haskell

IT WAS LATE. We were all tired from the day's hard work, but none of us were ready to go to sleep just yet. Instead, we'd said goodnight to the women and Mr. Thatcher and then retired to the bunkhouse where we could discuss what Thatcher had learned from his father and the implications it had for our team's mission.

We all agreed that it would be foolish to pretend this was still a simple travel team assignment. Getting Alex to the school remained our end goal, but it was secondary to making sure she stayed safe long enough to get her there. So, from here on out, we would be operating under the assumption that trouble could appear at any moment and that we needed to be prepared to deal with it.

To that end, I still had my phase pistol, but everyone else's weapons had been lost back at the base. Thatcher remedied that problem by borrowing weapons from his father's collection. They weren't military grade, but the rifles and pistols he gave us were in good condition and, in some cases, even better quality than the equipment the UFC normally provided for us.

It turned out that Thatcher's father took quite a bit of pride in his collection, only buying top of the line guns that were reliable and accurate. He had instilled that same pride in his son and then trained him to use them properly. It was that appreciation for fine workmanship combined with father-son range practices that had set the stage for Thatcher becoming the marksman he was today.

He looked a lot like his dad as well and it wasn't just because of his height and looks. First chance he'd gotten, he'd traded his hospital pants and T-shirt for well-worn denim jeans, cowboy boots, and a plain, sturdy phase pistol holstered at his hip.

I'd overheard Lilith call him a cowboy a few times today. I had to agree with her assessment of that. The only thing he was missing was the hat and a pair of riding chaps. Then again, Alex had pointed out a picture hanging in his parents' house that had shown a younger version of him riding a horse and roping a steer. In that image he'd been wearing the full cowboy get up and had looked like he could have ridden straight out of one of those old Western films I'd seen in the museum.

Wren said something that pulled my thoughts back to the conversation. "You're suggesting that the UFC is involved in this somehow?"

Thatcher nodded almost regretfully. "That cylinder proves it. There are only a handful of individuals trained to use it, and I know every one of them."

"Then we have a problem," Evans stated the obvious. "We'll be court martialed if we interfere."

Something in our expressions must have given him pause because he suddenly stopped what he had been about to say next and instead asked, "What don't I know about?"

Thatcher hesitated for just a moment before finally explaining. His hesitation was likely a result of trying to decide how much it was safe to tell a man who was only a temporary member of our team. "Our last *mission*," he stressed the word, "ended with us having to fight our way out of a UFC-led intrusion ordered by someone who either didn't know, or didn't care, that we were under orders of our own. If UFC forces come here, we may have to do it again."

"You're serious?" Evans asked in clear disbelief. Purposely firing on UFC forces or interfering with their assigned mission was grounds for immediate court martial. Or, at least it was for McLagan and me; Wren, Thatcher, and Evans might get away with a lighter punishment.

But even knowing this, we all nodded solemnly. We knew our job and we were determined to do it; no matter the cost.

Seeing it, Evans sat back slowly in his chair, a thoughtful expression on his face. I got the distinct impression that he was putting together pieces of a puzzle in his mind.

"How far up does the splintering go?" he finally asked.

Thatcher grunted softly as though he viewed the question with some type of twisted amusement, but the tone of his voice was very much serious. "Our orders come directly from the directorate's office. We don't know more than that."

"I see." Evans' expression matched the seriousness of Thatcher's voice. "Which Director are we answering to, then?"

"Beckwith," I answered when Thatcher hesitated. Evans had the right to at least know who was pulling the strings.

I was impressed with how quickly he was putting things together. Impressed, and annoyed. He had figured it out a lot faster than I had, and he didn't even have all of the pieces to the puzzle. What I had been slower to realize was that it wasn't just Icarus that Director Beckwith was making Alex invisible to. He had surrounded her by a team that would be loyal to the job of protecting her and he had arranged for her to be relocated to a secure location. Those two things alone would have been sufficient if hiding her from Icarus had been his only goal. No. The one that gave it all away was that he had changed her name and identity. There was only one reason to do that: He wanted her to be invisible to everyone, including the UFC.

I swore under my breath as something more suddenly occurred to me. If Beckwith was not doing this with the backing of the other Directors, then what had happened at my home would be interpreted through the eyes of a Directorate who had no idea that we had been protecting Alex and that she in turn had been acting to protect her team. They would only know that my family and the Scotsman there that night had challenged Remington's authority and had fought against the UFC soldiers that had been under his command. Viewed in that way, their response was likely to be swift and harsh. I felt the color drain from my face as the full reality of the situation hit me. Scotland was not ready for this.

"Haskell?"

I looked up to see everyone watching me.

"You doing okay?" Thatcher asked.

I hesitated, not sure what to say. Their concern was for Alex, not Scotland. And there was precious little I could do for my country in my current position. I had no power, no authority, no way to protect them. The only thing I could do was to hope that the Directorate would believe that what had occurred at my home had been the actions of a few, rather than the rebellion of the country as a whole. Regardless, it was not a concern I needed to burden my team with while they were trying to figure out the best way to protect Alex.

"Yeah," I lied. "I'm good. Just a little worn down is all."

Thatcher raised his eyebrow, clearly not believing me for a moment. But he also didn't challenge me. Instead, he said, "It's been a long few days for all of us. On that note, then, I think we'd better call it a night and get some sleep."

"Shouldn't we put someone on watch tonight? I'd be willing tae take th' first shift." McLagan asked, appearing somewhat surprised that no one had been assigned yet.

"No need," Thatcher laughed lightly. "Mazey and Turk will do a far better job of it than any of us could."

"Mazey and Turk?" McLagan asked in confusion.

"The dogs," Thatcher explained. "They're trained to alert us if anyone comes onto the property or if anything out of the ordinary occurs, and they're quite good at their job. I also don't suggest leaving the bunkhouse tonight unless Pa or I are with you. Turk doesn't take kindly to strangers on the property at night and you haven't been here long enough for him to learn that you're a friend."

McLagan's face paled slightly and he nodded his head. It looked like there was no question he'd be taking Thatcher's advice. Come to think of it, he had stayed several feet back when the two dogs had run up to Thatcher on our arrival and had steered clear of them each time we had been outside. Guess it was safe to assume he was afraid of dogs.

Ten minutes later I was lying on a bottom bunk, staring up at the wooden frame of the bed above me. Scotland, and the trouble I had created for it, was weighing heavily on my mind. I didn't doubt that my parents, wherever they were, would already be doing everything they could to mitigate the trouble that was certain to be heading Scotland's way. But it was hard for me knowing that I was at fault for what had happened. Thatcher had suggested that Remington made me pay for my choices already and that I needed to move on and quit blaming myself, but that was easier said than done.

On top of that, I was concerned about Alex. Once again, we appeared to be caught in the middle of an explosive situation that threatened our ability to protect her and keep her hidden. It felt like we just couldn't get a break. But at the same time, Beckwith must have known at least something of the situations he was sending Alex into. That suggested that he was purposely sending her into them. *Why? What was he hoping to gain from this?*

I didn't know those answers. What I did know was that Thatcher had told me to keep her out of whatever was going on around here, and that was exactly what I intended to do. The only problem was that I had no idea how I was going to do it.

Chapter 12: Cody Thatcher

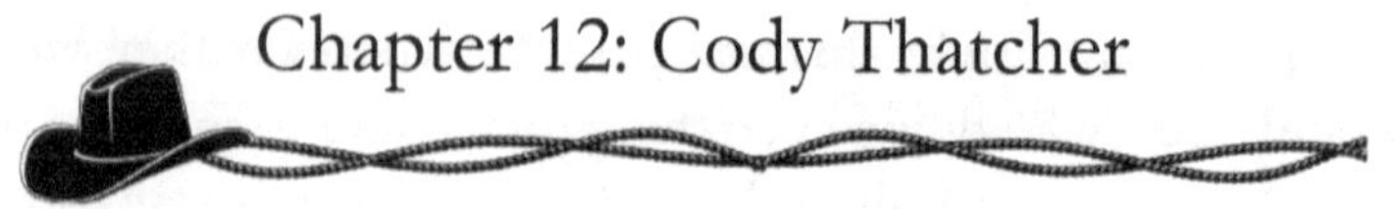

THE NEXT FEW days were relatively quiet ones. We spent most of our time helping Pa around the ranch, doing the things his ranch hands would have normally done. There were fields to be mowed, horses to be fed and groomed, one of the tractors needed repair work, the rest of the equipment needed basic maintenance, the chicken coop door had a loose hinge, and much more. There was plenty to keep the team busy.

Pa also took us over to Mr. Hillock's place to fix the door that had been busted in and to feed his livestock. While we were there, we looked for clues as to who had attacked him. It had been touch-and-go for a while there, but Lilith had pulled him through and Mr. Hillock was finally conscious. Unfortunately, he didn't remember much about what had happened to him.

We easily found the set of vehicle tracks and even some footprints that Wren said had come from his attackers. Wren, who had been a Tracker for the UFC prior to signing on to be part of the school's Special Ops Team, was able to tell a surprising amount from those two things. He said that the vehicle had an eleven-inch wheel width with an offset tread that was meant for off-roading, and that the front left tire was missing a chunk of that tread on the outside edge. He also estimated that the vehicle's gross weight was between eight and ten-thousand pounds.

From where the vehicle stopped, he was able to identify five sets of footprints that entered the house and then returned to the vehicle. He estimated that the vehicle's driver, and quite likely the group's leader, was just over six feet tall if their shoe size was any indication. They also walked with a slight pronation of their left foot and wore heavy work boots that were fairly new. The front seat passenger had a shorter stride than the rest of the group and a habit of not quite picking their feet up all the way so that those prints had a slight smudge at the top where the toes dragged with each step.

Of the three passengers in the backseat, one appeared to have dirt caked into their shoe's tread because their prints left several unique smooth spots and he had found a dried chunk of compressed dirt that matched the shape to the shoe's tread.

Another passenger appeared to be wearing a newer pair of cowboy boots. Wren said that the print was surprisingly similar to the print my own boots left, though the person who left them walked with a duck foot, that is to say that their feet angled ever so slightly outward with each step.

The final passenger's prints were considerably harder to read than the rest. Wren had almost missed it altogether, thinking at first that it had just been a smudge in the dirt. But then he had noted the faintest remains of a similar print in the house near the front door where the dust from the driveway must have fallen off of the sole of their shoe. Wren had remarked under his breath that it was interesting, but had not explained why to the rest of us.

In spite of all he was able to tell us, there wasn't much we could do with that information right now. According to Wren, there were an infinite number of people who would have similar shoes sizes and treads, and there were any number of vehicles with the same tire size. But if he saw any of these tracks in combination again, he would know them.

Back at the ranch, Lilith had sent her report in. There was an established line of communication between the travel teams, but it wasn't exactly straight forward as it involved Harry hacking into certain satellites to send and receive the encrypted messages that were designed to travel between the teams' command pads in emergency situations. It was how they had known we'd made it safely to the base after the attack at Haskell's home. I'd typed in a quick report while the base captain's assistant had been driving us to the MEDDAC.

Lilith had her own command pad; one she had been given before leaving the lodge. Her instructions to come to my folk's ranch and to check on our team had been delivered to her through that line of communication. But like our own, it was also not a direct line and she would have to wait for Harry to hack in, receive the response, and then send a reply. So far, the only response she had gotten back from her initial report were the brief instructions to lie low while they looked into McLagan, Wren, and Evans, and to await further instructions.

Right now, we were all sitting around the kitchen table eating lunch and talking. The plan, as soon as we finished up, was for me to head into town with Pa to get more fence wire and to get the parts for the tractor that the store said had come in. While we were gone, the rest of the team would be taking some much-needed down time.

I was listening in to the conversations going on around the table with half an ear in each of them. Ma, Alex, and Lilith were discussing dinner plans. McLagan and Evans were excitedly discussing a game of horseshoes and trying to convince others to join them. Wren declined their invitation, stating that he'd noticed an interesting book on Pa's shelf about horse breeds he wanted to take a closer look at, but Haskell sounded like he might join them.

Mr. Hillock had been allowed to join us for lunch, but only because Ma had suggested that it would do him some good to get out of that bed for a few minutes and Lilith had surprisingly relented after Ma had told the boys to carry in the recliner from the living room for him. He and Pa were talking about the plans to bring the cattle down from the grazing grounds.

It was a pleasant din of conversation that reminded me how nice it was to be home. But no sooner had that thought crossed my mind then Ma stopped talking, nearly mid-word, to instead look slowly around the table at those sitting there.

Uh-oh. I knew that look on her face. There was something Ma had decided needed to be done, and she was gearing up for battle in case anyone tried to tell her no.

"They announced at church last week that the young adult program is sponsoring a dance over at Thornberry's barn tonight. I think you should all go to it."

Silently, I cursed to myself. What was she thinking? We were supposed to be lying low; this was the exact opposite of that. The look Haskell gave me told me he was thinking the same thing. But the look in Ma's eyes was as determined a one as I'd ever seen there.

Not knowing Ma as well as I did, Haskell tried to politely decline her suggestion.

"Thank yae, Mrs. Thatcher, but that wouldn't be a good idea. We have…"

She cut him off. "But of course, it's a good idea. They would appreciate having you join them, and you kids deserve a night off to relax."

He tried again. "I'm afraid we wouldn't make very good dance partners considerin' th' shape we're in."

"Nonsense," she scoffed, barely giving him time to finish. "If you're in good enough shape to do all that work you've been doing around here, then you're in good enough shape to dance."

Haskell looked over at me, his jaw clenching in obvious frustration. I knew it was hopeless, but I had to try. "Ma, my arm is in a sling, Haskell's leg is injured, McLagan has stitches on his leg…"

She cut me off as well, her eyes starting to get that dangerous gleam they got anytime someone challenged her. "You can dance with one arm and they can take breaks between songs."

I looked to Pa for help. He was frowning, but didn't say anything. Instead, it was Lilith who interjected. "Beth, I'm sure these boys could dance just fine, but that is not the point. They have orders to lie low and they would stand out quite a bit if they showed up in those military fatigues they're wearing."

In truth, only Wren, Haskell, and McLagan were wearing military fatigues. Ma had scrounged up some clothes for Alex to wear, Lilith had brought her own, and there had been some spare clothes left behind by the ranch hands that Evans had chosen to take advantage of. But Haskell, McLagan, and Wren had been rotating each day between the fatigues they had arrived in and the ill-fitting jeans and shirts I had scrounged out of my closet for them. The clothes they had borrowed were currently in the wash, so they were back in their fatigues.

To my surprise, a faint smile of satisfaction twitched on Ma's lips. She nodded her head thoughtfully, as though considering Lilith's words. And then, for the first time in my life, she said something I would have never believed possible. "You know, you just might be right. Perhaps I was too quick in my suggestion."

I could have sworn in that moment that I heard Pa's jaw hit the floor. I know mine sure felt like it was wide open. Certainly, my mind was in shock. What had just happened? Ma never backed down once she got that look. Lilith, who mistakenly assumed the matter was settled, had turned back to Alex to continue the conversation they had been having. Ma's voice stopped her cold.

"But that doesn't mean you and Cody can't go. In fact, Lilith, I insist on it. The two of you will go to that dance representing our family while the rest of us enjoy a relaxing evening here at home. Cody would be expected to attend activities anytime he's home on leave, and Mrs. Sulley already knows he's here. She saw him with Pa when they went into town yesterday. So, if he doesn't show up tonight, she'll be sure to talk about the strangeness of it."

"All right," Lilith said carefully, her eyes narrowed in suspicion. "But that does not explain why I need to go."

Ma's smile grew triumphantly, joined now by a satisfied gleam in her eyes. It was the same look she wore whenever she got her way. "Because Mrs. Freeport saw you here when she came over on Wednesday to get her dozen eggs. If you recall, I introduced you to her as a friend of Cody's. If you don't go to that dance with him, she'll be sure to start asking questions at church tomorrow that might lead to someone noticing we have other guests. It could cause far more damage than just lying low would."

"I see," Lilith said coldly. "And just how long will we need to stay at this dance in order to avoid rousing suspicions?"

There was an uneasiness in the room that had started with Ma's suggestion. It was rapidly growing more uncomfortable with each word of the back and forth between Ma and Lilith. It felt like we were watching two gunslingers who had drawn their weapons but not yet fired. We were all nervously watching them to see which one would fire first.

"Oh, I suspect an hour or two will be plenty. Then you can come on home and the rumors should be laid to rest."

"And you'll be satisfied, and not make any further suggestion of this type while we're here? There aren't any other activities coming up?"

Ma smiled innocently. "But of course I would be satisfied. Why wouldn't I be? And no, I can't think of any other activities that would come up while you kids are here."

"All right, then. Cody and I will go to the dance tonight, to settle any possible rumors. In the meantime, from here on out, if anyone comes by, the team is to stay out of sight. We wouldn't want any more rumors starting."

Ma nodded her head in apparent satisfaction. She looked for all the world like she had just won the shootout. "I couldn't agree with you more. Such a good suggestion. The dance starts at 8:00 pm. So, I'll make sure dinner is ready early enough that you'll be able to eat before you go. Now, if you kids would clear the table, Pa and Cody can head into town and get the things they need so they can be back in time for Cody to get ready."

I felt the muscles in my jaw twitch as Ma stood up. It looked like I would be taking Lilith to the dance tonight. I debated the wisdom of trying once more to argue, then reconsidered. Once Ma got that look, the discussion was over. But, more than that, there was a similar look on Lilith's face.

At this moment, I wasn't entirely certain who had won the standoff. Ma had gotten her way, but there was the faintest hint of satisfaction in Lilith's expression as well. It was like she and Ma had come to an understanding and the stern set of her lips dared anyone else to challenge their agreement. None of us did.

***

THE BARN AT Thornberry's place had been decorated with pumpkins, glowing lights, and colorful streamers in shades of red, gold, brown, and orange both inside and out.

To my annoyance, we were arriving late. But Lilith had needed the additional time to finish getting ready, and I had to grudgingly admit that she had used it well. She was more than a little pretty tonight, as the admiring gazes of the men reminded me.

She had borrowed a patterned dress of Ma's, made a few adjustments to it, and then paired it up with a wide brown belt and the same stitched boots she had been wearing the day we arrived at Pa's ranch. She had also lightly curled her hair, put on makeup, and added some jewelry that complimented her outfit. I would never be accused of being any type of fashion judge, but even I could tell that what Lilith had put together looked real good on her.

When I got home from town, I had discovered that someone had set out an outfit for me as well. The dark blue button up shirt, denim jeans, and freshly cleaned leather boots matched her outfit surprisingly well. It was further paired up with the belt buckle I had won at the county fair a few years back and one of my wide-brimmed, brown felt hats.

Lilith had also insisted that my arm remain in a sling tonight, though she had found time to fashion a new sling for me out of some dark blue material Ma had provided her. It blended in with my shirt a far cry better than the white sling the hospital had given me did.

"Well just look at you, Cody Thatcher. My how you've grown. I'd heard a rumor that you were back in town and I was hoping you would come tonight." Mrs. Scott was one of the members of the youth committee. She was standing just inside the barn doors greeting people as they came in. "And who is this lovely young lady on your arm?"

"Evening, ma'am." I tipped my hat to her in greeting. "This is Lilith Alcott, a friend of mine. We're just passing though for a few days, but Ma thought I ought to show her how Texans throw a party since y'all we're kind enough to host this one."

Mrs. Scott laughed. "Well, you came to the right place. There's punch on the table in the back and bales of straw to sit on when you need rest. The band will be here till midnight and when y'all get hungry, well, the men have been sitting around barbecuing a pig since this morning. They'll be bringing it in for you kids later on."

I thanked her and tipped my hat once more, then led Lilith on in.

We made the appropriate rounds, introducing Lilith to old friends of mine and answering questions about where I'd been for the past two years and what I had done to injure my arm. I explained that Ma had decided I should serve a tour in the UFC military and most of them nodded their heads in understanding. I fudged the truth about how I had injured my arm, not telling them the conditions surrounding my injury, and only suggested that I had been given some leave time to come home while it healed. I didn't like lying to people, but telling them what had really happened was out of the question.

We introduced Lilith as one of the nurses I had met while in the hospital and added that she had been curious about the cattle ranch and family I had described to her, so I invited her home to see it. That got a few knowing chuckles as people drew their own conclusions about what that really meant. I mostly ignored them; let them think what they wanted.

Afterward, Lilith pulled me out on to the dance floor for a relaxed country waltz. It wasn't exactly easy to maneuver with only one arm, but she made the necessary adjustments look effortless and kept us moving smoothly through the steps. When the song ended and I tried to apologize for the difficulties, she only smiled patiently and reminded me that it had worked just fine.

We danced a few more turns that way before she finally allowed us to leave the dance floor and find a bale to sit on.

When I offered to go get us drinks, she only laughed at me and pointed out that I would have a difficult time carrying them. Instead, she went and got them for us.

When the band returned to the stage after a short break, I stayed seated. Lilith appeared ready to stay at my side, but then Gregory Farnsworth came up to us. Greg had been the football captain in high school. He had been popular with the girls then and appeared to still be so now.

"Evening," he nodded to me. "Mind if I take your girl out for a turn?"

My girl? I grunted in amusement at the suggestion that Lilith belonged to me. She was an adult and had the right to make her own decisions.

"If that is what she wants," was all I said.

Lilith looked at me with an arched eyebrow for the briefest of seconds, giving me the distinct impression that I had given the wrong answer. But, before I had a chance to ask how, she turned away from me, stood up, and said, "Sounds like fun. Let's go."

I was surprised by the twinge of jealousy that followed as he led her out onto the floor. She was laughing and smiling, clearly enjoying the dance with him. She even stayed out for a second song. Before Greg could ask for a third one, though, Bobby approached to ask her for a dance. Then it was David. Then it was some other man whose name I didn't know, followed by another man whom I had never even met.

She danced song after song while I sat on the bale, watching and quietly stewing in the unfamiliar emotion. I had no right to feel possessive toward her; no man did. But I really didn't like the way her current partner was dancing a little too close to her. For that matter, I didn't like the idea that she was dancing with anyone else but me. I shook my head in disgust at the thought; it wasn't my right.

Still, I was considering whether it would be appropriate for me to step back in on the next dance when movement in the back of the barn caught my attention. There were several people back there in the shadows, standing in a small huddle. I wasn't quite sure why, perhaps it was just a gut feeling, but I instinctively stood and reached for my gun. My hand found only air. I looked down, startled to remember that I was dressed for a dance, not combat.

I swore under my breath, my eyes darting back toward the shadowed forms. They had split apart and were starting to move toward the dance floor. *Lilith!* I surged forward, careless of who I bumped into as I pushed my way toward her.

Noticing the commotion I was creating, she turned to face me. Her eyebrow rose as though to challenge my interruption. I ignored it and stepped in close so that I was speaking up against her ear. *"We need to leave. Now!"*

As she pulled back, I expected her to argue. Instead, she just nodded her head and, without so much as an "excuse me" to the man she had been dancing with, took my arm and followed closely while I started to move us toward the front of the barn.

We'd only made it halfway to the door when there was a loud crash and a cry of alarm from the stage where the band had been performing. It was followed almost immediately by the sound of a phase gun firing into the air and a voice over the speaker shouting, "Everyone on the floor!"

I shot a quick glance over my shoulder to see a figure with a ski mask holding a gun to the lead singer's head.

I barely turned back in time to see another masked and armed figure step in front of us. "Where do you think you're going?" the man's gravelly voice asked scornfully in a strong Bronx accent.

There was something familiar about that voice, but I didn't pause to consider it as I pushed Lilith out of his line of fire and then pivoted so that I came up and under his arm. I rammed my shoulder into his stomach and tackled him to the ground.

He landed with an *"umph,"* the wind knocked out of him. I rolled off and pushed myself to my knees, punching him across the face before he could recover. But as I turned to grab Lilith's hand, I froze. A third masked figure was standing right behind her, one hand on her shoulder, the other holding his gun against her. He didn't have to say anything; he had Lilith. I slowly stood up and backed away.

Through the openings in his mask, the man's flint-hard eyes studied me coldly. There was a calculating intelligence in those eyes as they looked me up and down. Then they moved from me to the man still lying on the floor. His lips tightened into a harder line. Still not saying anything, he shoved Lilith at me. I caught her with my free arm, but allowed her momentum to carry her behind me so that I was between her and the gun.

Seeing it, the man's lips twitched ever so slightly. Unfortunately, the reality was that if he shot me at this close of a range, my body was unlikely to stop the bolt from striking Lilith as well. That didn't keep me from trying though.

Not taking his eyes off of me, he strode over so that he could nudge his fallen comrade with his toe; he wasn't very gentle about it. The crumpled figure groaned in response. The man kicked him harder. "Get up!" His voice was as hard as his eyes; it had an interesting effect.

The man I had laid out with my fist jerked back to alertness at those words and scrambled to his feet. Fury screwed up his face when he saw me, but the moment he noticed the flint-eyed man, the faintest hint of fear mixed in with that fury.

"Get your gun and get back into position," the flint-eyed man growled with disgust. His didn't raise his voice; he didn't need to. It was the type of voice that carried more weight when soft then it did when loud. This was a dangerous man.

The other man reacted as though a whip had been snapped, immediately spinning on his heel to do as he was told. His reaction was enough to make me suspect that the flint-eyed man was the group's leader, and a harsh one at that.

Turning back to us, the leader twitched his gun to the right, directing us back toward the center of the barn. I studied our situation as we walked.

I counted eight hostiles in total. All of them were wearing jeans and dress shirts suggesting they had entered the barn under the guise of being here for the dance. There were enough people here I didn't know that I doubted I would be able to identify them in a line up even if their masks were taken off. But each one of them would have been greeted by Mrs. Scott, and she probably knew just about everyone who had come in, so she might be able to pick them out.

I also noticed that each of them held their guns comfortably like they were extensions of their hands. Not unusual for boys from these parts whose father's had been teaching them to shoot since they were knee high to a grasshopper, but these men's accents identified them as not being from these parts. That meant they had likely trained elsewhere with those weapons.

For that matter, none of their accents sounded like they came from the same regions. I'd heard French, Hispanic, English, and New York Bronx accents, plus a few others. So, they were not a group brought together by territory.

They were also working together in coordination with minimal need for communication. That meant that they had been together long enough that they knew who was going to do what and could read each other's body language well enough to react accordingly.

Ex-military? That was a possibility. I'd heard of whole squads getting out of the service and then taking work together for one company or another. If so, the variety of accents suggested ex-UFC military.

We were directed back to the center of the dance floor where they were binding their prisoners' hands and then making them sit on the ground. Lilith did not look overly pleased when they made me take my arm out of the sling so that they could bind my hands as well, but she wisely kept her mouth closed. With nothing more to do but sit, I continued to study our assailants and to think.

It was possible that these men were still active duty. I'd seen enough in the last week that I wasn't taking anything for granted. But if that was the case, then why had the UFC sent in forces to break up a dance, and why do it with masks on? Unless…

My eyes narrowed as two things suddenly clicked in my head: the cylinder Pa had shown me and the familiar voice of the man I had punched. I remembered now where I had heard that gruffly accented voice before, and it was in the same place I had learned how to use those cylinders.

Another piece fell into place as I turned to slowly study the faces of the people huddled nervously around me. Gregory lived a few ranches to the south of my folks. Bobby's pa owned the vet clinic with several acres just eight or nine miles to our east. Jerry and Amber's parents lived side by side some six miles to our west. Daniel, Sarah, Lisa, Tommy and his sister Jessica, Theresa, Samuel, Tori, Bella—these were the kids of the ranchers whose properties were within a fifteen-mile radius of Pa's ranch. For that matter, most of those families who had kids close to my age were represented in this group.

I heard Pa's words again. *"Someone is trying to chase the ranchers around here off their land."*

Why? I questioned again. *For what purpose?* I still didn't know that yet. But if I was dealing with a group of stubborn ranchers who refused to be intimidated into leaving, then threatening their kids would be the next logical course of action. It was one of the strategies I had been trained to employ. I'd never liked it, but it was an effective tool if properly applied.

As if to confirm my suspicions, one of the soldiers stepped forward with a digi-pad and began scanning the faces of those around us. Based on what the pad told him, he started separating us into two groups. Sure enough, those I had already identified as rancher's kids with land near my folks were gathered into one group, while most of those I didn't recognize were sorted into another. I did not like where this was going. If I was right, then they would be separating Lilith from me. To make matters worse, I wasn't sure there would be anything I could do about it when that moment came.

"Thatcher's boy is here."

I had almost missed the words; they had been spoken softly, in a low, gruff voice. But now that I knew where I had heard that voice before, I was more attuned to it. Actually, I didn't just know where I had heard it before, I knew who it belonged to. Samuel Fischer was a mean-spirited bully whose skill with a gun was only matched by the size of his ego. We'd been in the same K-51 training group straight out of boot camp. He'd quickly developed a reputation for being ice-cold in his killings. He didn't care if it was a man, a woman, or a child. He would kill indiscriminately and even with a hint of pleasure so long as he had the protection of his military orders to hide behind. I'd never liked him much.

I turned my head so that I was able to better listen in on his conversation.

"You're certain?" That sounded like the leader.

"It's him." There was a hint of disgust in Fischer's voice. It didn't surprise me. As much as I didn't like him, his opinion of me was worse. Mostly because he had always finished second, just behind me, in all of our trainings. Last I'd heard, he'd been assigned to some squad in Egypt. It had not been the assignment he had wanted; I'd gotten that one.

"Call it in. Let them know we'll be following the protocol accordingly." I didn't hear the rest of what was said, the guard with the digi-pad had just stepped up to Lilith.

"Look this way," he ordered her. She obeyed, but her expression was one of cold disdain suggesting that she was only looking his way because it suited her whim. He didn't even notice; he was too focused on the digi-pad's screen.

Suddenly his eyes shot up to lock with hers. She raised her eyebrows in a silent question. "You're a soldier for the UFC?" he asked.

She answered with a hard edge to her voice. There was no hint of hesitation, fear, or nervousness; just cold distain. "Major Lilith Alcott, 48819237113. UFC Nurse."

I had to admit, I was impressed by her composure. At the same time, it really didn't surprise me that she wasn't the type to fall apart under pressure.

I heard footsteps approaching and turned to see the leader coming up behind us. He held his hand out for the digi-pad and studied it with tight lips. Then, after a few moments, he handed the pad back and turned to face me. I met his hard gaze with one of my own.

"Your name Cody Thatcher?" he growled.

"Yep." I nodded casually, trying to match Lilith's calm composure.

"She with you?"

I nodded again.

"You're both soldiers for the UFC?"

"Yep." Then I decided to take a chance on my earlier hunch and added, "same as you."

His only response was the faintest tightening of his eyes and lips. Then he raised his voice. "Tango. Foxtrot. Take these two back to the COP and lock them up."

COP? Now that was an interesting choice of designations. It was short for combat outpost, the term we used for any temporary base we set up in enemy territory. Most often we established one when we needed a secure base to work from.

Fischer and another man answered his call.

"Get up!" Fischer yanked on my injured arm making me wince. Lilith, who had gotten up on her own, started to take a step toward him. I shook my head ever so slightly, trying to warn her back. Her eyes narrowed dangerously, but thankfully, she stayed.

They led us to an old truck outside. Before loading us into it, they pulled hoods over our heads so that we couldn't see where they would be taking us. That meant I couldn't use my eyes to see where we were going, but I could use my other senses.

We left the property turning left onto the main road. About three minutes later we turned left again. That meant we were heading North, toward Miller's Pond. If we turned off before the sharp bend, then we would be heading toward the Scott's place. If we turned after, then we would be heading toward the hills. We turned after.

From here, there were three possible directions they could be going. Forkroot Road was the first turnoff. It would take us toward the lower grazing grounds. But we had just crossed over a second cattle guard, so they weren't going there. The next turnoff would take us toward lookout point. It wasn't much of a lookout, though it was a popular place with teens wanting to make out. The third cattle guard told me they weren't going there either. That left the river and the old abandoned hydropower plant.

It had been built more than a hundred-fifty years ago by the locals of that time and had produced enough electricity to power the nearby ranches during a period when the post-war populace had been unable to maintain the pre-war power infrastructures. New advancements in technology later left the plant as obsolete as the pre-war structures, but the buildings had been left behind as a monument to the ranchers' ingenuity during a time of struggle.

The truck finally slowed to a stop and the doors opened. We were pulled from the vehicle and guided along a gravel path. I was slightly surprised to note that I could only hear three sets of footsteps on that gravel. If the other guard was walking with us, he was either making too little sound to be heard, or he was far enough behind us that the sound of the river was covering his footsteps.

What I had no trouble hearing was the roar of the late season river flowing off to our left. It ran down a sharply graded slope at this point and had long ago exposed the larger rocks that it now noisily bounced off of on its way down. The river would be nearly at its lowest point this time of year, but that only meant that the water splashed louder as more of the rocks were exposed.

The power house and its supporting structures were located near the bottom of the slope where they could make the most of the energy produced by the falling water.

A door was opened and we were led inside the building. Based on the direction we had been walking I was fairly certain it was the main power house they took us into. How far we walked once we were inside of it confirmed my suspicions. The main powerhouse wasn't exactly small. Its two-story structure had been built into the side of the slope and went back some distance into it. They walked us through several rooms and corridors before finally bringing us to a stop.

"Watch them for a minute." That was Fischer's voice. So, the other guard was with us after all.

When Fischer's footsteps returned, he came up behind me and I felt the cold metal of military cuffs being snapped around my wrists. He didn't bother to remove the older bindings, nor did he take off the hood.

"Let's go." He grabbed my arm once more and shoved me forward. In seconds we were once again in what sounded like a hallway. The next time we stopped, it was followed by the squeaking hinges of a door being opened.

Fischer yanked me through the doorway, only to bring me to a stop several steps in. Judging by the sound of those steps, we were in a small room. There was also a damp mustiness to the air that suggested this particular room had not been opened in some time. Behind me, I heard Lilith being led in. But instead of leading her next to me, she was taken deeper in. Then I heard the faint rustling of cloth. It sounded like her hood was being taken off.

Next to me I heard Fischer whistle a cat call. "Would you look at that. Thatcher's got good taste in women. Too bad she doesn't have good taste in men. Hey, Tango, maybe we should teach her what a real man is like."

No! I yanked my arm out of his hand and surged forward so that I was positioned between him and Lilith.

Fischer laughed coarsely.

"You can't see and you can't use your hands, Thatcher. Do you really think you're going to do her any good?"

He was right, I thought bitterly. I would be hard put to protect her like this. But that wasn't going to stop me from trying.

"You touch her, Fischer, and I'll break both of your hands," I said coldly.

He went silent for half a second as he realized that I knew exactly who he was. Then I heard him take a step toward me as he growled, "You know, Thatcher, I never did like you."

I can't say as it was unexpected, but the fist in my side still knocked the wind out of me. Then another blow to my head sent me to my knees. But it was the kick to my ribs that sent me sprawling. After that, I lost track of how many times he hit me or kicked me. I couldn't do much to protect myself. I could only groan and accept the punishment. In the background, I heard Lilith's furious voice, yelling at him to stop. He ignored her.

I could taste the blood in my mouth and feel the sting of sweat in my eyes as his blows kept coming. I would have prayed for it to end, but I knew that if he was focused on me then he wasn't threatening Lilith.

When it finally did come to a stop, my pain-fogged mind struggled to reconcile the end of the torment with the scuffling sounds and the deep howls of pain that I could barely hear through the ringing in my ears.

Lilith's furious voice came unexpectedly from above me, "Come near him again and it will cost you more than that."

Fischer was swearing obscenities, only it was coming from much further away than I had expected it to. And then I didn't hear anything more as unconsciousness overtook me.

Chapter 13: Alexandria Jaquette

THATCHER'S FATHER HAD been pacing back and forth for the last hour. He hadn't said anything in that whole time, but his uneasiness was visible in every line of his body. Cody and Lilith weren't back yet, even though the dance had ended more than two hours ago. We were all starting to get worried.

Even so, Aiden had tried to get me to go to bed a few times now. I laughed softly to myself; there was little chance of that happening. I wasn't going anywhere until I knew they were safely home, and I wasn't alone in that line of thought. No one in the house had gone to bed yet, not even Mr. Hillock.

At the moment, Aiden and the other members of my team were off in the corner quietly talking. Although they sounded calm, there was a stiffness in their stances and an alertness on their faces that suggested they were on edge. The few snatches of their conversation I had caught suggested that they were discussing possible courses of action.

Mr. Hillock appeared to be reading a book, but I noticed that he hadn't changed the page for at least twenty minutes and he kept glancing at the C-DACS on his wrist.

The military used tactical bands to communicate; civilians used C-DACS. It was short for Communications and Digital Access Control Systems. They came in a variety of designs and styles that ranged from super simple wrist bands to diamond encrusted designer bands. There were also a lot of different brands. The most popular ones were made by a company that had labeled them Alpha Bands, named after the elite group of Alphas the world seemed to think we were. Some of the less popular brands had names like, George Bracelets and Digi-Watches. I'd never been able to afford even the most basic versions, but most of the kids back at school had worn them.

Thatcher's mother was the only member of the group who appeared to be completely at ease. She was sitting on the couch, quietly reading from her Bible. She'd been doing that for almost as long as her husband had been pacing. Sitting there, she projected an air of calmness that suggested she was not at all worried about her son's absence. It was like she was simply waiting for him to walk through the door, which she knew he would do at any moment, with a perfectly reasonable explanation for why they were coming home so late.

Trying to emulate her calmness, I was distracting myself by trying to think of all the reasonable situations that would explain their delay: The power cell in their vehicle had quit working, leaving them stranded on the side of the road; Lilith and Thatcher had come across a car accident on the way home and Lilith was busy taking care of someone who had been injured; Thatcher had insisted on holding the car door open for every girl there…okay, that one was stupid. Maybe I was more tired than I thought.

Suddenly, Mrs. Thatcher closed her book and stood up. "I'm going to go make us some coffee."

That was a great idea. I was glad she was going to do that. But, as I watched her go, fully intending to stay where I was, Aiden caught my eye and tipped his head slightly toward the kitchen door. For just a second, I was tempted to ignore him. I preferred to stay where I was, knowing that this room was most likely to be where news of their position would be heard first. But then I thought better of it. If Aiden had a reason for wanting me to follow her, I should probably follow his signal, even if it wasn't what I personally wanted to do.

"I'll go help her," I said with a heavy sigh as I stood. Aiden responded with a smile of amusement, but he also nodded his head to me, to show his appreciation. I just barely caught myself in time to not roll my eyes.

I found her standing in the center of the kitchen with her back to me. Hearing me open the door, she wiped at her eyes and hurried over to the stove. I realized with sudden understanding that she had come in here to cry alone, where no one would see her. I was embarrassed for intruding on her privacy, but at the same time, my heart ached for her. Thatcher wasn't just another member of the team to her, he was her son.

I crossed the room and put my hand on her shoulder. "He's going to be okay," I promised softly. It wasn't that I had any crystal ball to assure me that it would be so, but I hoped it would be true, and that hope would have to be enough, because I had nothing else to offer.

She smiled in appreciation, and patted my hand. "Thank you, dear. I'm sure he will be. He's such a capable boy…" I had stopped listening; my attention had been caught by something else. Outside the window a flash of light was streaking toward us; it was moving incredibly fast. *What is that? It almost looks like…*

I reacted on instinct, lunging forward and tackling Thatcher's mother to the ground. As I did so, I heard the familiar *whoosh* of phaser fire and the tinkling shards of shattering glass.

I hadn't even had a chance to roll off of her before the door from the living room slammed open.

"Alex!" Aiden was standing in the doorway, gun in hand and a frantic look on his face.

"I'm okay," I hurried to assure him, even as I turned to check on Mrs. Thatcher. She was slower than me to sit up, but she appeared to be otherwise uninjured.

Thatcher's father came through the doorway a split-second behind Aiden. Seeing his wife on the ground, he pushed past Aiden to get to her.

"Wait!" Aiden reached for him, but he was already beyond him. The instant he stepped into the open, a second phaser bolt streaked through the air.

Had I paused to think, it would have been too late. Thankfully, I didn't. My hand was in the air slamming down the gravity in front of him before I even realized what I was doing.

The blast arced sharply downward, scorching the ground just in front of his feet. In the next breath I yanked downward on the gravity under him, dropping him to the ground and out of the line of sight of the shooter.

From the corner of my eyes, I saw Aiden's expression morph from dread to awe. "How?" he started to ask, only to catch himself. "Never mind." His hand shot out for the switch and killed the lights. "Out of the room, now!" he ordered, even as he did the opposite and came to my side.

In the living room, we found that lights had already been darkened and the curtains closed. It made sense. Unless the shooter had infrared capabilities, they would have a much harder time seeing anyone inside the house now.

I could barely make out the shadowy forms of my team scattered throughout the room. It looked like they had spread apart so that there wasn't a single grouping of targets for the shooter to aim at. They also each appeared to have weapons in their hands and were guardedly watching the avenues of approach outside the windows.

Aiden immediately began issuing orders. "Wren, McLagan, go out there and find the shooter! Evans, you're with me. Alex…"

"Wait!" Mr. Thatcher interrupted him in a low, angry voice. He crept over to the back door and cautiously cracked it open, gave a low clear whistle, then turned and crept over to one of the nearby cabinets. He left the door slightly ajar.

What is he doing? We watched in confusion as he pulled something flat and rectangular out of one of the drawers. When he turned back to the door a moment later, I was startled to see two angular noses poking through it. I realized with astonishment that it must have been his dogs he had called with that whistle. They had come so silently that I hadn't even heard any sounds to warn me they were there.

Mr. Thatcher's expression was stern as he looked up from the digi-pad he had just powered on. "Mazey and Turk need to know you're friends before you can go out there. More than that, they're trained hunting dogs; they'll lead you straight to that shooter."

Aiden nodded his understanding. "How do you teach them we're friends?"

"Hold out your hand to them, palm up."

Aiden did as instructed, allowing the dogs to sniff it.

As they did so, Mr. Thatcher said firmly, "Friend."

Next, he had McLagan, Wren, Evans, and I repeat the process.

Finally, he ordered softly, "Mazey, Turk, protect!"

The two noses lifted slightly as though acknowledging the command, then they were gone in an instant. He eased the door shut behind them and began working the digi-pad. Seconds later it was backlit by the faint glow of a satellite view of the property. Two dots were visible on the screen as well, gliding smoothly in a coordinated pattern as they began to work their way around it.

The dots would occasionally pause, as though responding to a sound or examining something they had come across, but then they would continue to move, following their previous pattern. Had I not known better, I would have thought I was watching a military operation in action.

Mr. Thatcher held the pad out to Wren, "Let them do the hunting for you."

Wren accepted it with a slight upward twist of his lips. I'd come to recognize it as his version of a grin. "I like this plan." Then he turned to McLagan. "Let's go."

The next few minutes were nerve wracking for me. We sat in near silence, listening for any sounds that might warn us trouble was coming. The whole time, Aiden kept a sharp eye out the back door while Evans kept one out the front. The only interruptions to the silence came from the almost inaudible tapping of Mr. Hillock's fingers as he sent out messages on his C-DACS, warning nearby neighbors about the shooting and telling them to stay alert and keep their eyes open.

While we waited, I tried to distract myself from my nervousness by running through what had just happened in the kitchen, trying to figure out what the goal of the shooter must have been. I was fairly certain the shots had not been aimed at me. In fact, considering the angle the blast had come from, I may not have even been visible to the shooter. Well, at least not completely visible. They would have likely seen my hand on her shoulder, but probably not who the hand belonged to.

So, the shooter had been aiming for Thatcher's mother. And the second shot had clearly been aimed at his father. But was that because the shooter had known their targets or because they had been the only ones visible?

Both shots had also appeared to be head shots, though I wasn't a hundred percent certain about the second shot considering that the angle I had seen it from had not been ideal, and the fact that I had been more concerned with stopping the blast then measuring the angle at which it had come from.

But even if they had both been body shots, they would have resulted in serious injury had I not intervened. The full realization of what could have happened settled on me. If I had not heeded Aiden's suggestion and followed Thatcher's mom into the kitchen, she and her husband might have been killed. I shuddered, no longer wanting to consider what could have happened.

Thatcher's mom must have seen the shiver because she scooted over to put her arm around me. "Thank you for protecting us," she said softly. "What you did in there was nothing short of a miracle."

A miracle? I scoffed lightly. What I had done had been instinct, not a miracle. There had been no divine intervention, nor had I thought through what I was doing; I had just reacted. I didn't tell her that, though. Instead, I replied softly, "I'm just glad I was there."

She seemed to see through my words and shook her head sadly. "God has given you a gift child. You may not see it for what it was, but I do." She squeezed my shoulders before moving back to her husband.

A gift? No. I couldn't agree with that either. And if there was a God out there who thought that giving me this ability was a good thing, then I wanted to give them a piece of my mind. This "gift" was the reason I'd been raised without a family, the reason people were trying to turn me into a weapon, the reason more than a hundred men had been killed by that Talos machine while I watched.

No! It's not a gift! I thought bitterly. *It's a curse!*

But I also couldn't deny that it was the reason I had been able to stop those phaser blasts from killing them. For the first time, it occurred to me that maybe, just maybe, even a curse could do good once in a while. If that was the case, then I was determined to do as much good as I could with it. Maybe by doing so I could atone in some small way for what my siblings had done.

A sharp rap on the front door made me look up with a start. It was quickly followed by two thumps and then another sharp rap. Aiden released an audible sigh of relief.

"That's th' signal; we're clear. Evans, let them in. Alex, turn th' lights on."

There were deep frowns on McLagan's and Wren's faces as they came in, like they were both bothered by something.

"What is it?" Aiden asked.

"Whoever it was, they're gone." Wren looked toward Thatcher's parents. "But they've got Cody and Lilith."

Thatcher's mother gasped; his father stiffened.

"How do you know?" Aiden asked soberly.

Wren held out the object he had been holding tightly in his hand. "This was fixed to the tree out front, where the shooter was positioned."

I hadn't even noticed the object in his hand before that moment, though it wasn't exactly small. Even after seeing it, it took me several seconds to realize what I was looking at. Once I did, my heart sank. The dusty, crumpled object was a brown felt cowboy hat—one that had been stabbed through with a large hunting knife.

Mr. Thatcher stiffly crossed the space between them and took the crumpled shape from Wren's hand. His expression hardened as he tenderly straightened it back into the semblance of its original shape. "It's Cody's," he finally confirmed.

Mrs. Thatcher collapsed heavily onto the couch. Her expression was a cross between stunned emptiness and horror. It tore at my heart.

Wren nodded; he had already known. "The dogs led us to where the shooter had been. We were able to see the tail lights as they sped away. The tire tracks and the shoe prints there matched those I saw on Mr. Hillock's property."

"That does it. I'm calling the police," Mr. Hillock announced angrily. But Thatcher's father reached over and pressed the end button on his C-DACS before it had even begun to ring.

"No," he said softly. "I don't believe we want the police involved in this." He met Aiden's eyes as he said it, then he looked at me meaningfully. "Am I correct in my belief that you boys have been assigned to protect this young lady here?"

Aiden met his gaze stonily, clearly intending to not answer the question. Then he seemed to reconsider. "Aye sir, we have," he finally answered.

Mr. Thatcher nodded his head once; he had clearly just been looking for confirmation of something he had already recognized.

"This was Cody's assignment as well?" he continued.

"It is."

"And her safety is more important than my son's life?"

Aiden looked regretful, but didn't hesitate. "Aye, sir. It is."

"What? No!" I took a step forward, intending to argue with him, only to have Mrs. Thatcher startle me as she reached over to take my hand. The horror was gone from her face, replaced by a look of calm acceptance. "So, you're the reason my Cody had to join the UFC. God was putting him there to protect you. Now I understand what's happening to him. This is part of God's plan to keep you safe."

I was speechless. *How could she possibly believe that? What God would think me more important than her son? What mother would believe that this was God's plan?*

Mr. Thatcher swore softly under his breath. I looked over at him, hoping that he would be correcting his wife's misunderstanding. But instead of telling her how foolish she was being, he turned and crossed the room to the cabinet under the window. He took a control fob out of the drawer and held it out to Aiden. "The foreman's truck is parked out back by the barn. Its power cells should have enough fuel in it to get you anywhere you need to go within six hundred miles of here. Beth will get some food packed while I help you boys load the supplies you'll need for your journey."

I looked from Thatcher's mother to his father. *They were both crazy! I had to stop this!*

"No!" I pulled my hand free. "We're not leaving here without Thatcher and Lilith."

Aiden's jaw clenched as he turned to face me. "Alex, Thatcher told me tae keep yae out of whatever is goin' on here. He knew th' risks and he didn't want yae involved."

I cut him off incredulously, "The risks?! He knew that his family was being threatened and he was okay with that? He knew that his parents were going to be shot at and that had I not intervened they would both be dead? You seriously think he would have wanted me to run away and let them die?"

Aiden looked slightly taken aback. "That's not what I meant."

I cut back in before he could say anything else. "No, Aiden! I'm not okay with this. I won't run away and abandon my teammates. And I won't stand by while someone takes shots at innocent people. I can't!"

Didn't he understand? I couldn't leave without Thatcher and Lilith; I wouldn't just abandon them. If I did, what difference would there be between me and my siblings? They cared for nothing and no one. They would not hesitate to leave their teammates behind. The thought of taking so much as one step in that direction terrified me.

But, even as that fear raced through me, another emotion was rapidly burning it away. Anger had begun to sear through me. Anger aimed at all the things that were so very wrong with this situation. I was angry with Aiden and the others for even considering leaving Thatcher and Lilith. I was angry with Thatcher's parents for believing that I could possibly be more important than their son. I was angry with the people who had taken Thatcher and Lilith. I was angry with whoever it was that had beat up Mr. Hillock and damaged the other ranchers' property. And I was especially angry that no one was doing anything to put a stop to it.

At the same time as that anger was growing in strength, another part of my mind was screaming at me that I needed to get it under control. That small voice was desperately trying to remind me that, if I didn't, I would end up doing something I would regret. *I need to get control!* Only, the fire was rapidly burning away my ability to think; it was chasing away the warnings my mind was trying to scream at me.

Having no idea what was happening in my mind, Aiden tried to reason with me. "We have our orders, Alex. Yae are our priority."

Orders? His excuse was his orders?! That was the last straw; I exploded with fury. *"Orders be blasted!* I have seen far too many of my friends die because of orders. I am not going to stand by and let it happen again! And I am not going to allow these people to be threatened any longer. You can try to stop me or you can help me, Aiden. Either way, I *am* getting my teammates back and I *am* putting an end to this!"

The room had gone silent. Everyone was staring at me uneasily. Even Aiden was clearly startled by my outburst. I was beyond the point of caring, but he at least tried to get through to me.

"Alex, please. Let us do our job." His eyes searched mine desperately for any hint that I would back down; there was none. If anything, my resolve hardened.

We stood that way for several seconds before Aiden finally swore under his breath and gave in. He turned to Mr. Thatcher with a defeated look. "How dae we get tae th' dance hall?"

Chapter 14: Cody Thatcher

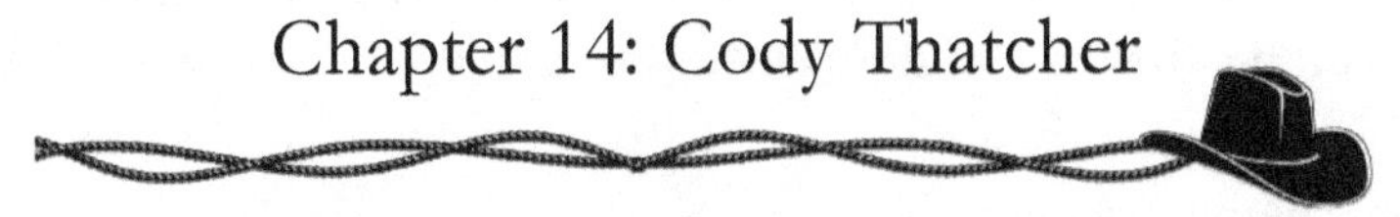

I WAS DRIFTING on a pain-laden cloud. Everything hurt. Every now and then I thought I felt something cool touch my forehead, but it was only there for a moment before I drifted on. Time passed. Eventually I opened my eyes to darkness and an eerie sense of aloneness.

"Lilith?" my voice croaked out her name with sudden raspy fear. Had Fischer taken her while I was unconscious? I frantically tried to force myself up into a sitting position only to be stopped by a hand on my chest.

"No you don't, Cowboy."

Relief flooded through me and I allowed her hand to press me back down. Then she placed her cool hand on my forehead.

"You're warm," she muttered under her breath.

I wasn't surprised. Fischer had worked me over pretty badly. It had been worth it, though. Lilith was still safe.

"How long was I out?"

"Maybe an hour, though I can't say for sure. There's no way to be certain in here. And they haven't come back in since I chased them out."

The room was pitch black. There didn't appear to be any windows and they had not turned the lights on for us. There also wasn't any warmth. The cement floor I was lying on was leeching the heat from my body, causing me to shiver. At least, I hoped it was the cold floor causing the shiver. The alternative was not a good one.

I'm not sure when I had first noticed it, but at some point, my hands had begun to tingle from lack of blood flow. Lilith had removed the hood for me, but the military cuffs would have been impossible for her to remove without the code. I tried rolling carefully to my side to take the pressure off of them. That made my injured arm hurt more. My other side wasn't much better. I needed to distract myself from how much I was hurting.

I asked the first thing that popped into my head. "How did you chase them off?"

She laughed bitterly. "They made the mistake of assuming I was helpless, so they didn't think to check me for weapons."

Their mistake. I thought with amusement. I had already learned the hard way not to underestimate her and I wouldn't soon make that mistake again.

The new position was becoming increasingly uncomfortable, so I tried shifting once more, looking for something less painful; it didn't help. I asked the next thing that came into my head. "You had a weapon on you?"

"I always do," she answered simply. Then I heard her moving and felt her reach under me to lift my shoulders. "Here. See if this helps." She eased me upward just enough to slide her body behind me so that I could lean back against her. The new position took the pressure off of my arms and my hands, allowing the blood to flow more freely. I sighed with unanticipated relief. I still ached everywhere, but it was more manageable in this position.

"I had trouble with a boy in high school who kept trying to get handsy with me. My dad found out about it and took me in to be fitted with a garter belt dagger and an ankle sheath. I've been wearing them ever since."

Somehow, that didn't surprise me to hear. I'd always been taught that it was my job to protect the women around me. But at the same time, it was no secret in our home that Ma was the better shot between her and Pa. When I'd asked Pa about it, he'd explained that he was glad his wife was such a good shot. That way he knew she would be able to protect herself if trouble ever came while the men were gone. Lilith was a lot like Ma. It made sense that she would have a way to protect herself when needed.

"What happened to the boy that was giving you trouble?"

She laughed softly. "The next time he tried touching me, I cut him with my knife. I got suspended for it, but my dad took me fishing as a reward. Of course, I had trouble getting a boyfriend after that, but I also never had anyone try to touch me again."

I started to chuckle, only to immediately suck in a breath from the sharp pain it caused. When it subsided enough that I could speak again, I asked, "Did you ever find a boy who wasn't intimidated by you?"

She hesitated just long enough that I began to worry I had asked something too personal. I was about to apologize when she answered, "It took me a bit. But the right one did finally come along."

I was startled by the wave of sadness I felt hearing those words. In spite of it, I felt the need to ask, "What's he like?"

Her voice adopted a hint of tenderness, and I could almost hear a smile in it. "Well, he treats me like a lady. He's a hard worker. He's one of the best in his field. He respects his parents and is respectful to others. A lot of people like him and I've only ever heard good spoken of him. He's thoughtful, caring, considerate."

I sighed, "He sounds like everything you deserve." A small part of me truly was glad she had found someone good. To my surprise, though, the rest of me was disappointed that she was already taken; I realized that I was jealous of that man.

But she only laughed and said, "He will be, once I convince him that he wants to be."

That confused me.

"How long have you been together?"

"Oh, we're not together yet. I've been waiting for him to figure it out and ask me, but he's a bit of a cowboy in that regard: the perfect gentleman in every way, but slightly oblivious to the hints from the women around him. I'm beginning to think that I may have to just tell him directly."

I started to ask, "Is he really that oblivious?" but a cold chill shook through me before I could finish the last word. The shudders hurt and I gasped softly.

She wrapped her arms around me, almost protectively, and said gently, "Hush now, Cowboy. It's time for you to get some more rest."

Suddenly, her words clicked. *Cowboy! I'm the cowboy she's talking about!* A smile began to tug at the corner of my lips.

"Yes, ma'am," I replied, as I settled back into her arms, allowing myself to bask in the warmth of the realization that I was her cowboy.

Chapter 15: Lilith Alcott

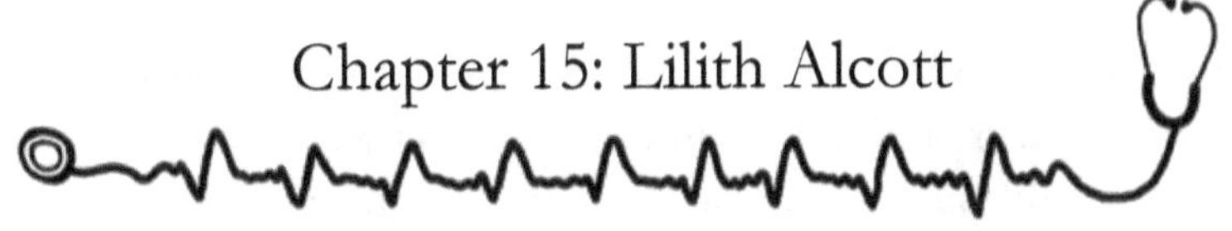

I WAS GETTING worried. His fever was growing. In the short time he had been conscious, I had been able to assess that a concussion was unlikely. His thought process had been consistent and logical, and also sweet. In the midst of his pain, he'd chosen to focus on me as the source of his distraction.

I smiled to myself. Yes, this was the one. Mee-maw had told me to find myself a good cowboy who would put me first, and Cody had done just that. I just had to keep him alive long enough to help him figure out that I was the right one for him.

My smile slid away. He had slipped back into unconsciousness several minutes ago, but his shivering was growing stronger. I suspected there was internal bleeding fueling his fever. *How could there not be after the beating he had taken?*

The first thing I had done once those men locked the door behind them, was to check him over for injuries. The pitch black of the room had made it extremely difficult, but I had trained hard over the last six years to be able to use my hands to detect damage that lay beneath the surface of the skin.

With a firm touch, I could feel the placement of the muscles and bone structures. I knew what they were supposed to feel like. So, when something was off, I could usually identify it. In my hurried exam, I hadn't felt any major breaks in his bones, but that didn't mean there weren't fractures.

I could also feel the site-specific increases in body temperature that accompanied most injuries. Cody had two of those hot spots. One on his injured arm, the other where his liver was located. The latter made me nervous. Blunt force trauma to the liver had the potential to be life threatening when it was severe, and the beating he had endured had indeed been severe.

I held him tighter as another series of shudders swept through his body. Internal bleeding was almost certain at that second site. If there had been any light, I would have been able to check for the bruising that would have confirmed my suspicions. But even without being able to see it, everything else indicated that it was there. Unfortunately, without my medical bag, there was little I could do about it, except to keep him comfortable and hope that his body was strong enough to deal with it on its own.

In hindsight, I wished that I'd done a lot more to that man then just cut him across his forearm. Fischer, Cody had called him. If he came back, I would ensure that he had a few less fingers for what he had done to Cody.

When he had started beating on him, Fischer's partner had held me back. I smiled bitterly at the memory of how that man had been surprised when I used my head to smash his nose. He'd let go of me long enough to allow me to jump my legs through my arms, and to grab the knife that was hidden in my boot. After that, it had been a simple matter of cutting my bonds and then chasing the two of them away from Cody and out of the room.

What I hadn't told Cody was that my dad was ex-military and had trained me how to use my knives. Mama might have objected to her daughter learning to fight like that, but she had died several years before.

She was the reason I had decided to become a nurse. I'd been ten when the horse she was riding had thrown her. I'd watched it happen and rushed to her side, only I'd had no idea back then what to do to help her. The doctors had later told my dad that if she'd had medical attention sooner, they might have been able to save her. I'd decided then and there that I would never find myself in a similar situation, not knowing how to provide the medical care that might save someone's life.

Only, here I was, holding someone in my arms who desperately needed that medical care, and I was once more helpless to provide it. I felt a single tear of frustration escape and slide down my cheek.

He'd better survive this! I thought fiercely. Because it wasn't fair that I'd finally found the man I'd been searching for, only to have him die in my arms.

# Chapter 16: Aiden Haskell

SOMETHING WASN'T ADDING up. We'd already been to the barn. The scene inside had been a horrific one, with dead bodies everywhere. At first glance, it had looked like the work of one of Icarus' Alphas. Light knows I'd seen enough of those when I'd been assigned to the squads hunting them. But then I had started to notice some inconsistencies that made me question my initial assumption.

First, each of Icarus' Alphas have a specific M.O. when torturing and killing their victims: a modus operandi that was consistent and identifiable. Every time we surveyed one of their killing sites, we looked for the signs of those M.O.s. Once we established which method had been used, we knew which Alpha was responsible. I was intimately familiar with all of their M.O.s. Only this time I hadn't identified just one, I had counted three of them. But that didn't make any sense to me. Icarus' Alphas never killed in groups. Three different Alphas might hit three different sites at the same time, but there was never more than one Alpha in the exact same location.

Second, all the sites of previous attacks that I knew about had been at established locations where people regularly gathered. Schools, government buildings, sporting venues, and churches were the most common. Parks and other popular public gathering spots were the second most common. This location was a private barn that would normally have been used to house animals, not people. Never before had I heard of an Alpha attacking a site like this one.

Finally, whoever had attacked here had taken a non-Beta prisoner. Icarus' troops never left anyone alive who was not a Beta. Thatcher made sense; he was a Beta. Miss Alcott was a Charlie. If the attack had been done by Icarus's troops, they would never have left her alive, at least I was hoping she was still alive, and they certainly would not have taken her as a prisoner. No. There had to be something else going on here.

Wren was also troubled by something he had seen, though once more I wasn't entirely certain I understood it. He seemed to be concerned about a particular set of tracks he had identified, or rather the lack of them. That is where he was losing me. The part I understood was that the same set of vehicle tracks and footprints he had found at Mr. Hillock's house were also visible at the barn, suggesting that the same group of people were responsible for both events.

Then he had started to tell me about a set of prints that appeared to be missing from them. How he could tell that footprints were missing was beyond me, but he was adamant about it. He'd gone so far as to show me several places where he said the prints should have been. Unfortunately, where he saw patterns he could make sense of, all I saw was dirt. He'd also used the phrase "ghost walker" while trying to explain it to me. Like the patterns in the dirt, that phrase also meant nothing to me.

The group as a whole was becoming increasingly solemn; even Alex's anger had finally dissipated. I understood her frustration. None of us wanted to abandon Thatcher or Alcott. But the way she had exploded was something I had not expected; it was so completely out of character for her. Or, at least, it was almost completely out of character for her. If I was being honest with myself, I had seen it before; twice before.

The very first time had been when Corporal Callia had suggested that Alex had done something in the barracks with Specialist Lance. The second time had been when she was shaking her head at me, telling me not to interfere with Roisin's plans for Remington. Both times, there had been a hardness in her eyes; the same hardness that had been there tonight.

I wasn't sure how I felt about it. Part of me knew she needed that hardness if she was going to survive what the UFC was trying to do to her. But the rest of me was worried by the implications it held. I had seen that same hardness in the eyes of every Child of Icarus I had ever faced. What I didn't know was whether the hardness had been in her eyes tonight because it was a basic human emotion or whether it was there because she was also a Child of Icarus.

I sighed as I looked over at her. She was sitting in the space between Wren and me. It was still dark, but there was enough light from the truck's dashboard to allow me to see her. Her head was down and she was looking at her hands as she absently twisted the ring around her finger. There was a defeated slump to her shoulders as well. That, at least, was not an emotion I had ever seen in any of Icarus' other children.

Alex had been this way ever since the barn. Seeing the devastation inside had taken its toll on her and had left her visibly shaken. I'd tried to protect her from it, but she had stubbornly refused to stay outside. So, instead, I'd watched her closely, knowing there wasn't much else I could do. As a result, I had seen the change as it happened.

She had gone into the barn, the hardness clearly in her eyes. But, as she had walked from first one corpse and then to another, it had melted away. It had only taken three or four minutes for it to disappear completely, replaced instead by a visible shaking of her shoulders and a silent trickle of tears down her cheeks. Seeing it, I had tried again to get her to leave the barn. Once more she had insisted on staying. She had continued to walk from body to body as though she were memorizing the faces of those who had died there. Only when she had studied the last one did she finally allow me to take her by the hand and lead her out. She had been silent ever since.

Come to think of it, none of Icarus' other children would have cried over those people. Unlike her siblings, Alex had not reveled in the pain and death in that barn, instead the opposite had been the case. The scene had cut through her hardness and replaced it with tears; tears that I sincerely doubted the rest of Icarus' children were even capable of.

Suddenly, I had my answer. The cold hardness of the children of Icarus came from their lack of empathy for others. Alex's hardness had faded because of her empathy. I felt a smile of satisfaction lift my lips as I realized that truth: she had empathy for others! It set her apart and made her unique among the Children of Icarus.

I realized that the truck was slowing and looked up to see where we were. We had been traveling primarily north along the same country road ever since leaving the barn, with an occasional brief detour down one side road or another. Wren was taking us down yet another.

I was not ashamed to admit that I was in awe of his tracking skills. I knew from talking to other trackers in the past that once a vehicle traveled onto a paved road there would be precious little to be seen of its passage from there on out. Yet somehow, Wren seemed to be able to identify nearly nonexistent clues in spite of the vehicle having moved onto a paved road, and he was piecing them together into a trail he could follow. He said it had to do with his Charlie ability. I'd just have to take his word for it.

Regardless of how he was accomplishing it, each of the times he had turned us down one of these side roads he had eventually found a spot in the dirt off to the shoulder where the tire tracks of the vehicle we had been following would randomly reappear once more. Each time they did so, the vehicle had made an obvious U-turn and then returned to the main road, but not before stopping for someone to get out. The footsteps, a single set each time, always led to a nearby house and then returned, still alone. Since none of the footprints were Thatcher's or Alcott's, we assumed that they had not been taken into those houses, and so we hadn't wasted time searching them.

As our truck came to a stop in front of yet another house, I noticed that Alex's head had finally come up. She was studying the house with a thoughtful furrow to her brow. Curious what had caught her attention, I studied the house as well. I didn't see anything out of the ordinary. It was similar in style to the other homes we had seen tonight; all of them had been single-story ranch styles. Several of them, like this one, had wraparound porches. This one even had a few rocking chairs and benches scattered at intervals along that porch. Also, like the other houses, the windows of this one were dark, indicating that anyone inside was probably fast asleep. Not surprising given the hour.

"How many people do you think were at that dance?"

Alex's unexpected voice in the otherwise relative silence made me jump. It was the first thing she had said since leaving the barn. I also noticed that she had stopped twisting the ring.

"There were fifty-two bodies in there," I answered, curious where she was going with her question. "Why?"

"I counted forty-eight vehicles parked outside that barn. Wouldn't at least some of those have carried more than one person?"

"I suppose so."

"Then where were the rest of the bodies?"

I started to tell her that Icarus' forces had probably taken more prisoners than just Thatcher and Alcott, but then I hesitated. I had my doubts about whether Icarus' people were responsible for those murders. Either way, though, she had a point. There should have been more people there than just the number of bodies we had seen. But if they had not been kidnapped by Icarus' forces then where were they? Would someone else have taken them prisoner? If so, why?

As though reading my mind, she went on. "What if Thatcher and Lilith weren't the only people kidnapped tonight? What if they're using the murders to cover up what they are really doing. And what if they stopped at these houses because they were doing to them what they had done at Thatcher's house?"

I stiffened as her questions suddenly connected in my mind with the inconsistencies I had seen in the barn. What had Thatcher said? That someone was trying to run the ranchers off of their land? Was this another tactic they were using to accomplish their goal? Hostages and Murder? Is that why they had stopped here? *There's an easy way to find out,* I thought bitterly.

"McLagan, yer with me. We're goin' tae check th' house and make sure everyone there's okay. Evans, Wren, stay with Alex."

The lights were off as we cautiously approached. A small part of my mind hoped that meant they were asleep and had not experienced any trouble. But even in the darkness, I could make out the broken window of the front door.

Suppressing the wave of fury that was aimed at those who were doing this, I knocked on the door and called out, "Is anyone inside? We're here tae help."

I heard a faint shuffling sound coming from the other side of the broken window, followed by a woman's voice. "Who's there?"

"Me name is Aiden Haskell. I'm a friend of th' Thatcher's."

I heard more sounds that suggested someone was moving closer to the door, then the front porch light flared to life.

"Open the door slowly and stay where I can see you." The woman's voice had a hard edge to it.

I glanced at McLagan. He took several steps back so he could cover me better and then nodded that he was ready. I opened the door.

The woman standing on the other side of it was a tiny thing, but the rifle she was pointing at me was more than big enough to do some damage. Despite her small size, she held it easily. She frowned as she looked me up and down. Her frown deepened when she took in McLagan and saw the gun in his hand.

"Y'all are military?" she asked coldly.

I wasn't surprised she had jumped to that conclusion. We were both in the military fatigues we had been wearing when we left the base and we were both carrying weapons, though I made a show of putting mine away now.

"I'm Specialist Aiden Haskell and this is Specialist Logan McLagan." I said it as reassuringly as I could, holding my hands out in front of me so that she could see that I was no longer holding a weapon. "We serve with Cody Thatcher in th' UFC Special Forces. We were visitin' his family's ranch for our leave, only he and one of our other teammates went tae the church dance this evenin' and didn't come home."

Her brow creased slightly, suggesting she wasn't sure whether she believed me, but that at least something I had said had resonated with her. Not looking away from us, she called over her shoulder, "Emma, call Beth. Ask her if they have guests staying with them."

I could hear a young girl's voice making the call, though not the words that were exchanged. While we waited, the woman never let her rifle drop and she never took her eyes off of us.

"She says they do," the girl finally answered back. "A few of Cody's military friends are in town. They're out looking for Cody."

The stiffness in the woman's stance relaxed ever so slightly and she lowered her rifle several inches so that it was no longer pointing straight at my chest, though I noticed that she didn't drop it completely. It was enough to tell me she was ready to hear more.

"Somone tried tae shoot th' Thatcher's in their home about an hour ago," I explained.

Her eyes sharpened with concern, so I hurried to assure her, "They're both safe, but whoever did th' shootin' left Cody's hat pinned tae a tree with a huntin' knife. We've been trackin' them ever since. Their tracks led us here, so we came tae check on yae and make sure everythin' was okay."

She glanced briefly at the hole in her window, then looked back at me. "They've been here," she said it coldly. "They threw a brick through the window, then took off. The brick had Tori's necklace tied to it with a piece of twine."

She pulled a plain silver chain with a cross on it out of her pocket. Her expression was a mixture of fury and concern. "Tori always wears this. She would not have taken it off willingly."

So, her daughter had either been kidnapped or was among the dead back at the barn. For her sake, I hoped it was the former.

"Did yae report this tae anyone?"

"I called the police," she laughed bitterly. "But they're not going to be sending anyone out tonight; not with what's happened at those other sites around the city."

"Other sites?"

She cocked her head. "You said you boys have been out searching for your friend for the last hour?"

"Aye," I answered in confusion.

"Emma, bring your C-DACS over here."

A small figure of a girl came into view. She was perhaps eleven or twelve. Though, considering her mother's small size, the girl might have been older than she looked.

"Show these boys one of the news channels."

The girl nodded, adjusted the settings on her band, then turned her wrist so that we could see what it was displaying.

The screen showed a reporter standing in front of a line of police barricades. Behind the reporter was the smoking remnants of what looked to have been a church. The stained-glass windows had been shattered and the once ornate doors were now little more than chunks of burned wood hanging on their twisted metal hinges.

As I watched, I caught snatches of what the reporter was saying:

"We can confirm three sites so far…"

"…a coordinated strike by Icarus' forces…"

"…president has activated the national guard…"

My attention, however, was focused on what was happening behind the reporter more then on what he was saying. It was like I was seeing a scene straight from the déjà vu of my memories. Surrounding the church was a flurry of activity as soldiers and first responders worked together to secure the attack site. It was a scene I was very familiar with.

Shortly after my brother had been murdered, I had requested assignment to a unit responsible for hunting down Icarus' Children. The first unit I had been assigned to was a "first-on-site" platoon like the one I could see on the screen right now. After any attack by one of Icarus' Children, it was their job to secure the site and then identify which Alpha had done the killing, as well as to gather all of the data they could about the who, how, and why of their killings.

Each member of those units wore a different colored arm band depending on the specific job they did. Blue bands were responsible for securing the area. They worked with the local authorities to establish a perimeter around the site and to keep the gawkers from accidently destroying possible evidence or stumbling into harm's way. White bands coordinated the bagging of the bodies, ensuring that they were properly tagged and arranged for later examination. Red bands, the color I had most often worn, were responsible to search the site for evidence of the Alpha's M.O. whether it was found on the victims themselves, in the way the attack had occurred, or in the form of a piece of equipment the Alpha had left behind. If it was the latter type of evidence, we would tag it, catalog it, and then store it in a tent set up nearby for that purpose. Gold bands, the final color, were responsible for establishing and maintaining the command center where the intelligence related to the incident was gathered and reviewed, and then putting together as complete a picture as they could with the data we gathered.

On the girl's C-DACS screen, soldiers were crisscrossing back and forth like bees in a crowded hive as they worked to secure the attack site. But the jobs they were performing were so familiar to me that I could instinctively tell who was doing what.

Wait! What was that soldier carrying? Without thinking, I snatched the girl's wrist so that I could zoom the screen in on the soldier with a red armband who had just come out of the church. *That can't be right! Why would that be…*

The thought broke off mid-word as the cold hard barrel of a rifle was pressed harshly against my head.

"Let her go!" the woman ordered angrily.

Startled, I looked up from the screen to realize that there were tears of pain in the eyes of the girl and she was whimpering softly. Stunned, I quickly let her go. As she snatched her arm back, I caught a brief glimpse of purple bruises forming where my fingers had been holding her. *Surely, I hadn't been gripping her that hard. I couldn't have been.*

"I...I'm sorry," I stammered an apology. "I didn't mean tae..."

The woman cut me off. "It's time for you boys to be leaving," she said coldly.

I wanted to say more, to make her see that I hadn't meant to hurt her daughter, but the look in her eyes made it clear that she didn't care what I had to say; she just wanted us gone. With a nod of my head, I backed up carefully, all too aware with every step that her rifle remained pointed at my chest. McLagan had his gun up as well, aimed at her in return. As I reached his side, I placed my hand on his arm and shook my head. I was worried that he would insist on keeping his weapon zeroed on her. Instead, he only glanced at me briefly before nodding and holstering it.

When we reached the far end of the walk without her shooting us or saying anything more, I released the breath I had been holding. If she'd let us get this far, then it was unlikely she would fire on us now, so long as we kept moving. I spun on my heel and kept retreating toward the truck. McLagan followed my lead.

The others were anxiously waiting for us. Because of the porch light, they had been able to see everything. I was pleased to see that Evans and Wren had instinctively taken up defensive positions around Alex, but I didn't miss the fact that Alex had still managed to position herself so that she had a clear line of sight, and she was holding her hands slightly raised at her side as though she were ready to reach for one of the gravity fields, if she hadn't taken hold of them already.

When I was close enough that they could hear me without my needing to shout, I called out, "We need tae get back tae th' Thatcher's house. Th' situation has changed."

"But Cody and Lilith…" Alex started to argue.

I didn't let her finish. "This is not open for debate, Alex!" I'd said it more harshly than I had intended to, but I didn't have time to argue with her. Time was running out for Thatcher and Alcott. If we didn't get backup immediately, there was going to be nothing more we could do for them.

"Everyone in! We're leavin' now!"

To my surprise, not a single one of them argued with me, not even Alex, though her frown warned me that she was not happy about it.

As Wren started the truck and pulled back onto the road, I rapidly weighed our options. I could tell Wren to turn north on the main road and drive us out of town or I could send him south and back to the Thatcher's. But which one should I tell him to do? My job was to protect Alex, and normally that would mean going north so that I could get her as far away from this situation as I could. Unfortunately, I was beginning to understand that she placed her friends' safety above her own. She might have relented temporarily just now, but the fire was back in her eyes. Her submissiveness was only going to last for as long as she believed I did not intend to leave Thatcher and Alcott behind; she was too loyal to abandon her friends. It was a loyalty caused by that same empathy that made her so much more innocent than her other siblings were.

I sighed with a sad smile. I knew which direction I would have to tell Wren to turn. I would do whatever it took to protect that innocence in her, even if it got me court martialed or killed.

South it was then, straight into the raging inferno, though I doubted anyone else here suspected what we were really heading into; they didn't know what I did. The technology that soldier had been carrying was only a few months old and still classified by the military as special designation only. So far as I knew, only the company I had last been serving with was authorized to use it in the field. Its presence at the church could mean only one thing: the attack had been the work of the UFC, not Icarus, and there was a good chance that my previous unit had been the one to do it. If that attack had been their work, then the scene in the barn had probably been their doing as well. That meant that Thatcher and Alcott were being held by UFC soldiers.

Worse, I had the gnawing suspicion that this was the reason Beckwith had sent us here. That thought made my blood boil. I was quickly becoming more and more certain that he was using Alex as a pawn in some bloody game of political chess, purposely putting her into no-win situations in the hopes that she could somehow conjure a victory out of it for him. Just another reason to hate that man, not that I needed more.

Beckwith was the UFC Director over Western Europe. He'd been serving in that office for almost thirty years now. As such, he was the director that was supposed to be protecting Scotland. Instead, he had betrayed us. He, along with the other fifteen directors, had signed his name to the Scottish Accords, condemning myself and every other firstborn son of Scotland to the UFC war effort. *I'm here because of him!* I thought angrily. But no sooner had those words crossed my mind then the tone of the them changed completely to one of stunned understanding. *I am here because of him!*

The only reason I was sitting in this truck right now, with this team, with Alex at my side, was because two weeks ago he had made the arrangements to have me transported to the cabin where I had been given a chance to make things right with Alex. Even though I was Scottish, he had still included me in this team. It was the complete opposite of what I had expected from him.

I felt a small part of my anger toward him begin to deflate. I still hated him, but now that hatred was tinged with the recognition that I owed him something I would have a hard time repaying.

As Wren turned south onto the main road, another unexpected thought crossed my mind: What if the chess game Beckwith was playing wasn't just about politics? What if he had sent Alex here to help a group of people he could not have helped in any other way? I may not like the man, but I'd long ago grudgingly admitted to myself that he was probably the least corrupt of the fifteen directors. Aside from his signature on the Scottish Accords, most of what he had done for those within his zone of responsibility had been good.

My birthright put me in a unique position to understand politics better than most people did. With the information that was available to me because of my position, I had learned that Beckwith was often the one responsible for guiding the other UFC leaders toward decisions that were beneficial for the world as a whole, leading them away from the other selfishly motivated options that they all too often put on the table.

But occasionally, our sources would also report that a decision which had been unanimously made by the directorate was one that Beckwith had privately not agreed with, and yet which he had publicly given his support to. It occurred to me now to wonder if this was one of those situations. If I assumed, for a moment, that Beckwith had known about the plans for this attack and had disagreed with them, but had been unable to stop it at the political level, what would he have done? Would he have found some other way to send these people help? Had sending Alex and our team been his way of doing that? If so, then wouldn't he have placed us, his playing pieces, into a location on the political chess board where we would be most capable of acting from? *Wait! What if he had?*

As Wren turned the truck off of the main road and onto the Thatcher's property, I considered the Thatcher's home more seriously. What was it about their property that would make it the best location for us to be at? Why would he have sent us here? The cut fences and the attack on Mr. Hillock popped into my mind. Thatcher had told us that the ranchers in these parts were being harassed. Wren had already confirmed that the vehicle and attackers at Hillock's house had been the same ones at the dance and again at the Thatcher's. So why would the UFC be attacking ranchers in

Austin, Texas? What would they be hoping to get out of this? Support? Concessions? Location?

Location! That last word repeated itself in my mind with searing intensity as the answers to my questions clicked into place. These ranches were inside of the American capital. America had allowed the UFC to build bases on their east coast, and even allowed a few UFC forces to operate out of the American bases further inland, including one here in Texas, but they had adamantly and consistently refused every request to build a UFC base anywhere near their capital. *These attacks are aimed at getting the United States to change that policy!*

By making it appear that Icarus' forces had somehow slipped into their capital and successfully committed a series of probing attacks without being detected prior to the attacks, or caught following them, they could then build on the fear and uncertainty of those attacks to argue that America needed to grant them emergency authorization to establish a base nearby. And if there just happened to be large chunks of land conveniently for sale in the perfect location?

My heart sank as the full ramifications of our situation finally became clear to me. First, this was a large-scale UFC operation against one of its own member countries, and we were caught right in the middle of it. Second, Thatcher and Alcott, if they were still alive, were in the hands of those UFC forces. Finally, there was no backup for us to call on because Beckwith had already done all he could by sending us here.

We were in trouble, and I had no idea how to get us out of it.

Chapter 17: Icarus Argyros 

IN THE GAME of chess, you must play by the rules. But if your opponent does not know the rules, allowing you to take an advantage you might not have otherwise had, that's on them. In the 1987 world championship chess match, legendary player Kasparov forgot to stop the clock after making his move. His opponent could have reminded him, but was not required to do so by the rules of the game. The result was that Kasparov wasted three of his remaining four minutes, causing him to have to rush his remaining moves in poorly thought-out actions; he eventually lost the game.

As I reread the message on my screen, I realized that my opponents had likewise blundered. They were playing their own pieces against themselves. The result was that they were now fighting each other instead of fighting me.

Like Kasparov's opponent, I realized with delight that I was under no obligation to remind them how they should be playing the game. Only too happy to let them continue battling each other, I sent a coded message to the forces I had positioned in America: *Belay previous orders. Do not follow through on planned assault. Remain in safe houses and await further instructions.*

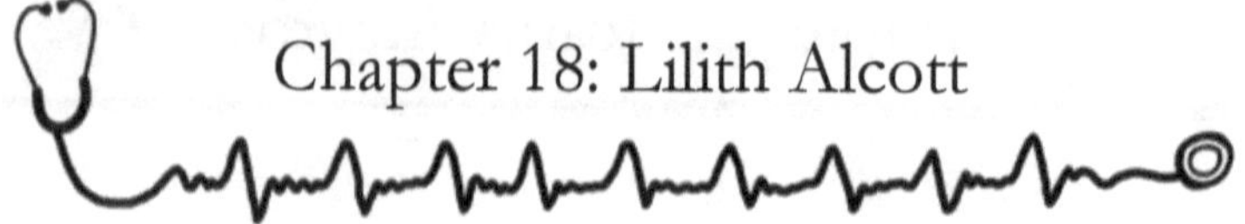

Chapter 18: Lilith Alcott

I ONLY REALIZED that I had drifted off when I woke to the sound of footsteps in the hall. Someone was coming! My head shot up and I hurried to shift Cody back to the ground so that I could get to my feet. If anyone came through that door, I wanted to be ready.

The footsteps came to a stop outside the door. I pulled my knives from their sheathes. But the door handle only jiggled for a few seconds; it never opened. Then the footsteps were leaving.

Behind me, Cody groaned softly. I let go of the breath I had been holding and slid the knives back into their sheathes so that I could bend down to check on him. He was still feverish. I about jumped out of my skin when his head suddenly jerked upward.

"Lilith?" his voice croaked out my name even as he struggled to sit up. There was a desperate edge to his voice that told me his first instinct on waking had been my safety.

"Hush, Cowboy. I'm here," I reassured him softly, even as I tried to gently push him back down. He relaxed the moment he heard my voice, no longer fighting me to sit up. With my hand pressed against his chest, I could feel a hint of dampness to his shirt that had not been there before. I frowned as I considered what that meant. If he was sweating…

"Is someone in there?" A voice from outside the room startled me. The door handle was wiggling again. I scrambled back to my feet and pulled the knives from their sheaths once more.

"Who's there?" I demanded. If this was one of our attackers, they were playing a twisted game and I intended to remind them the cost of messing with me. But if it wasn't them…if it was someone who could help us?

"Name's Paul Taylor," the man's voice answered. "What's yours?"

To my surprise, Cody's raspy voice responded from behind me, "If you're Paul, then what's the name of Blake's horse?"

The voice on the other side hesitated for just a moment before answering guardedly, "Ringo Starr. How do you know Blake?"

I heard Cody struggling to get to his feet. *Oh no you don't!* I thought in exasperation as I turned around. He ignored my protests and instead took several unsteady steps toward the door.

"I went to school with Blake and helped him choose that name after Pa gave the roan to him."

"Cody?" The man's voice sounded startled, as though he couldn't believe what he had just heard.

"Yes, sir." Cody answered. But the second he said it, he started coughing. I swore as he stumbled against me, nearly knocking us both down. The wracking cough shook his whole frame.

"Cody?!" The man shouted in concern. "What's happening?"

"He's been hurt," I grunted, trying to support him while the coughing fit ran its course. "He needs a hospital."

Paul didn't waste time asking anything else. Instead, I heard his footsteps hurrying away. A few moments later they came hurrying back. There was a sharp rapping sound followed by something metal landing on the ground. The sounds were repeated a second and third time. Then the door was wrenched off of its hinges.

In the pale light of a lantern that had been set on the ground, I was able to make out a grizzled older man holding the door in his hands. At his feet were the pins he had forced out of their hinges so that he could pull the door free. The man had that lanky, bandy-legged look of someone who had lived his life in the saddle combined with the sinewy muscles and weathered skin of one who worked outdoors for a living. Seeing Cody doubled over, the man tossed the door aside and rushed in. He helped Cody to straighten up so that he could breathe easier.

For the first time, I was able to see Cody's face; it looked worse than I had expected it to. His face was bruised and swollen with two distinct splits in the skin, one above his right eyebrow, the other on his left cheek. I felt my jaw tighten in anger, wishing I had acted faster to stop the beating.

"It's good to see you, sir," Cody greeted him between coughs.

Paul grunted dismissively, but his voice carried faint hints of emotion. "Save the pleasantries for after we get you out of here, son. I doubt we have long before they come back."

Chapter 19: Cody Thatcher

I GRITTED MY teeth and forced myself to keep moving. In addition to the painful bruises and split lip Fischer had given me, I'd woken to a deep, sharp pain in my left side where he had kicked me. Combined with the persistent, painful shivers that kept sweeping through me, I was rapidly being taxed of my strength. If that wasn't bad enough, my hands were still bound behind me throwing off my balance. Even with Paul and Lilith supporting every step I took, it was taking all I had to stay upright.

Paul was no fool; he could see that I was in trouble. Every time I stumbled, he would remind me that his camp was just across the river and that, if I could make it that far, there was a two-seater hidden in the bushes that would take us the rest of the way down. I was certain he meant the words to be reassuring, but we both knew that getting that far was going to be a problem.

The only river crossing within three miles of here was the old turbine housing. Back when the hydro plant had been in use, the housing had been designed to double as a way to cross the river. Unfortunately, what remained of it today was little more than broken sections of cement interspersed with gaping holes and rusted rebar for the river's playful current to race through. The crossing was still possible for anyone who was sure footed and wasn't afraid to swim if they misstepped; I'd even crossed it a few times myself in the past. But tonight, I was in no shape to do so.

The problem was that we didn't have much choice. Fischer and his companion could come back at any moment. If we weren't gone before they returned, then any chance of getting Lilith to safety would evaporate like mist in the morning sun. I was not going to let that happen. And if I fell trying to cross the river? Well then, I'd just have to rely on Paul to take care of her. Because if I fell, there was no chance I'd have the strength to escape the river's grasp alive.

"You better go first, miss," Paul said when we reached the river's edge. "Take this lamp and stay a few steps ahead of us so we can see where we're going."

Lilith, who had likely assumed Paul was leading us to a more secure crossing, looked up at him in disbelief. "You're joking, right?! There's no way he's going to be able to cross that."

"Ma'am," Paul said patiently, "I know this walkway doesn't look like much, but I crossed it myself just an hour ago, so I know it's passable. Now, I'm going to need both my hands to make sure this boy doesn't go for a swim, but we're also going to need that light to see by. So, you're going to take the lamp and guide our way while I help him."

Lilith's eyes narrowed and I could see that she was about to argue with him. We didn't have time for that, so I cut her off. "Lilith, just take the lamp. And Paul, if I fall, I want your word that you'll take her down the hill and back to my folk's house. Don't waste time trying to save me."

"Now hold on!" Lilith rounded on me, continuing with a steady stream of angry words that told me exactly what she thought of my request. I ignored her furious tirade, and instead held Paul's gaze. I was determined to have his word on it. Better to have her angry with me than have her back in Fischer's hands.

Paul raised an eyebrow as she stormed on. It was an impressive tirade that Ma would have been proud of, but Paul didn't look away from me. It was obvious that he was weighing my request against our situation. He knew, as I did, that we needed to cross here, and we needed to do it now. He must have also known that the odds weren't good that I would make it without falling, so it was safe to assume that his plan had been to follow me into the river, to pull me back out when that happened. Instead, I was telling him that I wanted him to let me go; to place Lilith's life ahead of mine. The hard lines of his frown showed me exactly what he thought of that idea. I was going to have to force him into it.

I made my voice as cold and hard as I could manage, given that I was struggling to keep going. "Paul, I'll have your word on this or I'm not going any further. I'll find some other way to get her to safety."

His expression darkened. He was not impressed by my demand, but I wasn't going to back down. He must have sensed it too, because he suddenly swore and said angrily, "You stubborn son of a mule. Fine, you have it."

Lilith stiffened at his words and went silent the way the charged air does in the nano seconds before the lightning strikes. Then she said in a soft, ominous tone, "Cowboy, when we get back to your folks' house, we're going to have a talk."

I nodded wearily. What else could I do? But she clearly thought I should have done something else because her eyes were narrowed dangerously as she stared at me for several seconds longer before finally turning to snatch the lamp out of Paul's hand. Paul wisely didn't say anything, though I noted the slightest upturn of his lips as he watched her step out onto the housing.

"Come on, son. Let's not keep the lady waiting."

The crumbling structure was about as difficult to cross as I had been expecting it to be. I quickly lost track of how many times I stumbled on an uneven edge or slipped on loose rubble. But Paul had a firm grip on me, and, in spite of my awkwardness, we were making good progress. Unfortunately, my dizziness was increasing in equal measure so that it was taking more and more of my focus to place my feet correctly. My vision was getting worse as well. It kept shifting out of focus and I found myself having to squeeze my eyes shut and then reopen them to bring things back into focus. All the while, the river churned and roared below us in a constant reminder of what awaited if I slipped. *Just keep putting one foot in front of the other,* I told myself. *Trust Paul to guide you.*

No sooner had that thought crossed my mind then I misplaced my foot again, sliding on some loose rubble instead of landing on the clear patch I had been aiming for. I grunted as I fell hard to one knee, my other foot continued to slide until there was no longer anything solid beneath it. The shock of the icy water grabbing at my leg sent painful chills through my whole body, making me gasp.

"Cody!"

Lilith's cry sounded so far away through the ringing in my ears. Paul was the only reason my forward momentum didn't carry me all the way in. His vice-like grip yanked me upward and I stumbled back against him. I was breathing hard as pain and adrenaline coursed through me.

"Are you all right?"

Lilith was in front of me, searching my eyes. It was a struggle to bring her face into focus, but I nodded my head anyway, trying to reassure her. The truth was that I couldn't seem to calm my breathing or get the pain back under control. I might as well have been trying to herd a gaggle of geese, because it wasn't doing any good. The burning pain in my side had intensified as well when my knee slammed down. Now it was radiating upward into my ribs and shoulder. I shook my head in frustration. I needed more time to rest, but this was not the place.

"Let's keep going," I finally said between gasps. Paul understood; he patted me on the shoulder knowingly. Lilith probably suspected as well, because she was slow to turn away.

I'm not sure how we made it the rest of the way across without any further slips, but we did. It was with a huge sigh of relief that we stepped back on to solid ground. However, we'd only made it about twenty feet past the river's edge when my strength finally gave out. This time, Paul wasn't able to keep me upright. In my head, a voice was screaming at me to get up and keep moving; I needed to get Lilith to safety. But that voice was becoming increasingly drowned out by the pain and the dulling sense of disorientation that accompanied it.

I shook my head, trying to bring my thoughts back into focus. *Get up!* At the same time, the darkness at the edges of my vision was enticingly drawing me toward it, dulling my thoughts even more. *Why do I need to get up?* I suddenly couldn't remember. Maybe what I really needed was to just rest here for a bit.

A stern voice cut through the disorientation, bringing a lifeline of clarity with it.

"Cowboy, don't you dare quit on me now!"

Lilith! She's the reason I need to get up! My determination hardened once more and I called on every hidden reserve of strength I could find to get myself back to my feet. I sensed her at my side as I struggled upward and took that first shuffling step forward. She had a hold of my arm.

Take another step! The words in my head were like instructions to my feet. I stepped forward once more.

Paul took hold of my other arm.

Another step!

"It's not far now, son." I heard his reassurance as though it were coming from a great distance. "Think you can keep going?"

I didn't respond; I couldn't spare the energy for that.

Take another step!

My mind couldn't focus on anything but the next step.

Another step!

My vision was beginning to blur again. This time, I couldn't get it back into focus.

Another step!

I would have to trust Lilith and Paul to guide my steps.

Another step!

Another step!

Another step!

I couldn't say how many steps I had taken or how long I had been walking. All I knew was that I needed to take that next step.

Another step!

Another step!

Unexpectedly, my attempt to take another step was hindered by Paul's grip on my arm; he had stopped moving. Through the dullness in my mind, I registered that he was swearing violently, but my mind was already locked on its two-word command and couldn't process the change.

Another step!

I tried to take that next step forward again. Once more, Paul's grip stopped me.

Another step? The thought shifted in confusion. I tried again. This time it was Lilith's hand on my chest that stopped me.

Another…step? The confused thought was disjointed. My eyelids began fluttering, fighting to stay open. I started to sway.

"Cody!" Lilith's alarmed voice shouted at me from somewhere far away, even as her face swam in and out of focus right in front of me. Then I felt my legs give out and my body hit the ground. This time, I had nothing left to hold back the darkness.

# Chapter 20: Aiden Haskell

THE TRUCK'S HEADLIGHTS came to rest on a small, brown, all-terrain vehicle that was parked in front of the Thatcher's kitchen door. It was the two-seater type, designed to take two passengers and their gear off-roading. It had not been there when we left an hour ago, and it looked to have arrived in a hurry if the skid marks behind it were any indication.

I looked to Wren. "Dae th' tracks match?"

He shook his head in the negative, then nodded toward the house. "Someone's coming."

The kitchen door had opened, allowing light to spill through it. Framed by the light, I could see Mr. Thatcher's purposeful strides as he quickly covered the distance between us. I opened my own door and stepped out to meet him. As I did so, I noted that two others had come through the door behind him. I recognized Mr. Hillock, but the third man was unfamiliar to me.

"What did you kids find?" Mr. Thatcher asked without preamble.

"Trouble," I answered bitterly. "I know who has yer son, but gettin' him back is goin' tae be a problem." Then I hesitated. How do you tell a man that the government you serve is the one that has kidnapped his son as part of a covert mission designed to steal his land? I opened my mouth again, not sure what I was going to say, but intending to somehow try and explain, only to have Alex's soft voice cut in.

"Who has them, Aiden?"

I looked over in surprise to find her beside me. I hadn't heard her getting out of the truck, but she must have done so right behind me to hear what I had said.

"Who's responsible for the attack in the barn?" she asked again.

I didn't want to give her that answer; I was afraid of how she would respond to it. But I also knew that lying to her would be far worse. Mr. Thatcher's eyebrow had come up as well, still waiting for me to explain.

"The UFC," I finally answered regretfully. "It was part of a coordinated attack on sites throughout th' city."

Mr. Thatcher grunted in surprise, but it was Alex who asked in confusion, "How can that be?"

Well, if she was going to hear it, then I better let the whole team know what we were up against.

"Wren, McLagan, Evans," I called to them. "Yae better come join us; you're goin' tae need tae hear this as well."

Once everyone was there, I began. "When we stopped at that last house, they showed me a live news feed about multiple attacks throughout Austin. The reporter blamed Icarus' forces, but I saw somethin' on th' screen that proved otherwise."

I proceeded to explain to them what it was that I had seen and how I knew what it meant.

"We called it C.H.A.O.S., short for Combat Hallucinations via Auditory, Olfactory, and Synapse. Me company was field testin' it for th' UFC lab that had designed it. It's not much bigger than a shoebox, but its effect on those we used it on was intense."

I went on to explain that, when it was triggered, it released a fluctuating pattern of soundwaves just above 18hz that induced fear and panic, airborne pheromones that triggered intense emotions of anger and aggression, and electromagnetic signals that disrupted the brain's ability to think clearly. Together they caused anyone in close proximity to begin acting irrationally and aggressively toward each other. Adjust it to release at high enough levels, and the scene around it rapidly devolved into literal chaos as they began to tear each other apart.

"It was still in th' early phases of field testin' when I transferred tae Ghana Base, but I recognized it when I saw it, and I know what it can do. The scenes they described at each of th' attack sites also line up perfectly with what I saw in the field. Me previous company, the Caledonians, was th' only group authorized tae use it, and then we were only tae use it in direct attacks on high-level enemy combatants." I paused for emphasis. "Its presence here means that me old company is as well. Th' UFC is responsible for these attacks."

"So, my son is in the hands of UFC soldiers," Mr. Thatcher said coldly; his jaw clenching angrily in the same way his son's did.

"Aye, sir," I confirmed.

"And it was likely UFC soldiers who caused all the trouble we've been experiencing?" Mr. Hillock asked.

"Aye, sir."

The two men looked at each other. Mr. Thatcher's jaw clenched again. He seemed to be thinking something through. After a few moments he nodded to Mr. Hillock. Mr. Hillock nodded back.

"So be it," he said coldly. "Call the men, Garth. Tell them what's happening. We'll be heading out in thirty minutes. Any of them who want to join us would be welcomed."

"Yup," Mr. Hillock agreed with a nod. Then he turned to the man at his side, "Bill, go to the house. Get the guns and the truck."

For just a moment I was confused. Where were they planning to go? Then it clicked. "Yae know where they are, don't yae." It wasn't really a question.

Thatcher's father nodded, but it was Mr. Hillock who explained. "Bill and Paul have been watching a large group of outsiders for the past few days. They were pretty sure the group was the one responsible for Blake's death and the mischief 'round these parts, but they needed proof. They figured they had just about enough evidence to go to the police with, and were fixin' to do so in the morning, but then something changed tonight. The whole group of them outsiders altered their routine and headed out in their vehicles in mass, something they'd not yet done before.

"So, the boys split up. Paul stayed to search the buildings the group had been using as their hideout while Bill took the vehicle and followed one of the groups to see what they were up to.

"He followed their truck around town for about two hours. They stopped at a few places, but each time only two or three people got out of the truck to go inside. And each time they all came back out not long after. About thirty minutes ago they left town and started to head back this way. Bill was going to keep following them to see if they went back to their base, but then his C-DACS came alive to alert everyone to the attacks. One of the sites they named as having been attacked was the bar he had just seen them at. He decided to come find me after that. He'd just finished telling us what's been going on when we saw you kids pulling up."

"Can you take us to them?" Alex asked hopefully.

Bill, who hadn't left yet, nodded his head, "They're using the old power plant."

I knew how my old company operated. If they had a base set up somewhere, then that was where we'd find Thatcher and Alcott. But getting them back was still going to be a problem. I tried to explain. "If this group is who I think it is, then they're a well-trained company of more than fifty soldiers. The five of us won't be enough tae take them on alone."

"Well, that's just it, son; You won't be alone," Mr. Hillock assured me. "Folks round these parts don't take kindly to having their homes attacked and their families put in danger. All we needed to know was the who and the where. Now that we know those things, we're fixin' to put a stop to it. We may not be trained soldiers like the five of you, but I think you'll find that we can hold our own."

I hesitated, not wanting to offend him. Texans had a reputation for standing firm against trouble; that was one of the reasons the American capital was now located in the middle of Texas. But there was a big difference between trained soldiers and untrained civilians. I was not keen on leading this group to their deaths.

While I was still trying to decide what to say, Evans interjected, "You said the other night that the UFC is split. Can we assume that the UFC operations here are not necessarily supported by all of the leadership, but that the side who supports us would be unable to send help to back us up?"

Once more, I was impressed with how quickly he saw into the heart of the problem and identified the real issues. I confirmed his suspicions then added as an afterthought, "I'm beginnin' tae wonder if we aren't th' backup that was sent. Why send us here where we might interfere with their planned operations, unless someone wanted us tae interfere?"

Several of their faces showed that they had not considered that possibility. Alex, in particular, became especially thoughtful.

"But if that was their intention," she asked slowly, "why send us in blind? Why not give us enough information to allow us to stop those massacres before they happened? All those people in the barn; we could have saved them."

"What's this?" Mr. Thatcher asked with a start.

I groaned inwardly. I hadn't intended for them to find out this way.

Alex didn't seem to notice the small shake of my head. She kept going. "We went to the barn where the dance was held. They'd killed everyone there."

Mr. Thatcher eyes narrowed and the muscle in his jaw twitched angrily. "Garth," he said in quiet anger, "go make those calls. I want everyone here, now!"

Thirty minutes later, the Thatcher's place was a hive of activity. At the center of it all was Mr. Thatcher, calmly organizing everything. It was impressive to see how he did it. I'd seen many others leaders in the past marshalling their troops for battles, but never before had I seen one accomplish so much while saying so little. When he spoke, it was concise while still providing exactly the details that were needed.

There were perhaps thirty or forty people who had answered his call. Most looked to be men in their thirties and forties, but there were also a few silver-haired grandfathers among them and at least one boy who couldn't have been older than fourteen. Then there were the women; about seven of them. Three or four had brought young children with them. I watched as they took their children into the house and then came back out. I'd thought at first that they had done so intending to stay outside only long enough to see their men off, but it quickly became evident that they intended to stay and fight alongside them.

As I watched this, I wondered if these people truly understood what they were preparing to do. How could they? I doubted that many of them, if any, had ever experienced war. How could they understand that choosing to fight against trained soldiers tonight meant that most of them wouldn't be alive to see the sun come up? That those who were leaving their children behind were likely leaving them to become orphans?

The more I thought about it, the more it bothered me. Maybe it was sadness for these children who were likely to be parentless in the morning. Maybe it was jealousy because these people had children, something I could never have. Whatever it was, it left me with a deep uneasiness.

But, as I rounded the corner of the house looking for Alex, I found myself intruding on a tender moment between a young couple. The man was holdings his very pregnant wife closely to him, with one hand gently touching her swollen belly. He couldn't have been much older than me and she certainly wasn't much older than Alex. I didn't mean to listen in on their conversation, but there was no way for me to miss it from where I was.

"If I don't make it back," he was saying softly, "tell this little one how much I love him and that I died to make sure his freedom stayed intact."

Her eyes were glistening, but she promised in a determined tone, "He'll know."

I froze mid-step as what they had said hit me: these people did understand. I was suddenly ashamed. I had underestimated them. Worse, I had been reluctant to share things I knew about my old team. It had felt like I would be betraying friends, but the reality was that every detail I shared had the potential to ensure that at least one more of these people would come home tomorrow morning. What did my feelings matter when compared to what they were willing to give up? I sighed. There were a few more things I was going to need to share with Mr. Thatcher. But first, I wanted to find Alex.

I found her in the back of the barn, sitting on a bale of hay, thoughtfully twisting the ring on her finger. She looked up as I came in.

"How are yae doin'?" I asked, moving to sit next to her.

She smiled nervously. "Does it always feel like this before you go into a fight?"

"Yae mean like yae've got a dozen butterflies tryin' to get out of yer stomach?"

She laughed lightly. "Yeah, like that."

"Well, I think I've got about two dozen right now, and they keep flutterin' between me stomach and me throat. So…no. Either it never goes away, or someone keeps puttin' new ones back in there."

She rolled her eyes at me, but her smile was a little less nervous. Then it faded completely and she asked, "Do you really think he sent us here on purpose? To help these people?"

Now it was my turn for my smile to fade. I probably should have kept my mouth shut about that, but it was a little too late now. I sighed heavily. "It's a real possibility and I'm not at all happy about it."

She looked down at her hands thoughtfully and absently started to twist the ring again. After a moment she said, "The day I met him, he told me that there was no shame in not wanting to hurt others, and he said that sending me to the school in New Los Angeles was meant to give me another option. At the time, I thought he meant an option that didn't include hurting other people. But what if what he really meant was an option that allowed me to help other people, to protect them instead of just hurting them?"

"How dae yae mean?" I wasn't sure I liked where she was going with this.

"What the UFC has done to these people is wrong, Aiden. They have a right to defend themselves. But if they go up there tonight, a lot of them are going to die, aren't they?"

"They will," I answered hesitantly, definitely not liking the direction her questions were leading.

"They won't die if I help them." She said it so simply, so sure of the truth of it. "I would hurt some of the soldiers, but I would also be able to make sure that these people came home to their families. I think…" she took a deep breath before finally looking back up at me. "I think that's a tradeoff I can live with."

"That's not a choice yae were supposed tae have tae make," I said with a frown.

She shrugged and said sadly, "Maybe not, but I like it better than the alternative of not having a choice at all."

Not having a choice? Well, I couldn't say that I didn't understand her reasoning, but this wasn't just about having a choice. "Alex, no one is supposed tae know who yae are. Claire can't dae th' things yae're talkin' about. If these people see what yae can dae, it will blow yer cover and our mission."

"I know," she said miserably, looking away once more. "But if I turn my back and walk away, I'll be just like all the rest of his children. I can't do that."

I sighed. I'd been afraid she would see it that way. *Fine!* I reached over to take her hand. "Then let me be yer tool again. Let me be th' one they think is controllin' th' gravity."

She looked up in surprise. "But if this is your old company, they'll know you can't be the one controlling the gravity."

I squeezed her hand gently. "Yae just worry about keepin' these people safe. I'll take care of foolin' me old company. I told yae. Where yae are, that's where I want tae be. And if this is somethin' yae need tae dae, then let me help yae dae it."

She seemed stunned by my words, unsure how to respond. But then the corner of her lips lifted slightly into a gentle smile. "Thank you," she said softly.

I squeezed her hand once more with a smile of my own before finally letting it go.

"Now that that is settled, any idea where th' rest of yer team went? We should probably let them in on th' new plan."

At that moment, the almost inaudible sound of a faint movement only a few feet from us reached my ears. My head shot up to find Wren standing in the shadows about fifteen feet away, silently watching us. He nodded his head to me as our eyes met.

Alex appeared to have already known he was there as she laughed lightly. "He followed me in here. Said it wasn't safe for me to be alone."

I was impressed that Wren had been able to blend in so well that I hadn't even seen him; it was rare that I missed someone like that. I was also impressed that he had taken the initiative to keep an eye on Alex; impressed and grateful.

"What about th' others?" I asked as I turned back to Alex.

"Last I saw, Nate and Logan were out there with the ranchers. I think Nate may have even made a new friend," she laughed lightly. "One of the toddlers escaped the house and was wrapped around his leg last time I saw him. He was struggling to get the kid to let go."

My lips twitched upwards in amusement. Somehow, I liked the idea of Evans struggling to unhitch a toddler from his leg.

"Well," I slapped my knee absently as I stood up, then reached back to offer her a hand. "Let's go find them and then talk tae Mr. Thatcher and Mr. Hillock about how tae make this work."

Chapter 21: Lilith Alcott

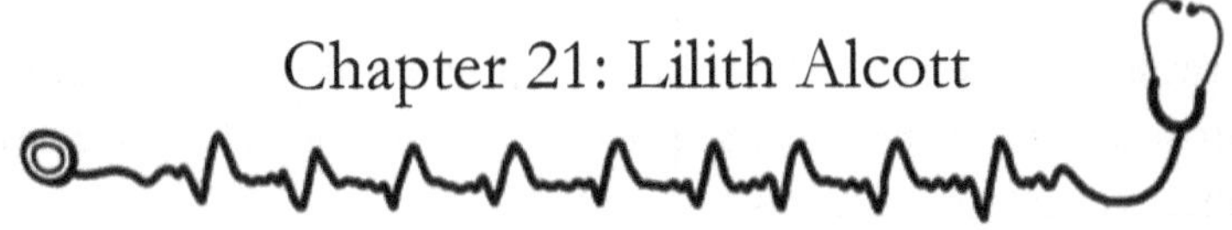

I PRESSED MY hand to Cody's forehead. He was burning up. At my touch, he muttered something inaudible and his head turned from side to side, but the movement was the result of the fever, not consciousness. He'd pushed himself to the end of his strength getting here. Now his body was paying the price. It would have been worth it if a vehicle had been here the way Paul had promised it would be, but it wasn't.

Paul was cursing himself and someone else named Bill, muttering under his breath about what he was going to do to him when he got hold of him. Well, he could deal with Bill later. Right now, I needed to get Cody somewhere secure then go for help.

"Do you have a bed?"

"A bed?" Paul looked at me in confusion.

"Yes," I said in exasperation. I didn't have the patience for this right now. "Somewhere we can get him settled; somewhere not out in the open. If we can't get him to a hospital, then I want to get him stabilized and then I'm going to bring help to him."

Paul seemed to consider my words. "You have medical training?"

"I'm a nurse," I said simply. The word was deceptive in its simplicity. The truth was that my training was quite a bit more thorough than that title implied, but it would take far more time to explain than it was worth.

A look of hope came into his eyes and he nodded. "You get his feet," he instructed. "We'll put him on my bag."

It was a struggle for us to lift him. Cody was in excellent physical condition, but at six-foot-two he was still some two-hundred pounds. Luckily, it turned out that we weren't going far.

What I could see of Paul's camp in the lamp's light was tidy, but sparse. Aside from a small tent, the only other camping supplies were a food preparation area that consisted of a small table, a small electric coil cooker, a medium-sized solar battery, and a small but organized arrangement of kitchenware.

Inside the tent were two sleeping bags, neatly laid out and ready for use. Next to each bag was a small backpack, probably filled with their clothes and other personal belongings. We laid Cody on one of the bags. It was a little awkward with his hands still bound behind him, but there wasn't much I could do about that. I did my best to instead straighten his arms and his hands and to roll him slightly to his side so that his body's weight wouldn't be on them.

From the corner of my eyes, I saw Paul's head come up as though something had just occurred to him. "I'll be right back," he said as he hurried out of the tent. He returned a moment later carrying the battery I had seen and a handful of tools.

"What's this for?" I asked as he straightened out the battery's lead wires, cut off the connectors that were on them, and then began to strip the protective coating from the wires.

"My Pa wanted me to be an engineer; said I had a mind for it. It turned out that it wasn't my breed of cattle, but I took a few engineering classes before I eventually quit school. One of them was electrical engineering. Didn't care much for the class itself, but I enjoyed playing around in the lab."

He had turned his attention to the military cuffs on Cody's wrists and began to carefully work the tiny command screen free of its housing.

"These cuffs were a new-fangled device back at that time, and they had a few prototypes in the lab that one of the professors was working with. We weren't supposed to touch his projects, but one day I got it into my head to see if I could find a way to open them without the code."

He slid the stripped wires under the small opening he had created, one to each side.

"It took me the better part of a week, but I eventually discovered that if I gave it just the right amount of voltage, in just the right places, I could short-circuit the control pad and then pry them open."

He adjusted the battery's voltage setting down low and released a short burst of electricity. I heard a soft pop followed by a click. Paul's lips twisted into a grin of satisfaction, then he grabbed each side of the cuffs and grunted as he slowly pried them apart. He held them up triumphantly for me to see.

"School expelled me and made me sign a non-disclosure agreement. Said they'd file litigation 'gainst me if I ever told anyone what I had discovered, but I didn't mind; didn't want to be there anyway. And I was satisfied knowing that I had succeeded. Funny, isn't it, how small things in yer past can turn out to be so important later on."

His smile was infectious. I found myself smiling softly as I rolled Cody onto his back and laid his arms gently at his side. But my smile slid away again when I unbuttoned his shirt to check underneath. The whole right side of his torso was an ugly shade of purple and yellow, confirming my earlier suspicions. I heard Paul's breath hiss when he saw it.

"He tried to protect me," I explained, running my fingers over the bruised skin, trying to feel the extent of the bleeding. "They beat him for it. Now he's bleeding internally and I can't stop it without my kit." I sighed in frustration as I pulled my hands away. The bleeding was dangerously severe, already causing his abdomen to slightly distend. The pressure would need to be relieved soon. If I had to, I could use one of my knives to do it. But without my medical supplies, I wouldn't be able to stop the source of the bleeding. I needed those tools!

"Watch over him," I said as I started to stand up. "I'm going for help."

"No, Miss," he interrupted me. "I'll be the one to go. I'd wager Cody stands a better chance of surviving if yer the one here watching over him. 'Sides that, I know where to go for help. I'm guessing you don't since yer not from these parts."

I laughed bitterly. He was right, of course.

"Figured as much," he said with a half-smile. "You just keep him alive till I get back." Then he turned to leave, only to stop in the tent's opening as something seemed to cross his mind. He walked back to me, unbuckling his belt as he came. "I'll leave this with you, just in case."

As he pulled his belt free, I was able to see a gun holster I hadn't even realized he was wearing. He handed it to me. Then, with a final glance at Cody, he turned away and jogged off into the night.

Chapter 22: Alexandria Jaquette

THIRTY-EIGHT PEOPLE. That's how many I would be protecting. Four were my own team members, but the other thirty-four were the men and women who were fighting for their families, their lives, and their homes. Those were the ones that were going to need me the most. It was a daunting task I was setting for myself, and I was worried about whether or not I would be successful.

It had only taken a twenty-minute drive to reach the river the hydro plant was built on, but then they had chosen to leave the trucks some distance back in favor of traveling the rest of the way on foot, so that we wouldn't be noticed. We'd followed an old hunting trail through the trees for that. One of the ranchers had known about it and led the way. It had allowed us to get close enough to see the impromptu base undetected, but this was about as far as we could go until the sentries were taken care of. Aiden and Wren were out there right now doing just that.

The rest of us had taken up positions inside the tree line, waiting for their signal. I had chosen a spot about halfway up the hill where I had a reasonably clear view of the grounds around the buildings. Aiden had helped me choose it before he took off. But when I had glanced upward at a nearby tree, considering the improved visibility I would gain by climbing it, he had harshly whispered, "Don't even think about it!" In spite of the tenseness of the situation, I'd chuckled to myself. He was probably right; we'd already learned that lesson the hard way.

Instead, we had quickly worked out a few signals he could give me if there was something he could see that he didn't think I could. I might not be able to control the gravity waves that I couldn't see, but I could still drop something from above and let gravity do the rest of the work for me when my line-of-sight was otherwise hindered.

Aiden had also left Evans and McLagan to guard me. He'd made it very clear that if anything went wrong, they were to get me out of here, whether or not I wanted them to. I was more than a little annoyed with him over that last part; I would not be abandoning my team, no matter how bad it got. But for now, I wasn't complaining about having someone I could trust watching the woods around me, leaving me free to focus on what was happening in front of us.

The large open area between the buildings was well lit with portable lights. We were probably thirty or forty minutes still from the first hints of morning light entering the sky and an hour or so from sunrise, so the lights were necessary if they wanted to see anything. Even so, I was a little surprised by the choice to use them. It seemed like a bad idea for a group operating in secrecy. But I didn't take the time to dwell on the inconsistency of it and instead took advantage of it.

The main structure was old, while still appearing to be reasonably sound, at least so far as I could see from here. It also looked to be where the soldiers had established their primary base of operations. At the moment, it was pretty obvious that they were packing up to leave. Men and women were rapidly moving into and out of the building, loading supplies into their trucks.

Aiden had confirmed that the people down there were indeed members of his previous company, removing any lingering doubts that this might not have been a UFC operation. Yet, in spite of being soldiers, none of those people down there were in uniform, and, at first glance, I could have easily mistaken them for an average group of civilians. But the longer I watched them, the more there were little things that jumped out at me to remind me how wrong first impressions could be. Like the fact that every one of the men had a military haircut and every one of the women had their hair either cut short or tightly pinned up. Or that every single one of them walked with a sure-footed cadence.

And then there was Red Shirt, the man standing at the building's entrance. He wasn't leaning against the wall or lounging about. Instead, his posture was erect and his feet were shoulder-width apart, evenly spaced and pointed straight in front of him. And Hips, the woman directing traffic, didn't just casually point with her finger to where she wanted something to go, she pointed with her whole arm. It felt a little like déjà vu as I watched them and began to pick out the unique traits that I could use to identify each of them, just as I had done with the soldiers at the clearing in Ghana.

I'd already picked out the leader of this group as well. To my surprise, even from this distance, I had recognized him. It was the same man that had been at the track the day I had met Aiden; the one who had told him he was to keep running.

If I remembered right, Aiden had called him Major at that time, so Major would be his name now.

Major was currently reprimanding two men, though I suppose reprimanding them would be putting it lightly. He was shouting obscenities at them, berating them for something they had done. But even if he hadn't been shouting, I still would have been able to hear him. In spite of the turbulent river and the distance between us, the horseshoe shape of the hill surrounding the buildings was causing sound to travel up it surprisingly well. I could hear nearly everything being said. And from what I was hearing, it sounded like those two men had acted on their own, disobeying the direct orders they had been given. Major seemed to think their actions had the potential to put their mission in jeopardy and he was telling them exactly what he thought of their choice.

The two men on the receiving end of the tirade had diametrically opposite responses to it. The shorter of the two men seemed to cower under Major's tirade. But the moment Major turned away from him, there was a balling of his fists and a tensing of his shoulders that suggested he was angry with the treatment. Fists. That's what I would call him.

The man next to Fists had the long, silky black hair, dark skin, and long, prominent nose of an American Indian. His expression never altered, either during the tirade or after it. There was something about the way he held his head erect that suggested he knew his value and was not intimidated by Major's ire. Iceman—that would be his name.

As Major walked away, Fists and Iceman put their heads together and seemed to be discussing something. Then they surprised me by turning toward the river and disappearing into the darkness around it. Where were they heading? The satellite images hadn't indicated that there was anything of interest in that direction. But I didn't have much time to dwell on it as a soft warbling sound broke the silence.

That was the signal. I took a deep breath to steady my nerves then squared my shoulders; it was time to begin.

At the signal, several of the Texans began moving into position at the backs of the buildings, while a few others began working their way up onto the roofs. The rest of us waited for Aiden to make his move.

Right on cue, Aiden's voice called out from the darkness. "Carter, I want tae talk tae yae!"

Major, who had been speaking with one of the soldiers by the trucks, looked up sharply, his eyes quickly scanning the darkness for the source of the voice. "Haskell? That you?"

"Aye, Major. Mind if I come out?"

Major held his fist up and nodded slightly, I assumed to let the sentries know that they were to let him through; he didn't know that his sentries were already out of commission.

Aiden walked from the darkness into the light. He was still in his military fatigues and looked every bit the quintessential soldier. He strode out confidently, only stopping when he was about ten feet away from their commander.

"What are you doing here, Haskell?" Major's tone carried hints of caution. He obviously wasn't sure what to make of Aiden's unexpected appearance. "Thought you signed on with that group in Africa?"

Aiden shrugged as if the question was unimportant. "I got reassigned. Unfortunately, though, me new team has run intae a wee problem."

"Oh? What's that?"

"It seems yae have two of our teammates in yer custody, and yer operatin' against a member country."

Several of the soldiers around Major looked at each other uncomfortably. I got the impression that Aiden's accusations had hit a nerve. But Major only raised his chin and responded innocently, "Not sure what you're talking about, Haskell. We're here at the invitation of the US Government and all of our training exercises this last week were sanctioned by them."

Aiden scoffed lightly. "I've no doubt yae have all th' proper authorizations, Carter. Yer tae thorough fer anythin' less. But that doesn't alter our situation. Yae have me teammates and I'll be needin' them back. How we get them is up tae yae."

Major's eyes narrowed as his guarded watchfulness shifted toward an ice-cold hardness. "I see. And if I'm not inclined to release them to you?"

Aiden sighed as though he had been expecting that answer. "As I said, that's up tae you. But yae should know that I'm not askin', Carter. I will be takin' them out of here with me. Just thought I'd offer yae a chance tae return them without trouble, for old times' sake."

Major's voice grew dangerously soft and I had to strain to hear his next words. "Haskell, I don't know what game you're playing at, but we have our orders and I'm not about to let you interfere with them. If I have someone in my custody, it's because those were my orders. And those orders came straight from the Directorate's Office. So, I suggest you go back to your commanding officers and let them know that you need to withdraw before you walk into a mess you won't be able to extract yourself from."

Aiden shook his head sadly; he'd warned us this was how it would go. "Well, that seems tae be th' crux of th' problem, doesn't it, Carter? Yae see, we're also here on Directorate orders. Th' difference is, yae were sent tae harm these people. We were sent here tae protect them."

Major's back stiffened and his expression grew harder. His hand moved to rest on the phase gun he had strapped to his leg. "If you get in the way of my job, Haskell, I'll shoot you myself."

Aiden's expression morphed into a small smile, as though he were mildly amused by Major's threat. "No yae won't, Carter. Yae should have realized that th' only thing that could have pulled me away from yer group was a better way tae take down Icarus. The scientists in Ghana gave that tae me."

Aiden's hands had been at his side, but now he slowly began to lift them as though he were picking something up. That was my cue. I had already chosen the waves I wanted. I grabbed hold of them now and lifted. Several basketball sized boulders smoothly rose from the ground in motion with Aiden's hands, moving to levitate at chest height in front of him. Even over the sounds of the river I was able to hear the gasps coming from both the soldiers and the Texans.

"What is this?" Major demanded angrily, his eyes darting from the stones back to Aiden.

Aiden's smile grew wicked. "Tell me, Carter, who are they givin' credit tae for Talos? I'm bettin' th' plaque is still blank on that one. Cause, accordin' tae th' official UFC records, me team doesn't exist."

I wondered briefly what plaque Aiden was talking about, but I didn't waste time dwelling on it. The soldiers around

Major had started murmuring again. This time they didn't silence completely when Major shot a look at them.

"This is yer last chance tae resolve this without a fight, Carter. Return me teammates, then take yer soldiers and leave. Let yer leaders know that th' people of Texas are under our protection now."

Major shook his head. "I can't do that, Haskell."

Even before he had finished speaking, he made his move. His reflexes were lightning fast as his hand whipped his gun from its holster and fired on Aiden, but I was ready. I slammed down the gravity immediately around Aiden causing the phase bolt to arc sharply into the ground. In the same movement, I sent the boulders flying forward. One of them flew directly at the major, so that he had to drop to his belly to avoid it. The others were aimed at the soldiers nearest him.

I was only somewhat surprised by how quickly they reacted to my attack. Aiden had warned us that the men and women we would be facing were well-trained and used to working in dangerous territory where attacks could come at any moment. They would not be easily surprised and they would not hesitate to shoot back. The speed with which they reacted to my assault confirmed what he had said; they were back on their feet and scrambling for cover almost immediately. Not a single one of them had been injured by the boulders.

Further, in spite of the fact that no weapons had been visible on them only seconds ago, several of them now had phase guns in their hands and had already fired on Aiden. They'd had hidden weapons ready to draw at a moment's notice.

After downing the bolts, I made those guns my next priority, ripping them out of the soldiers' grasps and sending them flying toward the river. The stunned looks on their faces were priceless. Before I had time to take any pleasure from it, though, movement inside the main building caught my attention.

Another group of soldiers had already moved to take up positions just inside the windows and doorways. This group had rifles and were firing them almost as quickly as they got into position. I focused first on catching their bolts and slamming them into the ground, ensuring that none of them could reach Aiden. It didn't take a lot of my strength; mostly it felt like I was swatting down flies. But it did require a lot of concentration to make sure that I didn't miss any.

At the same time, I realized that I could hear sounds of phaser fire coming from behind the buildings. That suggested that the soldiers had finally discovered the Texans there. Well, I couldn't see what was happening back there, so I would have to trust that they could handle their own safety for the moment.

The Texans positioned among the trees, however, had also joined in the battle; those were the ones I could help. I was glad to see that they were taking aim at the soldiers in the building, forcing them to take cover and freeing me up to do more than just swat down their bolts. Now I could start pulling the weapons from their hands as well.

Up to this point, everything I had done was relatively easy. I was breathing a little heavier than normal and I had a light sheen of sweat on my forehead, but I was in no way in danger of passing out. So, when Aiden lifted his hand, palm down, and pointed at a space between two of the trucks, indicating there was something over there I couldn't see, I decided it would be safe to push myself a little harder. It was the truck that was preventing me from seeing whatever was happening behind it. Therefore, it was the truck that I needed out of my way.

Thinking that the bulk of the truck's weight was likely to be in the front where the engine was located, I focused on the gravity waves under the truck's back end and began to lift them. It was a strain, but not impossible. Unfortunately, while I had some theoretical training in the movement of heavy objects from the physics classes I had taken, I had never seen the practical application of lifting a truck too high at one end. What I didn't anticipate was that, as the truck's center of gravity shifted, the gravity waves on that side of the truck became stronger than the ones I had hold of.

Okay. I should have seen this one coming and compensated for that shift; I really do have a firm understanding of how gravity works. But at that moment I was in the middle of a pitched battle, so you'll have to excuse me for my momentary lapse into stupidity.

I had thoroughly disrupted the truck's center of gravity without accounting for that change. The result was that I lost control of the truck as the unplanned for gravity wrenched control of it away from me.

Time seemed to freeze in my mind as I saw the scene play out. With the truck on its nose, I could finally see the small knot of soldiers Aiden had seen; that much had been successful. But when I lost control of the truck, I momentarily lost the ability to determine which way it would move next.

Aiden had to dive to the side as it toppled and began to roll in his direction. He was back on his feet in an instant, but I was left more than a little shaken. So much so that I didn't register McLagan's shouted warning or see the shadowy figures creeping toward us until it was almost too late.

The expanding glow of supercharged air at the tip of several gun barrels was the last warning I got. I reacted on instinct, slamming down the gravity in front of us and sending those bolts into the ground. Then I ripped the weapons out of their hands and sent them flying.

But, before I could do anything more, the breath was knocked out of me as I crashed to the ground, tackled by another figure I had not seen. Months of training kicked in allowing me to wrench myself free of the man's grasp and to roll out from under him. As I did so, I kicked out the way Aiden had taught me to do and was satisfied to hear a grunt of pain as my foot made contact. Then I scrambled to my feet and turned to face him. The broad-shouldered man was on his feet just as quickly.

Another grunt and several thuds in the darkness behind me told me that Evans and McLagan were engaged as well. As much as I wanted to help them, though, I had to deal with my own assailant first. As he lunged toward me for a second time, I pushed off the ground, lifting myself backward and into the air out of his reach. The startled look on his face as he stumbled through the space I had just vacated, assured me that he'd not known what I was capable of.

He slowed to a stop; a considering look on his face as he looked up at me. "What are you?" he growled suspiciously.

"Angry!" I answered sarcastically. Then I lifted a large rock behind him and brought it back down on his head. His eyes rolled up and he collapsed to the ground. *One down, two to go,* I thought wryly.

I turned to find McLagan and Evans still engaged. McLagan had his back against a tree, struggling to hold off the knife his attacker was pushing toward his chest. Evans was ducking the roundhouse swing coming at his head while trying to get in a punch of his own. I wondered for the briefest of seconds why they hadn't simply used their guns to shoot the two soldiers. Then I remembered that I had been positioned directly in front of them; they would not have wanted to take the chance of hitting me.

I yanked the soldier back from McLagan first, sending him into a nearby tree. Then I froze the gravity under the soldier attacking Evans so that he couldn't move his feet. Evans appeared confused for the briefest of seconds as his opponent suddenly lurched to a stop. Then his confusion morphed into a wicked grin and he ducked the other man's windmilling arms to step inside and land a blow across the chin. I released the gravity at just the right time to allow the man to stumble backward, sprawling to the ground.

McLagan and Evans took it from there. Very quickly, they had the three soldiers bound, gagged, and ready to move. The one I had hit with the rock was still unconscious, but they had tied him up and moved him off to the side, out of the way.

While taking prisoners had never been at the forefront of the plan, Aiden and Mr. Thatcher had agreed that if the opportunity came, we should gather anyone who fell into our hands on the off chance that they could be utilized in a potential prisoner exchange. To that end, they had established a rendezvous point about a quarter mile back where prisoners could be handed off to a small group who would secure them until needed.

"You want to take them, or should I?" Evans asked McLagan.

Leaving them to work out the logistics, I quickly turned my attention back to the clearing below. Aiden had taken shelter behind the flipped truck. He had his phase pistol out and was firing toward the group of soldiers I had uncovered, though I noticed that he kept throwing worried glances in my direction between shots. He had no way of knowing why the truck had fallen the way it had and was likely worried. I hurried to reassure him by lifting a crate that two of the soldiers had abandoned at the start of the fight. I sent it soaring through the air and then let it go, allowing gravity to bring it down on top of the group Aiden had been shooting at.

As that knot of soldiers scattered, I saw the brief flash of a predatory grin cross Aiden's face. He slowly holstered his gun and stood back up, no longer bothering to hide. I quicky deflected the shots that came his way.

Aiden appeared unconcerned by the phaser burns that randomly began to scorch the ground around his feet. Instead, he took his time to slowly look around the courtyard. As he did so, the fighting around him seemed to slow, as though he was commanding everyone's attention. He turned back to face the main building, staring at it with a hard expression. Then he raised his chin and called out, "Had enough yet, Carter?"

It occurred to me that I hadn't seen Major since the fight had started. *Where had he disappeared to?* I was surprised to hear his voice coming from out of the building's open doorway;

he didn't strike me as the type that abandoned his troops to hide.

"That depends, Haskell. Are you surrendering?"

Aiden snorted. "Yae know me better than that."

Major laughed dryly in return. "Didn't think so. But if you change your mind, you just let me know. Until then, there's someone else I need to have a talk with."

Before I could figure out what he meant by that, Major stepped through the doorway pushing a dark-haired woman in front of him. The woman was gagged, but her expression was fierce with barely contained anger as she walked stiffly in front of him. Though I couldn't see it, I was fairly certain he had his gun pressed into the small of her back. At her side, a terrified little girl clung to her arm.

His eyes searched the darkness beyond the light even as he raised his voice and shouted, "I warned you that there would be consequences for not fulfilling your assignment."

Your assignment? What assignment was he talking about? Who was he talking to? I had no idea what was going on, but Aiden's eyes suddenly narrowed and his jaw clenched in anger.

"Now you have to choose. Either you deliver it or I shoot these two. You have three minutes to decide."

It? What was he talking about? And who were the woman and child? Were these two of the Texans we had come to rescue? But a sharp hiss of breath next to me brought those thoughts up short.

Startled, I looked over to find McLagan standing next to me, his face unexpectedly pale and his hands trembling. His eyes were locked on the two figures that the Major was herding in front of him; horror and fury were etched on his face in equal measure. He began to swear vehemently making no effort to keep his voice quiet.

My heart dropped. Those weren't Texans Major had brought out, were they?

"Logan?" I said his name nervously.

His squeezed his eyes tightly shut at the sound of my voice, as though trying to block out the reality of his situation.

"Who are they?" I continued even though I was pretty sure I already knew the answer.

He opened his eyes and began to search my face imploringly. His voice sounded choked. "It wasn't supposed tae be like this. I told them I was out, that I wouldn't dae it anymore."

"Do what? Logan?"

"They said it was an object I was supposed tae bring tae them; they never said it was a person. I didn't know it was yae they were after till it was tae late."

Me? My heart fell as understanding dawned on me.

"Why?" I whispered, horror at what he had done preventing me from being able to push out anything more than that single word.

He shook his head bitterly, too ashamed to meet my eyes any longer. "They caught me just before Director Beckwith's team did. Said they would execute me if I didn't cooperate."

My mind felt numb. *He had joined my team only to betray me?* I had trusted him. A part of me still wanted to trust him. Even as the pain of betrayal swirled through me, disbelief stirred as well. I didn't understand. McLagan had always been so friendly to me. He had willingly stayed behind so that Thatcher could get me to safety at Aiden's home. He had worked beside me, smiling and laughing, on Thatcher's ranch. He had warned me about the attackers just moments ago. Had it all been a pretense?

"Why didn't you ask for help?" I was reaching for straws, hoping that Evans would get back quickly.

"From who?" He spat out bitterly as he turned angrily to face me. "They were from th' Directorate's office, Alex. Who was I supposed tae ask? Beckwith? I thought he was part of it."

"You could have asked your team," I said it automatically, still desperately searching for anything that would distract him until Evans got back. But he just shook his head in disgust, dismissing the suggestion even before I finished speaking it.

"We're Scots, Alex. Everyone knows we're th' expendable members of th' team. No one cares what happens tae us."

His frustration was palpable, but it was his words that stunned me. *Expendable?! How could he think that?* The question reverberated through my mind even as I took a step backward, instinctively placing more space between us. Suddenly I froze as the point of view unexpectedly shifted inside my mind. Always before, when I had tried to understand why someone did something, my understanding had been clearly tainted by my own way of thinking. It was like I cast my own voice onto their choices and saw their actions through a mirror that reflected myself. But, for the first time, I could see the moves and countermoves that had been forced on him and the corner he had been backed into from his point of view, completely free of my own voice.

He had been forced into the military at the age of fifteen. Forced to fight for a government he didn't agree with in a war he didn't want. He had a wife and child, but it was a family he would only ever be allowed to love from a distance because the bonds forced on him by the Scottish Accords would never allow for anything else.

I had read through the Accords for the first time a few days ago, trying to gain a better understanding of Roisin's bitterness toward them. What I had read had stunned me. The requirement that most people were familiar with, the one that forced their young men to serve in the UFC military, was only one of the many punishments the Accord outlined. A second punishment was the limitation of travel for the rest of the Scots; they were not allowed to travel outside of Scotland's borders. So, while most career soldiers could choose to have their families establish homes on or near their assigned bases, Scots didn't have that option.

A third punishment outlined in the Accords was the recognition that those young men that were given into military service were property of the UFC until such time as the UFC released them, and they were given few rights or privileges within that required service. They received no pay, little to no say in what they were called on to do, and no recourse when wronged. Logan would have had no way to support his family. It meant that his wife would have had to carry the burden of providing for herself and their daughter.

But my disgust at those punishments paled in comparison to what I had read next. I had struggled to believe it was possible even when the haunted glow in Roisin's eyes had left me with little doubt that she, at least, believed it to be true. I struggled to believe it still, even after I had read the words that could leave little room for doubt in my own mind: If any of the Scot's firstborn sons failed to fulfill their obligation to the UFC, the UFC had the right to execute them, and their families, as traitors.

So, if someone in the UFC Directorate's office had gone to Logan and told him that he was expected to report back to them on the location of an object, or even to deliver it to them, he would have had little choice but to do exactly that. Knowing that, if he didn't, they could execute him and his family for it.

I could see now why he had done exactly what they had told him to do, assuring himself the whole time that it was just an object. What did it matter if the UFC leadership played their little games with him as their pawn or if he was forced to carry out their whims even when it was contrary to what he himself wanted to do? The truth was that it hadn't mattered. Not really. At least, not until he had finally realized what was really at risk in this game of theirs. It wasn't an object he was being forced to betray to them; it was a person. And not just any person, but a person he had come to think of as a friend.

McLagan did not betray his friends or abandon them; he was not that type. So, he had tried instead to extract himself from their game, telling them that execution was preferable to continued betrayal. Only they had called his bluff. It wasn't his execution they were going to carry out, it was the execution of his wife and child.

My eyes shot up, meeting his as I finally understood. Cold, hard anger began to churn deep inside of me. I was not going to let this happen. As the fury rapidly raced through me, so did a buzzing sensation; as though electricity were flowing through my veins instead of blood. My fury was aimed at the

UFC and what they had done to Logan, but he had no way to know that.

A look of terror crossed his face as I stepped toward him. He took an involuntary step backward, at the same time fumbling to draw the gun holstered at his side. He pointed it at me shakily. "Alex, please. I didn't know. I didn't mean for this tae happen."

I almost laughed at the absurdity of the situation. His gun would be worthless against me; I knew that I could easily deflect any bolt he fired from it. Surely, he must know that as well. But then it occurred to me that he was just frightened. So, as gently as I could, I explained. "I do, Logan."

Confusion joined his fear. "Yae dae what?"

"I do care what happens to you and your family. And I am not going to let the UFC do this to you. So, if I'm the cost of your freedom, then you are going to give me to them."

His eyes widened as understanding dawned on him. Then his shock morphed into horror as he looked from me to the gun in his hands. "No," he said in sudden alarm, throwing the gun away like it was a snake that had reared up to bite him.

This time I did laugh as I looked at the gun at my feet with amusement. *He's refusing? Now, when he'd being told it's okay?* I knew exactly why he had thrown the gun away; that explanation was playing like a recorded lecture in the background of my mind. But that understanding didn't stop the frown that began to replace my laughter the longer I studied the gun. It represented all that was wrong in the UFC.

No! I thought in sudden anger. *He does not get to refuse this!* I took several steps toward him. "Like it or not," I told him coldly, raising my eyes to hold his, "you are going to give me to them."

Logan was shaking his head desperately, continuing to back away from me. I grabbed hold of the waves under his feet and locked them into place. Then I used more gravity waves to force his arm upward and the gun back into his trembling hand. Sweat beaded on his forehead as he fought to resist me.

"You will do exactly what I tell you to, Logan McLagan," I pushed on without pity. "Because if you don't, they will execute your wife and your child, and you will be forced to watch it happen." I was purposely being harsh. I didn't have time to argue with him. I didn't have time to explain the rest of the things that had clicked into place in my mind.

The same shift in point of view that had given me insight into his actions had given me the reasons behind the Major's as well. He would kill that woman and child without hesitation because he was the type of soldier who always found a way to carry out his orders, no matter the cost. He had been ordered to recover an asset and he believed that this was the surest way to get it done. He wouldn't understand McLagan's willingness to let his family die instead of completing the job they had given him because it was not something he himself would have ever considered doing. The only way to save McLagan's family, then, was to give Major exactly what he had asked for: *me*.

"Please, Alex," McLagan whispered shakily.

But I was not going to let him go. I refused to let his family die for me, and I refused to stand by and allow the UFC to destroy him.

I took the final step forward, closing the distance between us, and placed my hand around his trembling fingers so that they had to close on the gun at last. "You are going to have to trust me, Logan," I said gently. "I can save your family; I can save them all. But I need your help to do it. You still have my trust. I just need yours in return."

The faintest hint of hope had returned to Logan's eyes while I was talking. But when Major's voice called out, *"One minute,"* that spark of hope seemed to waver. He looked away from me, his eyes returning to his wife and child. I firmly reached up to turn his face back to mine. "Trust me, please."

That appeared to do it because he swallowed hard and finally nodded. "I trust yae, Alex. Tell me what yae want me tae dae."

Chapter 23: Lilith Alcott

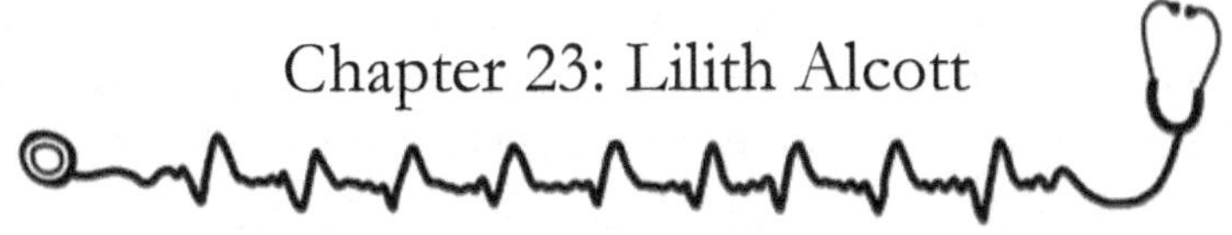

CODY'S HEAD WAS rocking from side to side, fever-sweat glistening on his brow. With each shift in direction, more incoherent words flowed from his lips. It was hard to watch, knowing that under normal circumstances I could have prevented this. Unfortunately, without the necessary medical supplies, there was little more I could do now then watch his decline.

The one thing I had been able to do was to relieve the pressure in his abdomen that had been continuing to build because of the internal bleeding. I'd used my knife and some tubing I'd found to accomplish that. But if his body didn't get relief from this fever soon, I risked having his organs start shutting down. Then there really would be nothing more I could do for him.

There were very few options available to me at this point. I had already searched the camp for any form of medicine and found none. I'd even considered trying to drag him back to the river so I could float him in its icy waters. But it had been hard enough just to move him sixty feet to this tent, and that had been with Paul's help. No. It was unlikely that I'd be able to get him back to the river on my own. The only other thing I could think of was to go looking for a natural remedy among the nearby plants.

I knew from my field medicine training that feverfew was a plant that could be used to reduce fevers. So was Mimosa pudica. And I was pretty sure that both of them could be found in this part of the United States. But the chance of finding them at night and in the dark wasn't good. Yet what choice did I have? If I waited till sunup, it might be too late.

I glanced back at Cody only to realize with a start that his head was no longer rocking. When had it stopped? Instinctively, I reached out to touch him. His chest was still moving, but he didn't otherwise respond. *He's getting weaker!* My fists clenched as I came to a decision. He couldn't wait; I needed to go now.

I grabbed the lamp and hurried out of the tent. It didn't matter which way I started walking. After all, any way was as good as another when I didn't know where to start. But it just happened that the tent was facing the general direction of the river, so that was the direction I walked.

As I moved away from the camp, I considered more carefully what I should be looking for. I quickly abandoned the idea of searching for the Mimosa pudica. Its leaves would have curled up for the night making it almost impossible to spot. So, feverfew it was. That meant I was looking for a short, bushy plant that had feathery leaves and small, white, daisy-like flowers.

The words of the field book drifted through my mind as I searched: *"While not native to the Americas, feverfew has spread throughout both continents since its introduction in the nineteenth century. It is commonly found along roadsides, fields, and on the edges of woodlands. It is also popular in home gardens due to its decorative nature and fragrant aroma. It can be identified by its fern-like feathery leaves, yellow center, and white petals. Its flowers can measure up to three-quarter inches. For fevers, ingesting two to three leaves should be sufficient."*

The book went on to outline additional ailments the plant could be used to treat, but I wasn't interested in those right now. Instead, I allowed my mind to move on to other textbooks as I continued to search.

Few people knew that I had a photographic memory. It was a big part of the reason I was so good at my job and why my training was so much more complete than the title "Nurse" implied. Once I read something, it was locked into my memory.

Back when I was in school, I had spent a considerable amount of time reading every medical text I could get my hands on. It had made me successful in my classes and later allowed me to become one of the top nurses in the military. At some point, reciting those texts in my mind had become a way to calm myself down during stressful situations. I guess that explained why the texts were running through my mind right now.

I had been walking for a while, stopping every now and then to look closer at one of the plants, when my thoughts were interrupted by an old, rusted, metal sign that glinted the lamp's light back at me from the darkness. Curiously, I walked around to the front of it so that I could read what it said. *Caution! Covered Well.* I looked down at the ground, almost in the same direction I had just come from, to see a rotted, wooden lid, about four-feet wide, partially covered by low spreading plants.

Well, that's not very safe, I thought to myself. I was glad I had not stepped on the rotted wood in the process of going around the sign. But then something else caught my attention. Some of the plants at the lid's edge were tightly curled in similar fashion to what the Mimosa pudica would do at night. I bent down to unfurl the leaves, hope rising in my chest, only to have the hope doused a second later by a jolt of fear in response to a faint sound I had just heard.

I hurried to turn the light off and duck behind the closest tree I could find, even as I silently prayed that I had reacted fast enough to avoid being seen. I cursed my stupidity for not being more conscientious about shielding the lamp's light so as to ensure that no one else out there could see it. The sound I'd heard had been the soft *whooshing* of air that happened when someone tried to muffle their sneeze. I heard it again, closer this time. Moving carefully, I set down the now dark lamp and reached for my knives.

A twig snapped nearby. With my senses heightened by fear, it sounded like the cracking of thunder. I tightened my grip on my knives and pressed my back harder against the tree.

A deep, coarse voice broke through the silence, almost too soft for me to hear. "You're louder than a herd of buffalo."

"Shut up," a Bronx accent retorted, not nearly so quietly. "You don't even know what buffalo sound like."

I recognized that voice! *Fischer! How?!* I fought down a wave of panic. How had they followed us?

The first voice countered softly, "Only because your people killed them all off."

"Just find them," Fischer snapped crossly. "Do your job so I can do mine."

There was another snort, but it sounded like it might have been further away than the first one had been. I prayed fervently that they were indeed moving away.

I stayed frozen against the tree for a long time. Were they gone yet? I strained to listen for anything more that would tell me they were nearby. The only thing I heard was the whisper of the gentle breeze in the leaves around me. Gradually, I took a chance and cautiously peaked out. The rush of adrenaline that accompanied my fear had caused my pupils to rapidly dilate, greatly increasing my ability to see in the darkness. There was no one there.

I closed my eyes and let my head fall back against the tree in relief. That relief was short lived as I suddenly remembered Cody. My heart lurched into my throat and I shoved myself off the tree. I had to get back before they found him!

I took off as quietly as I could. I was far from being silent, but I had grown up near the woods and had gone hunting often enough with my papa and brothers that I knew how to avoid stepping on anything that would make loud noises. I was also willing to give up some silence in favor of speed because they had a head start on me. But, unlike them, I knew where the camp was. And I was not about to let them anywhere near it.

Chapter 24: Aiden Haskell

A STRING OF curses rang through my head as I watched Carter push the woman and child ahead of him. I'd seen him use this tactic before and new what it meant. But who was he targeting?

My mind raced to find the answer. He'd said their job was to deliver an item. *What item?* The situation with Remington flashed through my mind. Remington had known we were transporting an item of power, even though no one should have known about it. Had someone on our team betrayed us to him? That possibility had not occurred to me before now, but it would sure explain a lot. If so, then who would it be? Evans had only joined us recently, so he didn't seem likely.

"Two minutes," Carter called out.

Thatcher? No. Carter wouldn't be addressing the trees if it was Thatcher.

Wren? As far as I knew, he was still on the other side of the river. He and one of the Texans had crossed it just before I made my move, following the two men Carter had been chastising. If he was Carter's target, then it was unlikely he was within hearing range to respond to it.

McLagan? He was old enough to be married and have a child, but he'd never said anything about having a family. We'd even been in Scotland. Wouldn't he have made an effort to see them while we were there?

"One minute!"

I shook my head in frustration. *What am I wasting time for?!* No amount of time spent trying to figure out who the traitor was would help me save her so long as she was already out there with them and I was still over here. *I need to get to her, now!* I took several slow, careful steps backward toward the trees.

"Take another step, Haskell, and I'll shoot the kid."

I froze. I knew all too well that he would do it; he would do whatever he thought it took to accomplish his mission. He'd always looked at the death of innocents as a necessary cost in war and looked down on those who weren't willing to pay that price as well. Because he respected me in every other way, he had decided early on in our association that my failure to see it the same way was my Achilles heel, my only flaw. Well, only flaw or not, he wouldn't hesitate to use it against me. I clenched my fists in frustration. This time it was going to keep me from being able to help Alex!

With a cold smile, Carter turned away from me to scan the tree line once more. "Times up!" he shouted a moment later as he shoved the woman to her knees and pointed his gun at the back of her head.

"No!" I yelled, automatically stepping forward even as I knew there was no way I could help her.

At the same time, McLagan's voice called out, "Wait!"

McLagan? What is he doing?! My chest constricted as a figure stumbled out of the trees, blindfolded and hands bound.

Alex! McLagan followed her out. He grabbed her by the arm and shoved her forward once more. As he did so, she tried to yank her arm free, but he only tightened his grip and forced her forward once again.

It was then that I noticed the dirt stains on her elbow and shoulder, a dark smudge on her forehead, and the tousled state of her hair and clothes. Anger began to mingle with my alarm. McLagan had clearly not been gentle with her.

"What is this?" Carter asked in obvious irritation. "You were told to bring me the asset you were transporting, not some woman."

"I couldn't brin' yae th' asset; Haskell has it." McLagan called back nervously.

I have it? What in blazes is he saying?

"But this is his girl," McLagan continued without pause as he forced her forward once more. "He'll dae anythin' tae protect her."

Carter's eyes narrowed angrily; he knew me too well to believe McLagan's claim that I had let a woman into my heart, and he had no patience for liars. "Haskell doesn't have a woman," he retorted coldly.

McLagan shook his head insistently as he asserted again, "He has this one. Please, I'm tellin' yae th' truth." His eyes darted nervously from Carter, to the woman, and then back again.

Carter was clearly not inclined to believe him, but he had once told me that only a fool wouldn't consider the possibility that even a liar tells the truth once in a while. So, when Carter turned back to me, I knew what he was looking for. I needed him to continue to believe that Alex couldn't possibly mean anything to me, so I shook my head as though amused by

McLagan's claim and tried to project an air of disgust. Unfortunately, Carter must have seen something that tipped him off because his expression slowly morphed into a wicked smile accompanied by an amused chortle. "So, someone finally broke through those impregnable defenses of yours."

My heart sank. *He knows!*

Still chuckling to himself, he turned back to McLagan. "All right then, I'll make a trade with you. Haskell's woman for yours. But I'll be keeping your kid until I have that asset."

McLagan's wife began furiously shaking her head and pulled the girl in front of her to wrap her arms protectively around her. Carter only nodded to two of his soldiers. I knew one of them: Dillon. He was like Carter in his view of innocents on the battlefield, just more mean-spirited about it. Inwardly I cringed as he roughly grabbed the woman's arms and forced them open, allowing the other soldier to grab the child away from her. Even through the gag, I could hear her furious screams.

Ignoring her cries, Dillon next grabbed her by the hair and forced her over to McLagan where he shoved her to the ground at his feet. Then he turned to forcefully grab Alex's arm and yank her away. I expected her to resist him as well. To my surprise, she didn't. Instead, she meekly allowed him to pull her along. That didn't make sense. Why wasn't she fighting him?

McLagan ignored what was happening to Alex and hurried to help his wife back to her feet. He ignored her furious glare and pulled her into a tight hug. Her back stiffened as he did so. She clearly was not happy with him. I hoped bitterly that she never forgave him for what he had just done.

Dillon shoved Alex toward Carter, causing her to stumble against him. Carter didn't seem bothered by it. Instead, he studied her for a moment, taking the time to brush a loose strand of hair away from her face before finally turning her around to face me. The muscles in my jaw twitched angrily.

"Well then, Haskell," he said through lips still twisted in a faint smile. "Shall we try this again? I believe you have something I want."

On the outside I tried my best to keep my expression calm, but inside I was fighting a raging torrent of fury, frustration, and fear. He had Alex! And he had her because I had left her in the care of a traitor!

McLagan! I thought furiously. He was still holding the woman he had betrayed Alex for. I was going to kill him! I…W*ait! What in the Light is going on?*

McLagan had just let his wife go then moved his hands so that they were in front of her where Carter couldn't see and was dramatically pointing to his wrists and then to me, followed by the sign to regroup. *Regroup? Regroup what? And why was that traitor signaling me to do anything?*

But, before I had time to come up with any type of explanation, something small bumped against my fist. I glanced down sharply to see a flat, smooth stone, perhaps an inch in diameter, hovering in the air next to me. My confusion deepened. How was this possible? The only person who could make this happen was Alex, but she was blindfolded. She couldn't possibly see the waves to control it with. I looked up at her and had to immediately backpedal on that assumption. In spite of the blindfold, she was looking straight back at me. The only answer that made any sense was that, somehow, she could see through the material covering her eyes.

Moving discreetly, I opened my fist. She smoothly moved the stone so that it was now nestled in the palm of my hand. It fit there perfectly as I closed my fingers around it.

"Well, Haskell?" Carter reiterated. "What will it be?"

I quickly considered this new information, desperately trying to make sense of it. McLagan had obviously betrayed Alex, but now he was trying to tell me something without Carter seeing it. What was he playing at? *If he's hoping to earn back a measure of forgiveness, he's a fool!* I thought furiously. And what did it mean that Alex was able to see through that blindfold? If McLagan had truly wanted to make a prisoner of her, he should have never left a way for her to use her gravity against him.

Then I had to shake my head to clear it of those thoughts. *Focus!* Right now, I needed to answer Carter. He wouldn't wait around while I figured everything out.

There was no chance in the Light I was going to tell him that Alex was the asset he was looking for, and telling him that she was a Child of Icarus was absolutely out of the question as well. So, what then? What would he believe?

McLagan was watching me intently. He pointed to his wrists again. Instinctively, I glanced down at my own wrists. My eyes focused on the damaged skin there. It was no longer red and raw from my attempts to escape the chair Estradé had strapped me into so that I couldn't interfere with the procedure they had done on Alex, but the three-inch wide scabs that were forming as part of the healing process were readily visible. *My wrists? Regroup?* Suddenly I understood.

Carter and his soldiers didn't know what the asset was or he would have recognized that he already had it. That meant it could be anything I told him it was. And McLagan had just told them that he couldn't bring it to them because I had it. A cold, hard smile lifted the corners of my lips as I looked back up. I still wouldn't be forgiving McLagan for what he had done, but at least now I knew exactly what I was going to tell Carter.

"Whoever gave yae yer orders, Major, was either a fool or didn't have accurate information. The asset yae were told tae recover is not somethin' yae can simply take away from me. It's not a box like C.H.A.O.S."

I raised my wrists to eye level in front of me. Even from this distance, the three-inch-wide scabs would be clearly visible to everyone.

"The scientists implanted th' asset intae me arms. They gave me a new way tae fight Icarus. Now *I* am th' asset." I emphasized the word "I".

Carter's smile slid off, a frown taking its place. I seriously doubted that he believed me, but the truth was that this particular show wasn't just for him; it was also for all those soldiers around him who were second guessing their orders right now. This was for my old company.

I'd been with them for more than a year. In that time, they had come to know me reasonably well. They knew me as a seasoned soldier, tried and proven in combat. They knew that I had always been the one they could trust to have their backs. They knew that I hated Icarus and his children and they knew the reason behind that hatred. They also knew that I had taken on any mission that had anything to do with one of those children and they knew that I had accomplished every single one of those missions. I wanted them to remember that side of me right now and to decide that it was in their best interests to get out of my way.

Several of them began to shift nervously. I was pushing the limits of plausibility with my story, but then, so had C.H.A.O.S. when the scientists had told us what it would do, and every one of them had since seen that asset's effectiveness. Beyond that, there had been rumors of scientists running experiments on people for years, and these people knew that the Ghana Base's primary group which I had left them to join was put together for the purpose of finding a better way to fight Icarus' Alphas. So, many of them would buy my story, if I could just sell it to them the right way.

"I wasn't th' first one they tried tae dae this with, but I am th' first one they succeeded with. I and me new team were created tae bring down Icarus. But we can bring yae down just as easily if yae stand in our way. So yae will return our teammates tae us, as well as th' others yae kidnapped tonight, or we will march through yae and take yae down one by one till there is no one left standin'.""

Carter was not at all impressed to hear my speech; I watched his lips tighten into a hard line. When he finally spoke, it was with that quiet, dangerous tone of his. "This is all you're going to get from us, Haskell." He stepped forward and roughly shoved Alex down to her knees.

My façade of confidence faltered for the briefest of seconds as my terror flared to new heights, only to have it replaced a second later by confusion as an unexpected flicker of movement at Alex's side caught my attention. She had just moved her hand beside her leg and was signaling for me to hold position. *First, she can see through the blindfold and now her hands aren't even bound?! What in the Light is going on?!*

The answer hit me like a nuclear shockwave immediately followed by a raging wildfire of fury. *Of all the Light forsaken, stupid things to do! Alex was not a prisoner; she was exactly where she wanted to be! She had planned this!* It took everything I had to keep my expression steady as that realization settled on me.

Alex began lifting her hand ever so slightly and slowly spread her fingers apart. I gritted my teeth in frustration. I knew what she wanted me to do; it all made sense to me now. But how could she expect me to stand here, unable to do anything more than pretend, while she was in very real danger? My fists clenched tighter. They were now so tight that the small stone was biting into my skin.

As though reading my thoughts, she increased the gravity under my feet for just the briefest of seconds before returning it to normal again. The muscle in my jaw twitched in response; the only other outward sign of my internal struggle. Alex's lips lifted ever so slightly into a sad smile as her hand closed into a fist that then moved in a tight circle again. *Hold position.*

I wanted to scream in frustration, only I couldn't. The only way I could help her now was to keep the deception going. So, I took a calming breath while I rapidly fought to pull myself back together. Then I looked back up to meet Carter's eyes.

In spite of my best efforts, some of my fury and frustration leaked through into my voice as I angrily said, "Yae should have given me what I asked for. It didn't have tae be this way; I don't like hurtin' friends." Then, making a show of it, I slowly raised my tightly clenched hands until my forearms were level with the ground. *Alex had better be right about this!*

Carter raised his gun in time with my hands, pointing it at the back of Alex's head. My jaw was clenched so tightly that my teeth ached.

"Say goodbye to your girl," he said coldly.

I shot my fingers apart, flaring them out. The rock that had been fitted there stuck to my hand for a full second before it finally fell to the ground. Appearing to be in response to the motion of my fingers, Carter's gun was suddenly wrenched from his hand. It landed with a heavy thud and sank into the soil deep enough that only the tip of the barrel was visible.

Carter swore fiercely, cradling his hand tightly as though the gun had wrenched his fingers on its way down. At the same time, the soldier who had been holding McLagan's daughter yelped as his gun was likewise inexplicably jerked out of his hands and he was thrown back against the truck behind him. With no one holding her back any longer, the little girl ran for her mother. The moment she was wrapped up in her mother's arms, McLagan hurried them to safety.

In spite of my anger with Alex, I watched in awe as she continued her assault. She moved her head from side to side as though trying to hear what was happening while yanking weapons from the hands of soldier after soldier and sending their guns flying into the river. If any of them got a shot off before she was able to get their weapon, she slammed the bolt into the ground then sent that soldier either flying out the window or flying back against the closest vehicle or building depending on where they were. She didn't stop until there was no one left to fight back.

Then, appearing to have somehow freed her hands, she pulled the blindfold from her eyes and stood up. She turned to face Carter, looking him up and down, clearly unimpressed by what she saw.

"Where are they?" she said coldly. Her tone surprised me; I had never heard it so icy before. In a small corner of my mind there were alarm bells going off again, but I wasn't focused on that right now. When Carter didn't immediately answer, she took a step toward him. To my complete shock, Carter stepped back. It was the first time I had ever seen him retreat from anything. Then he shook his head as though uncertain himself why he had just retreated. His lips drew into a snarl.

"We were following our orders," he growled; another thing I'd never seen him do before. He was the type of man who always had complete control of his emotions.

"Orders?!" Alex spat back furiously. "Your orders were to kill innocent people and make prisoners of your fellow soldiers?"

For the briefest of seconds, a look of discomfort crossed Carter's face, but it was gone just as quickly as it had appeared. His expression hardened and he was in control of his emotions once more. "I don't have to explain anything to you."

Alex laughed without mirth, shaking her head in obvious disgust. "You're right," she replied coldly. "You don't have to tell me anything. But you will have to explain it to them. They want to know where their children are, and they aren't going to be nearly so nice about it as we would have been."

From the corner of my eyes, I saw several figures stepping out from among the trees. With the gray light of the pre-dawn sky finally lightening the shadows, I was able to make out the figures of the Texans as they emerged from the tree line. They had their weapons trained on the soldiers around Carter and were pushing several more in front of them that they had captured during the fighting. Thatcher's father strode ahead of the rest, clearly the leader of the group. Alex stepped back to allow him to take her place in front of Carter.

Carter was not a small man, but Mr. Thatcher towered over him. Like Carter, he showed very little emotion on his face, yet that somehow made him even more imposing.

"I'm only going to ask this once," he said softly. "Where is my son?"

Carter's lips drew into a tight line as he squared his shoulders and stared straight ahead, refusing to meet his eyes.

Mr. Thatcher nodded to himself, his lips tightening ever so slightly. Then, before I had time to register what he was about to do, he drew his gun in a fluid motion and shot Carter in the leg. Carter gasped, collapsing to the ground as he clamped his hands over the gaping wound. Mr. Thatcher turned away from him, ignoring him now as he walked over to the next soldier.

"I'm only going to ask this once," he said softly.

The man shot a desperate look at Carter, but clenched his mouth shut. Mr. Thatcher raised his gun, pointing it at the man's shoulder. "Where's my son?"

"Stop," Carter called out in a strained voice. Mr. Thatcher paused to look back at him.

Though I didn't let it show, I felt a flash of satisfaction. Carter might not have a problem with injuries to civilians, but when it came to his own soldiers, that was a whole different matter.

"Avery," Carter called out between steadying breaths, "take him to them."

Mr. Thatcher nodded and holstered his gun. He looked to several of the closer Texans. "Go bring them home."

While Avery led the group into the building, Mr. Thatcher turned back to Carter.

"I want your people off our land immediately, and you are to take this message with you: If the UFC comes back here, they'll find they've dug up more snakes than they can kill."

Carter nodded and said through gritted teeth, "I'll pass on your message." It was obvious he wasn't happy with the situation, but I also got the distinct impression that he had gained a measure of respect for Mr. Thatcher.

Mr. Thatcher nodded once more, then glanced down at Carter's leg consideringly. "You should probably do something about that. Don't want you bleeding out before you deliver my message."

Carter grunted in mild amusement. Mr. Thatcher's comment had sounded exactly like something he would have said had their positions been reversed.

Well, Mr. Thatcher clearly had things in hand. It was time for me to deal with other individuals; or, rather, one person in particular. Now I knew how the UFC had known about the asset of power and our location. But I had just turned away, fully intending to find McLagan and shoot him, when Carter's strained voice stopped me. "Your team really the ones who took down Talos?"

I didn't bother to turn around, but answered over my shoulder, "Aye. We did."

"Thatcher and Alcott are part of your team?"

"They are," I nodded, not sure where his questions were leading.

His next question clearly wasn't aimed at me. "You Thatcher's father?"

I didn't hear a verbal response, but suspected that some type of response had been given because Carter went on a moment later, "Figured as much." He paused for a second to catch his breath again before going on. "Then I guess the two of you should probably know that they aren't with the rest of the prisoners."

I spun around angrily, only to find that Thatcher's father had beaten me to him. "Where are they?" he asked coldly, towering over him once more.

"They escaped," Carter said with the faintest hint of amusement. "Fischer and Three Bulls bungled their job locking them up. Last I saw, those two boys were heading across the river, looking to clean up their mess."

My back stiffened. So that's what those two had gone across the river for. Out of the corner of my eye, I saw Mr. Thatcher's hand clenching next to his gun. I suspected he was considering the benefits of shooting Carter again. But then he seemed to change his mind and he instead hollered, "Hillock! Get this piece of filth out of my sight. Samuel, Craig, I want you boys with me." Just before turning to walk away, he looked over at me. "You coming?"

I nodded. "Right behind yae, sir."

As I turned to follow him, my gaze fell briefly on Alex. She was still standing upright, though there was a slouch to her shoulders and a sheen of sweat on her brow that told me she had pushed herself too hard once again. Part of me felt the desperate need to go over there and make sure she was okay; to wrap my arms around her protectively so that no one could threaten her again. But the rest of me was still burning with fury.

I wasn't beyond understanding why she had done it. Because of her decision, this battle was over and McLagan's family was safe. But it had been the stupidest, Light-blinded, foolhardy decision she could have possibly made. And, because she had done it, I had been forced to watch, helpless to do anything to protect her. I was furious with her for putting me through that.

I felt my jaw clench tighter as our eyes met. There was a look of uncertainty in hers that had not been there five minutes ago when Carter had been holding a gun to her head. *Now she's concerned about what I think?* I shook my head in frustration. No. Now would not be a good time for me to talk to her. Right now, what I needed was some space; I needed time to cool down before I said something stupid that I would regret later. So, I paused only long enough to pointedly say, "Stay here. We'll talk when I get back." Then, ignoring the flash of worry in her eyes, I kept walking.

Chapter 25: Icarus Argyros 

WAS IT POSSIBLE that I had been mistaken? I reached forward to replay the video, watching it more closely for the answer to my question.

The video had been sent to me by one of my pawns in the UFC strike force, the Caledonians. She had begun filming the attack as soon as it became evident that an Alpha was involved. Unfortunately, the angle of the video was not ideal, and she had not been able to film the entire encounter, but it was sufficient to raise doubts in my mind regarding Alexander.

It was the look of concern on his face as he glanced toward the tree line that had caught my attention. Who was out there, and why had his concern for them started only after the truck had nearly fallen on him?

I fast forwarded to the moment McLagan had pushed Alexander's girl out into the open. She exited the tree line from the same spot Alexander's previous glance had been directed.

I sat back in thoughtful contemplation, then nodded my head as understanding came to me at last. It was time to take a closer look at this young lady.

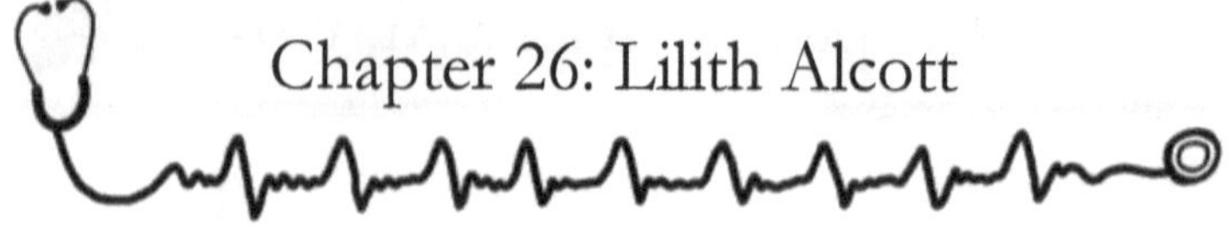

Chapter 26: Lilith Alcott

MY BROTHER BEAU would have been proud if he could have seen me tonight. He'd always said I was the best in the family when it came to moving silently through the woods so as not to spook the animals we were hunting. Tonight, I'd managed to keep two men from knowing I was there while still running for all I was worth through the trees at night. I'd made it to the camp ahead of them, if only by a minute or two, but it had been enough.

I had foolishly left the gun in the tent at Cody's side when I had gone looking for the feverfew. I grabbed it now, pausing only long enough to assure myself that he was still alive, then I made a beeline for the spot where the side-by-side was supposed to have been hidden.

It had occurred to me that one of those two men must be a tracker. There was no other explanation for how they had found us so quickly. But that also told me that they would be following the same trail we had taken to get here. In other words, I knew where they were going to be next and I planned to use that information to my advantage.

I got into position just in the nick of time as the bright beam of their flashlight cut around the bend. I carefully aimed the gun. I wasn't a bad shot with a phase pistol, but I also wasn't a great one. I was only likely to get one clean shot off before they scattered; I needed it to count.

Come on! I thought anxiously as the moment stretched into seconds without anyone stepping into view. *What's taking them so long?* I could see the beam of their light, sweeping back and forth across the ground, but they hadn't rounded the corner yet.

It was instinct that saved me as I felt a sudden prickling sensation at the base of my neck. I spun around, just in time to see a dark shadow rising up behind me. Before I could even squeeze the trigger, the gun was knocked from my hand.

It was the Indian, the one whose nose I had broken. A small, disappointed thought flashed through my mind: I must not have been as successful as I had first thought; they had known I was there. I dove to the side, narrowly avoiding the blow he swung at me. I came up with my garter belt knife in hand, the way papa had taught me to do. Seeing it, he scoffed and pulled out his own, bigger knife. His thrusts were swift and smooth; he knew how to use the blade. It was all I could do to block him.

I kept backing up, doing my best to stay out of his reach. I didn't dare take my eyes off of him long enough to make sure there was nothing behind me, so I wasn't surprised when I bumped into something solid. I was surprised when it reached around me to pin my arms at my side.

"Got her!" Fischer shouted triumphantly as he lifted me off the ground. I screamed in frustration and struggled to break free of his hold. The more I struggled, the tighter he squeezed.

In front of me, the Indian approached and forced the knife from my hand. He tossed it away with a tiny self-satisfied smirk.

"Where's your boyfriend now?" Fischer sneered in my ear. "I'm guessing he's not coming to protect you this time; Three Bulls says his tracks were getting pretty unsteady back there. Why don't you show us where he is so I can finish what I started."

Not on your life! I thought furiously. But I couldn't seem to break his grip; his hold was too strong. I wanted to scream. If I had thought it would do any good, I might have. Except, Papa's instructions had just begun to replay in the back of my mind like an audio recording. I heard his stern voice. *Calm down, Lil! The more you struggle, the tighter I'll squeeze. You want me to relax, so you need to relax first. Trick me into thinking that you are no longer a threat.* I forced myself to heed his words and stop fighting. As Papa had promised, Fischer's hold began to relax in response.

"That's a good girl," he laughed coarsely as he set me back down, no longer holding me off the ground, but still holding firmly to my arms. "See, that's how a woman should respond to a man."

How a woman should respond?! I was disgusted, but didn't bother to answer. Instead, I kicked back suddenly with my heel. It connected with his shin. He swore, his hands reflexively letting go of me in response to the pain. The instant I was free, I spun around and showed him how a woman should respond to a man like him by kicking him in the groin. Then I ran.

Behind me, his furious howls were intermixed with shouted demands for Three Bulls to shoot me. I kept running, praying the trees and the darkness would be enough to shield me from their phase bolts. There were a lot of those blasts lighting the darkness around me.

Wait! That bolt just came from in front of me! My steps faltered and my heart dropped. I was trapped!

A familiar voice shouted from somewhere ahead of me, "Keep running! We've got you covered."

Wren? Another phase bolt streaked past my shoulder, providing just enough light for me to make out the speaker. It was Wren! He was kneeling on the ground next to a tree, along with another man I didn't know, firing back at Fischer and Three Bulls. I redoubled my effort and ran for the safety they offered.

"Where's Thatcher?" Wren asked between blasts as I slid to a stop behind him.

"Injured," I got out between relieved gasps of breath. "I need to get back to him soon and get him to a hospital or he's not going to make it."

Wren seemed to consider my words for the briefest of moments. Then he turned to his companion. "Continue laying down fire; keep them distracted. I'm going to work my way around and get behind them." The man nodded his understanding between shots. Wren turned to me next and handed me his gun. "Help him with that cover fire so they don't realize anything has changed." Before I could respond, Wren disappeared into the shadows.

It was a relief to know that I now had help, but it only slightly improved my position. Assuming everyone's weapons were fully charged, this could easily turn into an impasse that would delay getting Cody the medical help he needed. I couldn't afford that. Worse, Fischer and Three Bulls were now between me and Cody.

As I fired shots toward Fischer and Three Bulls, I considered possible alternatives. Was there a way I could create a distraction? Something that would help Wren to be able to sneak up on them and not get me shot in the process? And then it hit me. A cold smile crossed my lips as I made my way to the man who had come with Wren and told him what I had in mind. He laughed softly and said, "Go. I've got this covered." That was all I needed.

Chapter 27: Lakota Wren

HASKELL HAD WARNED me about these two men before I crossed the river to follow them. Fischer, he had said, was a sharpshooter, similar to Thatcher though not quite as good. He'd warned me that, even so, what he aimed for he usually hit, and that he had an ego the size of Texas because of it.

Three Bulls was another story; this one I knew. Haskell had said that Three Bulls was a tracker like me. It was clear that Haskell did not know our ways. Three Bulls was more than a tracker; he was a Ghost Walker. I had suspected that a Ghost Walker was working with the UFC when I searched Mr. Hillock's property. I was certain of it after searching the barn tonight. Tracks had been missing in both of those places at key points where tracks should have been. Only a Ghost Walker was capable of that.

To be a Ghost Walker was to walk like the wind. To leave no sign of one's passage. To know the Earth around them so well, that they became one with it. But it was also to walk half in this world and half in the world of the dead. Our legends teach that they are the guides to the world of the dead. In my tribe, the Ghost Walker works closely with our Shaman when sickness comes. Together, they would either guide the sick back to health or they would guide them into the afterlife. It was not so for all tribes.

I knew of at least one tribe whose Ghost Walkers had abandoned the old ways and were using their training for personal gain and honor, and I had heard rumors that there were others. I believed that Three Bulls belonged to one of these; he would not be in the military otherwise.

It also meant that he was going to be a dangerous opponent and I would need to be cautious. There are few alive who can follow a Ghost Walker's trail; I am one of those few. It is a skill that has been passed from father to son in my tribe. I had been trained by my father, as he had been trained by his father before him. But it was also a highly guarded secret. Not even the Ghost Walker in our tribe knew that we could track him. It wasn't a matter of pride; it was a matter of life. If a Ghost Walker knew there was someone who could track them, they would see that person dead before nightfall.

I spared a step to glance up at the sky. The stars were gone and the black had lightened to a deep gray. The sun would be rising soon. I would have to be careful that they couldn't see me against the increasing light.

It was my intent to come up behind Three Bulls and Fischer. I was a silent enough walker that they were unlikely to hear my approach, and so far it was working. I had circled to the east and moved past them in the dark. Now I could see them in front of me and neither seemed to be aware of my presence. Fischer was my first target. His skills with the gun meant that I could not leave one in his hands. But just as I was about to step out into the open, Miss Alcott's voice startled me as it called out tauntingly, "Hey Fischer, how are you feeling? Still think your man enough for me or did I do some damage to that precious manhood of yours?"

To my surprise, her voice had not come from the location where I had left her. Instead, it seemed that she had moved to the west by quite some distance. Her taunt surprised me as well. It was not something I would have expected to hear from her, especially not in this situation. But Fischer's reaction suggested that she had chosen her words wisely.

He spit in the dirt next to him and said with an angry tone, "That wench is mine. You can deal with the other scum." Not giving Three Bulls an opportunity to stop him, he stormed off in the direction of Miss Alcott's voice.

I was impressed by the boldness of her move, and the success of it. She had just divided an enemy that should have known better than to separate. Grinning to myself, I silently pulled my knife from its sheath and rose up. Like a coyote hunting, I stalked toward Three Bulls. Unfortunately, I had underestimated the level of his skill.

I had not made any sounds, but he spun around to face me while I was still several steps from him. I dropped to the ground to avoid the phaser shot he fired at me, then rolled to my knees and released my knife in a fluid motion. The heavy handle of my knife struck his gun squarely on the side of its barrel, knocking it from his hands.

He growled and lunged at me, knocking me to the ground. We grappled hand to hand in the darkness; strength against strength, skill against skill. It was a warrior's fight, like our ancestors of old had fought. His training pitted against mine.

For a moment, he had the advantage as he rolled me onto my back, using his free hand to pull his own knife from its sheath. His lips split into a cruel smile, and his gruff voice laughed, "What tribe should I send your scalp to when I am finished here?"

I didn't allow myself to become afraid, but I did tell him who he was facing. "I am of the coyote," I said, just before I used my arm and leg to throw him off balance and kick him over my shoulder.

"Nex Perz," he spat back in disgust after coming to his feet. Then he shook his head and laughed. "A worthy opponent then. I shall enjoy skinning your hide all the more, pup."

Our words ceased and we continued the fight. When his strength forced me to step backward, I called on the spirit of the coyote to empower me and I stepped forward, gaining ground. When his blow struck me in the face, I did not bow down, but rose up once more. It was the spirit of my people that carried me forward each time.

It soon became apparent that I was the stronger fighter, a fact that brought him no joy. With a growl of anger, he took a final swing at me then turned and ran away into the darkness.

I pursued him through the trees, only to lose him some distance later; he was a fast runner and it was still dark among the trees. Knowing that he could have gone anywhere, I stopped to listen to the sounds. I closed my eyes so that I could focus deeper. The wind whispered through the trees. A barn owl hooted; its call returned seconds later by the higher pitched hoot of its mate. A woodpecker drilled into a tree. These were the sounds that belonged. But then a mourning dove cooed off to my left, its call was the one it made when it was disturbed by something too close to its nest. I opened my eyes and moved in the direction its call had come from. As I walked, I searched the ground. There were no footprints; I knew there would be none. Instead, I searched for a different type of track; the type my father had trained me to see.

There it was. It indicated that he had moved toward an outcropping of rocks that were big enough to hide within. I placed my feet carefully so as to not make a sound and circled around to the backside of the rocks. My skill was rewarded as one of the shadows nestled among the rocks moved ever so slowly, so that the man it belonged to could peak toward the road. He did not suspect that I was behind him.

Without warning, I lunged. The startled look on his face just before I slammed him against the rocks was very rewarding. Before he could recover, I swung my fist up under his chin. I watched with satisfaction as his eyes rolled up into his head and he slumped to the ground.

I bound his hands with the length of rope I had been using as a belt. But as I bent down to lift him to my shoulders, a movement on top of the rocks caught my attention. I looked up sharply to see a large silvered coyote looking down at me, its eyes seeming to be backlit by a faint golden glow. When our eyes met, it blinked, then lifted its head and emitted a series of yip howls that were answered seconds later by several others some distance away. With a final look down at me, it turned and disappeared into the trees.

Chapter 28: Lilith Alcott

FISCHER WAS FASTER than I was, which meant that I was having to run extra hard in order to keep far enough ahead of him. If I'd had more time, I would have gotten things ready first and then come back to taunt him into following me, but that hadn't been an option. So, instead, I'd tried to give myself enough distance to give me the head start I needed, while praying that I could run fast enough to maintain it. The truth was that even if I wasn't successful at my end goal, I had at least gotten him to follow me, which meant that Wren only had to deal with one of them now; at least that much of my plan had worked.

I was starting to gasp for breath as I ran, but I didn't have much further to go. Giving it all I had, I put on a final burst of speed, not slowing until the metal pole was finally in front of me. Then, not wasting time to see how close behind me he was, I used Wren's gun to heat the metal near its base. I kicked it hard, snapping it cleanly off. Next, I picked up the pole and threw it as far away as I could; unfortunately, not before Fischer rounded the corner.

He slowed to a stop, eyeing me mistrustfully. "What was that?" He lifted his chin to indicate the direction I had sent the pole flying.

Well, darn it. I'd hoped to be far enough ahead that he wouldn't have seen any hint of what I was up to. But, since he'd seen me throw something, I was going to turn it to my advantage. I knew from years of practicing on my brothers that I could be very annoying when I wanted to be. And right now, I would take Fischer focused on anything except for his surroundings. So, I started to back away from him while smiling coyly and pouring on all the Southern charm I could muster, "Well, bless your heart, but that's not really any of your business now is it, Sugar? After all, I can't think of any reason why I should tell a polecat like you anything at all."

His scowl deepened and, for just a moment, I had reason to think my plan might work as he took several steps toward me. But then he stopped, his expression morphing into a wicked smile.

"That's fine," he said with an oily tone. "You go ahead and keep your secret. Just know that I'm going to enjoy making you pay for your insolence all the more. Then I'm going to go find that man of yours and make you watch while I finish the beating you interrupted."

Somehow, I kept that sickeningly sweet smile on my face, in spite of wanting to claw his eyes out, and kept talking, all the while continuing to take careful steps backward. "Oh, I sincerely doubt that." I even managed to force a giggle. "From what I've seen so far, there's not much difference between you and the Babcock brothers back home: all talk, no real skills, and not a lick of a brain between them."

He took a single angry step forward, only to stop again. *Come on!* I thought in silent frustration. *What's it going to take to get you to come this way?* I decided to change tactics.

"Actually," I said, dropping the coy smile and the southern charm, "I think I'm not being fair to the Babcock brothers. They at least have a set of morals. You're just an arrogant, yellow-bellied dirtbag who's too cowardly to face anyone in a fair fight. You talk about being a man, but you're not even half the man Cody is."

I kept talking, throwing out more and more insults about his manhood with every careful step I took. But, instead of following me, his smile grew increasingly colder until finally he raised his gun and pointed it at me. I froze, feeling my insides go cold. I knew in that instant that I had failed; He was going to shoot me instead of coming after me.

Before I could even squeeze the trigger to defend myself, he had already released two blasts. The first one knocked the gun from my hands. The second one sliced an inch wide trail across the surface of my upper arm. I cried out in pain, instinctively reaching up to cover the injury.

"That," he said with a wicked chortle, "is for the cut you gave me on my arm. This one is for your insolence." He shifted the aim of his gun in less than a heartbeat and gave me a second burn across my thigh.

I cried out again, even as I staggered sideways. This burn was deeper than the first, and both were very painful, but the truth was that neither of them had cut through to muscle and neither was life threatening. He was just toying with me. I realized that I still had a chance. I gritted my teeth and limped back another few steps, this time being especially careful of my footing and the terrain beneath me.

Finally, he started to come toward me with a self-assured saunter. In an arrogantly confident tone he ordered, "Now. You're going to tell me where Thatcher is. Of course, you can either tell me willingly or I can torture it out of you. Personally, I'm hoping for the second option; it's more fun that way."

"I'm not telling you anything," I spat back acridly, no longer pretending. As I limped backward another few careful steps, I reached down to pull the knife from my boot and held it out in front of me defensively with my good hand.

"I was hoping you would say that," his smile broadened. He had fired another scorching blast before he had even finished speaking. This one took me full in the leg, knocking it out from under me. I collapsed to the ground with a cry of pain. I didn't need to look at the wound to know it was a bad one.

Finally, Fischer closed the distance between us and crouched down beside me. With one hand, he pushed his gun into my shoulder. With the other, he wrenched the knife out of my hand and tossed it behind him. Then he lifted my chin so that I had to meet his eyes. There was a hunger there that made me feel sick. Almost feverishly, he crooned softly, "I'm really going to enjoy teaching you some manners."

Not happening! I thought triumphantly as I jerked my chin out of his hand and flung myself onto my back. I coiled my good leg to my chest and kicked back out as hard as I could. My foot caught him in the shoulder and sent him reeling sideways. His arms windmilled as he tried to regain his balance, but the dull thud of rotted wood under his feet gave way to the sound of splintering, followed immediately by the ground giving out from underneath him. I had pushed him on top of the rotted wood of the covered well I had discovered while looking for the feverfew.

He cried out in alarm as he suddenly dropped through the shattered remains of the cover.

Chapter 29: Alexandria Jaquette

I WAS EXHAUSTED. It had taken almost everything I had to put an end to the standoff. Now it was taking all I had left just to keep standing. Unfortunately, there was still more that needed to be done. Mr. Hillock and the other Texans were busy rounding up the UFC soldiers and herding them into their vehicles, then ensuring that they were headed out of town. At the same time, somewhere across the river, Aiden and Mr. Thatcher were searching for Lilith and Cody. I would have preferred to be part of that search, but Aiden had made it clear that he didn't want me with him.

To say that he had not been happy when he left would have been an understatement. Somehow, I had fooled myself into thinking that he would understand the need for what I had done; clearly, he had not. Now, instead of being there to help my team, I was doing my best to stay out of the way of the mop up efforts and anxiously twisting the ring once again while I worried about what he would say when he got back.

I sighed and purposely let go of it as I closed my eyes and leaned back against the wall. I was pretty sure I knew why he was upset; I'd seen the clenching of his jaw when he finally figured out what I was doing. But what other choice had there been? To let Logan's family die? To let the UFC destroy a friend? No. That was not a choice I could have lived with. Now I could only wait to see if the consequence of that choice, the one thing I didn't get to choose, would also be one that I could live with.

"You doing okay?"

I opened my eyes with a start to see Evans standing in front of me. I hadn't even heard him approaching.

"Yeah," I answered, even as I pushed off the wall and shook my head, trying to make myself more alert.

His eyebrows came up doubtfully.

"Okay," I finally admitted with a half-hearted laugh. "The truth is that I'm exhausted, but too worried about my team to rest."

He smiled in understanding. "Kind of figured it was something like that. You've been oblivious to the fact that several people have been trying to get your attention over the last little bit."

"They were?" I didn't remember anyone trying.

He shrugged. "People just want to make sure you're all right. You had us all worried when that man put the gun to your head."

"That's kind of them," I said with a small smile. "But I was never really in danger."

"How…" he started, only to stop almost immediately, as though thinking better of it. "Never mind," he mumbled and started to turn away, looking suddenly embarrassed.

"Nate, what is it?" I called him back wearily. I could have just let him go; I was sorely tempted to do so. But he'd made the effort to come check on me. I didn't want to repay his kindness by ignoring him when he obviously had something he wanted to say. Even so, I braced myself. I guess I was expecting him to berate me the same way it seemed obvious that Aiden planned to do when he got back.

He surprised me by instead saying, "I…well…I was curious how you did all that. That was you, wasn't it?"

A little startled, I replied, "Uhm, it's not really something you're supposed to know I can do."

Now he laughed, appearing genuinely amused. "Claire, this isn't the first time I've seen you use your abilities. It's not even the second time."

"I guess not," I smiled back sheepishly. "How much do you already know?"

Now his smile broadened mischievously, "Let's just say that your boyfriend wasn't happy when he learned how much I had figured out."

My smile faded as my nervousness returned with a vengeance. "I see," I said softly.

"No worries," he hurried to assure me. "I'm on your side." Then he laughed again, this time with a strong hint of irony. "Besides, I think your boyfriend would kill me if I ever tried to betray you."

His smile suddenly faded as he realized what he had just said. "What I mean is…uh…that is to say…"

"It's okay, Nate," I cut in. "Logan didn't have a choice in the matter, because I didn't give him one. I wasn't going to let his family die for me."

"What do you mean you didn't give him a choice? I thought he was the one responsible for giving you to them?" he seemed genuinely confused.

I shook my head sadly. "It was quite the opposite. The UFC ordered him to betray me, or rather to turn over to them the asset that our team was transporting. When he discovered that the asset was me, he tried to get out of it. They kidnapped his family and brought them here to force his hand. I was the price of his family's freedom."

"So, he asked you to trade places with them?" Nate was still confused.

"No," I laughed bitterly. "Logan was going to let them die instead of turning me over. I couldn't let that happen. And the only way I could stop Major from killing them was to trade places with them. Logan tried to refuse me, but I'm a little more persuasive than the UFC is. Unfortunately, I don't think Aiden sees it the same way."

Evans' head was cocked again. It seemed to be a trait of his, to cock his head when he was faced with something confusing. "What makes you think he doesn't?"

I shook my head in frustration. "The tone of his voice. His clenched jaw. The way he stiffened when he met my eyes. It was pretty obvious that he wasn't happy with me for taking their place."

"Wait. You think he's angry with you because you risked yourself for McLagan's family?"

"Well…yeah." It was my turn to be confused.

Evans' expression morphed into a wicked smile and he started laughing. "Wow. You really don't know men very well, do you?"

"Excuse me? What does knowing men have to do with Aiden's anger?"

He was still chuckling as he answered. "You're the most powerful Alpha I have ever heard of, able to control things with your mind, but you don't have a clue the control you have over him do you?"

The amusement in his voice annoyed me. At the same time, though, there was a strong hint of astonishment mixed into that amusement that left me even more confused. I shook my head as though doing so would clear the confusion.

"I'm not trying to control him," I started in exasperation, not having a clue what he was getting at. But I trailed off as he started laughing even harder; so much so that there were literal tears in his eyes.

I was just about to throw up my hands and walk away when he managed to get it under control enough to say, "In all seriousness, Claire, he's not upset because of what you did out there, or at least he wasn't for very long. He's upset because of what you put him through."

"What I put him through?" I asked hesitantly.

Evans' wiped a final tear of laughter from his eyes. "Let me explain something to you about how the mind of a man works. We are fixers. We see a problem and we find solutions to fix it. Kind of like the way Aiden made it possible for you to help these people while keeping you hidden. But when our plans fall apart, it becomes very frustrating; especially if they fall apart because of a lack of communication from others. He's not going to be upset that you went out there; it obviously worked and that's what matters to us in the end. But he is going to be bothered that you didn't communicate what you were doing so that he knew what was going on.

"We're also protectors. We protect the things that are important to us. And make no mistake, Claire, you are important to Aiden. His whole plan tonight revolved around keeping you safe while allowing you to do what you needed to do. But you stripped him of any ability to do that when you purposely put yourself into those soldiers' hands. You left him feeling helpless. Do you have any idea how hard that was for him? To stand there, unable to do anything to help you while a gun was being held to your head? That would have left him angrier than anything else you could have done tonight."

I left him feeling helpless? How did he think McLagan felt?! I thought somewhat bitterly. I began shaking my head, ready to tell him what I thought of his argument, but I didn't get the chance as he continued.

"All I'm suggesting is that you try to see it from his perspective. Maybe even consider apologizing to him. I doubt you've ever had to stand on the sidelines, helplessly watching someone you love being threatened. But you could at least try to imagine what it must have been like for him out there tonight."

I didn't have to imagine it. His words had triggered a memory buried so deeply in my subconsciousness that I had forgotten its existence. It was the memory of helplessly watching from behind a glass window while Remington tortured Aiden in the driveway below. In the background of that memory, I began to faintly hear his screams of agony. It was not a memory I wanted to recall. I shook my head, trying to chase it away.

Evans must have thought I was still shaking my head in response to his words because he suddenly changed tactics.

"On the other hand, you could always just kiss him," he said mischievously. "That would give you control over his emotions real fast."

I rolled my eyes. I was not going to use a kiss to control him; it was too close to what a Child of Icarus would do. But even as I denied it, a shiver raced through my spine and a sinuous voice began to whisper: *But you are a Child of Icarus. You were quick to play with Aiden's emotions before, using Evans to make him jealous. And you killed those soldiers you threw off the hospital roof. You even sent the collar to Rosin in order to cause Remington's pain. You can deny it all you want, but none of those were accidents. You did each one of them on purpose. You are just like the rest of his children.*

Icy tendrils began to slowly spread outward from the frozen core that had settled into my chest with those thoughts. The more I tried to ignore them, the louder they were becoming.

Evans was still talking, oblivious to what was going on inside my head, but I wasn't really listening to him anymore. Instead, I was finding it harder and harder to ignore the memories the voice in my head was dredging up. The icy tendrils were spreading further, growing stronger with each memory. I rubbed my hands on my arms trying to warm them.

The voice in my head kept taunting me in spite of my efforts to ignore it. *How many people will you hurt before you finally admit who you are? How many times will Aiden let you hurt him?*

The image of Aiden thrashing in pain rose back to the surface. I realized with dismay that it had never truly gone away. Instead, it had been playing in the shadowed recesses of my mind, waiting for me to realize it was still there. This time, the memory of Aiden's screams were loud and clear.

No, please. Not again! I thought desperately as those screams began dancing in and out of Evans' words. They were like the counterpart of a discordant melody and they were growing stronger by the second. At some point, my hands had raised to cover my ears and I had begun rocking slightly. I squeezed my eyes tightly shut, praying that it would force the vision out of my head.

This isn't real! I silently screamed against the cacophony of noise. But it was too late to matter now; the vision had control once more. Only, this time, Aiden wasn't here to pull me out of it; because this time I had hurt him too badly. This time, he wouldn't be coming back.

From somewhere beyond the nightmare, I heard Evans' voice rising in concern. "Claire? What's wrong? Can you hear me?"

The only answer that escaped was a desperate sob. I realized frantically that I couldn't breathe anymore. I was suffocating, unable to draw enough oxygen into my frozen lungs. All the while, a new vision had begun to haunt me. It was the sight of Aiden angrily turning his back on me, walking away and taking my hope with him.

Evans' voice was shouting now. "Someone help! I need help!"

As darkness closed in on me, the final words in the discordant melody shifted. It was no longer the word *helpless* that was accompanying Aiden's screams. *Helpless* had become *hopeless*.

Chapter 30: Aiden Haskell 

IT WAS HARD to push my anger aside so that I could focus. I needed my attention to be on the trail ahead of me and the forest around us, but all I could think about was what would have happened if Carter had been faster to pull the trigger, or if Alex had run out of strength before she had disarmed everyone. Everything could have ended so differently.

I shook my head in frustration. *This is not what I need to be focusing on right now!* We were hunting Fischer and Three Bulls, two men that I knew from personal experience could be deadly if I allowed myself to be distracted.

Three Bulls was a skilled tracker who had been instrumental more than once in guiding our team to the hidden bases of enemy troops. He was also very skilled at sneaking up on enemy soldiers. At one point, we'd held a contest between us; to see who was the best at sneaking up on others. The outcome of that contest had been for him to acknowledge that I was good, but I'd had to admit that he was far better. He wasn't what I would consider a friend; he held himself too far aloof from everyone else for that. But we had mutual respect for each other's skills.

Fischer, on the other hand, was just an out-and-out jerk. No one liked him much. He was a braggart who was only good at two things: getting revenge on his enemies and shooting the targets he aimed at. He had developed a nickname among the team, though not one we used when he was around. He'd gotten it because, first, he took offense more easily than a drunk Irishman, and second, because his only redeeming grace was that he was the best shot the team had. His knack for always hitting the target was like everyone else's knack for accidentally offending him; they both seemed to happen with the same frequency. Thus, the nickname we called him under our breaths: Easy Target.

Thoughts about my old team brought with it a sense of déjà vu. How many times over the past five years had I traversed through unfamiliar territory with them, in the middle of the night, while hunting for a hidden enemy? I'd lost count. Yet, here I was once more, tracking an unseen enemy, in the late hours of the night, in a place I'd never been before. Only this time, the enemy I was hunting were my old teammates, and the new team I was hunting with were strangers to me.

To be fair, I was passingly familiar with Mr. Thatcher, having lived in his home and worked with him for the last few days, but I was completely unacquainted with either of the other two men. What I did know was their names: Samuel and Craig.

Sam was the younger of the two. He couldn't have been much older than I was, but he walked with a surefooted confidence that suggested he was capable of taking care of himself. That suspicion was reinforced by the fact that Mr. Thatcher had specifically called on him to help in the recovery his son. I also suspected he might be the man who had been privately saying goodbye to his pregnant wife; he certainly looked a lot like him.

Craig, the other man with us, was probably in his late forties. At least I was assuming so since his closely trimmed mustache and beard were streaked with silver. He also appeared to have some skills in tracking because he was the one carrying the flashlight and halting our progress periodically while he searched the ground, and because Mr. Thatcher deferred to him each time we came to a fork in the trail.

In spite of periodically losing time while he searched the ground, we were moving fairly quickly. During one of those brief stops, I had taken a moment to gauge how much time we had left till sunrise. The sky above the trees was steadily progressing from a dark gray to a pale gray, and I could hear the warbling of a few early rising birds. That suggested to me that we were only five to ten minutes away from sunup.

We had just taken the left fork in the trail and were starting to pick up our speed once more when a sudden cry of pain cut through the silence, freezing us in our steps. It was followed almost immediately by a second cry. It had come from somewhere off to the right of the trail, but the echoing quality of the sound suggested that it wasn't from within our immediate vicinity.

"Alcott," I said softly. Mr. Thatcher nodded in agreement. Without another word, we took off in the direction the cry had come from. At first, I matched my pace to that of the other men, knowing that arriving in a group would be better than arriving strung out. But when a third, more desperate cry cut through the darkness, still some distance ahead of us, I stopped holding back.

I crested the final hill to see Fischer crouched down, holding a gun to a clearly injured Alcott. I surged down the hill, not sure whether I should shoot him or tackle him, only knowing that I would need to be closer before I could do either. But, before I was close enough to do anything at all, she abruptly rolled onto her back and kicked out at him. He staggered away from her, windmilling his arms as he tried to regain his balance, only to have the ground underneath him suddenly give out with a resounding crack. His cry of alarm cut off in a sharp grunt as his desperately outstretched arms slammed into something strong enough to support his weight. If the moment hadn't been so desperate, I might have laughed at the sight of him dangling half in and half out of a hole, shouting in furious anger even as he scrambled to keep from falling deeper.

Alcott struggled to her feet, grimacing in pain as she limped heavily on her injured leg, making her way over to the phase gun he had dropped. She picked it up, determinedly aiming it at him, only to rapidly shift her aim as she suddenly realized that someone was racing toward her.

"Alcott, hold yer fire," I shouted even as I ducked out of the way of her first shot.

"Aiden?!" she called back in surprise, not trusting what she was seeing enough to lower her gun yet.

"Aye," I hurried to assure her. There was a definite look of relief on her face as I skidded to a stop beside her.

Recognizing me as well, Fischer called out in desperate hope, "Haskell! Get me out of this!"

This close up I could see that the thing he was precariously holding on to was a rotted piece of wood. The decayed timber was all that was keeping him from falling into the darkness beneath him. A more secure ledge was potentially within his reach, but each time he shifted his weight to grab for it, the wood beneath him groaned dangerously, leaving him afraid that too much movement would cause it to shatter under his weight.

A slow, wicked smile spread across my lips as I watched. "Looks like yae picked on th' wrong target this time, Easy Target."

His hopeful expression melted into one of hatred and he began spitting out curses at me. I ignored him with more than a little satisfaction and turned to help Alcott.

The gaping wound in her leg was an ugly one; she was going to need a surgeon to repair it. But until we could get her that, we needed to bandage it so that she didn't bleed out. I was grateful I had taken the time to reload my gear back into my pockets while we'd been at the Thatcher's house. I pulled out the Medi-kit.

As she reached to take the supplies from me, the sleeve of her dress shifted just enough that I noticed a burn on her arm. The muscle in my jaw clenched in sudden anger as I realized what that burn meant. I'd seen Fischer do it before; he took a wicked sort of pleasure in torturing the helpless. He'd even been reprimanded for it on several occasions, but always had some excuse that got him off the hook. Knowing the burn on her arm was not likely to be the only one, I did a quick visual check and discovered the one on her hip as well. Three cries of pain; three wounds.

I spun in fury, aiming my gun at Fischer's head. "Yae no good, Light-forsaken…" The rest of what I was going to say was cut off by Mr. Thatcher's stern voice, "No! Not yet!"

My eyes shot up to see that the others had finally arrived. Mr. Thatcher was breathing hard, but he hurried over to me and put a calming hand on my shoulder. "We still need him, son." I growled in disgust, but lowered my gun. He nodded in approval then turned to Sam and Craig. "Get him out of there and bind him." Then he turned his attention to Alcott. "Let me help you with that, miss."

As he gently wrapped the bandage around her leg, I heard him ask, "Where's Cody?" His voice was calm, but it was also laced with the faintest hint of worry. We both knew that Cody was not the type to abandon a woman. If he wasn't here with Alcott, then something must have happened to him. The worried look on her face confirmed our fears.

"He's not in good shape," she said with a faint shake of her head. "He needs medical help as quickly as we can get it to him." Then she saw the glint of silver on his wrist and said excitedly, "Your C-DACS! I can use it to call in a medical transport."

Mr. Thatcher met her hope with hesitancy, but he unlatched the strap and handed the device to her. The instant the computerized voice answered, she was speaking. "This is UFC Major Lilith Alcott, authorization code Charlie-Recon-Delta-5-3-3-8-9, calling for an immediate Medical Emergency Transport to my location. I repeat: This is UFC Major Lilith Alcott, authorization code Charlie-Recon-Delta-5-3-3-8-9, calling for an immediate Medical Emergency Transport to this location."

In seconds, a live person had replaced the computerized recording. "Major Alcott, this is Lance Corporal Johanson out of Fort Hood. What is the nature of your emergency?"

"I have a level 2 priority patient with blunt force trauma to the thoracic cage and abdomen. Internal hemorrhaging is extensive in the abdomen. Possible hyperpyrexia as well."

"Copy that Major Alcott. I'm routing a MET vehicle to your location. ETA is seven minutes."

She handed the C-DACS back to Mr. Thatcher with a faint sigh of relief. It was a relief that quickly changed into a grimace of pain as she tried to stand. We were going to need to carry her out of here; she was not going to be able to walk any real distance on that leg.

She had just wrapped her arms around our shoulders, and was sitting back into the seat we had created with our linked arms, when a cry of alarm cut sharply through the air. My head shot up and I was craning to look back over my shoulder.

The last time I had glanced over at him, Fischer had been sitting against a tree, his hands bound in front of him. But his hands weren't bound anymore and he was lunging toward Craig, a silver gleam reflecting off the knife in his hand. *Where had that knife come from?* I'd watched Sam checking Fischer for weapons; he'd done a very thorough job of it. Regardless of where it had come from, Craig didn't react fast enough to dodge it. He grunted in pain as Fischer yanked his arm back, a bloom of red suddenly spreading outward from the stab wound in his side.

Sam was already in motion, blocking the second thrust Fischer had aimed at Craig. He followed the block by stepping in close to Fischer and quickly trapping the knife against his own hip so that Fischer no longer had the leverage to use it properly. No matter how Fischer fought to break his knife hand free of Sam's grasp, Sam was ready to counter it. I was impressed. Sam had clearly been trained to fight against an opponent with a knife. But I also knew the level of training Fischer had received while with the Caledonians. Sam was going to need help.

I didn't quite drop Alcott, but it was very nearly so as I released my grip on Mr. Thatcher's arms and turned to charge Fischer. I was still several steps away from him when Fischer seemed to suddenly stop fighting to free his hand, giving Sam a momentary advantage. Only, Fischer wasn't giving up. He instead shifted his weight and used his free hand to steal the gun holstered on Sam's opposite side.

The flash of the phase bolt seared the horror of the scene into my mind. I watched as Sam's facial expression morphed in the blink of an eye from determination, to shock, to horror, to slackness. In that same blink, it was as though I could see the reflection of his pregnant wife in his eyes. *No!* I thought in fury. *Not him!* But his lifeless body was already toppling backward as I crashed into Fischer. I didn't hold back as I knocked the gun from his hand and then allowed my fury to vent with each swing of my fist. Some part of my mind registered that Mr. Thatcher was firmly telling me to stop, but it was Alcott's hand on my shoulder that drew me back from the haze of my fury.

I looked up to see her concerned face. "He's had enough," she said, almost regretfully. For just a moment, I was confused by her words. But when I looked back at Fischer, I realized that his face was a bloody wreck. I had broken his nose and probably his cheek bone as well. He had multiple splits in his skin and at least one tooth had been broken. It would be a long time before his face resembled anything close to its normal appearance.

In spite of the beating, he was still conscious. He moaned in pain as I rolled him over to his stomach and bound his hands with the length of rope I pulled free of my belt loops.

Assured that I was back in control, Lilith limped over to Sam to check for a pulse; I already knew she wouldn't find one. With a sad shake of her head, she turned toward Craig and started caring for the wound in his side.

The muscle was twitching angrily in Mr. Thatcher's jaw as he picked up the pistol Fischer had dropped and handed it to the man Lilith was patching up. "Keep an eye on this one for me, would you, Craig? He doesn't get to leave with the rest of them."

"I'll do that," Craig said with a grimace as Lilith wrapped the bandage around his torso. "You just go find that boy of yours."

With a final nod, Mr. Thatcher turned to Lilith. "Take me to my son."

***

TWO HOURS LATER, I was wandering the halls of the hospital. Thatcher was finally out of surgery, but they had placed him into an induced coma so that his body could continue to heal. It had been touch-and-go during the surgery; he had even flat-lined once. He really had been in bad shape. But in the end, they had succeeded at pulling him through.

Now we were just waiting for Lilith's surgery to be finished. She had refused to go into hers until Thatcher was out of his. Interestingly enough, I'd gotten the impression from watching her that, at the bare minimum, a strong friendship had developed between the two of them during their captivity. In fact, the more I watched her, the less it would have surprised me to learn that their relationship ran deeper than simply that of friends. The biggest clue had come when she told the doctor that they might as well go ahead and set up her recovery bed in Thatcher's room because she would not be leaving his side until he was strong enough to walk out of the hospital with her.

In truth, however, it wasn't her surgery that had me on edge. No. What had me pacing the halls was the memory of the heartbroken sobs of Sam's young wife when she had learned that her husband wasn't coming home. It didn't seem fair. A lot of people had been injured in the night's fighting, but Sam was the only one who had been required to give the ultimate sacrifice.

Now, as I wandered blindly through the halls, a single thought had begun to coalesce in my mind: I didn't ever want to put Alex through what Sam's wife was going through. And yet, if I were being totally honest with myself, that was exactly what I was on track to do. That left me in a dilemma. The only way I could protect her from that pain was to leave her before I earned enough of her heart to cause it. The problem was, she already had all of mine. Leaving her would be the hardest things I had ever done. I ran my hands though my hair, unsure what I should do.

"Haskell!" A familiar voice pulled me from my thoughts. I looked up in a flash of fury to see McLagan hurrying down the hall toward me. My fists clenched as I turned toward him; that traitor had a lot to answer for. I was swinging my fist before he even had a chance to speak.

McLagan reeled to the ground amid several gasps and even a scream from one of the nurses. I took another step toward him, intending to pick him up and slam him into the wall, but someone grabbed me from behind before I had the chance. I automatically moved to throw that person off, only to discover that they had a more solid hold than the average person was trained to take.

"Easy, Haskell," Wren's voice said firmly in my ear, not relaxing his hold on me. "This is not the place for that." If it had been anyone but Wren, I probably would have adjusted my stance and broken their grip. Instead, I forced myself to calm down and held my hands up to show that I was cooperating. Wren's hold relaxed in response.

McLagan had begun to stand up as well. He was rubbing his jaw tenderly and watching me warily, but I was surprised to note that there was no anger in his expression, only concern. "Claire needs yae," he said without any further preamble. "They have her downstairs in th' emergency room."

My anger vanished in a heartbeat, replaced by a jolt of fear. "What's wrong?"

"She's unconscious. She started having breathing problems, then she passed out and we haven't been able tae wake her since."

I didn't wait for him to say anything more as I turned on my heels and ran for the emergency room.

Chapter 31: Alexandria Jaquette

I WAS DRIFTING on a cloud of thick fog, not really caring where I was or how I had gotten there, only knowing for certain that I did not want to return to the place I had been. At some point I began to notice sounds and scents floating to me through that fog. I could hear a soft, steady *beeping* and a gentle, rhythmic *whooshing*. I could hear faint *squawks* and lilting *chirps*. I could also smell a salty tanginess mixed with a sterile sharpness. Yet, even though the sounds and scents were all vaguely familiar, recognition of their actual identity remained just out of my reach. It wasn't until someone took hold of my hand and began gently running their thumb across my knuckles that the fog finally began to lift. My fingers twitched in response to that touch, causing the hand holding mine to tighten its grasp.

"Alex?" I heard Aiden's voice call out anxiously.

I slowly opened my eyes to see his worried face.

"Hi," I said groggily.

"Hi, yerself," he smiled back with obvious relief.

"Where are we?" I asked in a half-dazed tone as I looked around. I was far from being fully alert, but I didn't recognize the pale blue wallpaper or the gauzy curtains that were flapping playfully in the soft breeze coming through the open window.

"Yae're in th' hospital," he answered with a small shrug. "Yae pushed tae hard and collapsed again."

"Well, that wasn't very smart of me," I said with a small laugh. As an afterthought, I added, "How long was I out?"

His smile slid away, replaced by a nervous tightening of his eyes. "It's…well, it's been a little bit," he said hesitantly.

I might have been groggy, but it hadn't escaped my attention that he hadn't given me a straight answer. Unfortunately, before I could ask what he meant by that, there was a swishing sound as the room's door opened.

"Well, it's about time," a gruff voice said. I looked over in surprise to see Dr. Paxton approaching my bed. "How are you feeling?" he asked brusquely, even as he promptly began to check my vitals.

I was suddenly more alert. Dr. Paxton was not supposed to be here; he was supposed to have gone straight to New Los Angeles.

"Uhm…fine, I think." I answered his question automatically, but my thoughts were more focused on trying to understand what was going on. "Why are you here?" I asked.

He paused what he was doing and met my eyes.

"Here?" he asked, a hint of concern in his voice. "Just where is it that you think you are?"

"In Texas," I said slowly, suddenly not so sure.

His lips twitched upward and he barked a gruff laugh. "Afraid you've got it backward, young lady. I didn't come to you; you came to me."

"I came to you?" I started to ask, only to stop as several things finally clicked into place. The steady *whooshing*, the *squawks* coming through the room's open windows, the salty tanginess of the air: we were near a beach; we were in New Los Angeles.

I sat up suddenly and turned back to face Aiden. "Just how long have I been out?" I asked it more firmly this time.

"Two days," Dr. Paxton answered for him, at the same time pressing the button to raise the bed behind me. He continued in his no-nonsense tone as though he hadn't just dropped a bomb. "You experienced a traumatic event that sent you into a state of shock. Your brain tried to adapt, to protect you from the trauma, but it overcompensated, causing you to hyperventilate and lose consciousness. I don't know yet why you stayed unconscious for so long; the results of all the tests I've run have been inconclusive. But, since you're awake now, I'd say that whatever was keeping you under has resolved itself. So, we'll chalk it up to your unique physiology for now. In the meantime, I'm going to keep you here overnight. Then, if everything still looks good, I'll release you in the morning. But I will also be setting you up to meet with a counselor who can help you through the trauma so this doesn't happen again. Any questions for me?"

I shook my head, almost too stunned to think. *Two days?!* But as Dr. Paxton left the room, questions finally did begin to filter into my mind. Foremost was the question of what had really caused me to pass out. I hadn't missed the look of consternation that had flashed across Aiden's face when Dr. Paxton had said that a traumatic event had caused me to go into shock. He'd not intended for me to hear that detail. Why?

Then another thought popped into my head. I didn't have any memories that I would consider to be traumatic. My last solid memory was wandering around the clearing outside the power station. The fight against Aiden's old team had been tense, but not traumatic. Was there a memory missing? And why did the memory of waking up in the tent just pop into my head as though it were somehow related?

Slowly, I began to make the connection. "This has happened before, hasn't it?"

Aiden seemed even more hesitant, but he eventually nodded his head. "It has."

"Why didn't you tell me about it before?"

"Uh…well…Lady DuCain said that I wasn't tae bring it up till yae did."

Until I did?! How did they expect me to bring something up I didn't even remember?! A little heatedly, I huffed, "Fine. I'm ready to talk about it now. What happened?"

If I had thought he looked nervous before, it was nothing compared to the anxiety that flashed across his face now. But, to his credit, he took a steadying breath and answered.

"Yae went into shock when yae watched me bein' tortured. It was me screams that did it tae yae. Yae were able to pull yerself out of that one at first, but when Roisin put th' shock collar on Remington, Lady DuCain said his screams triggered yae tae relapse."

There was a haunted look in his eyes as he continued to explain, like he was retelling a nightmare.

"We carried yae intae th' house, tae get yae away from Remington's screams, but it didn't seem tae make any difference. It was like yae were hearin' them in yer head. It was terrifyin' tae watch, Alex, not knowin' how tae help yae."

As he explained, flashes of memories began to filter through my mind. I saw him kneeling in front of me, desperation in his eyes as he held my hands away from my ears. I heard his voice as he talked about America, trying to pull my thoughts away from the false images in my head. I remembered the warmth of his arms when he had wrapped me into them to fend off the icy chill that had spread through me.

"You pulled me out of it that second time," I said slowly as the pieces started to fit together. "I remember your voice, talking me through it until I calmed down."

"I was just followin' Lady DuCain's instructions," he countered with a depreciating shrug. "She's th' one who pulled yae out of it."

I opened my mouth to argue with him, only he was already speaking again.

"I didn't see th' next one. It happened Sunday mornin', after I crossed th' river tae go lookin' for Thatcher and Alcott. Evans saw it, though he wasn't sure what started it. He said that th' two of yae had been talkin' about th' way yae had taken down th' soldiers, when yae suddenly went pale, covered yer ears, and started rockin'. Th' next thin' he knew, yae were havin' trouble breathin'. He said yae passed out before he could get help. When they couldn't wake yae, they rushed yae tae th' hospital."

My head tipped slightly in confusion. Without being able to say why, I knew that something wasn't quite right in that explanation. Not that it was wrong in and of itself, but rather that it was missing an important piece of information. I just wasn't sure yet what that was.

Like my memories of the events in Scotland, flashes of scenes from that night in Texas had begun playing in the background of my mind. I allowed my attention to focus on them now, searching for what it was that was missing from Evans' explanation. I saw Major holding McLagan's wife and child hostage. I saw McLagan's fists clenched in frustration and the horror in his eyes. I heard Major telling Aiden that he would trade me for the asset and saw Aiden's jaw clenched in response. I remembered wandering around the buildings afterward, trying to stay awake. I even heard Evan's voice explaining to me why Aiden had been angry with me. But, as I heard his voice, a different word flowed into my mind: *hopeless*. Suddenly, I knew what was missing.

A faint chill washed through me, like a whisper of the fear that had caused me to pass out last time. I pulled my legs to my chest and wrapped my arms around them as I looked back up nervously. "I know what caused it," I said softly.

His eyebrows came up questioningly.

"We weren't just talking about what I'd done to the soldiers that night," I continued apprehensively. "We were talking about what I had done to you, and why it had made you so angry. But something he said triggered the memories of your screams and the panic started to return. Only this time, I knew you wouldn't be coming back to help me escape it, because I knew that this time I'd hurt you too badly."

I felt my heart fall as the muscles in his jaw began to clench. It suggested that an apology would be too little, too late. Still, I had to try.

"Oh, Light. I didn't mean to hurt you, Aiden. If there had been more time, if there had been any other way to save Logan's family, I would have taken it. But it was the only way

I could think of, the only way I could get close enough to ensure that I could control the waves I needed. If I had known what it was going to do to you to have to watch it…" I choked out remorsefully. "If I'd just understood, maybe I would have looked for another way. But I didn't know, at least, not until Nate explained it to me. And once I understood, it was too late. You had already left, and I didn't think you would be coming back, and I knew it was hopeless, and I…oh, Aiden," I finished weakly, "I am so sorry."

As I finished, he looked away from me, seemingly no longer willing to even meet my eyes. Up to that moment, I had harbored a faint hope that he might forgive me, that my apology would somehow be enough. Now I knew for certain that it wasn't. So, I did the only thing left to me: I tried to steel my heart for what I knew would be coming next. I refused to cry, but that didn't stop the unshed tears from stinging my eyes.

His own eyes closed as he took a deep, steadying breath. Opening them once more, he finally turned back to me. "Look, Alex," he started hesitantly. "I've spent th' last two days thinkin' long and hard about what happened back there. I had even almost convinced meself that I could stay, that I could make it work. But th' truth is, th' longer I stay, th' more damage I'm doin' tae you."

"To me?" I was suddenly very confused.

He only nodded dispiritedly and went on. "Every time I was th' cause of yer pain. First, it was me turnin' me back on yae in Ghana. Then it was me screams when I was bein' tortured. Then it was me walkin' away and leavin' yae afraid I wouldn't come back. I'm supposed tae be protectin' yae, but instead I keep hurtin' yae. I don't want tae dae that tae yae anymore. And I don't ever want tae hurt yae th' way she's hurtin' now."

"She?" My confusion only grew. "Aiden, what are you talking about?"

He looked away again, this time looking up to the ceiling as though he could find answers there. When he finally looked back down, the pain in his eyes caught me off guard. "I was there when they told her, Alex. She was inconsolable." His voice was halting as he recounted the memory. "Th' hollow emptiness in her eyes when she finally stopped cryin', it was th' same look I saw in yer eyes back at th' lodge. I can't dae that tae yae again; I won't." He said the last part determinedly, as though he were trying to convince himself. Though what exactly he was trying to convince himself of, I couldn't figure out.

"Aiden, I don't understand…" I started, only to have him interrupt.

"Sam's dead, Alex. Fischer killed him. His wife's not even twenty-two and now she's a widow with heartache she should have never had tae feel. Just like yae will be if I stay. I won't dae that tae yae. He wasn't even a soldier; just a man fightin' for what he knew was right. But I'm never goin' tae be allowed tae leave th' military. I'll be required tae keep fightin' until one day I don't come home from th' fight." Nervously, he ran his hand through his hair. "This isn't easy for me, Alex. I'm tryin' tae protect yer heart. If I leave now, before yae let me in tae far, I can't hurt yae like that. But I don't…I don't want tae leave; I love yae. It's just that I know stayin' will only dae more harm. And I…it's tearin' me apart." Now his eyes were imploring. It was like he was begging me to understand.

I was too stunned to speak. I did finally understand what was bothering him, only it was not at all what I had thought it was. As my mind continued to process this information, it also began to instinctively identify what needed to be done to help him. Very much afraid, but at the same time refusing to let him suffer when I knew I could ease his pain, I let go of my knees and climbed down from the bed so that I could stand in front of him. He watched me nervously as I placed my hands on either side of his face and then pulled him gently into a kiss.

I didn't let him go until I felt his tenseness begin to relax. Only then did I finally pull back to meet his stunned gaze. "We'll work through this together, Aiden. I'm not going to let you walk away from me again; not this time. Because I'm stronger with you at my side then I will ever be standing alone."

'But…" he started to argue. So, I kissed him again. As I pulled back for the second time, I firmly repeated, "Together." This time he only nodded. I could see that he was still worried, but there was a new resolve in his eyes; he trusted me and my promise.

Unfortunately, I didn't feel that same sense of trust in myself. A small voice was whispering that I had done exactly what I said I wouldn't do: I was controlling his emotions with a kiss. *I really was a Child of Icarus.*

Chapter 32: Cody Thatcher

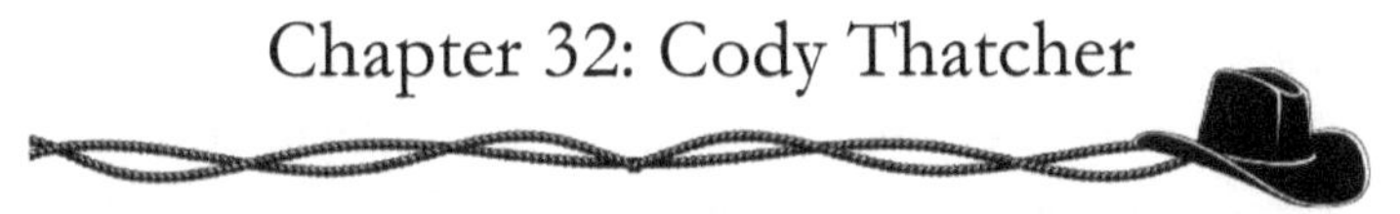

I WAS FINALLY home from the hospital. It had taken much longer than I would have liked, but Lilith had refused to budge on letting me leave until I was able to walk out of there under my own strength. Tired of being forced to stay in bed wasting time, I had stubbornly tried to prove I was ready several days before I actually was. The result had been an embarrassing fall followed by an overly patient look from Lilith as she had done everything except say, "I told you so." It had been another few days of frustrating inaction after that before she finally deemed I was truly ready.

Despite the tedium, I had to admit that one good thing had come out of it: I'd had all the time in a wide-open prairie to talk with Lilith about what it meant to be her cowboy. Turns out, even though we'd grown up more than a thousand miles apart, we hadn't been raised all that differently. God was important to her, family was everything, and if something was worth doing, then it was worth taking the time to do it right.

That meant we'd be taking our relationship slow and easy for now; getting to know each other better before we made any serious commitments. But if everything still looked good come spring, she'd take me to meet her pa and her brothers. And if I survived that encounter, then we would discuss the next step in our relationship.

We also discovered that we both liked playing dominoes; even more so once I taught her how to play the Texas Forty-Two variant. Having her there made my down time more bearable.

Unfortunately, getting home did not provide the relief I had been hoping for. Instead, Ma had taken over coddling me and controlling my activities. By the end of the second day home, I'd had about all I could handle. But it wasn't until the next morning that things finally came to a head.

We were at breakfast. Pa, Paul, and Mr. Hillock were preparing to head into town for Fischer's and Three Bulls' arraignment. I might have gone with them, except that both Ma and Lilith had made it clear that they didn't want me to. Ma was worried I wouldn't have the strength for it. Lilith was worried I might follow through on my threat to break Fischer's hands. But just because I wasn't going, it didn't mean I had to sit around the house doing nothing.

Pa was telling Ma that he planned to swing by the feed store on the way home from the court house to get chicken feed and a replacement heat lamp for the one that went out yesterday. Thinking it would give me something to do, I offered to take care of it for him.

Pa nodded, but Ma cut in, not even looking up as she continued to cut my pancakes into bite size pieces. "I don't think so, Cody," she said with a firm tone. "You shouldn't be behind the wheel of a vehicle until you have the use of both your arms again."

The truth was that my arm was mostly healed, and I was getting impatient to ditch the sling. The only reason I still had it on was because Lilith had seen me come out of the room without it and had sent me right back to get it. But she seemed to have forgotten that was the case as she countered, "Now, Beth. I think Cody can decide for himself whether or not his arm is strong enough to drive a truck."

Normally, like my pa, I was slow to anger. But the truth was that my frustration had been building for more than a week now; their conflicting arguments were just the final straw. Yanking the napkin from my lap, I shoved my chair back and stood. Not looking at either one of them, I turned to my pa and said in quiet anger, "I've changed my plans. I'll be going with you after all." Then, not waiting for his response, I turned to leave. As I opened the door, I heard chairs scraping.

"Thank you for breakfast, ma'am," Mr. Hillock said, followed immediately by Pa's voice, "We'll be back in time for dinner, Beth. And don't worry, ladies. We'll keep an eye on him."

As I walked past the kitchen window on my way to the truck, I found myself glancing in. I was surprised to see Ma and Lilith smiling at each other with satisfied expressions. If I hadn't known better, I would have said that they looked like their goal had just been achieved. Though what that goal would have been, I couldn't imagine.

Then something startling occurred to me: that was the first time in my life I had done something contrary to what Ma had told me to do. My steps stumbled for just a second as that realization sunk in. Then a second thought occurred that made me stumble again: those two had set me up! They had purposely forced me to choose between them, and they had been happy with the outcome. What in the blazes were they up to? One thing I was certain of, I didn't like being caught in the middle of whatever it was.

Shaking my head, I opened the truck's door ready to climb in, then paused and look down at the sling on my arm. A small streak of rebellion coursed through me. I pulled the sling off, scrunched it into a ball, and tossed it into the nearby garbage can. Let those two make of that what they would.

***

THE COURT ROOM, when we got there, was standing room only. Quite a few of the locals had shown up to see the arraignment, as had a surprising number of reporters. We had just found places near the back door when the bailiff called out, "All rise for the honorable Judge Carson."

"You may be seated," the judge said in a gravelly voice as he took his own seat at the front. Not wasting time, he got straight to the point.

"Samuel Fischer and Todacheene Three Bulls please stand. It is my duty to advise you of your rights. You have the right to know and understand the charges against you. You have the right to a trial by jury. You have the right to council…" he continued to outline more rights before eventually moving on. "Today we are here for your arraignment. In the next few minutes, you will be informed of the charges against you. I will set your bond, and you will then be given the opportunity to enter your plea as it relates to those charges. As your name is called, please step forward. Todacheene Three Bulls.

332

"You stand accused of felony kidnapping and accomplice to first degree murder. Your bond is being set at ten million dollars. How do you plead?"

Three Bulls was holding his head proudly, but without any other expression. "Not guilty," he said simply.

"You may sit down," the judge nodded. "Samuel Fischer, please rise."

Fischer stood. Unlike Three Bulls, there was arrogance in every line of his stance.

"You stand accused of felony kidnapping, felony assault, and murder in the first degree. Your bond is set at one hundred million. How do you plead?"

"Not guilty," he said smugly. But then, unexpectedly, he added, "However, you may want to wait a moment before you continue with this charade any further. The lawyers have something they need to discuss with you."

There was a low murmur as the unimpressed judge looked from Fischer to the prosecutor's table where one of the lawyers had just stood.

"Your honor," the woman said, "if I might approach the bench, there is a matter I need to discuss with you."

"Approach," the judge said testily. The two of them talked in hushed tones for several seconds before she handed him a digi-pad and walked away. The judge studied what was on it for a long moment. There was a distinct frown on his face as he set it down.

"Todacheene Three Bulls and Samuel Fischer, stand up." This time his tone was short and curt, clearly angry. "All charges against you have been dropped. You are free men. Bailiff, remove their cuffs and get them out of my courtroom."

As the gavel came down, there was an uproar of furious voices. In the middle of it all, Fischer turned and met my eyes with a smug smile. In a different situation, I might have found pleasure at seeing the wreck Haskell had made of his face. But any pleasure I might have felt was washed away in a wave of fury several moments later when he walked past. "Give my regards to that girl of yours, Thatcher," he said just loud enough for me to hear. "I'll be sure to look her up next time I get the chance." My father and Paul grabbed my arms; they were the only thing that held me back from punching him. Fischer was laughing as he walked out of sight.

The moment he was out of the building, though, Pa let go of me and turned to push his way through to the prosecutor's table.

"What in blazes in going on, Richard?!" he demanded angrily.

Richard Starky was a well-respected lawyer among the ranchers. He had been instrumental a few years back in settling a land dispute when a city official had gotten it into his head to sell some of their prime grazing land to a group of developers. He and Pa had been on a first name basis ever since.

The lawyer shook his head, sadly. "It's out of my hands, Dale. Turns out several key officials met behind closed doors this morning and hashed out a plea deal. I don't have all the details, but the gist of it is that those two boys get to walk out of here without any further recourse while the UFC agrees to pay an undisclosed compensation to the injured parties. I wish I could tell you more, but that's all I know right now." Just before turning away, he added, "You can expect a payment to show up in your account sometime this week, for the damages done to your property and to your son."

Chapter 33: Aiden Haskell

"WELCOME TO NEW Los Angeles, otherwise known as the City of Angels," the tour guide announced as we filed off the bus at our first stop. Captain Marcellus had arranged the tour for the team, to show us around the city we would be living in. Prior to leaving for America several weeks ago, the team had been divided into five separate travel squads of five to six team members each. The other squads had been trickling in throughout the week, but Thatcher, Alcott, Evans, and McLagan hadn't made it here until late last night; they had been the last to arrive.

I hadn't been overly pleased to learn that McLagan had been permitted to stay; I still held a grudge against him for turning Alex over to Carter. But Alex had insisted he remain on the team. She had explained to the group what had really happened that night, and I guess a part of me understood the position he had been placed in. But the reality was that the rest of me didn't care; I doubted that I would ever trust him again.

Evans had gotten his wish as well and been formally invited to join the team two days ago. He was now the team's designated pilot and drone operator. I had kind of hoped he would change his mind when he learned that our team was more defensive in nature than the attack force he had first assumed we were. But, to my surprise, he hadn't been the least bit bothered by it. It turned out that the pilots and co-pilots of Hawk Wings were inseparable when it came to flying those things. With his co-pilot dead, he was grounded for the foreseeable future.

There were, of course, other candidates who were compatible matches for Evans and could have taken Hocket's place, but Evans said it would have taken several weeks to find the right match and several months more of simulator training, teaching them to work together in sync, before they would be allowed back into the cockpit of the real thing. I got the impression that he had decided to instead throw his lot in with a team he seemed to think destined for greater things than was evident in its declared purpose. I hoped he was wrong. Because, if he was right, that would mean that Alex would be forced deeper into this war. Regardless, he was here to stay.

The tour guide waited until everyone was gathered in front of the water fountain before starting her memorized script. "In post-bellum one, North Korea launched a nuclear missile straight into the heart of downtown Los Angeles. In the flash of its horrific light, two-million people were instantly sent heavenward to join the angels. That was the start of a war that would go on to devastate the world as a whole, and take humanity in particular nearly to the brink of annihilation.

"Fortunately for us, it was not the end of our race. We came back stronger, smarter, and with the fervent desire to ensure that such a war would never happen again. To that end, our forefathers formed the global alliance that came to be known as the United Federation of Countries. Today, the leaders of the UFC continue to work tirelessly to strengthen the bonds of friendship that bind us together. The rebuilding of this city where the first bomb was dropped is their latest and, I dare say, greatest effort yet to bring about this unity.

"The Hope of the Angels Memorial in front of you is a reminder of all those who lost their lives in that war. But more importantly, it is a symbol of the hope that this city is meant to give us and the hope that we bring to the UFC's efforts for peace."

The guide continued to expound on the hope we each carried within us, but I found myself paying less attention to what she was saying and more attention to the memorial itself. It was truly a work of art unlike anything I had ever seen, and that was saying a lot considering the art work I had grown up with back home.

At its center was a large sphere of water, slightly raised above the basin beneath it. The water flowed from its top so smoothly, and arced so perfectly, that its spherical cascade appeared to be almost glass-like. The basin beneath it was a low rectangle about twenty feet wide on each side. Throughout the walls, narrow troughs had been cut so that the water drained out of that basin and into the recessed area beneath the large plexiglass walkways we were standing on. It gave the illusion that we were standing on the water itself.

The final touch to the fountain was the silver spires that arced and twisted gracefully over the globe of water. They had been polished to such a brilliant gleam that I could see Alex's reflection in the one she was standing next to. There was a look of thoughtful contemplation on her face as she reached up to place her hand reverentially on the spire. But then, almost as if she sensed someone was watching her, she suddenly turned away from it to look around. Seeing me, her expression melted into a shy smile and she quickly pulled her hand back.

Under normal circumstances I might have chuckled at her embarrassment and the faint hint of a blush that bloomed on her cheeks, but the anxious fear that had been haunting me ever since Texas was still weighing heavily on my mind. Her kiss several weeks ago had reminded me how much I loved her, and her words had given me a new determination to find an alternative to leaving. But that determination was being slowly eroded by the fear that staying was only going to make it worse for her in the end. I realized that my hands were clenching again, so I took a deep breath and forced them back open.

"Hey, Haskell!"

I looked up just in time to be hit full in the face by a spray of water. Evans was standing next to the fountain, shaking water off his hand with a mischievous grin.

I wiped the moisture from my face, flicking it off in annoyance. "What was that about?" I growled.

"It's hot out here," he said with an innocent shrug that was betrayed by the devious twinkle in his eyes. "Thought you could use a hand cooling off."

"Mind yer own business," I growled back.

He only grunted an amused laugh. Then, appearing satisfied with his mischief, he turned away and started walking back to the bus.

I'm not sure what came over me in that moment, but I had reached into the fountain and scooped up my own handful of water before I even thought through what I was doing. Only it wasn't just a handful of water that hit him. As my hand flew forward, I felt the faint shift of gravity around it and watched in startled surprise as a trail of water followed behind that was much larger than physically possible for my hand to have made. I had to force myself to keep a straight face and to not look at Alex as Evans was hit in the back by nearly a bucketful of water. He stopped mid-step, water dripping off of his now soaking hair and T-shirt.

I expected him to turn around in anger. Instead, he only chuckled as he stripped off his shirt, wrung it out, and then put it back on. Not even looking back, he continued on to the bus, leaving a trail of soggy footprints behind him.

Only when he had disappeared from view did I finally turn to look at Alex. She was not supposed to be using her abilities out in the open like this, but she stared back at me with an eyebrow raised in challenge. There was not even a hint of remorse in her expression.

A lot of things crossed my mind in that moment: anger that she was putting herself in danger for such a petty act of revenge, amusement that she had thrown so much water at Evans, and fear that her actions might have been seen by the wrong people. But the emotion that stood out the strongest, overruling the others, at least for the moment, was a surprising sense of satisfaction. Alex had taken my side over his, yet again. Whether or not I deserved it yet, she was still choosing me. My frown relaxed into a grin as that realization settled in.

Seeing my grin, her challenge relaxed into a coy smile as well. "Come on," she said as she walked over and took my hand. "Let's not keep the team waiting."

Epilogue: Icarus Argyros 

MOVES AND COUNTER moves; kings and pawns. The board was set and the next move was mine to make. The game waited only for me to set the play in motion. But I wouldn't do so quite yet; this was not the right time. Instead, I set down the coffee and signaled to the waitress that I was ready to leave.

Across the plaza, the group I had been watching was loading back on to their bus. Once they were gone, I would leave as well. For the moment, though, I permitted myself the indulgence of watching a little longer as my missing child walked away from the fountain, hand-in-hand with the young man I would be using to trap her.

I had come here to confirm my suspicions. The evidence I had seen was irrefutable. As the bus drove away, I rose, confident at last that I had played the game correctly; it was now mine to win. The only move left was checkmate!

ALPHA RATING LIST

Alphas α	Genetically modified to have 6th lobe in their brain; can see and control waves otherwise invisible to humans. *Approximate Population: 200
Betas & Charlies β & Γ	1% of genetically modified who keep enhancements after puberty, but then experience a leap forward in one or more of their enhancements. *Approximate Population: 300,000
Deltas Δ	10% of genetically modified who keep enhancements after puberty. *Approximate Population: 300 million
Echoes ε	90% of genetically modified who do not keep changes after puberty. *Approximate Population: 2.7 billion

Digi-Pad 300

BETA/CHARLIE CLASSIFICATIONS

Physical (P)
- Fine Motor (FM)
- Balance (Ba)
- Coordination (Co)
- Body Awareness (BA)
- Strength (St)
- Reaction Time (RT)
- Speed (Sp)
- Endurance (En)

Intellectual (I)
- Cognition (Co)
- Speech (Sp)
- Sensory (Se)

Physiological (Ph)
- Cellular (Ce)
- Chemical (Ch)

Digi-Pad 300

UFC ALPHA RATING REGISTRATION
SECRETARY OF ALPHA REGISTRATION
28839 FEDERATION WAY
LONDON, ENGLAND

REPORT DATE : 15 OCTOBER 188

Name	Country of Origin	Alpha Rating	Classification
Alexandria Jaquette	N/A	α/β	Gravity Waves Ph-Ch; I-Co
Icarus Argyros	Greece	α/β	Radio Wave Ph-Ch; I-Co
Talos	Unknown	α	Radio Wave
Nate Evans	England	β	I-Co,Se; P-Co
Cody Thatcher	USA	β	P-Co; I-Se
Samuel Fischer	USA	β	P-Co; I-Se
Aiden Haskell	Scotland	Γ	P-Sp
Huang Zhaohui (Harry)	China	Γ	I-Co
Lakota Wren	USA	Γ	I-Co
Lilith Alcott	USA	Γ	I-Co
Todacheene Three Bulls	USA	Γ	I-Co
Patrick Paxton	England	Γ	P-Co
Paul Lopez	USA	Δ	N/A
Logan McLagan	Scotland	Δ	N/A
Beth Thatcher	USA	Δ	N/A
Dale Thatcher	USA	Δ	N/A

PRONUNCIATION GUIDE

Aiden Haskell   Ay-dehn Haa-skohl
Alexandria Jaquette   Owl-eh-xaan-dree-a Juh-keht
Alistair Buccleuch   Ow-lih-stair Boo-kih-loh
Callia Ubuqua   Kuh-lee-uh Oo-boo-kway
Captain Marcellus   Mahr-sehl-uhs
Cepheus Jonsson   See-fuhs Jahn-suhn
Claire DuCain   Klare Doo-Kayn
Dimitri Sobrien   Dih-mee-tree Soh-briy-ehn
Eithine Buccleuch   Eh-tih-nay Boo-kih-loh
Garth Hillock   Gärth Hill-uck
Huang Zhaohui   Hwawng Jow-hway
Icarus Argyros   Ih-kuh-ruhs Ahr-ree-yohs
Lilith Alcott   Lihl-ihth Aal-kaht
Maria Estradé   Muh-ree-uh Ehs-staw-deh
Nate Evans   Nayt Ehvins
Roisin Buccleuch   Roh-sheen Boo-kih-loh
Samuel Fischer   Sam-yull Fish-er
Talos   Towl-oes
Todacheene Three Bulls   Toe-duh-shayn Three Bulls
Troy Durnham   Troi Duhrn-haam

Coming 2026

BOOK 3:
BATTLE LINES

Alex and her team are just getting settled in at the City of Angels University, but Icarus now knows who she really is and he won't stop until she is back in his possession. When he sends one of his best Alphas to reclaim her, her team will have to fight with all they have if they're going to keep her safe. But will an injury bring an end to Alex's chances at freedom, or is there more to her than meets the eye?

www.ingramcontent.com/pod-product-compliance
Lightning Source LLC
Chambersburg PA
CBHW051318190726
48290CB00001B/212